I0583592

DRAGON BOUND

REUNIFICATION BOOK TWO

GLENN BIRMINGHAM

STET PUBLISHING, LLC

This is a work of fiction. Names, characters, organizations, places, events, and incidents are either products of the author's imagination or used fictitiously.

Interior graphics by Crystal Gafford of Crafty as a Coyote.

Published by STET Publishing, LLC, Denver

WWW.STETPUBLISHING.COM

WWW.GLENNBIRMINGHAM.COM

Trade Paperback Edition
ISBN: 1-64392-028-6
ISBN-13: 978-1-64392-028-3

To my readers
who have felt helpless amidst the chaos of life.

Be brave. Seize your control.

And to those touched by the COVID-19 pandemic:
I grieve with you.

NEW RESPITE
ARTEN

Arten was asleep; she knew it was a dream, but the hands around her throat felt solid and hot. She kicked at the knife embedded in the man's thigh, but he ignored it. He pressed down on her with crushing weight, his breath hot on her cheek. She couldn't breathe, couldn't get away, couldn't wake up. She felt like she was dying.

"I could have freed you," Ergin said, his voice mournful, his face confused. A glitter of demon-metal shavings cascaded around him, a grisly halo. "Why did you kill me?"

She jolted from the dream, eyes flying open. The sheet was tangled around her, binding her limbs, restricting her breath. She struggled free of it, clawed her way out of the too-soft bed to brace herself on her hands and knees against the solid stone floor.

It wasn't me, it wasn't me, she reminded herself, *I didn't kill him!*

She clawed fingers into the stone as though it kept her tethered to the world, forced her breathing to slow, and gradually her heart stopped jumping.

Her nightshirt, damp with sweat, clung to her back in a

way that reminded her too much of another, thicker fluid. She scrabbled free of it, pushing down the panic.

Stekin killed him. He's dead, she told herself, staring at the crumple of pale cloth in front of her. It was clean. She was safe.

You're being foolish.

With a frustrated sigh, she pushed herself to her feet. Her skin itched and crawled. She needed a bath.

She lit the candle next to the bed—her bed, now. Its warm light pooled on the polished blade of the knife that sat on her night table. It, too, was clean. She picked up the candle, grabbed a fresh nightshirt from a stack of clothing on a chest of drawers, and left the room. The only sounds in the compound were the sticky noises of her feet on stone and the whisper of doors as she slid them open. She didn't bother to close them behind her; she was the only one here.

The dark gray stone ate the light as she crept down the long corridor lined with doors. If she weren't alone, this was where her fellow sources would sleep. She'd seen inside a few other compounds since she arrived five days ago, and the long hall in each of them had been filled with voices and laughter and warmth.

Not here.

This might be the biggest, finest compound in the circuits, but it was also among the least used. From what she'd gathered, even before Stekin had left to find her, he'd stopped acquiring sources, letting his number dwindle to nothing. She felt sorry for whomever was left in this dreary place at the end. Being the last when all her companions were gone must have been terrible.

Maybe that's why it feels like a tomb.

As she passed through the cavernous common area, she heard the clock bells chime second-night.

Everything here is so different, she thought, the refrain a common one in her mind these days. *A proper clock, not just an initiate ringing the bell to work and to rest.* They even spoke of time differently here. At home, an hour had been a long stretch of time: how long it took to walk to the temple or do a round of deliveries. A minute was a small slice of time: how long it took to help a customer in the shop or to curry down the horses. Here, minutes were regulated like currency. They added up to hours, hours added up by fives into the day quadrants—morning, afternoon, evening, night —until a whole day was counted. All tracked and tolled by the clock in the upper city.

I'd like to see it, see how it works. I wonder how they make the sound carry all the way down here. She hadn't been allowed into the town yet. Stekin insisted she go nowhere outside the compounds alone, but seeing as she was a pariah and Stekin had abandoned her, it was proving challenging to find anyone to show her around.

She passed the kitchens and turned into the next corridor, which took her past some storage spaces and the library before ending in at door to the bathing room. There were two doors, actually, the inner one tighter in its track, to keep the moisture out of the rest of the house. She closed these behind her with care, thinking of the books in the next room down. She'd never had access to books like this before.

I could barely even read until just before I left. Not that there was any reason to learn.

She set the candle down by the door and stepped into the stone bathing stall, drew a bucket of water, and started scrubbing the sweat from herself. Everyone here was meticulous about cleanliness. Matron drilled it into her repeatedly every time they talked. *Like I didn't already know dragons are sensitive to smell, after being on the run with Stekin for the whole summer!* She scrubbed her short hair vigorously, scratching the prickly sweat free.

To be fair to Matron, I guess most people have never met a dragon before they show up. They don't get personally escorted through the network by the kaz himself.

She poured the clean water over herself, washing away soap residue. It swirled and scudded down through the grate in the corner of the stall. Then she went over to the oblong of dark water that ran most of the length of the room and slipped into the pool. With just her there, it was long enough to swim in. She had done some estimates a few days ago and determined that if this compound were full, the pool would have been able to seat all of the occupants at the same time, but without any wiggle room. She passed over the benches and went to the deeper middle to swim the length.

Juro had taught her to swim, but she was never elegant about it. Her arms and legs thunked against the water, the noise echoing back at her from all sides. He wasn't here to sigh at her. So she kept swimming, letting the sensation of her limbs plunking through the water dull the memory of her nightmare.

The nightmares had started after Stekin had left. Had it only been three nights ago? He'd stayed on a couch in the sitting area of her absurdly large suite for two full days after they arrived, shuffling outside only to let Kylik heal him. While he'd been in the next room, she'd felt safe. She'd slept off the exhaustion of their months of travel and rejuvenated a little.

He'd just started to perk up from his injuries and seem a bit more like himself when he'd said, "Arten, I must remove myself to my own home." That was the first time she'd heard that this place was, essentially, hers. He'd asked her if she remembered what he had said about expectations. She had —he was kaz, so people ascribed meaning to his actions, intended or not—and he'd said this was an example of one of those times. "If I stay, it will send a message. People will talk."

People always talk. I still don't see why he had to banish me away from him for it.

He hadn't been back, and she didn't know where he lived, nor was she able to slip off the premises without being spotted. She'd found *that* out two days ago, when she tried to go up into the city. A woman from across the boulevard and one from next door had both dashed out of their houses and intercepted her, asking what she needed, insisting they would take care of anything. When she told them she wanted to go into the city, they both looked at her with differing degrees of alarm, and one said, "I don't think the lord kaz would like that," then all but shoved her back inside.

So this was, for all its grandeur, another type of cell. She'd had enough of stone rooms for her whole lifetime in the months she had gone through the network, locked in every night, not knowing if she would be released in the morning. She always had been, but the fear had never left her.

At least here there are no locks. I can go outside when I wish, as long as I don't try to do anything silly like go somewhere. Prison it may be, but it's better than the alternatives. For now.

She hadn't forgotten the promise she'd made to herself one night closed up in a stone bunker. She'd been struggling to come to terms with her forced relocation, with giving up everything about her life to come to this place, a place she'd had only the vaguest assurances was "safe" but nothing more. She'd vowed that she would make it here, and, if the situation for people like her—Tainted people whom the temple wanted to kill and dragons wanted to possess—was bad, she would burn the place to the ground. At the time, she'd meant it literally.

But she'd never expected anything as big as a city. A secret city in the mountains? She would have laughed if someone had tried to tell her it existed.

She stepped on one of the long benches submerged on either side of the pool, stepped out of the water, dried herself, and donned her clean nightshirt.

The alternatives to staying here were all bad. She could leave—and succumb to the conflagration of her wild power within days or weeks. If, that is, the temple didn't find her first and burn her on the pyres as a sacrifice to the saviors. She could have Stekin remove the kernel of her power, like he'd done with Ergin, *but Ergin murdered hundreds of people trying to get his power back.* Not that he had been a model citizen before—Stekin had stripped his power away and banished him after Ergin had been found responsible for a series of assaults on female sources, the last of which resulted in the woman's gruesome death. The punishment for "interfering with a source" here was severe. *Maybe the desperation of losing the power, the Taint, wouldn't drive me to become a killer, but if Ergin is any example, it would certainly ruin me.*

She slid open the door to the library, edged inside. *You should be trying to sleep*, she chided herself.

Tomorrow was an important day, she'd been warned. She would be getting her tutor. The dragon who would train her in learning to control her wild power so she wouldn't flare-out when it built up. So that she could become source to someone here and funnel them power for the rest of her life.

She didn't want to think about all that, didn't want to think about how the choice she made in the next few months would be permanent for the remainder of her life. Dragons, she'd been told, were possessive. Sources were property, for all that they were given comfortable compounds and were purportedly cherished. The dragon she picked, once she had tamed her power, would be the dragon she sourced to forever.

She set her candle down on a small table, curled up in the chair beside it. There was a book on the table, one she had started reading earlier that day—she had nothing else to do but read these days. Her hands were too damp to open it right now, so she just leaned back in the chair and let her thoughts drift.

If dragons are so possessive, why is Stekin giving me a choice about whom I source to? By all rights, including the law of the temple—the ruling institution beyond this hidden city—he owned her. She could still hear the heavy clink as he stacked the gold pieces on her parents' table, could see the five columns of ten and two of five. More money than she had ever conceived of before that point.

Maybe after travelling with me, he's decided he doesn't want me after all. I mean, he searched for some mysterious power for thirteen years and only found me? I would be bitter about that. Or maybe he had no further need of her after she'd stumbled onto Ergin's trap and solved the mystery of how the sources were disappearing. Or maybe he thought she wouldn't be sufficient for whatever purpose he had hinted at. Or maybe he just didn't like her.

Her thoughts spun down a dozen paths of unhappy speculation before she reined them in. Her hands were dry enough, so she grabbed the book to distract herself. It was an adventure novel, the sort Juro had started her reading.

She'd found that wanting to know what happened next forced her proficiency to improve in a way that struggling through fact-filled books did not. Even so, she read slowly— more slowly because she kept getting distracted by her thoughts. Thoughts now of Juro.

Now that she was out of danger and settling into this new life, she missed Juro quite a lot. He'd always made things interesting, kept her pushing herself, kept her pushing him. He wouldn't take these restrictions with the complacency she had. If he were here, he'd be enticing her to sneak out, to scramble through the city at night, to get out of this mausoleum and spend the night down in the valley fields under the stars. *Or he'd be lounging about in here all day, wanting to know why I can't just relax.* Juro could be a wastrel at times.

She gave up trying to read. She curled up around her knees and thought of him. Of Maruko. Of her family. All the people she'd never see again. The people who she couldn't even contact to tell that she was alive. Both her family and Juro's knew that Stekin had followed her into the network, so they had more assurance than most that she would make it. Juro's family was part of the network and knew that Stekin was one of the people they served. They didn't know he was a dragon. Outside this city, she doubted anyone did.

The four bells from the clock roused her; she'd drifted off. She picked up the candle and padded back through the dark halls. Not to her suite of rooms but to one of the smaller ones. Bigger than the cells she'd stayed in while traversing the network. But those cells had been a home, of sorts, and the memory of them was more comfortable than the opulent bed and grand rooms Stekin had appointed her. She pulled the coverings off the bed, made a pallet on the floor, pillowed her head on her arm. There was no lock on the door, and the room had a window she'd pushed open, but otherwise, she could have been back in one of the nicer bunkers. She could almost imagine Stekin waiting outside, listening for her call. Almost.

She thought about calling out for him. To see if he would come, as he had always done before. She didn't. Didn't want proof that he wasn't there.

The Words were her only companion. She welcomed them, knowing that the stone walls of her prison would contain them if they escaped and consumed her. The Words swirled, a warm, soothing caress circling her chest. They lulled her to sleep. Where Ergin was waiting for her.

THE PROBLEM WITH MORNINGS, she decided, was they came too soon after nights. Especially nights interrupted by nightmares. It was the panicked footfalls racing up and down the long hall that woke her. Back and forth, back and forth, echoing up through the stone under her ear. It took her some moments to pull the cotton off her thoughts, to remember why she was sleeping on the floor, to remember seeking out the smaller room. It seemed silly, now that daylight streamed in from the window, to be afraid of the suffocating bed and the memory of a dead man. She stretched and yawned and scrubbed her hands over her head and face. Thus fortified, she peeked out into the corridor.

A very feminine shriek greeted her. While she was still reeling from the blast of sound, she was assaulted by a tumult of words.

"What are you doing in there? Demons, I thought you were a burglar! No, never-mind-that. Do you know where

Arten is? I have been looking all over for her but she's *gone!* Oh, I'm supposed to find her and take her up the Hill, but she's just *gone!* Do you know? Have you seen her? What were you doing in there? Who let you in? No, never-mind-that! Have you seen her!?"

"I *am* Arten," she said slowly, not certain which question to answer. *A burglar?* she thought, still wrapping her sleep-slow mind around the girl's words. But there was no time to catch up, because she was off again.

"You can't be! You're a *boy.* Besides, Arten does not sleep in *that* room. Who are you? What are you doing here? Who let you in? What have you done with Arten!?"

It was too much, too early. Arten's patience snapped. She channeled her best Stekin impression, let the frost crisp her words as she demanded, "Who are *you,* and what are you doing racing through my halls like a mad woman?"

"I *told* you, I'm looking for Arten!" the girl wailed.

"I *am* Arten," she growled, adding *you twit* only internally.

"Oh. Oh! Well, then you'd better hurry and get ready! I'm supposed to take you up the Hill."

"You've said," Arten ground out. The girl was dragging on her arm, pulling her back to the end of the long hall where her suite was situated.

"Then why did you make me say it again!?" the girl cried, exasperated. "Hurry, hurry. Why were you in *there?* You've got dirt all over you—did you sleep on the floor? Why would you do such an absurd thing? No, never-mind-that, you've got to dress! I'll get your breakfast. You'll have to eat on the way. We're late!"

Arten stared at the doorway to her bedroom, even after the girl had vanished, dazed. *Who was that?* she wondered. *And how can she have that much energy?*

She shook herself, picked up her freshly laundered clothes from the top of the chest of drawers, stuffed her legs into the trousers, then, quickly, lest the girl return mid-change, pulled off her nightshirt and wriggled the tunic on.

The clothes were much nicer than the ones she'd crossed the country wearing. Those were tucked away at the back of the bottom drawer—she'd salvaged them from the rag bin. Stekin'd had three sets of clothing delivered her first day here, though how he'd managed to arrange it, as injured as he'd been, she didn't know. This was the plainest of the three—dyed cotton with a simple geometric pattern embroidered around the edges. This tunic was blue, the color of his scales, another was the emerald of his eyes, and the third was black. She didn't think it was coincidence. Didn't know what he meant by it—why garb her in his colors just to ignore her?

She was pushing her feet into her boots when the girl returned. Pointedly trying to ignore the bloodstains on them and the knowledge of whose blood it was.

"What are you *doing!?*" the cry came from the doorway. "We're *late!* I've been waiting for you."

"Dressing," Arten said, strangling her temper.

"Demons, you've been forever! We have to go, *now!* Are you finally ready?" She barely waited for the response before she was dragging Arten back down the hall by her hand, out the front doors. "Here." She pushed a napkin at Arten. "You'll have to eat while we go. Can you walk any faster?"

Arten jogged to keep up with the girl's longer limbs, nibbling the flaky breakfast pie in the napkin. It was delicious. All the food here was. Stekin had employed a cook to feed her and the woman did not disappoint. She felt a little guilty that he was going to such expense for her. Not just letting her live in an enormous, well-appointed house, but with servants to do her laundry, make her meals, tidy up the place.

They followed the curve of the wide boulevard, which was already swarming with people despite the early hour. They were greeting each other, pulling out chairs into the middle of the road into the impromptu clusters that the scarred-faced sources would drop into throughout the day for a quick chat with their neighbors. Some of the older sources seemed to sit there most of the day, while the younger ones could be seen doing the more strenuous work of keeping the compounds running. Except for hers, all the compounds were self-sufficient. She felt guilty about that, too, and saw the eyes of the other sources on her as she passed, felt their judgement.

No one called out to her or greeted her. She tried not let it bother her, but didn't manage well. It was getting worse every day. That first day, the day Stekin had abandoned her, she'd gone out and spoken to a few people. Or tried. As soon as she'd revealed who she was, they'd looked shocked and made a disapproving, "Oh!" But no one had bothered to explain what they disapproved of, even when she'd pressed. And pressing had just alienated them faster.

The boulevard formed a complete circle, with compounds on the inner and outer rings. Stekin's compound—for the moment, *her* compound—was backed by the cliffs, atop which the dragons lived. It was in a prime spot—of course it would be, for the kaz. The girl led her clockwise until they reached a gap in the outer ring, impossible to miss with the towering stone arch framing it. It was farther than Arten had been allowed to go before. Here the boulevard sprouted a smaller road that slipped under the deep arch and stretched into the world beyond the walls of the circuits. As she passed beyond the arch, past thick, rusted gates thrown fully wide, Arten felt a thrill of freedom.

She peered down the road, vaguely remembering from her rushed flight into the compound days ago that the road curved away north and east, following the cliffs, doubling back with them. Kylik, the dragon from whose claws she'd dangled, had told her the city—New Respite—lay around the bend of the cliffs. He'd been winded from the emergency healing he'd done on Stekin after their encounter with Ergin, but he'd had enough breath to give her a brief verbal tour of her new home.

Arten thought the girl would be taking her there, to the city she had glimpsed only briefly, but no. They hadn't gone halfway to the bend when the girl turned left off the road, taking them onto a smaller track which ended at the cliffs. A narrow stairway had been carved out of the stone, zagging back and forth at irregular intervals.

Arten had tuned out the girl's babbling while they walked once she realized no input was required on her part and nothing useful was being said. But as they climbed, she focused on the steady stream of words—let it distract her from the height and the fall that loomed. She was huffing by the time they reached the top, wondered how the other girl had the breath to keep talking. *Does she ever stop?* But there was no time to rest, she was being dragged by the hand onwards.

The streets here were not as wide as the boulevard, but wide enough to accommodate dragons. They wound up the hillside, trees and flowering shrubs obscuring glimpses of great houses from their view. Every now and then, they would pass a gate or an archway through which Arten could see exotic manicured gardens and the gables of tall build-ings. She automatically noted landmarks as they went, a habit from her months on the run through the wilderness. Finally, where a broad-leafed tree shaded the road across from a circle-cut hedge threaded through with purple trumpet-flower vines, her escort exclaimed that this was it.

They turned off the lane, passed through an unlocked gate. The gates were all human-sized, Arten noticed. *I suppose it makes sense—dragons have no need for a gate; they can fly. But then why have one at all?* The path was a bit overgrown, the gardens they passed through unkempt. When they reached the broad stretch of lawn in front of the house, she saw it had bare patches and had grown up in weeds. But the house itself was impressive enough to make up for its shabby surroundings.

Situated on the ridge, nothing but the rocky cliffs pocked with tenacious trees and morning-blue sky behind it, it was as open and appealing as Stekin's compound was dark and closed. The stone walls were of a soft pale stone, more blue than gray, but not so light as to blind when the sunlight struck it. Right now, the sun was still rising, hadn't yet cleared the western ridges, and the house was in shadow.

The girl didn't seem impressed with the view or the house and didn't stop to take it in as Arten had. The girl marched up the door and banged a metal knocker against a strike plate. She looked tiny beside them. And Arten realized just how large the house actually was. All the proportions were dragon-height—the doors, the windows, the walkways. She felt strangely vulnerable standing in its shadow. Exposed.

A dragon lives here, she realized.

The girl was hissing for her to hurry up. Arten shook off her cold fear enough to trot to her side. The door slid open a crack, a polite voice enquired, "May I help you?"

"The lord kaz said I was to bring her here." The girl jerked her thumb at Arten.

"I see," the man said. "Please follow me," he said to Arten, then, "You may go," to the girl. She looked like she was going to explode into words at being left out of whatever was about to happen but turned on her heel with a huff and stalked away. Arten let out a sigh of relief.

"Please," the man repeated, beckoning her inside. The door slid closed behind her on squeaky wheels. He winced. "Apologies, we're doing maintenance."

"It's fine," she said, because he seemed like he needed an acknowledgement. He bowed slightly, then led her through the echoing atrium, through a vast open courtyard beyond. A blue and gray and white pattern made of tiles stretched across the gaping space, leaves and debris obfuscating the design. She knew it ended, could see the far side, but she felt they made too little progress as they crossed it. The proportions of the space and the house had her senses confused. "How many dragons can fit in here?" she wondered aloud, gawking at the size of it.

"All of them," he said, startling her in a completely different way, "if they're friendly."

All of them? Surely not. It's not that big... But then, until two weeks ago she'd not known dragons actually existed. Why did it surprise her that their numbers were small? She was still wrapping her head around it, trying to equate the size of the area to numbers of dragons, when he announced their arrival.

"Best not keep him waiting," the man said with a friendly smile. He slid open the doors enough to admit her, propelled her gently through when she hesitated, and closed them behind her.

Closing her inside with *him*. Whomever that was. Her

tutor. A dragon. The feelings of awe curdled inside her into dread.

She turned from the doors that had just swallowed her escort's reassuring face, braced herself, and took in the room. It was a library. Shelves lined the walls, floor-to-remote ceiling, filled with books as tall as she was. Some of the ones that rested on their covers were twice her height. She moved quietly into the room, peering down the dragon-wide rows of shelves. Carpet runners patterned in swirling blues similar to those in the expansive courtyard muffled her footsteps. The shelves branched out to either side, but at the end of the runner she crept along, there was an open space set with two incongruous human-sized chairs and a little table between. The chair backs were high, obscuring her view of any occupants, but she could see an elbow protruding over the arm of the left chair. On the table was a white-wrapped box.

She felt tiny, like she imagined a mouse in her own house might feel, as she approached the chairs. She edged around them, jaw clenched.

And let out an undignified squawk.

She wouldn't have recognized him if not for his unchanging, bristly hair.

His well-worn robe was gone, replaced with clothes much finer than her own in an antiquated but recognizable style. Trousers, a neatly pressed shirt with buttons down the front, and a thick vest, all a little loose, though she suspected they had once been well-tailored. Glossy boots covered his feet, not his familiar cracked, stained sandals. Even the sharp angles of his face seemed different—more refined, somehow.

"Stekin?" she asked, incredulous. His eyes flashed emerald through his lashes. *Definitely Stekin...*

"Were you expecting someone else?" His tone was impassive, but she knew him well enough by now to know he was amused. The small sharpness at the edge of his mouth gave him away.

"You know I was," she snapped, irritated by the relief that coursed through her at hearing his voice.

"I did try to find another," he said, "but your power would have overwhelmed those who volunteered. So until you have some basic control and I feel confident in turning your tutelage over to a less-skilled person, I will teach you."

She scoffed a little internally at his arrogance but quickly sobered. *He* has *proven he can handle my power; he's saved me from flare-out several times.*

But seeing him...remembering the lonely desperation last night as she wondered why he had disappeared... She felt foolish, pathetic. She flushed with embarrassment. "Fine. Let's get this over with."

"No," he said, his eyes now open, scrutinizing her with the intensity of the predator he was. "You are upset."

"I'm fine," she lied.

"You are not. And I will not endanger both of us by entering this while you are emotional. Your power is close to flaring."

Is it? The statement startled her. The Words inside her normally rioted and swarmed, and she constantly battled to keep them down. How long had it been since she'd felt their motion? Even now, thinking about them, focusing on them, she could feel that they barely stirred. *Since Ergin.* Since he'd wanted to take them, and since she'd learned what life without them would be like. *It's like they're afraid I'll have Stekin rip them out if they're ill-behaved. I know he says the Words aren't sentient, but how else do you explain it?*

"They're fine," she protested. "They're quiet. Nothing will happen."

His voice took on that icy edge that told her he was disappointed in her. "I do have experience in these matters, Arten." He didn't add *hundreds of years of it,* but she didn't need him to—it was difficult to forget.

It was easy, however, to forget that she was his slave, that he had a contract signed with her parents giving him legal guardianship and indenturing her into his service for the next three years. Except when he used that tone and his cold disdain spiked that particular knowledge into the forefront of her thoughts.

"Very well, *master,*" she said, unable to keep the bitterness at bay. "What do you want me to do?"

"I want you to tell me," he said, unfazed, "why you are suddenly angry with me. Unless I mistake your tone?"

"I don't want to talk about it," she evaded.

"Nevertheless, you will," he said with the confidence of someone in the habit of being obeyed. She growled under her breath and paced, stalking along the runner that ran along the windows opposite the chairs. "I do have all day," he noted, with that hint of amusement again. When she refused to answer, added, "The longer you avoid this, the more you postpone your training, the longer you must be unwilling source to me."

That sparked her tongue. Because unwilling source she was, and he had promised her he would take nothing she didn't give freely. While her power was wild, that was a promise he couldn't keep, for her own safety. And she still didn't have an adequate answer to what he, and dragons in general, did with their sources' power. Didn't trust that it wasn't used for nefarious purposes. But that was a

"You do not work for Kylik," Stekin snapped, and his man began unwinding the long linen strips, his arms passing around Stekin's torso in a slow rhythm. Stekin's shirt flowed around the motion, like a strange tide. Stekin hissed as the last layer of bandages were peeled away.

"Come," he said to Arten. "Come see what has kept me away the last three days." He motioned to his man. Claude frowned and glanced anxiously at Arten but, after a hissed warning, gingerly lifted Stekin's shirt away, exposing his left side.

Arten felt her eyes widen. His chest and side were traced with thick, abrupt slashes, as though some large child had practiced their clumsy stitching on him. A bright drop of blood trailed down the ridges and valleys of his ribs from a scab that had just broken open. Arten moved closer, drawn by the ghastly sight.

"This," he gestured down his torso, indicating the fresh cuts across his chest that followed the line of his ribcage and traced the spaces between his bones—everywhere but over his heart—"was yesterday. This," he lifted his left arm briefly, sending another glob of blood trickling over the prominent curves of his bones, "was the day before. And this," he flicked his hand and Claude moved to show her his right side, where the scabs were harder, a little less red, "was the day I left you."

"What happened?" she breathed, transfixed by the raised, arcing lines.

"Kylik has been working to get the demon-metal filings out of my lungs."

"I...I didn't know it was that bad," she admitted. "You were getting better."

"I am. But it is dangerous for me to shift while they remain, and much easier to retrieve them in this body."

Without scales, he means.

"Are you...did Kylik get them all?"

"Not yet. There will be more treatments. My body must recover between them. He has retrieved enough that I will do so more rapidly now. They have been corrupting the flow of Kylik's and my power." Was he out of breath?

"Oh," she said, felt the Words churn deep inside her, was almost glad for their now-familiar turmoil.

"Claude," Stekin said, a request, and the man practically jumped to his aide. Arten noticed the tremor in Claude's hands as he wrapped the dressing around Stekin's torso again.

"I did not intend to abandon you, Arten. I thought you would want some time to yourself, to adjust, to meet people without my interference. I know the sources can find me...intimidating."

Do they? Is that why they're avoiding me?

"You are not my, nor anyone's, pet. Nor will you be."

"Oh," she said again, thoroughly chagrined.

Claude finished with the bandages and began putting Stekin's clothes back to rights. "Shall I send for Kylik, my lord kaz?" he asked after he had helped Stekin ease back into his chair.

"No." Stekin, dismissed him with an abrupt wave. The man slipped away, glancing briefly at Arten and throwing her a tight smile as he left.

Stekin gestured her to sit. She perched on the edge of the other chair. It was angled slightly towards his, conversationally. She stared at his side, where the bandages had drunk up the fresh trails of his blood.

"This," he indicated the white-wrapped item, his hand trembling slightly, interrupting the silence, "is for you. A gift."

It was not one, but two items, stacked neatly atop one another. Books, by the feel of them. "Why?" she asked, holding them in her hands, still in the pristine paper.

"Unless I am much mistaken, today is your birthday."

"How...how did you know?" the question blurted out. She immediately regretted it.

"I was not certain, but it is the day I first felt you. The day I set out to find you." His voice was soft. At first she thought it was emotion and looked up sharply but saw his face drawn and taut, and she knew that it was fatigue or pain. "I seem to have over-exerted myself."

"I'll go," she offered.

"I need rest," he agreed. Alarming her further. She had expected him to protest. "Return at apex bell."

"Okay," she said, standing.

"Arten," he started, hesitated. His fingers twitched as though they were going to reach for her but the effort was too great. "I...have become accustomed to your presence every day. Your absence has been noteworthy."

She left, gifts tucked under her arm. Wondered, as she crossed the empty courtyard, if she should have said that she'd missed him, too.

Her escort hadn't returned by the time Stekin's front door screeched to a close behind her, so Arten was left to her own devices. Away from the prying, unfriendly eyes on the boulevard, she hardly minded. She retraced her steps, following the landmarks she'd noted, until she stood atop the stone stairway. Below her, the compounds followed the curving of the cliff wall, and the curving of the boulevard. There were three circular boulevards in all, connected by short stretches of straight, equally wide road. The pale flag-stones were already gleaming in the risen sun. She wondered how blinding it must have been before years and use had smudged their surface with grime. On the far edge of the circuits, the compounds were backed with a masonry wall, not nearly to the scale of the cliffs but high enough to disincline someone from crossing it.

From here, the cliff and the wall of joined stones formed the edges of a box canyon. The wall ran all the way up to the road on either side—she had walked under the arch of it this morning. And at the far edge of the last circuit, the wall curved around until it abutted the cliff, sectioning the compounds from the valley beyond. Inside the canyon, inside the box, there was activity, a gentle swirl of motion. People moved about the boulevards, congregating in the middle, dispersing. Others working in their compound's functional gardens, weeding, harvesting, watering. Others hanging clothing and bedding to dry or taking it down. A gentle, steady stream of industrious labor and socialization.

Something seemed wrong about the scene. It niggled at her for some time while she observed the people from her high vantage. While she wondered what her place would be among them. While she imagined herself in all sorts of drudgery roles.

That's when she realized: no one ran, no one played. There were no children, no pets, no erratic bursts of spon-taneity.

Where are the young people? she wondered. She knew the power that made her, made them, sources didn't manifest until most people were between sixteen and twenty. *For that matter, where are the old people?*

Those in the middle of the boulevards supervising and socializing were the elders among the sources, but they were all not much older than her parents. *In their forties, maybe*, she guessed; it was hard for her to judge age. But she knew they weren't *elderly*, just old.

She was puzzling over this imbalance, and something else that was just beyond her grasp, when someone behind her spoke.

"Well?" the voice, cross and bored, said. "Are you going down or what?"

Arten jumped, whirling. A tall, gangly girl with shocking blonde hair stood a few paces behind, tapping her foot, arms crossed tightly.

"S-sorry," Arten muttered, scampering to the side of the path, clearing the way to the steps.

The girl rolled her eyes, made a noise of impatience. "Sure," she said, made to sweep by Arten. Paused. "Hey. You're the kaz's girl, right?"

Arten pressed back against the hedge behind her, moving a few inches away from the piercing look that was now turned on her. "Not exactly," she said carefully.

The girl's eyes flicked to the left side of Arten's face, where her brow and temple were unmarked. The girl's fingers tightened on her thin arms. "I heard you wouldn't let him brand you," she said, impressed.

"Not exactly," she said again, shifting uncomfortably. "I'm not his source." *Not yet, at least.*

"Hah, I knew it! You're too young to have power. So why are you even here?"

Arten shrank back from the look of vindication that had passed over the other girl's face. "I do have power," Arten corrected, "I'm just not his source."

"That doesn't make any sense. If you have power," she said, in that special tone reserved for explaining plainly obvious things, like how fire is hot, to people of marginal intelligence, "then you're a source. They claim us the second we get here. You can't expect me to believe the kaz found you and *didn't* claim you."

"He didn't. At least, not like that." The girl's eyes narrowed, her face went suspicious. Arten stammered quickly, "He bought me."

"Bought you?"

"Yeah. I'm indentured to him." *Even though he still hasn't told me why or what he needed me for. Other than saying I'm 'special.'*

"Why would he do that?" She was skeptical.

"I don't know," Arten said, prying up a rock with the toe of her boot.

"That's weird. But then, I hear he's...strange." She seemed to expect Arten to say something.

"I guess," she offered. "But I thought that was because he's a dragon."

"What's he *like,* though?" she asked eagerly, leaning in like she expected to hear a secret.

Frozen glimpses of memory sparked.

A dedicate lying dead, glassy eyes staring at her above the cheek Stekin had fractured with a casual blow.

The flash of a knife, blood flinging away from the edge, as Stekin ripped it from Ergin's thigh and sliced it across his throat.

His jaw stretched wide, teeth gleaming as he leaned over her, inhaling not air but the power that was escaping her.

A cool palm resting on the bridge of her nose, long fingers curling through her hair.

The tight, sharp smile as he stared at her mother over stacks of gold.

"He's quiet," she said.

The girl rolled her eyes again. "Well, if you're going to be uptight about it..."

"No," Arten said quickly, anxious not to alienate this person who had spoken more to her than anyone else, "I just mean I don't know him very well. At all, really."

"But I heard you travelled together...?"

"We did. But we didn't really talk."

"What did you do, then?" the girl had that suspicious look again. Arten felt her face heat.

"Walked a lot. Climbed. Tried to stay dry." Arten shrugged.

"You, what, just walked along in silence? Every day?"

"Mostly, yeah. He told me a little about the Words—I mean, my power—a little about this place. In the mornings, I'd tell him what the cell was like and how hospitable it had been. That's really it." It sounded tame, when she said it aloud. Almost like she hadn't been on the run, fleeing the temple, terrified of dedicates and forcing herself to enter the cells each night. Almost like she hadn't nearly died, hadn't stumbled across a few monsters that were wholly human.

"That sounds dull," the girl commented, bored again, looked down over the valley.

"Was your trip through the network dull?" Arten bristled.

The girl's eyes cut back to her, her brows pulled down. "No."

"How long...?" Arten started, realized it might be a sensitive subject, and stopped.

"I was in the network for five weeks. I've been here nearly two years. Sourced to Hiranyath."

"Hiranyath—that's a dragon?"

"Obviously," she snorted, then said a little more kindly, "I guess you don't know all that, though, considering how no one really likes you."

"What? Why not?" *They don't even know me!* Arten thought unhappily.

"Oh, it's nothing to do with you." The girl waved a hand dismissing the concern. "They're a bunch of fussy old hens when it comes to outsiders." Her eyes flicked to Arten's temple again. "Until you're branded, they're probably going to continue to be...well, how they are." She seemed to think about something, fingers tapping against her arm. Then they stilled, and her mouth set in a resolved line. "I'm Natalia."

"Arten," she returned, gratefully.

"Come by sometime. I'm sure you've got questions that no one's bothering to answer."

Arten grinned, "I do. I will!" Natalia looked like she might already be regretting her offer. "Wh-where?"

"Oh, right. New," Natalia said to herself with a resigned sigh. "I'm on the last circuit." She pointed to the farthest of the three circular boulevards. "Just look for my dragon's mark."

"What does your dragon's mark look like?" Arten asked.

Natalia looked at her askance, a disbelieving grimace about her mouth. She simply tapped her temple with a finger, drawing Arten's eye to the scar that swirled from beside her eye up onto her forehead. Arten's face was hot, but she kept her chin up while she studied the mark, fixed it in her mind. "Got it?"

"Yeah," Arten said.

"Good. I've got to get back. See you around, Arten."

"See you," Arten said as Natalia set her feet onto the steps. The girl scampered down them at a pace that sent Arten's stomach twisting.

Arten watched Natalia dwindle in size, followed her progress as she approached the boulevard entrance from the road. Saw her bright head pass under the archway, become part of the motion inside. That's when she realized the other thing that had bothered her: people were moving about inside the stone walls, but no one left. And no one from the city had come in. She wondered why. Felt it was significant.

The Words churned uneasily.

Arten settled down at the edge of the cliff to watch the compounds below, wondering, *What have I fallen into?*

2

THE KAZ RETURNS
STEKIN

The library doors hissed open behind him, rousing Stekin from his doze. This body fatigued easily, and it had been in bad shape even before the demon-metal tore through his sinuses and lungs. He chose not to reflect on how close Ergin had come to actually killing him, but Kylik's expressions had conveyed that message clearly enough.

"Nhemith." He knew the sound of her claws, the weight of her tread without looking.

"Kaz Stekin." She rounded to stand in front of him, blocking the windows. The light cascaded around her, darkening the soft gray of her scales, the sharp lines making small movements seem sinister. She inclined her head just enough to indicate respect, but a shade too little for deference. For all Kylik claimed Nhemith had supported him as kaz while he was scouring the world for Arten, for all she verbally acknowledged him so now, he had the suspicion his return rankled her.

I must keep an eye on her, he reminded himself, tamping down on the complex tangle of emotions she inspired in him, *and determine what she has been up to in my absence.*

Nhemith had tried to supplant him as kaz before. And failed. Whatever her tactics had been while he was out in the world, they had been subtler than the last time. That she had been up to something, he had no doubt.

And yet, despite his distrust, he felt something inside him uncoil. A tension he had carried all the years he was away finally relaxed. He was back, his people were alive, and Nhemith...Nhemith was just the same. She had come to see him a few times before, he had been informed, but he had been too exhausted to be roused. Seeing her now, smelling her—he had needed this. The knowledge irritated him.

"You will need to make an appearance soon," she cautioned him. "They are wondering why their kaz hides upon his return. They fear that you have returned unfit."

"Is that what you are telling them?" he asked, letting the cold snap in his otherwise neutral words.

"You insult me, Stekin," she said, unfazed. "I have supported you in your long absence, unquestioningly. I have staved off the panic, assured them of your return, kept this place flowing along when everyone else was ready to tumble into chaos and despair."

Chaos and despair... The words lodged in his chest, heavy and accusing.

"I apologize, Nhemith," he said sincerely. "That was thoughtless of me."

She huffed down on him through her long nose, her breath warm as it passed around him. Memory unfurled its wings and swept through him: the cool wind on a warm night, above the clouds, her teeth scraping his throat, his neck bared to let her. *Machinations aside, I have missed her,* he thought with a purely internal sigh.

"Yes," she agreed angrily. But shifted into her human form with a hiss of scale and creak of joints and sat on the arm of his chair. She placed the edges of her now-soft palms under the line of his jaw. He let her tilt his head back, looked up at her. She looked worried, aged in some indefinable way. He wondered if she thought the same of him. She murmured, "I would not say this to anyone else, but you *do* look terrible."

"I would not say this to anyone else," he said, feeling a wry expression twist his mouth, "but I feel terrible."

"Can Kylik not help?"

She sounds genuinely concerned. His suspicion heightened.

"He is. I am no longer in danger, it is just a matter of retrieving the last shards and allowing this form to heal. A few weeks, at most. Less if Arten's power flares and I can use it to supplement Kylik's healing."

She stiffened at his mention of Arten. He reached his own hand up and laid the short side of it along her jaw. He could feel her pulse threading against the side of his hand. "You dislike her?" he asked.

Her jaw tightened against his fingers.

"I do not know her," she dismissed.

He brushed his thumb over the ridge of her cheek. "Then what is this reaction in you?" Her skin was soft, warm, fragile. He preferred the feel of her scales against his own, the muted clicking as their cheeks slipped past each other, the armored resistance against his teeth... He wrenched his thoughts back from that path.

She brought her forehead down, pressed it against his. He breathed deeply of her as she said, "You left us, Stekin. For her. For the dream of her. They may not say it, but I will: you abandoned us. We are not so long-lived anymore that thirteen years is a trivial thing. Our sources are dying more quickly, fewer are reaching us. So many small things have been neglected in your absence. We are dependent upon you; yours is the diamond will that guides us, the unbreakable teeth that protect us. And you left—stole away in the night with barely a word to anyone."

He was torn. He wanted to protest her accusation, wanted to inquire about the sources, and wanted to transform so that his senses could take her in fully. *If the transformation did not kill me, Kylik might*, he thought with a frustrated growl. He knew she heard it by the sudden alertness that thrummed through her. *This is dangerous.* He pulled away from her, moved his hands to her shoulders and pushed until she was sitting upright on the chair arm. Her nails scraped along the skin of his jaw as she drew her hands away, sending a strange shiver through him.

"No one here is dependent upon me," he said, more harshly than he intended. "I abandoned no one."

"Say what you will," she said with a shrug and moved to sit in the other chair. "You cannot change what has passed. You do not yet realize how much has shifted." She sounded almost pitying.

"Then tell me," he demanded.

"You should have branded her," Nhemith warned.

Stekin did not miss the evasion. "Why?"

"They are skittish these days. More than usual."

"Have there been attacks from the city?" he asked.

"No. As their numbers decrease, we are more dependent upon each of them. They are noticing the increased burnout; a few primes have shattered. They are scared. And humans are herd beasts. The brand tells them where they belong. Helps them feel safe."

"They are not beasts, Nhemith, they are people," he said with the heavy dullness of often voiced, often unheeded words. "Why should they feel unsafe without a brand? They have not complained before now."

"You were here before," she said caustically. "You purged the corruption from our kind once, and the memory of that is long. Not long enough to last beyond your shadow, however."

He hissed in an alarmed breath. "Speak plainly, Nhemith. What happened?"

"After the first prime shattered, many of us panicked. Those with sources became increasingly possessive and protective. New acquisitions started going only to those who had already proven they could care for their sources."

"That could not have gone over well with the younger generations..."

"No." The way she said it, Stekin knew there was more she did not want to say.

"Tell me," he insisted.

"It is better if you do not know," she said. "Now that you have returned, all will settle into rightness, again. And since that fiend Ergin—did I not council you to destroy him at the time?—can no longer intercept our sources before they reach us, the drought will cease. There is no need to upset yourself over what is done."

He growled a warning. Even if he could not follow it with action, at the moment. "Tell me."

She sighed, a long-suffering sound. Her eyes warned him that he would not like this, even as she said, "There was a group of the un-sourced, young and angry, that bought or stole human forms." Stekin jerked, appalled, listened in mounting horror as Nhemith continued, "Three took the forms of sources, two of humans from the city. They started going into the compounds, forming relationships, siphoning away power undetected. Small amounts at first. But they grew bold. One eventually seduced a prime, but she pushed him too hard, pulled too much. He shattered. She was beyond distraught and confessed to me what she and the others had been up to..."

"And?" he pressed when she trailed off.

"She ended her life shortly after the prime died. By all accounts, she was genuinely grieved."

"The others?"

"Were watched. Until we could get them a source. You have no right to hiss at me like that! It was a compromise that kept everyone—dragon and source—alive and safe. People were preparing to war over this, and I cannot be you, Stekin."

He felt his eyes blazing, forcibly curbed his temper as he asked, "The brand?"

"The sources' idea. I agreed. Detest me if you will, but it has prevented any further problems and will continue to keep them safe."

Sickened, he asked her to leave.

Before she did, she gave him the names of the dragon youths. They were all familiar to him. Of course they would be—they were his people, the last of his kind, and few enough now in number that he knew them all.

Graug's name settled in him with inevitable certainty. The young dragon was a descendent of the massive southern plains tribes, but as smart as he was strong, unlike his brutish, simple parents. His father had died before he was born, his mother lived only long enough for Graug to become attached to her. He had been raised by Kikkyo and the community, but his resentment toward all three of his parents had turned as black as his adult scales. Stekin had intervened countless times during Graug's adolescence to redirect his sharp intellect away from paths dangerous to himself and others. He had been relieved, gratefully laid down that responsibility, when the phase ended and Graug had seemed to settle.

I should have warned Nhemith about him before I left, I should have seen that he was too isolated, that his mind would rebel against our ordered, simple life.

The others were a surprise.

The ringleader, still a juvenile when he had left, he knew only through the affection of her parents. With her death, he would never get to know her himself.

Alectros he had always felt a kinship toward, if only for the fact that his bones and scales were configured like Stekin's own. They could have been cousins, outwardly. *I never made the effort to know him.* Looking back, he could see that a part of him had liked the illusion, had found comfort in the false idea of Alectros as family. The few times he had visited Alectros, he had seen what he wanted—a sensible, thoughtful dragon, with a glimmer of mischief that would have made Stekin's clan proud.

Nyyrikki was a mongrel, as most were these days, though he could be said to resemble the eastern jungle dragons more than anyone else. Stekin had often wondered, when Nyyrikki had first hatched, if he was some genetic relative of Nhemith's son. They had the same long, round-barreled shape, the same elegant arms and long jaw, the same sweeping brow. But Nhemith's son had been same-bent and had borne no offspring. Other than his similarity to Nhemith's clan and his vibrant coloring, Stekin had not found Nyyrikki remarkable, and could now find no indicator for his deviance.

And the last name, Hiranyath... He should not have been shocked. Hiranyath had been cursed from the moment she cracked open her shell. Still, until Nhemith had spoken that name, it had been unthinkable for Stekin that their daughter would number amongst the source-thieves.

He turned his power in his chest, wrapping wide bands around the agitation in his core.

I must fix this. Diamond wings rustled deep inside. *Is this my fault? For leaving them unsupervised for so long?* He could not have predicted it. *I have been superfluous for a century or more. There was no indication that anyone had a particular reliance upon me.* He could not have predicted that his people would fall apart in his absence. *How did things get so bad so quickly? What will happen after I'm gone?*

Then, a doubt. *Am I strong enough to do what must be done?*

The scrape of diamond scales brought no comfort.

STEKIN WAS DISTRACTED, brooding, when Arten returned. She was in a similar mood. His frown deepened when he saw the books under her arm, still wrapped, unopened. He should have turned her away again, but Nhemith's words rang in his mind, and he knew it was urgent that Arten get her power under control. Wild as it currently was, she was vulnerable to any dragons who might still be stealing power. Despite Nhemith's seeming confidence that the thefts were limited to the five she mentioned, Stekin was certain that was not the case.

It would not be so simple...

"Your power builds," he told Arten, "but does not know how to flow. You must give it direction, turn it to your will, carve out the pathways it will follow. That will come later. Today, you will simply touch your power. Reach inside to your core, find some of your power, and try to touch it."

"Touch it with what?" she asked.

"Whatever you wish." He shrugged. He saw her jaw clench, heard the grind of her teeth, but did not offer more. Any other instruction would limit her. She must find the way on her own.

He watched through his lashes as she closed her eyes, turned her focus inwards. *I thought it would be easier to protect her once we were here.* It disturbed him that he did not know what was going on, where the dangers now lay in his own city. He needed her to be safe, needed her to be settled into her new life. But did not know how to assure either at the current moment. *I must heal faster. Perhaps I should post- pone the rest of the surgeries.* He toyed with the idea as he studied her. She winced, jolted.

"Good," he said. "Again. Without getting burned."

She drew her features down into a determined scowl.

No, he thought, *I need to have access to my real form as quickly as possible. If this investigation goes the way I think it will, I must be prepared.* Besides which, while Arten's power was still wild, he needed to be able to get to her quickly when it flared. *I cannot lose her,* he thought, felt his power constrict in response. Forced his hands to release their grip on the arms of his chair. For a moment, he imagined a mark across her temple, and he felt a surge of possessive- ness, of urgency. He forced it down, tore his eyes away from her.

I understand why my *people would want the brand, but it does not make sense that the humans would come up with it.* Even if it prevented a dragon from passing as a source— such a marking, born of pain, was imprinted on the self, not the body, and would be impossible to copy in the transfor- mation—surely there was a less permanent and less painful alternative to keep the compounds safe.

Another answer to demand of Nhemith, he thought with a silent sigh.

Between needing to get the network cleansed, needing to train Arten to tame her wild power, and now needing to find and eliminate the corruption from his people, he did not have time to be weak and recovering.

I will ask Kylik tonight if his sources can handle the strain of accelerating my healing.

Arten yelped.

"Again," he said.

She opened her eyes to glare at him this time before diving back into herself.

Each time she touched her power, he could see the backlash as it struck at her. He had hoped that her efforts today would agitate it free from the tight knot it was keeping at her core. But as she touched it again and again, it remained still and deep. *If it sparks tonight as it did last night, it will flare-out. In my current state, I will be unable to get to her in time to stop it from consuming her.*

She could stay here, an inner voice whispered enticingly. *These rules were made for the deviant, not for you. You are kaz, you can do as you please.*

It was, for some reason, Nhemith's voice.

No, he thought, the words filled with ancient ice and a wind that tasted of all directions. *I am kaz, so I must set the example. In the days that come, I must be without fault if my investigations are to stand.*

It was as it had always been for him—setting the standard by which they lived, providing a template for his people to follow. The voice of strength as his race declined. Except for once, thirteen years ago today, when he had acted on instinct and impulse and left to seek the girl that now sat across from him.

I will fix this, I will fix all of it. And you will help me, Arten.
He felt his eyes flash. It was why he had sought her, why he
had purchased her indenture. She was unprecedented, new.
Younger than any source that had ever been. Her power was
blinding to his sight like no other he had ever experienced
or heard of.

The clock in the upper city chimed three-afternoon,
interrupting his scrutiny of her. "That is enough, Arten."

She wiped the sweat from her brow and sank back into
her chair. Her power stayed belligerently fixed at her core.

I have to do something, he thought, grimly. *I cannot allow
her to flare out tonight.* Once she was recovered, he said,
"Come here."

She approached cautiously until she stood in front
of him.

"Thank you," he said. "I need you to give me your assurance that you will not practice except in our daily sessions."

"Why?"

He felt his lip twitch up at the corner. There was no
falseness with her, no deference to his title or artifice to gain
his approval. "It is dangerous. Until your power is tamed,
any interaction you have with it can cause it to flare. While I
am in my present state, I will not be able to get to you in
time."

"Oh," she said, going still and pale. "Okay."

He could sense her panic in the increased tempo of her
heart, the scrape of breath through her constricted throat.

"There is something I would like to try, to help prevent
your power from flaring while you are away from here." He
added, studying her, "It could be dangerous."

"What...what do you plan to do?" she asked.

"Calm your power, I hope."

She squared her shoulders, braced herself. "Okay," she agreed.

She finally trusts me? he wondered as he pushed himself out of the chair. The scabs around his torso pulled; another one broke with a sharp pain. He ignored it.

He laid his palms along her jaw, tilting her head up. Closed his eyes, gathered his emaciated power and released it, breathed it gently into her. He had no idea if it would work; such a thing had never been done before. But what alternative had he? He would not lose her.

He felt the life-force leaving him, saw without his eyes as it flowed into her. It splintered in her throat and burned cold to her core. It met the knot of her power and melted. But it was enough to lance the pressure building there. He opened his eyes.

Hers were wide, her mouth gaped in awe, but her vision was turned deeply inwards.

"Do not reach for it," he reminded her, sharply.

She startled and focused on him.

"You gave me your word," he said, his voice trembling slightly. His hands were trembling, too. He withdrew them, sank gracelessly into his chair.

"Stekin?" she was at his knee, anxiety tight on her face where joy had been moments before.

"I must rest," he managed around a tongue thick with rapid fatigue. "You gave...your word."

"I did. I won't reach for it."

"Good," he whispered as his eyes closed, as darkness pressed close around him. He felt her nearby, felt her hesitate, then the light, warm touch of a palm on his forehead, the curl of narrow fingers through his hair. He was too exhausted even to smile.

3

A FRIEND & THE MATRON
ARTEN

Arten had retrieved Claude after Stekin had slumped, unconscious, in his chair. Kylik, the healer dragon, was being sent for, and she felt distinctly in the way. So she ambled back towards Stekin's compound, packages tucked under her arm. *Home*, she reminded herself.

Stekin's power felt shivery inside her. She could feel it there, wanted to reach down with the internal hands she had just found, wanted to touch it. But she didn't. She felt it passively in the way her Words rasped against it, not discordant but foreign. She was tingly and a little light headed, and the long stairs down didn't bother her a bit.

There was still plenty of daylight and she was feeling bold, not quite herself, so she didn't turn in at the gate to Stekin's compound but continued to follow the boulevard. Whispers and suspicious glances chased her around the curve of the second circuit, onto the third. She strolled by compounds, peering at the carved or painted signs that hung off the fence in front of each, displaying the owning dragon's mark—unlike the first circuit, where the marks were wrought into the iron of the gates or worked elaborately into the doors. When she looked more closely, she could see that there were other marks underneath the wooden placards. *New owners,* she realized.

She came to a compound that had not one or two, but four wooden shingles hung along the fence, two on either side of the small gate. One of which was twin to the brand on Natalia's brow. She let herself through the fence. There were fewer whispers, here. Almost no one sat in the road. The decorative gardens were wild, unkempt, as though someone had just not gone to the effort to tear them down. Around the side of this compound, Arten could see a vegetable garden. The masonry wall rose up close behind.

She knocked on the door.

A scrawny man about twenty years old answered. He scowled at her, all jutting chin and elbows, as he said, "What do you want?"

His rudeness tempered the fizz in her blood. "Does Natalia live here?" she asked, in a voice too small for her liking.

"Who's asking?" he demanded.

"Arten. She—said I could come by some time."

"Did she, now?" he muttered to himself. Then, to Arten, "She's round back, at laundry. Pitch it or get out."

With that, he closed the door in her face.

Arten found her way around to the back of the compound, passing carefully through the vegetable garden. It was nowhere near as grand as Stekin's place. Looked from the outside about the size of her parents' shop and home. A figure in a shapeless, colorless dress was bent over a tub on the patio, arms-deep in gray water. Only the shine of pale hair indicated that this was the same woman she'd met hours ago. That and the effortless scowl on her face.

"Natalia?"

A glare speared her to the spot for a moment. Then Natalia looked away, her face coloring.

"Demons, what are you doing here?"

"You said I could come by...?"

"I didn't think you'd come *today!*" she snapped, wringing out a pair of trousers with a single-minded intensity.

"Oh," Arten said, crestfallen.

"Look, it's just not a good time. I've got to finish this up before it gets dark, and the boys thought it would be funny to wrestle in the muck. Not only did they wreck our gourd garden, but they made this stupid job ten times harder for me this week." Natalia was standing, fists on her hips, glaring at the pile of mud-crusted clothing.

"I can help," Arten offered.

Natalia pierced her with that stare again. "Why?" she demanded, "Why would you?"

Arten shrugged. "Because you could use it. And I'd like to learn more about this place from you."

Natalia was still suspicious. "Why are you here, Arten?"

"You invited me."

"No...you're the kaz's girl. Why are you slumming it down here on the third circuit?"

"I'm not the kaz's girl. And you invited me," she said again, flushing.

"I think that was a mistake," Natalia said, snatching up another muddy item from the unwashed heap. "I think you should go." She dropped back to her knees and dashed the tunic in the water.

"Okay," Arten agreed, but didn't. She took the next item and knelt opposite Natalia, dropping it in the water.

"What are you doing?" Natalia snapped.

"I'm helping you, then I'll go," Arten said, agitating the cloth against the board in time with Natalia, who said nothing. Arten was burning with questions, but she held them in. Just scrubbed the mud out of the trousers, then a tunic. Helped Natalia empty the soiled tub onto the trampled gourd garden, hung the cleaned items to dry while she refilled the tub. Went back to the laundry with clean water and cleaner clothes that required less vigor. When the pile was gone, she helped Natalia empty the tub on the other garden, careful of the intact plants. Natalia stowed the tub inside while Arten hung up the last of the laundry to dry.

She turned around to find the young woman leaning in the doorframe, assessing her, arms crossed, eyes narrowed.

"Well, see you," Arten said, glum, turned to leave.

"Wait."

She stopped.

Natalia's face was contorted in that look of indecision she'd had earlier. "Look, if you want, you can stay for dinner. It won't be as posh as what you're used to—"

Arten cut her off, "I will, thanks. As long as it's not dried meat and travel bread. Or mint," she added with a little shudder.

"Why mint?" Natalia asked.

"The lady who poisoned me used something that tasted like spoiled mint."

Natalia had the twisted expression again.

"What, isn't everyone poisoned in the network?" Arten joked, but Natalia didn't laugh.

"Not poisoned, no," she said, guardedly.

Arten sobered. "Workshop men?" she asked.

"I don't—look, we're not supposed to talk about it. About whatever happened in the network. You should learn that fast." Natalia was drawing herself away, her face drawing up haughtily, her fingers rubbing an anxious line under her clavicle.

"Sure, okay," Arten agreed quickly. "Thanks for letting me know. But...if you *did*—talk about it, I mean—Stekin could help."

Natalia barked a bitter laugh. "The great kaz, deigning to listen to me? Right," she scoffed.

"You don't know him at all!" Arten was startled at how fierce and hot the retort came. Natalia recoiled, then covered the motion in a smirk.

"I thought you weren't the kaz's girl?"

"I'm not," Arten muttered, embarrassed.

"Right," Natalia started to say, skepticism drawing the syllable out. Just then a figure appeared behind her in the doorway. Taller and more muscular than the one who had answered the door. "What is it, Rac?" Natalia sighed.

"You've got a visitor. Viktor's keeping her company." He smiled facetiously, jerked his head over his shoulder.

"Great," Natalia snapped and pushed past him. Arten heard her stomped footsteps fade as she disappeared into the house.

He took Natalia's place against the doorpost, took up her arms-crossed stance. Arten was forcibly aware of the muscles that stretched the cloth of his tunic and that he was strikingly handsome. And how he was looking at her. And how far away and incapacitated Stekin was.

The last bothered her the most. *Why should I care where Stekin is?* she growled internally. *I can take care of myself.* A fist balled at her side, the other went to her pocket, grasping for the knife hilt that was no longer there. *I took on Ergin unarmed, this pretty boy is nothing compared to him*, she reminded herself. But she desperately missed the knife.

"Viktor," she said, filling the awkward silence, "is that the boy who answered the door?"

Rac let out a mirthless chuckle. "Scrawny, gangly little

shite? Hair like the business end of a broom—" He ran a hand through his own hair, as though to assure himself it wasn't contaminated by association. "—and a scowl to match?"

She thought it a harsh assessment, even though he'd been unfriendly to her. "Sounds right," she admitted.

"That's our Viktor, source to Nyyrikki. Little shite doesn't know how good he's got it here. And who might you be?" the man added, his voice turning low and rumbling.

"What's it to you?" she demanded.

He laughed, the sound skittered through her. She gritted her teeth. "Easy, I just want to know your name."

"You first," she said.

"Raccard, source to Graug." He smiled, showing teeth straight and white enough to make a dragon proud. He pushed away from the wall, took a step towards her. "And you?"

She stepped back. "Arten," she said and immediately regretted it. *Demons, why did I tell him my real name?*

"Arten," he repeated, trying her name out. "It's unusual. Where are you from?" He had advanced a few more paces, she retreated with each one. Her heel hit the wall. She glanced up, already knew it was too high to climb. Wasn't sure if she was fast enough to get past his reach.

But then Natalia's harsh voice cut across the small patio. "Demons, Rac, get away from her!"

Raccard scowled over his shoulder at the interruption. Arten took advantage of his distraction to dart away, until Natalia was between them, and her back was to the garden and the exit.

Natalia sneered. "You're disgusting, you know that?"

He shrugged, grinned lazily at Arten. "I'm just getting to know her, Goldie. Are you jealous?"

"You stupid ox." Natalia was within range of him, now. She reached up and grabbed a fistful of his glossy, perfect hair, dragged his head down to her level. "First, she's like twelve, and you know it."

Arten bristled at that—she was thirteen today, thank you —but Rac didn't seem to care.

"Second, she's a source," Natalia said.

That got his attention. He paled.

"She's not branded," he protested.

"Think with your head for once," Natalia snarled, shaking it roughly by the roots of his hair. "Really young. Unbranded. Put it together, idiot."

His face went green. "Oh, demonsfire..." His pupils contracted and the look he had turned on Arten changed from keen interest to fear.

"Yeah," Natalia snapped. "If you don't want his attention, I suggest you don't forget her face. And if you're that ener-getic, go up the Hill. Take Carl with you, he needs to get out." She dragged him towards the door, shoved him inside it. "And stop eating that junk they send down. How many times have I said?"

"I can't help it, Nat," he moaned, "I'm so hungry. And it makes me feel right."

"That's the point, idiot. Next time I might not be here to save your sorry carcass."

"You're right. You're right. I'll go." He sighed.

"Take Carl!" she called after his retreating back. Then turned to Arten. "Sorry about that. My compound-mate is, um, not himself right now. And that was someone looking for you, at the door. *Really* annoying. Sound like someone you know?"

Arten groaned. "I think I might."

"You should probably head home."

"Are you...going to be okay?" Arten asked, the alarms still tingling in her limbs.

"Yeah, I can handle them," Natalia said with a dismissive shrug. She looked older and harder than her years.

Arten didn't know what to say other than, "You can come to my place any time. I mean any time. For as long as you need."

Natalia stiffened. "I don't need your charity."

Arten had seen the same expression on Juro and Maruko more often than she could remember. The same injured pride at being offered kindness. "It's not," she said. "Goodnight, Natalia. Thank you for the offer of dinner."

Natalia said nothing, just watched as Arten picked her way through the garden. Arten looked over her shoulder to see a thoughtful scowl on the golden face. Waved once, then went through the gate, out onto the boulevard.

There were two men ahead of her, one large and the other withered. The large one was dragging his companion along the road. It reminded her of how she had dragged Stekin along the road, though he had been more emaciated and delirious than this man, who just seemed to be tired. And she had been small, just as she now was. She could still feel Stekin's weight on her shoulder, the compression of her spine in every limping step he took. She absently rubbed her palm, where his hip had cut into it, then her rib where the scab from the knife wound Ergin had given her was just starting to crack. The large man ahead glanced back over his shoulder. He recognized her the same time she did him; Raccard paled and pulled his friend along faster.

She let them draw ahead, thinking about what she had witnessed. *That must be Carl. And he is Raccard. Then there was Viktor, who opened the door.* There had been four wooden sigils outside the compound. One was Natalia's, the other three—*one was definitely like Raccard's. The other two might match the other guys.* That meant Natalia lived with at least three men, in a compound that, she suspected, held sources for four dragons. She'd never heard of that before.

Not that I'm an expert. She sighed. *What do I know about this place?* But what she had observed, so far, was that everyone with the same marking lived in one compound. One compound one dragon. So why were four dragons sharing a compound? *And, at least, I haven't seen any other mixed compounds. Everyone near me is all women.* The more she thought of it, the more she realized that any men she had seen on the boulevards had been unbranded— tradesmen of some sort from up in the city, who came and left quickly.

At the second circuit, Raccard and Carl turned right to follow the curve that swooped counterclockwise around the south and east sides of the boulevard. She had travelled down on the cliff-side, and it was a circuit, so it didn't really matter which way she went back... She followed them. And found the men.

This half of the circuit had a similar setup to the other, though with fewer people out in the streets, less gossip and more small crafts being worked in the idle time. Just like the other side, though, people stopped and stared at her, the low rumble of whispers followed her. She tried to ignore them, focused on not letting Raccard get too far ahead. She went far enough along the first circuit to determine that it, too, housed all-male compounds, then backtracked to the female side. It was getting dark, and she was getting hungry. So she scuffed along to Stekin's compound. She stopped under the delicate archway. A symbol was twisted into the metal at the apex of the arch. The same symbol carved in relief into the doors.

That must be Stekin's symbol, his brand. She rubbed the unmarred skin at her left temple and over her brow. Wondered why the sources were all fine with their slave-mark, and how long before she would have her own. She was only indentured to Stekin for three years, but she would never be able to go home.

A WOMAN WAS WAITING for her outside the age-blackened double doors of Stekin's compound. Her brand, now that Arten knew what to look for, marked her as one of Kylik's sources. The Matron, it seemed, had summoned her. Arten followed the woman back into the boulevard, around the curve clockwise, until they arrived at Kylik's compound on the inner ring. It was not so large as Stekin's, but much more comfortable.

The chattering women quieted as Arten passed through the common area on the heels of her escort. She felt their eyes on her. Felt her face heating. The long corridor was mostly empty, its denizens out in the common area or preparing the evening meal. They passed open doors; she glimpsed slices of the lives of the women who dwelt within. A new dress draped over a chair; a half-finished quilt; disheveled heaps of clothing and a rag rug; a precisely made bed and messy bookshelf; a collection of rocks on a windowsill; paintings drying against a wall. Each step down the hall made her feel heavier, each room a taunting reminder of what she did not have—companionship, family, a home.

The woman knocked, a voice inside called them to enter. She slid the doors open, bowed Arten through, closed them smoothly behind.

"Have a seat, child," the matron said warmly.

Arten lowered herself carefully onto one of the chairs. They were the sort that her friends, the Swains, had in their formal sitting area—a place she and the Swain children had been forbidden to play. She felt the same discomfort here, in the matron's receiving room, adorned with expensive furnishings that Arten felt she might soil just by breathing on them.

"You met your tutor today?" Matron prompted.

"Yes. It's just Stekin."

Matron Pasha swelled indignantly, "Do not be so ungrateful, child. He condescends greatly to teach you, and you must never forget to be appreciative to him for that. And you must always call him Kaz Stekin, or the lord kaz, never just *Stekin* like that."

"Why?" Arten asked, "Why do I have to call him Kaz? He's never said anything."

"Your...meeting," she said primly, "in the network, was highly irregular. Whatever casual address you used while traipsing across the continent, *here* you will call him Kaz Stekin. He is your better, you must show him respect. You must address all dragons except the lord kaz as Lord or Lady."

"Yes, Matron," she said dutifully. Even as she wondered inside if she should be calling him by another title, the one he had rightly purchased.

Matron had continued, and Arten wrangled her attention back.

"Two days ago," she had said, "I gave you a task." She had paused expectantly.

"Meet people," Arten answered.

"Good. And have you?"

"Not really. Everyone stares at me and looks away or

leaves when I go up to them. Except the people that tell me what to do. I did meet someone today, though." She brightened a little.

"Good! Who did you meet?"

"A girl named Natalia."

"Natalia?" The matron hesitated, drew back a little. "To whom does she source?"

Arten shrugged and admitted she didn't remember.

The matron looked horrified. "I can see you have much to learn of manners yet." Her voice dripped disapproval.

Arten simmered inside, her Words rasping sluggishly at her core. The matron's next statements incited them further.

"This Natalia person. Is she blonde, about eighteen?"

"Yeah. She lives down on the third circuit," Arten said, proud of her newfound vernacular.

Matron's frown solidified into a frosty censure that would have made Stekin proud. "It would be best, child, if you did not associate with her."

"Why not? She's nice."

"She's...not the right sort. Although," she mused to herself, "Lady Hiranyath is of relation... No," she resumed, firmly, "no, you are better to avoid that girl."

"Of relation? Lady Hiranyath—that's her dragon?"

"Yes," Matron said, wincing.

That must have been crass, in some way.

"Lady Hiranyath is Kaz Stekin's daughter. But..." She paused delicately. "There has been some...scandal surrounding Lady Hiranyath. If you wish to integrate into our community, if you wish to source to a dragon once your power is tamed, it is best to avoid the tarnish of Lady Hiranyath's association, or that of her source."

"What scandal? Her source? She has only one?" Arten pressed.

"For the former, it is not suited to your ears. For the latter, yes, she has been permitted but one." Matron looked distinctly uncomfortable, opened her mouth to change the topic, but Arten pressed another question.

"So the guys she lives with—they have their own dragons?"

"They *source* to other dragons, yes," Matron Pasha corrected harshly, her mouth compressed in the pauses. "How did you know that?"

"I saw the marks on the fence."

"You've *been* there? Child, you must not do so again!"

"Why not?"

"Because I have forbidden it! That is sufficient reason. Do you understand?"

"Yes, Matron," she agreed glumly. *The one person who talked to me, and I'm not allowed to see her? I hate this place.*

"Good, good." She smoothed her skirts, calming herself. "The lord kaz would be quite upset if you went down there, again. We mustn't upset him..."

"Why not? What does he do when he's upset?"

"He needn't *do* anything," Matron snapped. "He is kaz! He is law and leader in this city; there is no higher authority, no one with more influence or power. Whatever happened between you that has caused you to speak of him with such irreverence, you would do best to immediately forget it." Her voice was rising in volume and lowering in temperature. "You and I exist at his whim, to source his people. That is our sole function. He has granted you use of his compound until you can become sourced; he has fed and clothed you, housed you in comfort. He now deigns to instruct you in control of your power. You *will* be respectful, you *will* be grateful!"

"Yes, Matron," she said, cowed. Two memories crowded

into her mind: a crumpled cheek and lifeless eyes, a knife tearing through a throat. But she was not afraid of him, not anymore. He had killed the dedicate, killed Ergin, but that same hand had curled gentle fingers through her hair, had cooled her face when the poison burned through her.

Before Matron Pasha could start in on a longer lecture, Arten let some of her questions tear free. "So how many dragons have only one source? Is Stekin—*Kaz* Stekin—the only dragon without one? Why does he not have any sources? How many dragons *are* there? Will I get to see them? When can I go into the city?"

"Slow down, child. It's unseemly to harangue your elders. Now..." She paused for, Arten thought, too long, then said, "You must never go into the city alone. Within each compound we have designated chaperones that can, at their discretion, take people up to the city. However, as you at present have no compound, it is best if you do not go. If you require something, I am certain Kaz Stekin will arrange to have it provided for you.

"Don't look so put upon," she said, patting Arten's hand dismissively, "you'll source to a dragon before you know it."

The statement didn't comfort her.

"As to how many dragons there are, we don't keep an exact count. Not all dragons have sources, nor compounds. Some dragons share a compound, to keep expenses down. There are about a hundred that have sources. I suspect there are close to half that many again who don't."

"Why do they not all have sources?" Arten pressed when Matron paused. "Why do some, like Kylik—sorry, *Lord* Kylik —have lots and others like Natalia's dragon—yeah, Lady Hiranyath—not have many?"

"I don't presume to know the business of our betters." Matron sniffed. "But it is not only a matter of prestige as to how many sources a compound has. Not all compounds are as successful at keeping their expenses as mine, and require financial supplement from their patrons. My girls keep in line, so we are no drain to our Lord Kylik. It is not so every-where." Her pointed look indicated to Arten very clearly what she thought of the expense Stekin was going to on her behalf.

Servants, clothes, food—I wonder how much it is costing him to keep me. "So if a dragon is poor, they can't have as many sources?"

"Well, it's a bit more complicated than that. There aren't many of us in the world, you know. So clearly, those dragons with a *need* naturally acquire more sources than those without."

"What do you mean, a need?" She leaned forward. "What do they need us for? Stekin will never say."

"It is not a topic of polite conversation," the matron frowned severely.

"Please," Arten begged, unashamed.

"Hmph. Very well," she said, sounding so like Stekin for a moment that Arten's mouth twitched. "We source our power to the dragons whenever they require for whatever matters they deem necessary."

"But *why?* What do they do with it?" Arten pressed urgently.

"That is not our place to ask, nor our concern," she snapped.

"But surely you *know,*" Arten wheedled, "since you're Matron. You know everything about this place."

"I can tell you what you will discover yourself in time. Some of our dragon lords, like Lord Kylik, have roles which require a steady source of power. Our Lord Kylik is the primary healer on the Hill, and uses his power to heal not only the dragon lords but their sources. This is one of the reasons my compound is so full, despite the recent short-ages," she said carefully.

Since Ergin started killing about half of the sources that fled though the network, she means. Arten wondered if anyone had told the matron that the "shortages" had been addressed. She hoped that, if they had, her own role in bringing that to pass was downplayed. *The people here already avoid me—if they found out that I attacked Ergin, I doubt they'd like me any better.*

Well...Natalia might...

"Don't smirk like that."

Arten blanked her face immediately.

"Hmph. Well, aside from the dragons that use our power for their professions, the rest of the lords seem to require some small amount to do any magical workings. Don't ask me," she interrupted the question before it passed Arten's lips, "what magical workings they do. I am not privy to such things, nor do I want to be. Lord Kylik is my patron, my busi-ness is to keep him happy and content, to source to him whatever I can when he asks, and to keep this compound running efficiently. As prime, I also keep the girls in line and maintain discipline within the compound. As Matron, I help new ladies adjust to their new duties and make a home here.

"When you are sourced properly, you will need to do your part to help out in your compound. You must listen to your prime. And you must report any indiscretions you witness to myself or your prime."

"Yes, Matron," she said, because it was expected, as she'd learned the last three times she'd heard this speech. But inside, she chaffed at the invisible chains this new life was already drawing around her. *There are more restrictions from the matron than Stekin.*

"Good. In the meantime, you must do what you can to stay out of the lord kaz's way, minimize his expenses and inconvenience on your account, and make an effort to be neighborly. People don't think you're very approachable, you know."

"I'm not unapproachable," she protested, "they just keep staring and hissing behind my back."

"Of course they do; you're quite a spectacle! Running around in boy's clothes, with no hair to speak of. Talking of the lord kaz as though he were a commoner, living in his compound as though you were the prime of it. Appearing amongst us with no warning, no bell, no *attempt* at proper methodologies. And," her lip curled, "the lord kaz *staying* with you for days. It's unheard of. It's obscene."

"Wait, what? I'm not...I didn't do any of that! I mean, it happened, yeah. But it's all Stekin—yes, sorry, *Kaz* Stekin. *He* cut my hair off, he gave me these clothes, he shut me in that compound, he brought me here. It's not like I *asked* for any of this!"

"Don't shout at me, child!"

"Sorry, Matron," she ground out.

"I didn't say *I* thought those things, but that others do. Which is why you must make an additional effort to be civil and polite. Try to fit in. Wear proper clothing. Talk to people. They've complained, you know, to me—they're saying that you think you're too important to associate with us, since Kaz Stekin brought you in. They think you're putting on airs. They don't want their patrons to choose you, for fear that you'll be unhappy for the step-down from sourcing the lord kaz."

"That's crazy!" She winced at Matron's scowl, said, "Sorry. I just mean, that's not it at all!" She hated the plaintive tone in her voice.

"Well, the only one who can fix that, child, is you." The matron's tone had softened a little. Seemed almost caring.

"I'll try," she promised unhappily. "What do you mean, though, about the choosing? Kaz," she caught herself that time, "Stekin said *I* would choose who I sourced."

Pasha actually laughed, the sound of tinkling glass, "Oh, child, don't be absurd! *You* choose? No, no, no. You must have misunderstood. The lord dragons always choose their sources."

Stekin had clearly told her that she would be able to choose to whom she would be enslaved as a source, even if it wasn't customary. She resolved to ask him if that was still true, but either way, it wouldn't hurt to know more about this choosing process. "How? And when will it happen?"

"Generally, it happens when the source first arrives, that very day. Your power being wild complicates things a little. Until it is tamed, you are not fit to source anyone and are a danger to any compound. *Usually,*" she stressed, with that disapproving frown, "the wild-powered source lives in an empty compound on the third circuit until their power is tamed, then they may be chosen. That you are living in the lord kaz's compound is not unnoticed, and not unremarked upon."

"That's not my—"

"I *know* it's not your fault; I didn't intimate otherwise," she interrupted. "Let me finish." When Arten clamped her jaws together, Matron continued, "Once your power is tamed, the dragons who have earned the right to attain a source will examine your power in order to determine if it is compatible with them. Of those who remain, there is a small ceremony on the Hill to determine to whom you will source. It's all efficiently done, and nothing to fear."

"Is there something I *should* fear?" she asked, feeling anxious about something in the matron's tone.

"No, of course not!" she said, too quickly. "We're all safe, here. Our lords take prodigious care in protecting us."

"You just said that like you're expecting me to be afraid..."

"Well, the transfer can be...intimate. Most girls are nervous about that the first few times. But you will grow accustomed to it. And Kaz Stekin, like most of our dragon lords, has much experience in the transfer to minimize the discomfort for you. Even if you end up being chosen by a newer dragon, there is no reason to fear, as I assure everyone. The lords have strict laws of conduct in place. You can, of course, come to me with any concerns once you are sourced."

"Intimate? What do you mean?"

"It's...well, we can talk about that another time," Matron deflected, "when you're closer to being chosen."

But there was something else she had said that was bothering Arten and demanded her attention. "Why would it be obscene for the kaz to stay in his compound?"

"It's forbidden for the dragon lords to stay in their compounds. They rarely visit for more than an hour. So that he stayed there with you for two whole days—inside!—is quite improper. My Lord Kylik was distraught, even knowing how injured the kaz was at the time."

"That's a silly rule," Arten snorted. "They own the places, why can't they visit and stay?"

"It is the way, child, it is part of how life here is run. Accept it and abide by it quickly and life will be easier for you."

"Yes, Matron." It hadn't answered her question, not really. *Breaking a rule isn't the same as obscene.*

She frowned, then brightened. *Maybe Natalia will tell me.*

"Good. You'll adjust, child, everyone adjusts. You are fortunate, though—as young as you are, you have nothing to regret leaving behind—" Arten felt a flash of anger. "—unlike many of the ladies who come to us." The matron was about to say more, but there was a rushing of wind outside. Her eyes snapped to the patio doors. She rose swiftly and went to them, spread them wide, as something heavy and winged dropped onto the broad surface beyond.

"My lord!" Matron cried, with a warmth she had never shown in Arten's presence. She was looking out and up, arms still spread wide against the doors, leaning forward. *She looks...younger. Happy.*

The sound of something large scuffed across the patio and Matron backed into the room as the head of a dragon poked through the doorway where she'd just stood. The dragon peered at Arten. She froze under the stare.

"What," Kylik snarled, his teeth flashing in the low light, "did you do to him?"

4

AN ALLY

STEKIN

Stekin hissed as one of his myriad scabs caught on a bandage and cracked free.

"Apologies, my lord kaz." Claude cringed, freezing in place, the half-unwrapped bandage in his hands.

"It is nothing. Finish it," Stekin said. Claude continued changing the bandage, more slowly this time. Normally the pain from a small scab like that would have been beneath Stekin's notice. But normally, Stekin was not covered in them and lanced through with pain from the inside out.

Stekin locked his hands on the back of his chair and closed his eyes while Claude moved around him, applying soothing salve and clotting powder to his surgery marks. Kylik was insistent that while the demon-metal remained in his lungs, Stekin's body should be trusted to the do the long-term healing. The healer spent Stekin's power only when he was around to supervise it, to ensure the demon-metal did not twist it into something else. Which meant Stekin was stuck with the pain and stiffness for most of the day. Kylik had just left, and already Stekin could feel his muscles tensing against it.

By the time Claude finished, Stekin was more than ready to sit down again. The man helped lower him into his chair, a skeptical expression on his face.

"Shall you be retiring soon, my lord kaz?"

"No," Stekin said, willing strength he did not currently feel into his voice. "Fetch Kikkyo to me."

Claude hesitated. "Lord Kylik was most insistent that you not overextend yourself."

Stekin dismissed the concern with a flick of his fingers. "I know my limits. Send for Kikkyo, Claude, and make sure we are not disturbed."

A concerned look passed across the man's features, but he verbalized an assent, bowed, then trotted off.

Stekin closed his eyes and caught a short nap, too tired to be cross that he needed one, while he waited for Kikkyo to answer his summons.

When she arrived, he roused himself but managed little more than straightening in his chair. Kikkyo bowed her head deeply to him, the curving horns around her head nearly brushing the floor, respect and awe in the gesture. He realized he had never sought her out in particular before.

"Thank you for coming," he said. "As you see, I am not yet well enough to travel to you." The admission was more bitter than he had intended.

Kikkyo just acknowledged his words with one of the smiling, graceful inclines of her head for which she was so admired. All the more impressive for the weight of her horns. Grace on the ground was something Stekin had never found useful in a dragon, but he was just now begin-ning to appreciate its quiet appeal.

He wasted no further words. "Are you on the network council still?"

"Yes, my kaz." Her voice was smooth and low, easy to

listen to, like water flowing over old stones. He knew, because he had witnessed it, that it had taken her decades of practice to develop that voice. For the first time, he found himself admiring the result of her efforts.

"Good. What has Nhemith told you of Ergin?"

Her head tilted, confused. "Nhemith has told us nothing but that you are returned and recovering from a great battle, and that we are not to disturb you."

He felt his mouth compress. *Nhemith, what are you up to?* He pushed the flash of suspicion aside. "Kikkyo, I charge you with taking word back to the rest of the council of what I have discovered..."

He told her a condensed story of the discrepancy he had found while traveling in the south between the number of sources entering and leaving the network. Then of Ergin, who had been stealing those sources, murdering them, in a mad attempt to restore his own power. He told her that Ergin was dead by Stekin's own hand.

He paused as a spasm of pain shot through his lungs.

"So it is finished," she said. "This Ergin stole our sources, and he is dead. But, kaz, this sounds like a matter for the source council—why have you summoned me?"

"Because," he grunted, teeth clenched as the fire ebbed in his chest, "Ergin was not the biggest threat to our sources. The network is."

Kikkyo frowned thoughtfully then lowered herself to the ground, crossing her wrists before her, her forepaws draped with unconscious elegance. "I think you had better tell me, my kaz," she urged, her seriousness gratifying.

He drew a few shallow, pained breaths, until the worst of the spasm had passed and he could speak freely again.

"Arten was endangered several times while she was in the network. One node custodian would have tortured her, and had tortured many in the past, but released them all. Another wanted to keep her for his own. At another, the custodians had let four sources flare out and not bothered to scour the bunker between—had I not been there, Arten also would have died. I extracted her from those situations before she came to harm, but even I could not protect Arten from the custodian who poisoned her and had killed two others before her."

Kikkyo's head was reared back, disgust and horror warring on her face. "My kaz!" she exclaimed, as though the words could ward away the evil. "Is she well?"

With that, Stekin felt the last of his reservations about summoning Kikkyo crumble. "She is well," he assured, "but others are not as fortunate. Even accounting for Ergin, if we take the numbers that I observed enter the network in my travels and compare to the number that reach the final node, we are still losing at least ten percent, perhaps as much as thirty."

"We cannot guarantee that all who enter emerge," Kikkyo mused, "but what you have told me is troubling. Sickness, capture by a dedicate, these are things we cannot control. But once a source enters the network, they are under our protection. It is inexcusable that our network has caused their mistreatment and death!"

Stekin felt the corner of his mouth angle into a smile. "It relieves me to hear my sentiments in your words," he said. Then sobered again. "But there is more you must know."

Kikkyo cocked her head, attentive.

"We were diverted twice, on our way here, due to dedicate activity."

Kikkyo said carefully, "That cannot be so unusual, my kaz. You know, better than anyone, the lengths to which the temple will go in their thirst to eradicate sources."

Stekin shook his head minutely. "I fear it is more than that, Kikkyo. I will tell you, but you must let this go no further than between us, not even to the rest of the council."

"I trust my ancestors and my kaz to guide me," she said.

It was the strongest oath he could hope for. He nodded once. "Very well. You can see that I am injured, but I have asked the cause to be kept from public knowledge. When I came across Ergin, he had fashioned a weapon against our people. It was made from demon-metal." Kikkyo's breath left her in an appalled huff. He would not tell her about the filings—that knowledge was dangerous, and too many people knew of it already.

"What concerns me," he continued, "is not that Ergin acquired demon-metal. It is how he came by it, and how much he had."

Kikkyo recovered enough from her shock to ask, "How *did* he come by it?"

"He killed dedicates," Stekin said. "Dozens of them over the years."

"Is that not a good thing?" Kikkyo asked, confused. "A dedicate dead is one not harming our sources."

"That is true, but Ergin was entrenched in the mountains just beyond our southern border. He had been there for quite a long time, based on his dwelling."

Kikkyo looked puzzled, then gradually, horrified. "He has led them to us?"

"I cannot know for certain. But yes, that is my fear. There is no reason for dedicates to venture this far north, not with enough consistency to garner him that much demon-metal. Our southern border is impassable, and to the west there are only small scattered family communities."

Kikkyo asked, "Could he not have encountered them away from here?"

Stekin coughed a note of mirthless laughter. "Not and killed so many of our sources. No, the rate of loss was consistent; Ergin had not left these mountains for many years."

"I see," she said, her expression dark and concerned.

"I imagine after he killed the first dedicate, the temple sent another to investigate. Ergin could not have killed everyone they sent, otherwise we would have had an army on the road long before now. But with as many has he *has* killed...and with the increased vigilance that forced Arten to reroute...I fear the temple may find us soon. Or worse—find the network."

"But the custodians are all under compulsion to keep the network safe," Kikkyo protested. "A compulsion you yourself generated, and one that has kept it secret for centuries."

"Yes," Stekin agreed, his mouth tight and grim, "but the sources are not."

Kikkyo went still, her mouth gaped in understanding.

"They have only to take over one node, capture the next source to go through, and the network will crumble. Once they have tortured the source, they will trace its path back, destroying each node they find. And with each node, they will better learn how to find other nodes, each custodian they torture will reveal more of the compulsion. Until they are able to scout nodes on their own."

"But this has never been a concern before!" she protested.

"This has always been a vulnerability in the network," Stekin correctly gently, "but we can mitigate the risk."

"My kaz, what must we do?" Kikkyo whispered.

"First, we must not panic," he cautioned.

Kikkyo squared shoulders that had hunched and smoothed her wings back down. She nodded once, ready for him to continue.

"Good. Next you must tell the source council about the damage to the network. Tell them of the dangers from within, but do not mention Ergin or the increased dedicate activity; it will cause only panic."

She nodded again.

"Then start recruiting and training more network agents. We will need them, whatever course we take."

"That will take considerable time, my kaz," she warned.

"Then you had better to convince the council to start on it soon."

She bowed her acknowledgement.

"That is enough for tonight," he said, feeling the weight of his injuries press down on him and his energy drain away. "Leave me. We will speak again soon."

"Yes, my kaz." She rose, bowed to him again, then left.

Stekin was relieved to hear Claude's rapid step and more relieved for the solid shoulder that held up under his weight as the man helped him up to his bed.

The temple would not come in the night; the network would not collapse tomorrow. They had a little time. And now, more than anything, Stekin needed to rest. So that when the time did come he would be able to be the kaz his people needed.

5

A CONFRONTATION WITH KYLIK
ARTEN

"I didn't do anything!" Arten protested, taking a cautious step back from the bristling dragon whose head was thrust into the matron's sitting room. His scales were flared out in sharp ridges, making his massive head seem even larger and more menacing. Arten was fixated, however, on the long curve of his teeth.

Kylik's low growl rumbled through the room, then cut off abruptly. "My dear," he said, curling his head to look at the matron, "I must ask you to assemble the girls."

"At once, my lord," she said, curtseying to him. As she dashed past Arten, she launched a scowl at her, then hurried on.

Once the doors rumbled closed behind Matron, Arten realized she was very alone in the presence of a hostile dragon. She backed up another pace. Kylik's shoulders were too broad to allow him to enter the room, his neck was shorter than Stekin's, and while he couldn't reach her with his teeth, she wondered how far his arm could reach. She felt like a mouse with a cat at the door.

"What did you do to him?" Kylik repeated, lips drawn back.

"Nothing!"

His teeth parted. She wondered if he was calculating his attack the same way she was.

"Then why was he near comatose and drained after you left, when before your arrival he had been recovering nicely?"

"I don't know!" she snapped, edging farther back from the hot amber stare. "He—he gave me some of his power, then he fell asleep so I left!"

The sound that then escaped Kylik was unquestionably a snarl. It sent alarm down her spine, set her limbs crackling, her heart pounding as a need to *flee* seized her. She leapt back, edged towards the doors, unable to look away from the expanse of teeth that seemed to fill the room.

"Stop!" he commanded, and she froze, inches from the door.

I can't move! Why can't I move!? she thought, panicked. *He's going to kill me and I can't get away. I made it all the way here, only to die in someone's sitting room.* A bubble of hysterical laughter pressed against her throat, and she swallowed it down.

Instinctively, she also pushed down on the Words. The Words, which always sought to escape when she was distracted. The Words which now were not scrabbling for freedom but churning, like fish in shallow, too-muddy water. But she couldn't think about them, not with Kylik hulking in the doorway, not with his power holding her in thrall.

The door behind her slid open, the matron dashed back in. Took in the scene, dismissed Arten, and in a moment was by Kylik's side, her hand on his cheek, stroking smooth his moss-green scales. Asking what had happened, drawing his attention away from Arten, drawing his eyes to her. Arten would have sagged when the angry eyes released her, but the power that gripped her did not permit it.

Under the matron's hands and voice, Kylik's teeth disappeared, the tension in his neck and shoulders steamed away, the light in his eyes dimmed to a normal shade. Arten stared, amazed and disgusted, at the transformation that was occurring before her.

Demons, do they all do that for the dragons? Is that what they'll expect of me? What Stekin expects? The way she's fawning over him...it's revolting!

The matron's hands were stroking over his scales, and Kylik was rumbling something that sounded like a staccato purr while he nuzzled her.

I won't do it, she told herself. *I won't!* The thought of Stekin crouching before her with that wistful expression, arching into her touch, turned her stomach. The hand she had curled through his hair earlier, imitating the gesture of affection he had made so often to her, felt dirty. Her face heated.

"My dear, we are all assembled for you," the matron was saying, still in that warm tone. "Will you come into the garden?"

"Oh, Pasha," Kylik mourned, "what will I do when you're gone? I'll be bereft without you."

"You will be fine," she assured, "just as you were before I came."

"You're my favorite, you know," he murmured, nuzzling her.

She didn't say anything, just ran her hands over his eyeridges, smiled at him. The Words at Arten's core rolled sickeningly. There was something unspoken passing between them, a language between people that know each other well. It reminded her of Juro and Maruko, and what twisted in Arten's stomach was homesickness.

The matron placed a hand on Kylik's nose. He edged back from the door, his scales scraping against the stone lintel as he worked them free. Arten's mouth went even drier when she realized how hard he'd been pressing against the doorframe to get at her.

"You and I," the matron spoke sharply over her shoulder to Arten, "will speak tomorrow morning." There was a threat in her words that Arten didn't miss. Then, in the simpering tones, she said to Kylik, "Come, my lord," laid a hand on his neck and led him away. He followed, subdued and obedient. Before his wings disappeared from view, Arten heard Matron say, "You must release her, my dear."

A grumble from the dragon, then the vise of power around Arten broke. She fell forwards, limbs spasming but unable to coordinate. Her muscles twitched and cramped as she knelt, hands and knees cushioned by thick carpet. Once her limbs were back under her control, she pushed herself to her feet shakily and stumbled out of the still-open patio door.

Kylik's tail disappeared around the corner. She trotted after, putting a hand against the stone exterior wall to steady herself, trying to keep her footfalls silent. At the corner of the house, she peeked around. Saw Kylik lowering himself on a patch of lawn at the center of a ring of torches. Clustered around him, perched on the edge of stone benches, were his sources. All clean and neat, their brands dark in the flickering torchlight, wearing identical dresses, identical little slippers, hair bound in identical braids.

"How much do you require, my lord?" Matron asked, formal and reverential. No longer stroking his face, but merely standing near his shoulder.

"As much as you can spare safely, my dears," Kylik said, apologetically. He lowered his voice. "The kaz's injuries are extensive, but keep that between us."

"Always, Lord Kylik," Matron said with a smooth bow. "We keep your confidence gladly." She turned to the waiting women—Arten counted fourteen of them—said, "Ah, Rya. You first, since you are most recovered."

A young, nervous woman was pushed to her feet, and stumbled to a stop in front of Kylik and the matron. She curtseyed gracelessly to the pair and, with occasional nervous glances to the dragon, started to sing. Her voice was thin and high, her song was in a language Arten didn't understand and seemed to meander instead of following a rhythm.

Something barely seen, like the shimmer of heat, flowed out of her. *Her power, it must be.* To Arten's surprise, Kylik didn't draw the great breath to pull it from the air—Matron Pasha did. A shuddering inhale that forged the shimmer into a current between them which broke only when the girl stopped singing. She scampered away to the empty place on the bench, but Arten watched the matron, whose face was grim and pained.

What is this? Arten thought, shuddering at the sweat that sprung onto the matron's brow. Two more girls rushed forwards without prompting and began to sing in unison. Another formless song with nonsensical words, the two voices entwining easily. The shimmering current appeared again as power flowed into the matron. Twice more the women came forward to sing in a group of three, then two. Each song different, each opaque. The matron drew the power in, until her shoulders were curled, her face glistening, the strain written in the lines of it.

"That's enough, my dear," Kylik said after the last two sat down. "I will do the rest myself."

"Yes, my lord," Matron panted, her voice a croak. She turned to face him, laid a hand on his shoulder, and sang. Her voice was cracked and rough at first, but warmed up into something pleasant. Her eyes locked onto her dragon's as she sang to him, hers tired, his glowing with increasing brightness.

Arten saw the girls casting their faces politely aside as the power flowed out of their prime into Kylik. Matron had said the transfer was intimate—Arten's face heated to see it now, though she didn't know why. They were just standing there, Matron singing, Kylik drawing the power in, but Arten wanted to look away. Something more than just the power was passing between them, something vulnerable and private. She knew shouldn't be here, shouldn't be seeing this.

But she didn't leave. She made herself watch as the matron finished singing the power to Kylik, as Kylik drew the last in, his tongue curling through the air, wrapping around the invisible ends of it. Watched as Pasha lowered herself to lean along the outstretched forearm Kylik offered to her, and rested against his shoulder, head tilted back, eyes closed. Her arm stretched atop his. His sources continued to avert their faces, even the last group of six who stood in front of Kylik and offered him their haunting song as a single unit.

Only now did the transfer seem familiar as Kylik hissed in that not-breath, jaws opened to draw in the power. *Why was it different with the matron?* The dragon had seemed to make no effort to pull the power in when she had sung it. But now, he reached for it, pulled at it, in that way Arten had become accustomed to with Stekin. *But it's not the same as with me and Stekin. Stekin gets feral-looking, intense. His jaws go much wider than that...and he snaps at the Words.* But he had only drawn her power in his human body. *Maybe it's easier as a dragon?*

The women ended their song and began filing inside, taking the torches with them. Two of the younger helped the matron to her feet; she leaned heavily on them as they walked her back in through the side door. Kylik stayed in the garden, eyes half-closed and no longer glowing. A dark blot, lost against the backdrop of trees but for the outline of his limbs and tail on the ground.

"You can come out now," he rumbled. Arten saw motion of his head in the shadows, knew it was now pointed at her. "Come, come, I can smell you there."

Arten edged out from around the corner, kept her back to the wall as she crept towards him. *This is stupid, you should run*, she thought. But she was curious. She stopped well clear of him.

"Come closer. I wish to talk," he urged. "I will not attack you."

"You nearly did earlier," she countered.

"You have my apologies for that," he said elegantly. She thought she saw the dipping of his head. "I am feeling much more myself, now. I promise you will be safe."

"All the same, I'd rather know if I'm about to be eaten," she said.

He made a disgusted noise. "We do not eat *humans,*" he said, appalled. "Whoever gave you that notion? If the kaz told you—"

"No," she interrupted, "it wasn't him. I have eyes, and I'm not stupid. You could kill me in a second if you wanted to."

"Then what use is huddling against the wall?" He

chuckled—amused, but not cruelly so. "I can see why he likes you."

"Who?" she asked automatically.

"The kaz, of course, who else?"

"Why can you see that?" She moved a little closer. Now that he wasn't growling at her, she found his voice quite pleasant. Not frigid and stiff like Stekin, but light and easy. *Jovial.*

"I will answer your questions if you agree to stay and talk with me for a while." She saw the smoky smudges of his teeth as he grinned.

"All right," she agreed, "but you have to light up your eyes so I know where you are. I know you can do it."

"What an interesting request!" He sounded delighted. "I am happy to oblige you, of course." His eyes glowed softly as his head dipped in an incline and back up. "There, now, come here so we can speak without disturbing my poor sources."

Arten moved closer until she perched on one of the stone benches.

"You look good there," he said, his eyes flashing brighter for a moment. Arten's heart stuttered. "Will you sing for me?" he asked, slyly, his eyes narrowing to amber slits.

"No," she said.

"Ah, well. Probably for the best. I would not want to upset the kaz. And speaking of," his eyes opened, his pupils narrowed as he stared at her, "tell me what happened this afternoon between you two."

"I already told you," she said, "He gave me some of his power, then he fell asleep and I left."

"You said that, yes, but it makes no sense. Why would the *kaz* give *you* power? You're a source!" The thought seemed to genuinely distress him.

"I don't know, why don't you ask him?" She bristled, glaring at the glowing orbs of his eyes.

His pupils contracted to tiny points, lost in amber. "No, no, the kaz's business is his own," he said quickly.

"And my business isn't my own?" she snapped.

"Well, no. Of course not," he said, confused. "You are a source. All that concerns you is the business of the dragon you source." That seemed to be explanation enough for him.

"But I'm not sourced to a dragon," she said caustically. "So is everyone going to be edging in on my affairs?"

"Of course not! You may be unclaimed as of yet, but everyone knows you're to be the kaz's." He was being conciliatory, as though his news would soothe her temper.

"Am I really?"

"Yes, of course. His interest in you is plain. And he *is* the kaz, so of course none would stand against him."

Arten ground her teeth. "So that's it? Stekin wants me, so I have no choice in the matter."

"Goodness, child, why would you think that?"

"Because you just said—"

He wasn't finished, "Of course you have no choice! I wonder what gave you that notion. What I am saying is that no dragon will challenge the kaz in his choice of you, so you need not worry." He paused, lowered his head to peer closely at her, "Here, I have just given you good news, why are you so upset?"

"Good news?" She barked a laugh, "How is that good news? To know that my life is completely out of my hands, and that Stekin has gone back on his word?"

"Of course it is good news! You are to be sourced to the kaz, the most respected of all dragons. It is a placement others long for, yet makes you unhappy. You are very odd, even for a human. Does it not comfort you to know that you will be cared for throughout the rest of your life, that others will seek your friendship because of the prestige your association with bring them?"

"No, it doesn't," she muttered. "I am not some pet to be locked away and trotted out to impress the neighbors."

"Locked away?" he recoiled. "Stars above, child, no one is locking you away! But here, I can see you are distressed, so let us talk of something else," he added quickly. "I promised to answer your questions..." he offered.

"Fine," she said, crossing her arms stiffly. "Then tell me what you do with the power you take from us."

"I am a healer," he began, but she cut him off.

"Not you specifically, you dragons."

"Ah. Well, we need the power provided by our sources to perform our functions in the community. Aside from that, there is a very little we spend on private matters."

"Like what?" she demanded.

"Child, they are *private,* and thus of no concern to you."

"Like what?" she repeated.

"The health and reproductive necessities of my race are, as I have said, *private*, and you will oblige me not to ask again." His voice was edged with temper.

"Oh," she said, uncomfortable.

He mastered himself, said, "I apologize for raising my voice, I—"

The side door slid open, Kylik fell silent, his head snapped up alertly. A girl crept out of the house, candle in hand.

"Lord Kylik?" she said, her voice small. "Are you unwell? I heard you from inside..."

"Rya, my dear, I am well. I was just speaking with our newest arrival. But it is time for me to depart. Arten..." He turned his eyes on her, they flashed merrily. "I look forward to speaking again, soon. And, Rya, my dear, please escort Arten home so that I may be assured she is safe tonight. And tell no one that you saw us together. Do you understand?"

"Yes, my lord," Rya murmured, curtseying, her reflected light bobbed along the shiny surfaces of Kylik's scales. It caught the flare of his wings. Arten scuttled away from the bench, avoiding the worst of the downdraft of his wings as he launched into the sky. She watched the dark shape of him rise to blot out the stars, watched it until it disappeared into the night.

"I'M RYA," the girl said, tentatively. Arten dragged her eyes back from where the darkness had swallowed Kylik's form, down to the girl next to her.

"Arten."

"It's nice to meet you, Arten," she said, timidly. "Um, shall we?"

"I know the way," Arten said, feeling tired and not looking forward to even the short walk with someone who thought whatever it was the matron had said they thought about her. *That I'm weird and a snob.* She ground her teeth together.

"No, um, I mean...Lord Kylik said I need to escort you home, so I have to. Not that I don't want to!" she added hastily.

"Fine, let's just go." Arten sighed and stomped away, leaving Rya to scamper after her.

The girl drew abreast of her in the boulevard, candle still clutched tightly in her fist. Arten glanced at her from the corner of her eye. From the set of her face, Rya seemed to be working up her courage.

"Just ask it," Arten said, when the silence had grown painful.

"What's the kaz like?" Rya blurted, relieved.

"Why do you care?" Arten asked, suspicious.

"Well, he's been gone for thirteen years. No one knows him. I mean, a handful of people remember him from before he left, but even the matron hasn't been around long enough to have met his sources. She said that his compound has been empty since she came here."

"It's only been thirteen years, how can only a handful of people remember him?" she scoffed.

"What do you mean?" Rya asked, confused.

"I mean, thirteen years isn't that long, what do you think I mean?"

"But...it *is*. That's most of our life." Rya was speaking with nervous caution, as though Arten's sanity were in question. "Matron's nearly forty and that's practically unheard of."

"Don't be absurd," Arten laughed.

"I'm not! It's true," Rya protested.

"Are you seriously telling me that, what, all sources die before they're forty?"

"Not all, but most, yes."

"Look," Arten snapped, "just go home. I'm tired of all of you laughing at me just because I'm new. I'm sure you and your friends think this is really funny because I'm just the stupid new kid. Well, don't expect me to play along."

"Some of the people here *are* predisposed to be cruel," Rya said in a tiny voice that made Arten want to shake her, "but not everyone is. Not everyone wants to laugh at you."

"Yeah, like who?" Arten scoffed.

"Like me?"

Arten could tell from the way the candle shook how difficult those words had been to utter, but she was in no mood to acknowledge the girl. "I don't believe you," she said evenly.

"They—they don't like me much, either. I just...well, I just don't want you to go through the same thing."

They had reached Stekin's compound, stopped in front of the gate. Arten pushed it open, glanced back at the girl in her tiny halo of light. She looked as small and hurt as Arten felt, and a lump formed in Arten's throat. "Goodnight, Rya," she said quietly.

"Goodnight, Arten," the girl whispered back.

Arten went inside.

WITH A HEAVY SIGH, Arten closed the door behind her, putting Rya out of her mind.

It was dark but not late—the third bell of evening had only just rung—but she was ready to sleep. She scarfed down the plate that had been left for her in the kitchen—cold, but she didn't mind. It was her own fault for missing the meal. She would need to be more considerate in the future and send the cook warning if she was going to be out. Meal out of the way, she went back to her suite of rooms, passing through the long, deserted corridor. Remembering the comfortable, homey rooms at Kylik's. Remembering all those girls lined up like dolls to sing their power away.

She pushed open the doors of the suite then winced as a sharp screech greeted her.

"There you are! I've been looking for you *all day!* Where have you been?"

Arten groaned internally. *Not her, again. Please...* "Who are you? Why are you here?" Any pretense of civility had wilted in the garden with Kylik.

"What a question! I'm your maid, of course. Emilette."

"What are you talking about?"

"What are *you* talking about? The kaz hired me to be your personal assistant. To provide whatever you need, to be your intimate companion!"

"Oh," Arten said, at a loss.

"We're going to be such good friends!" Emilette gushed, clasping Arten's hands in hers.

"Oh," she said again, "yeah. Look, um, Emilette?"

"Yes?" the girl chirped brightly.

"I'm pretty tired. I'd like to go to sleep."

"Of course! I'm happy to help you—" she started.

"No!" Arten cut her off, alarmed. "No, I don't need any help. I just would like to be alone. Understand?"

"But...who will help you undress?" Emilette's eyes flicked over her clothes, she frowned confusedly. "Or," she recovered quickly, "dress your hair for the night?" She stared at Arten's short hair, her clothes, back and forth rapidly enough to make Arten wonder how she wasn't dizzy from it. "Oh!" she cried at last, "oh, I'm sorry. I didn't mean to...you know I would *never*...I mean, I'm sure there's a good reason you're trying to look like a boy. I'll leave you to yourself, then."

"I'm not trying to look like a boy," Arten said with forced calm, propelling the girl out of her room.

"Then why—?" Emilette started, craning her head over her shoulder to look down at Arten's head.

"Goodnight, Emilette," Arten said firmly, then slid the doors closed, cutting off the babbled stream of questions. They filtered through the doors in a muffled chain, then stopped. Arten heard quick footsteps disappearing down the corridor. She wondered, briefly, where the girl was going, if she planned to stay here in one of the rooms on the long hall or if there were servants quarters she had overlooked somewhere. Decided she didn't care for tonight.

She woke twice that night—the first time when she realized she'd left Stekin's gifts in Matron Pasha's sitting room. The second time when Ergin took the knife out of his thigh and drove it into her heart. After a bath and a swim, she fell back asleep in the same bedroom off the long hall she had used the night before.

There was no laughter here, no clothing discarded, no warm memories to soften the cell. She pressed her back against the cool stone, imagining Stekin outside waiting for her call. Knowing he wasn't. Her anger at him forgotten in the tide of her loneliness.

6

FRIENDS & WEAKNESSES
STEKIN

Stekin awoke abruptly, tensed with alertness. He was home—the luxurious bed, long enough to accommodate his tall human frame told him as much. Something was not as it should be. Notes of tuneless music were in his mind. It took a moment for him to process what his senses were telling him. He turned his head, met the colorless eyes that were watching him. Irises like fractured ice that had once reminded him of home.

"Why are you here?" he complained.

"I thought you might want some company last night," Nhemith said, sliding her foot along his shin. It was that motion that had awoken him. "But you were too tired to notice me. So I thought I should stay to watch over you."

"I do not need your protection," he growled.

"Oh? You have always been proud but never a fool, Stekin. If I had come intending you harm, you were incapable of stopping me."

He said nothing, kept his features neutral. She was correct, and that he had been so weakened as to not notice her entry into his room, much less into his personal space, was sending alarms pealing through him. She shifted closer until she was lying alongside him, her leg curled around his, her skin startlingly hot against his own.

"You are like ice!" she hissed. "Is that girl not giving you enough power?"

"That is none of your concern," he said, more harshly than he intended. Nhemith's proximity was unsettling him, and he could not understand why. Why should the warmth of her skin be so distracting, the lines her hand traced over his bandaged chest set his nerves tingling? And what was that scent—so familiar, yet new?

"Of course it is," she snapped back, "You are my kaz. You are too thin, your power is nearly depleted, and you are in no shape to defend yourself. You would be unwise to refuse my assistance."

"And what assistance do you offer?" he asked, flicking his eyes away from her throat, narrowing them. He wrapped her hand in his, drew it away from his hip.

"I will stay with you," she proposed, shifting, her thigh sliding higher, her fingers entwining with his, "until you are recovered. My presence here will keep others away and mask the reason you retire early and are frequently tired." She grinned.

"What do you want?" he bared his teeth in response.

"Nothing," she shrugged, "for now. But once you are more recovered..." Her teeth flashed again, and before he could stop her, they were closed gently over the column of his throat. He inhaled sharply at the sensation of her hot breath, the keen edges against his weak skin. Her teeth scraped closed and he felt shivers travel down his limbs, his flesh prickling.

"Stop," he croaked. Realized his hand was in her hair, pulling her closer. Forced the traitorous limb to push her away. His back arched more as she drew away, trying to follow her warmth. *What is wrong with me?* With an internal growl, he flattened his spine, ignored this body's protests.

"As you wish," she said with a hint of frost. She got to her feet, leaving his side cold and empty. His eyes tracked her as she made her way to the door, found her shape intriguing in a way they had not in her centuries of wearing it.

"I will not give you an egg," he said.

She stopped, hand on the door, gave him a look that held promise and teeth. "I did not ask you for one."

"What do you want?" he asked again.

Her eyes smoldered, burning with white light, lancing at him. "You are my weakness, Stekin. You have always been. For thirteen years, I have thought about what I would do if you returned. Now you have. What I *want,*" she said, her gaze raking over his body, teeth gleaming, "is to live that dream."

His mouth was dry, his body sending signals that threatened to cloud his thoughts. "You are not my mate, nor my consort," he said.

"No," she agreed, "nor have I any wish to be." Her eyes flashed, then she was gone.

Stekin lay back, mulling over her words. But the scent of her was too heavy, the memory of her warmth too immediate for him to focus. *What is wrong with me?* he thought again, dragging his hands through his hair. It felt wiry and coarse to fingers that remembered Nhemith's soft strands. He stared at his hands, repulsed.

He swung his legs around, pushed himself upright. The world reeled as he stood, and he clutched the bed post to steady himself. Then clutched his chest as the *wrongness* there shifted, doubling him over in pain. Each gasped breath sent ripples of fire through his lungs. *The demon-*

metal. It must be playing havoc with my senses. Why did it take so long to take effect? He took shallow, short breaths, trying to calm the pain.

Demon-metal had always worked quickly on him before because his power had been stronger than most since the Sundering. *But my power has been diminished since I returned, and yesterday I gave Arten what little I had left. I have not been this empty since those first days.*

He straightened with a groan. Snatched a robe from his wardrobe, not trusting his energy to hold out long enough to dress properly. He drew it around himself, managed to work enough loops of the belt for it to serve its function, then carefully made his way into the hall. A glance to his left showed the gray light of dawn over his balcony, too far gone to be the color of Nhemith's scales. He turned right, managed to get himself moving in a gait that was not a stumble, though he leaned heavily on the banister as he descended the stairs. Eased his way towards his library.

CLAUDE LOWERED him carefully into his chair.

"Thank you, Claude," he said, trying not to let the pain sound in his voice.

"I will get Lord Kylik right away," the man assured and, with a final check to make certain Stekin was comfortable, bolted away.

Stekin closed his eyes, tried to focus on anything but the pain. But it was too strong. All he could think was, *It was not this bad before. Not even while Kylik was doing the surgeries.* There was no question—Kylik must perform the final surgery today, before Stekin would not be able to undergo it. Part of him wondered, though, if it were already too late.

He opened his eyes, stared blankly out the windows. Let the shifting of leaves, the flutter of birds passing, the more distant glimpses of dragon-bright wings, distract him. The day grew brighter, but he was lost in a haze of pain and barely noticed.

Until a face was staring at him, full of worry. He blinked, blinked again, his eyes refocusing on the person in front of him.

"Arten," he croaked, cleared his throat and tried again. "Arten."

"What's wrong?" she asked, he heard the control she was exerting over her panic.

"Worry not," he said, "Kylik is coming."

"Is there anything I can do?"

"No."

Her face hardened in a familiar, resolved scowl. "I'll wait with you," she declared, then dropped to sit at his feet.

He curled his fingers through her hair, and she leaned her head against his knee. It was soft, softer than Nhemith's, and he let the motion of it through his fingers distract him from the tearing pain in his chest. He felt her arm wrap around his leg, her fist clenched in the folds of his robe.

He supposed she had spent many hours at her father's knee, just like this. His hand stilled on her head. "I am not your father," he said, felt compelled to say.

She stiffened, her jaw flexed against his knee. "I know," she said, clipped and full of hostility. But did not move away. Did not object when his fingers moved through her hair again.

She is not my daughter, she is not my source, he mused. *What is she to me? Why does this feel so...right? Natural.* He tried to turn his thoughts from that line. Because it did feel right to have her here, at a time when he would permit no one else but Claude and Kylik to see him, at a time when he was most vulnerable. It felt natural for her to lean against him, where he normally limited physical contact, just as it had when she had carried him here. He did not want to think about that, did not want to know what it meant, did not want to know if he had come to care for her more than he intended.

'You are my weakness,' Nhemith said. I...

His fingers faltered, and Arten's arms spasmed reflexively around his leg.

I wonder if this is my weakness. This human, this girl. If she was, he must be even more careful not to reveal her as such. *My research has always kept me apart from the others, made me impartial, given me the freedom to act for the good of my people without the bias other entanglements cause. But if people learn of her, they will use her against me. I cannot risk her being a pawn in the politics of my people.*

But how could he keep her safe?

He knew the answer. His stomach clenched in unhappy response.

I have to give her up.

STEKIN ROUSED when Arten shot to her feet, fists balled at her sides. "He's here," she said, her eyes locked on the far end of the room. Stekin heard the doors rattle open. Wondered how she had heard Kylik's approach from beyond them. But then there was the heavy tread of a dragon trotting the length of his room.

"Help me stand, Arten," Stekin asked. Had nearly managed it with her help by the time Kylik slid to a halt.

"Kaz—" the healer began, alarmed, but Stekin held up a hand to stop him.

"You must do the final extraction today, Kylik. Now."

"You are too weak," he protested, hissing. "You can barely stand!"

"Today!" Stekin barked, immediately regretting it as it set his lungs on fire. He doubled over, coughing, leaning heavily on Arten's shoulder. She was still and solid beside him.

"Very well," Kylik said unhappily when Stekin had recovered. "But I do not have enough power to heal you if I do it myself. Child, I will require your assistance."

"No," Stekin croaked, even as Arten said with firm resolve, "Okay."

"No," Stekin repeated. "Arten, you must leave."

"Kaz," Kylik stepped forwards, scowling down at him, "in these skies, I lead. She stays, she helps, or we do not do this."

Stekin felt his eyes burn as he glared up at Kylik. The younger dragon was correct, however, and not cowed.

"Very well," Stekin snapped, baring his teeth.

"Good," the green dragon said, then, to Arten, "Get him up on this table." He swept Stekin's journals and papers to the floor with a brush of his scaled forearm, ignoring Stekin's wordless protest. A bottle of ink broke with a scattering sound and Stekin knew at least one document was now lost forever. He was sitting on the table before he had even processed the loss of his work.

"What is his man's name?" Kylik asked.

"Claude," Arten supplied.

Kylik bellowed for the man, then bounded off to meet Claude at the door. Stekin overheard a brisk demand for supplies, then the dragon was trotting back.

"I cannot put you out for this," he told Stekin, "I will need everything I have to keep you from bleeding to death as we go. If you can do that trick you have for dealing with pain, now is the time."

"What is Arten's role in this?" Stekin asked.

"She will be performing the extractions." Kylik plowed through Stekin's protest once again. "She is much more deft than I am, even in human form. I will clear the way, heal after her, but she will retrieve the shards. Are you up to that, girl?"

Stekin saw her nod firmly, her jaw set. A warning glare from Kylik kept him silent. While the healer instructed Arten in her task, walking her verbally through it then with mimed actions in the air, Stekin sank down into himself. Summoned the diamond beast at his core.

It knew his weakness, surged up, wrested control. And he was looking out through a lens, hearing as though through crystal, as he fought to keep his own body under rein, to avoid giving over completely. The beast scented her, recognized her—the one who had killed, the one who had carried him. She smelled different, somehow. And then there was the healer. The beast saw what Stekin had missed —the easiness between the girl and the healer, the way he peered at her, the glimmer of interest on his face. *He wants her for his own.* A growl escaped before Stekin could check it.

Kylik looked up, his guilt clear on his features, gulped. Stepped back a pace.

The girl stepped forwards, concerned. "Stekin?" she asked, drawing his focus. "Stekin, why are your eyes glowing like that? What's wrong?" His hand reached out, touched her face. He expected her to draw away or brush him aside, but she did neither. She cast a worried glance over her shoulder —Kylik was back at the door, haranguing the people in the hallway to hurry—and stepped closer.

"You have to promise me," she whispered anxiously, "that

you won't die. Because—because if you do, it means I killed you. So you can't die. Okay?"

She was vibrating with agitation, the fire of her power was knotted in her core. There was something wrong there —something Stekin could not see, but his diamond instinct noticed. And there was another thing, looking out at him through her eyes, behind the worry and fear, something familiar that had him reaching for her, drawing her close, wrapping arms around her like wings. Again, she did not protest, only begged him for a promise, her voice muffled against his chest.

"I will not die," he promised. "I will not die."

The servants scuttled around them, laying out the supplies Kylik had requested. Stekin noted them from his small corner of perception. Boiled water and clean linens, tweezers of varying sizes, some small, precise knives. How had they gotten to Kylik's and back so quickly? He had no time to wonder. Kylik was staring at him, disgusted and alarmed—no, not at him but at the beast and at the way it had wrapped itself around Arten, claiming her. Stekin felt exposed, released her, even as diamond eyes stayed locked with Kylik's amber.

The healer cleared his throat, looked away. To Arten. Stekin strangled the growl this time. The eyes went back to him. "Bare to the waist," the healer said, "and face down. And since I don't want to put your teeth back together, put this between them." He passed a bit to Arten, who held it while Stekin threw his robe off his shoulders, and lay himself out on the table. The bit was primitive, a measure only still used by the humans. It was an indication of how earnest Kylik was when he said he had no power to spare for niceties.

"I am ready," Stekin said to Arten, placed the leather-wrapped dowel between his teeth, and curled his hands around the corners of the table.

He felt the healer's power flowing over him, seeking. "Cut here," Kylik told Arten. There was pressure on his skin, he felt the heat of her hands, the slice of a knife. But the beast was alert, was focused on Arten and Kylik and the words passing between them, and the pain was easily ignored.

When Kylik chastised her—"You're not buttering bread, this requires precision! If you keep up like that, I won't be able to heal him!"—Stekin growled. Hoped it was mistaken for pain. When she snapped back—"I can't see anything! How am I supposed to know what I'm looking for? Can't you make it glow or something?"—he growled again, pleased.

When Kylik later praised her—"Much better, very steady. Elegantly done."—the wood splintered under his nails. Still later, when the healer moved to her side, and they leaned over him, speaking and working as a team, his jaws tightened convulsively around the bit until it cracked under the strain. He champed it until the wood inside was fragments.

After what felt like an eternity, she appeared before him. Her clothes were dotted with his blood, but she had washed her skin clean. "You're done," she said quietly. "Can you sit up?"

He spat out the sodden leather, pushed himself upright. Knew there was pain, knew he would regret this when the beast retreated once more, but for now it was only knowledge. Distant and unfelt. Arten threaded his arms through his robe, lifted it to drape over his shoulders once more. He leaned on her as she helped him up, as she walked him back to his room.

His legs were heavier than they should be, and his head

swam disconcertingly. "Nearly there," she said, even though they had only just mounted the stairs. He recognized that it was more for herself than him.

"I will be fine, Arten," he assured her, his voice sounded hollow and cold.

She looked up at him, then back at the stairs. Said only, "Good."

"Where is the healer?" he asked, when she rested at the top of the stairs.

"Giving instructions to your staff. Talking to Nhemith, I think." She set her shoulders and pulled him forward again.

"Nhemith?"

"I guess she told him that you'd want to do something stupid like this today," Arten panted.

Did she? How could she have known?

They were in his room, Arten lowered him to sit on the bed, then tipped him sideways, arrayed his legs in a semblance of order. He was too heavy to help, sleep had claws in him and was dragging him down.

"Kylik says..." She plopped down on the floor beside the bed. "You've got to stay on your stomach or your side. Can't sleep on your back. Hey!" she shouted. "Do you hear me?"

He made a noncommittal noise.

"Not good enough." A finger jabbed into his chest. "Stekin, Stekin, are you listening?"

"No," he heard himself say. His hand closed around hers, halting the poking. "Stay for a bit," the beast asked. He barely heard her agreement before he stopped hearing anything.

WHEN STEKIN AWOKE, the pain hit him full force. Even half-healed, his torso felt like fire-hot skewers had been plunged into it. A groan escaped, then hands were helping him to sit. Lifted his jaw.

"Nhemith?"

"As you see," she said, her voice low and quiet. "Send the girl away, and I will deign to heal you." Her eyes flicked behind him. Stekin shifted to follow them, hissing at the consequence of the motion. Arten lay on his bed, curled into a tight ball, her back abutted against a wall of pillows and rolled-up clothing that had fenced his own sleeping movements. Nhemith sounded amused as she said, "She is resourceful, I will grant her that. She has been asleep since I got here."

"How long—?" he managed, his mouth thick and dry.

"You have been asleep all day. It is nearly midnight, I expect the bell any minute. Long past time for little sources to be abed. And quite the wrong one to be in," Nhemith warned.

"Yes," he agreed. Reached out and touched Arten's shoulder.

The girl awoke with a strangled yell, twisted like a cat and her fist connected with the barricade before he could more than withdraw his hand. She seemed startled that it yielded. Saw him. "Stekin? Oh...I'm sorry, I thought you were *him*..." She pushed herself upright, he could hear the pounding of her heart.

"It is late. You must go home, Arten," Stekin said.

"Will you—will you be okay?" she asked, still muzzy, rubbing her eyes. "You can't sleep on your back."

"I will be fine. Nhemith is here."

"Oh. Okay," she said, sliding out of the bed, pushing her feet into the boots that waited for her with the same motion.

"If you're sure." She avoided looking at him or at Nhemith as she edged around to the door. Kept her back mostly to the wall, even as she exited.

I frightened her, but why? he wondered as she backed through the doorway.

After the door had closed behind her, Nhemith said, "Skittish little thing..."

"Not generally." Stekin frowned.

"If you wish to take advantage of my generosity while it lasts, give me your back," Nhemith said brusquely. Stekin turned his back to her, crossed his legs in front of him, unwilling to lie down again just yet. He could feel her close behind him, the warmth and solidity of her. It was not an entirely comforting feeling. Her hands reached around to unfasten his belt, then drew his robe down from his shoulders, letting it fall around him. Her fingers were light as she unwrapped the bandages and pulled away the sponge-cloth. He hissed where his skin stuck to it.

"What butchery," Nhemith hissed, when the last tugged free. "Did he at least get the last of it?"

"I do not know," Stekin admitted. "I was not myself."

She made a disapproving noise, then piped a series of high, trilling notes. He felt her power swirl over his skin, then under, like the thick fogs of her homeland. As it pooled around the wounds, dripped into the deep injuries, he sighed. *I wonder if she even remembers it? I wonder why I am remembering it...* The pain had clearly muddled his mind. Her home was gone, and she had left it behind her long ago, as they all had done. There was no use dwelling on what was lost.

"Why are you doing this, Nhemith?" he asked when she finished, drawing his robe over him once more.

"I told you—" she began flippantly, but he interrupted her.

"No. Kindness is not your way. Why are you really doing this?"

"Very well." She sighed, settled beside him, her cracked-ice eyes searching his. "If you must know," her voice was bitter, did not match her concerned expression, "I do not want to be alone."

"You have many friends and lovers, Nhemith, you have never been alone."

"That is not what I mean!" she snapped. Touched his cheek. "We are the last, Stekin. Without you... For thirteen years, I have suspected that you would not return, that I alone would remember. But you *have* returned, and I do not wish to feel that way again."

"We are the last," he agreed. Touched his forehead to hers. "I thought of you often, while I was away. I wondered if I would come back to find you were no longer here. I wondered who would carry my bones to rest, if you were gone. No one else remembers."

"No," she agreed. "There is no one else. But I will not carry your bones, Stekin."

"Why not?" he asked, her statement cutting him more deeply than he would admit to her.

"You are too determined to die."

7

CONFRONTS STEKIN
ARTEN

A rten tried to meet people, she did. But if public opinion had been formed against her before she spent all day and half the night at Stekin's, it was now solidified. She had stumbled home past the night-apex bell, her clothes flecked with Stekin's dried blood, and someone must have seen her because the next day the whispers and stares were even worse than before.

After she had been turned away at Stekin's door this morning—he was still recovering and unable to see her—she had ditched Emilette and gone out into the street to talk to people. She tried to join their little circles in the road, but people refused to acknowledge her, turned their shoulders to cut her from the conversation. The gray-haired women, whom she discovered were indeed not as old as she had originally thought, watched her with tight frowns or open disgust. They urged those with their brand to avoid her when they thought she was out of hearing.

Rya stopped by that evening with Arten's wrapped packages, the ones she had left in Matron's sitting room. She invited the girl in, glum and discouraged, didn't expect her to accept, but she did.

"They're books, aren't they?" Rya asked, staring at them eagerly.

"Seems that way," Arten agreed.

"Are you not going to open them? Who are they from?"

"Stekin," she said, then amended, "Kaz Stekin," when Rya blanched. She wandered into the common area, staring at the packages in her hand. Hesitating to open them, though she didn't know why.

"Why would the lord kaz give you a gift?" Rya breathed, awed. She settled in a chair across from Arten's.

"It's nothing like that," Arten muttered, face heating. "I know...I know what people are thinking," she lied, "but it's not like that! It's just a birthday gift."

That didn't decrease the size of Rya's eyes. "The lord kaz knows your birthday?" she gasped, impressed.

"No, it's not—look, it's not a big deal!"

"Okay," Rya agreed quickly, "okay. But are you going to open them?"

Arten was relieved at how quickly her interest shifted back to the books. She pulled the paper off, folding it carefully. Even if it was a little dingy at this point, she could reuse it. *Assuming I ever have someone to gift something to, and something to gift.* She stifled the sigh, picked up the first book. It was small, thin; the cover and spine were blank and made of something flimsy and flexible. She paged through, looking for a title, but only blank pages met her. She shrugged and handed it to Rya before picking up the second.

This one was larger, had the blocky solidity of a proper book. Inscribed on the cover was the title: *A Brief History of Dragons, Reltat Age to Pre-Sundering.* Inside, the pages were filled with tiny, cramped letters—printed, to her relief, not hand-written. She thumbed through the pages, knew it would take her a long time to read.

Rya had gone very still. Arten looked over, saw the greedy look on her face. She covered it quickly, but asked, "May I read it when you're done?"

"Sure," she agreed. "But it's going to take me a while." The girl's face fell. *She must really like to read*, Arten thought, feeling guilty for her own indifference to it. "Maybe there's something in the library you'd like to read, now?" she offered.

Rya's mouth dropped open. "You have a *library?"*

"Don't all the compounds?"

"No."

"Oh. Well...do you want to see it?"

"Yes, please!" Rya jumped to her feet. Arten led her back, watched her gasp and flutter about the stacks. Wondered if she had made her first friend. She wondered if, once the books were read, Rya would have a reason to stick around. *I don't care,* she decided. For once, someone was looking at her with delight instead of suspicion.

WHEN THE NIGHTMARES woke her that night, she lit her candle and curled up with *A Brief History* on her lap. She didn't dare the hall for a bath and a swim, not with Emilette sleeping in one of the rooms there now. So instead she cowered in her room, read about dragons whose names she couldn't pronounce, and places she didn't know, fighting battles, making alliances, for reasons she didn't fathom. But she would, she vowed—Stekin had given her the book, a book about his people. Clearly it was important. She would read it again and again until it made sense.

She fell asleep with multi-colored dragons darting through her dreams, acid, frost, and fire pouring from their maws. They were savage and wild and hard.

ARTEN SAT ACROSS FROM STEKIN, probing at her power with raw, tentative hands. Nhemith perched on the arm of his chair, ignoring her for the most part, speaking with Stekin in low voices about business of some kind.

"When will you be able to come before them?" Nhemith asked. Arten's attention was divided between their conversation and her power, and she reached too far, scalded her ethereal hands.

"Focus!" Stekin's teeth clicked. "Again." Arten ground her own teeth. Then, to Nhemith, he said, "Tomorrow morning. It will be informal, do not make it a procession," he warned. "I will go to the amphitheater and anyone who wishes may join me there, but I am not giving a speech."

"You should," Nhemith cautioned. "It will present you as strong going into the investigation."

"The only investigation I intend is of the network," he said, his words clipped and brittle. "I will speak with the four, but privately."

Arten glanced up when the silence stretched. Nhemith was scowling at him. "You must at least announce that the source drought is ended."

"Word has already spread," he disagreed.

"Gossip! You must announce it officially," Nhemith pressed.

Stekin snorted a sigh. "You know I detest pronouncements."

To which, Nhemith said, "You are kaz," as though that settled the matter.

"Very well," he grumbled. "I will speak of Ergin, and before you insist, I will answer three questions. That is all."

Arten prodded at her power half-heartedly while Nhemith thought. She burned herself with her inattention, and Stekin barked a predictable, "Again!"

"Ten," Nhemith insisted, "and I will heal you beforehand."

They stared at each other, intent and calculating. "Ten," he agreed, "but none about Arten."

"That will be difficult," Nhemith mused, brushing her knuckles back and forth along her cheek as she thought.

Stekin's face angled into his thin, sharp smile. "Then let it be three."

Nhemith hissed angrily, her eyes darted to Arten, who ducked her head quickly. "Ten," she agreed, "and none about the girl."

"Agreed," Stekin said formally, then, "Now, please leave me, I must speak with Arten."

"Stekin..." Nhemith warned.

"Enough," he growled. "On this I do not need your council."

There was a small, silent battle of wills, which Arten watched from under her brows. Stekin must have won, because Nhemith stood, inclined her head stiffly, then stalked off, her robe fluttering out behind her in its liquid, weightless way.

"Nhemith's presence has distracted you," Stekin said once the doors rattled closed. "I will ensure she does not disturb us in the future."

Arten muttered an embarrassed apology.

"It is well," he said. "But are you? You are not yourself today."

"I'm fine," she lied, looking away. She was many things in turn—isolated, worried, angry, lonely—but none of them were fine. Even her Words were tangled in the confusing march of her moods.

"Very well," he said, "then continue. You may leave when you can hold your power for three heartbeats without burning yourself." He leaned his head back and closed his eyes. "Or," he added, "when you admit what is troubling you."

His demeanor, the touch of smug arrogance, reminded her of Juro. Reminded her of her weakness the last time they had sat here. How she had curled up at his knee, like a child. *'I am not your father,'* he had said. *No,* she thought, *and you're not my friend, either. Whatever we were out there, in the network, here...here you're the kaz and I'm your property.* She scowled and turned her attention inwards, tried to ignore him.

She dove into herself, plunged her fists into her power, held fast until she couldn't anymore. Then did it again. And again. Her power was sparking, lurching and rolling away from her clumsy attempts to hold it. She felt scalded inside, a faint reminder of the inferno that had nearly consumed her twice before.

Icy fingers wrapped around her own, jolting her out of herself. Her eyes snapped open. Stekin was kneeling in front of her, sitting on his heels. His eyes were brighter, clearer than they had been for several days. She jerked her hands away, balled them into fists in her lap.

"It will not respond to force," he said gently, "nor

emotion. Power is wild when ruled by instinct and emotion. You must be calm and rational to tame it."

"That would have been helpful to know before now," she snapped, her knuckles going white in her fists.

"Yes," he apologized. He reached a long finger forward, tapped it on the outside of her thigh. The metallic clank hung between them. "What is the reason for this?"

She drew the knife out from the slit she had cut inside her pocket, laid it across her palms and stared at it. There was no blood on it anymore; she had cleaned it many times since Stekin had given it to her. But even lying inert, her hands remembered the resistance as it pierced into Ergin's leg, the lurch as it hit bone.

"He is dead," Stekin said.

"I know."

"But you dream of him?"

"How did you—?" She looked up sharply. His mouth twisted wryly. "Ah...so Nhemith knows, too?" The thought made her uneasy.

"We did not speak of it."

"Oh."

"Would it help to see his body again?"

"No!" she yelped. Her hands were shaking. Stekin took the knife from them, placed it on the table so she didn't cut herself. His cool fingers curled into her palms again.

"Then what frightens you?"

She didn't want to tell him about Raccard. *He'll tell me I'm just jumpy from coming out of the network, that no one here would hurt me.* "Nothing," she said.

"If you tell me nothing, I cannot help," he chided.

"You've *helped* enough." She pulled her hand away again, glared at him. Anger she had tamped down for days boiled up. He looked puzzled, faintly annoyed. Her anger heated, a pressure inside her growing until it ruptured free. "Thanks to you, everyone hates me! They all think I'm weird because you cut off my hair and dressed me like a boy. And they think I'm some sort of pampered pet! They're telling their dragons to not choose me because they don't want me in their little compounds."

Stekin's mouth was a thin line. "Their words matter little —the choice will be yours."

She yelled a wordless frustration, jumped to her feet and paced away from him. "What choice? There is no choice. There never was! The choice is between you," she stabbed a finger in his direction, "and no one. You're the almighty kaz," she said witheringly, "no one is willing to challenge you for what you have already claimed."

"I have *not* claimed you, Arten." Stekin was on his feet, now, his eyes flashing. "I gave you my word that you will choose to whom you source, and that should be sufficient on the matter."

"Well, your *word,*" she sneered, "clearly hasn't reached the ears of anyone else. So instead of being the currency of most value," she threw back at him words he had spoken weeks ago, when he made the empty promise, "it is worthless."

He drew himself up out of the pained stoop he'd been in for days. His eyes were emerald fires. She felt a quaking inside her, *He must be really angry...* She fanned the flames on her own anger, used the heat to meet his stare.

"What would you have me do?" he asked, the words chipped at her as if she were a block of ice.

"Fix it!" she snarled. Stekin's mouth opened to reply, his teeth ready to slice through the air, but Claude interrupted them.

"My lord kaz, Lord Ktet is here to see you."

Arten and Stekin glared at each other.

"Shall I ask him to wait?"

"Yes," Stekin growled. His eyes flicked to the man, breaking the tense connection between the two of them. The fire in her fizzled, and she knew only one thing. That she didn't want to be shut in here with an angry dragon.

She jumped to her feet, dodged past a startled Claude, and ran. She heard Stekin shout her name, put on more speed. Barreled into the doors, shaking them in their runners, shoved them aside and spilled out into the walkway. A dragon stood in the courtyard, his orange and black scales shocking in the sunlight. He gaped at her, his wings half-raised as if to flee. She darted down the covered walkway, leaving him behind, racing for the main house and the exit.

She was halfway there when a roar caught her, propelling her legs to new speeds.

ARTEN MADE it to the lane, barely, before she stumbled to a gasping halt. Her lungs burned, sweat dripped into her eyes, poured down her face and back. She was too hot, couldn't get cool. She vomited onto a patch of grass, clinging to the iron fence. Another blistering wave of heat flashed through her, turning her knees liquid. She vomited again, squeezing out breath she desperately needed.

The poisoning had been worse, but at least she had been able to breathe then. She sat back against the fence, gasping, sweat and tears mingling.

"Demons, help me get her up," someone said. Arten cracked her eyes open, immediately regretted it when it sent her stomach churning. She groaned as two pairs of hands hauled her to her feet.

"N—Natalia?"

"Yeah, we're going to get you home, don't worry." There was an abrupt pat on her shoulder. "Come on, you ox, she can't weigh anything. What are you waiting for?"

"She's going to be sick," a male voice protested.

"Oh, get over yourself. I'm the one doing laundry this week. Now pick her up."

Arten was lifted awkwardly into a pair of stiff arms. Arms that wanted her nowhere near the body they belonged to and held her only reluctantly. To her credit, she only vomited on him once, when she cracked her eyes open on the stairs and vertigo seized her. To his credit, he didn't drop her.

"Hey, hey!" Natalia was shaking her shoulder. "Listen, you've got to walk in. If they see Rac carrying you, well, it'll just make things worse for you. Hear me? Arten!"

"Okay," she said. She was lowered to her feet, hands kept her from falling down before she got her legs sorted out. Natalia threaded her arm through Arten's and pulled her forward. She kept a brisk pace, which helped. Somehow it was easier to keep moving if her legs just had to stumble along.

"A little too much sun," she heard Natalia saying sweetly, and, "The altitude. Got to her." Arten knew they were drawing stares, she tried to keep her eyes open, tried to not look as sick as she felt.

"We're here," Natalia announced finally. "Do I knock or what?"

Arten shook her head, stopped quickly. "No, just go in." She reached out to push open the door. Natalia helped when the weight of it proved too much for her to shift. Helped her limp down to the bathing room.

"You can probably handle this on your own," Natalia said uncomfortably. "I'll uh, I'll drop by later to see how you're doing."

"Thank you," Arten said earnestly.

"No problem." The girl shrugged, rubbing her fingers against her palm anxiously. "Listen, whatever he did, you don't have to tell anyone. But...some people know what it's like. And it gets easier."

"He didn't do anything," Arten protested, listing heavily against the stone wall in one of the bath stalls.

"Yeah. I hear you," Natalia said glumly. "See you, then." And she darted off before Arten could say more.

Alone, Arten stripped out of her soiled clothes, managed to rinse off the sweat and most of the stink. She was neck-deep in the bathing pool, the cool water already warming around her, when Emilette found her. There was a shriek and a commotion, which Arten endured, eyes closed.

"I'd like to be alone, please," Arten said, when there was a rare pause in the girl's hysterics. "Will you clean those clothes for me? And, if you don't mind, go down to the third circuit and help Natalia—she's at Hiranyath's compound—with her laundry? I vomited on her friend."

There were variations on "are you okay?" and exclamations of dismay and disgust and "yes," and then, eventually, she left. Arten scooted down the bench to a cooler area, and felt a little more certain she wasn't going to die.

ARTEN DIDN'T TRY to go out for the rest of the day. She was tired and irritable and, except for the brief minutes when

Natalia came back to check on her, she stayed closeted in her room, reading or staring at the ceiling. She tried not to think about Stekin, tried not to remember the anger lit inside him. She kept wondering if he would still be angry tomorrow. If she shouldn't go up but practice on her own down here.

I promised that I wouldn't. She sighed, padded out to the kitchen. Emilette had disappeared after supper, to Arten's relief, on some errand or other, so the house was quiet and still. The kitchen had a plate of apple pies that the cook had worked up to tempt Arten's appetite. But whatever had ailed her earlier was gone, and she'd eaten like she was starved. The kitchen was still uncomfortably warm from the baking, so Arten wrapped her hand-pies up in a napkin to take back to her room.

It was quite late at this point, and Arten was beginning to wonder where Emilette had gotten to. She was new to this whole servants thing—the Swains had only had part-time servants, never anyone live-in. *Is she supposed to be here all the time? Surely not—she has a life and friends.* Not that Arten wanted much from her. Mostly, she wanted to be left alone. But Emilette did do a number of small things for Arten without being asked. Like laundry, and keeping these rooms swept and tidy, setting the meals out and clearing them away. Arten didn't know where the dust came from, but every time she saw Emilette, she seemed to have a broom in hand.

Arten pushed open the door to her suite with one hand. Stopped. An autumn wind gusted in through the patio doors. Patio doors that she'd left closed. And there, next to the hearth, the tall silhouette of Stekin. His back was to her. She thought about turning around, going to the kitchen or the library or anywhere but here.

Before she could, he said, "I should not have shouted at you."

A fearless, stupid part of her said, "And roared."

He turned, she couldn't tell if his eyes flashed or if they just caught the firelight. "That also." He seemed to be waiting for something.

"Why are you here?" she asked, suspicious. "Am I supposed to sing for you, now?"

"No. Why would you think that?"

"That's what Kylik wanted when he showed up at Matron's door." She shuddered, remembering the green body wedged against the doorframe. She thought hers was wide enough that Stekin's narrower dragon form could fit through. Wondered if that was by design.

"You are not my source; I am not here for your power," he said.

"Then why are you here?"

"To talk, to...apologize." He inclined his head. "If you will permit me."

She stepped into the room, slid the door closed behind her back. "So talk."

He moved from the hearth to the couch that faced it and lowered himself into its corner. Only then did a fleeting look of pain cross his features. *He looks much stronger. Whatever healing Kylik and Nhemith are doing, it's working.*

"I have thought about what you said," he began, gesturing for her to sit, "and your concern and censure is valid. I have not made my agreement with you public, primarily because I have not been well enough to be in public. However, the failure must be corrected. This afternoon, I met with the source council and informed them of your circumstance. They were," his teeth sliced through the air as he said delicately, "unhappy. But persuaded. Your choice is now on record and part of law—it cannot be taken from you. I will mention it in my announcements tomorrow."

"It's still no choice at all." She bristled, arms crossed.

He inclined his head in acknowledgement. The light cast his tight smile into sad lines. "I also intend to announce that I will not contend for you."

A pit yawned in her chest. "What do you mean?"

"You are more perceptive than I have been. If it is known that I would take you as a source, you are correct in your surmise that few will challenge me. Those who would are the sort I would not permit you to source, and, I believe I am not incorrect in stating, you would not choose anyway. The only way to resolve the issue is to remove myself from the equation."

The pit gaped wide a tooth-filled maw, shredding her as it pulled her in. *He doesn't want me? All of this—thirteen years of searching, buying me, giving me run of this house, this life-style...and he doesn't want me.* She sat heavily.

The infuriatingly rational part of her reminded, *But I wanted...this? I wanted options, I wanted out of this tomb. To live with other people, to be part of a community. A family. And I do, I do want those things.*

"Thank you," she said from the bottom of the pit.

Stekin moved closer, she felt the brush of his knee, the coolness of his hands as they covered hers. She stared at the long fingers that caged her palm. She wondered if her dragon, whoever that was, would be cold like he was. "I do not need your power, Arten. That is not why I sought you."

"Then why?" Her voice was flat, she could feel the pull of his gaze, didn't look up.

"You know that I am kaz," he said, "but not why. The humans will tell you nonsense; they will think the kaz is a kingship, no matter how many times I have tried to quell that misconception. As I have mentioned before, the kaz is an honorific given to the one my people choose to follow. I am kaz only because the dragons consider me so. I am not kaz to you, nor to any human.

"As kaz, I do not rule, I have no enforceable power. I set expectations—standards—of behavior, of ethics. If my people agree with them, they adopt them. If enough adopt them, they become law. Do you understand?"

"I think so," she said.

He squeezed her hand, continued, "The reason my people consider me kaz is because I have, permit me, a knack for survival. You know that I have kept this place secret from the temple for five hundred years. Many decisions I have made to that end have been controversial and often ruthless. Yet, these decision have kept us safe here. At this point, I have proven that whatever I do, however seemingly inane, however bloody, is in the best interests of this city and my people. That is why I am kaz.

"I tell you this so that you know when I say I do not need your *power,* I need *you,* that I do not do so lightly. I could have sources, if I choose, I could have a prime. That is not the value you hold."

"I don't understand," she said, "That's the whole reason you found me—my power."

"I found Juro Tsyaro's mother through her power, too. That is not significant."

"Then what is? Why won't you just tell me?" she heard herself yell.

"It is not so simple," he said, releasing her hand. His palm along her jaw tipped her head up until she met his eyes. "I cannot tell you. Not and have you understand. I must show you."

"So show me."

His smile was tight, grieved. "I am, the only way I know how. Have you started the book yet?"

"Yes," she said carefully. *What does that have to do with anything?*

"When you finish, I have another. One I cannot gift you, as I possess one of a few remaining copies. When you have finished both, we will have a basis on which to have this conversation."

"That doesn't make any sense," she complained.

"Be patient with me a little longer," he asked, his eyes imploring.

"Yes, kaz," she said, looking away.

"No," he said firmly, catching her eye again and holding it. "I am not kaz to you, I have not earned that."

"But Matron says—" she started.

"No," he said again. "I want no titles, no false honorifics. With you, Arten, I'm just Stekin."

She was confused; he didn't want her, and yet this...this intensity in him...felt like a claim.

He withdrew his hand, she felt a pang at its absence. "Tell me," he said in his usual tones. Only then did she notice how warm his voice had just been. "Tell me, what do you think of the book so far? Of the dragons?"

She frowned, searched for words past the void that was turning her insides to ice. "They're...not like you at all. Are there feral dragons in the world?"

"No," he said, sounding distant, "all the dragons in the world live in this valley."

"Then I don't understand. Where are these dragons? The ones that breathe fire and fly around the continent and have terrible battles between clans?"

"They are gone," he said. "Dead. That era passed long ago."

"All of them? What happened?"

"Demons killed them." He stood abruptly, faced the fire, his back to her. His hands were clenched together behind his back, knuckles showing pale through his skin.

"I'm...I'm sorry," she offered.

"It is no matter," he said, as though to himself, "it is past."

She had the impression that he said that often.

He turned back to her, his eyes dull. "I must leave. Before I go..." He reached inside his robe, drew out Ergin's knife. "You left this, earlier. Keep it hidden. Weapons are forbidden on the circuits and within most compounds. Here, of course, you may do as you wish."

She took it. Sat there, swallowed by the pit. Wished he would reach out, curl his fingers through her hair, or put his arms around her again. Something, anything, to show her that everything hadn't just changed between them.

He only said, "Goodnight, Arten," and left, closing the doors behind him. She sat in front of the fire, unable to move. She heard a heavy sound, then the pulse of wings, fading. He was gone.

Eventually, she got to her feet, shuffled into her bedroom. She lay the knife on her bedside table. Looked down at her other hand—fisted around a napkin. She forced her fingers open, the scent of cinnamon and baked apple wafted up. Her hand was sticky with the remains of the forgotten pies. She washed it in the little basin on her chest of drawers, left the gooey napkin beside it. Crawled into bed, snuffed the candle.

Stared up into the dark as her world fell apart.

When he'd agreed to let her choose who she would source, he'd misunderstood. She hadn't been upset about this dragon or that dragon, she'd been upset about the lack of choice in giving her power away at all. At the time, skulking through the network, she hadn't known about this place. Stekin had refused to tell her anything until they were practically arrived. She'd only just learned that he was a dragon, not a demon.

I wanted to know what they used it for, why I had to give my power away. Other than the fact that it will burn me up if I don't. But it wasn't...I never...

She'd never minded Stekin taking her power, not really. Yes, it had been alarming—*Intimate, Matron said.* Intimate was a good description. She thought of the transfer between Kylik and his prime—the way everyone had averted their faces, how she had felt like she was intruding. She didn't want to be Stekin's singing doll, didn't want to fawn over him and flatter him the way Matron Pasha did with Kylik. *But I don't mind giving him my power. He's never wasted it...but would I even know if he had?* He'd used what he'd taken from her to heal her, to heal himself, but nothing nefarious, nothing unnecessary. *If I could have, I would have given it to him every day we've been here to help him heal himself.*

He went without sources for the thirteen years he was looking for me, and long before that if Rya is to be believed. And he's right, he could have any source he wanted, so if he hasn't had them, it's been because he can and chooses to do without. Like he's choosing to do without me.

The Words flopped sickly in her abdomen.

Maybe when people find out he doesn't want me, they'll be nicer, she thought, miserably, rolling onto her side.

She kept seeing his jaws stretched wide above her, the fierce gleam in his eyes, the elation on his face as he pulled her power from her. Nothing easy like with Matron and Kylik, but a battle with flashing teeth and clawed hands clutching her shoulders with unintended strength. Intimate was the right word. The thought of being in the grip of another dragon, of other eyes boring into her, of a stranger's fingers curling through her hair... She felt tears sliding from the corners of her eyes. Buried her face in her pillow.

It won't be like that, she reminded herself, *once my power is tame. It'll be like Kylik's sources.* But that was almost worse to imagine. Being a face in a crowd of similar faces, a stamped template. Or being like Matron, a prime, playing the role that best pleased her dragon and only her true self behind closed doors. Would any other dragon just let her be herself? Or had she thrown away her best chance at that?

She turned her pillow over to the dry side.

She didn't dream of Ergin that night, but of the Words rising, tearing free, burning her. Of Stekin standing back, holding his hands out in refusal. Of another dragon, one with Ergin's yellow gapped teeth grinning, leaning over her, pulling the power out of her. Pulling too much, the knot that was the source of her power slipping with that bone-shuddering wrongness. Of Stekin standing over the empty shell of her, saying, "This is what she always wanted."

8

THE KAZ SPEAKS
STEKIN

The door whispered open. Stekin's eyes flicked there, confirmed what he already knew.

"Why are you here, Nhemith?" he asked, irritated.

"Ah, so you have been to see the girl." Nhemith grinned.

Stekin exhaled sharply through his nose. "Whatever you think you detect to draw that conclusion, it is incorrect."

She glided to the bed; he watched through narrowed eyes. The mattress sank as she perched on the edge in the void of his loose curl. "You are brooding, Stekin. Only humans make you brood this much."

"First, I am not brooding. Second, you could not possibly tell if I were within moments of your ingress. Third, I contest your generalization." He was in no mood to spar with her tonight. He was, probably, brooding, and it soured his mood further that she would hazard the cause so quickly.

"Deceive yourself, if you like." She shrugged.

He felt a familiar prick of bitterness. *She wears this form so easily, so naturally.* He had never mastered the nonverbal communications of humans; it was always an effort. He could read them, certainly, but it was a studied pantomime to reproduce them. Whereas for Nhemith, it had been as easy as breathing. Even when she had first bought this form, she had taken to it within hours. *She would have known how to act with Arten.*

"Goodnight, Nhemith," he said, rolling over to his other side. He swallowed the hiss of pain as he passed over his back.

"You are in a foul mood tonight," she complained.

"Say what you came to say," he snapped, ice in his words, "or go."

"I thought we would talk *after,*" she suggested.

"I cannot fly tonight, even if I were so inclined. You are wasting your effort."

The bed sank more, he felt her press against his back. Again, the prick of bitterness. She was so warm; he could feel the slither of her power under her skin where it touched his own. He had hoped Arten's power would flare today. He had let her practice while she was clearly emotional in the base hope that it would. A selfish act, and one which had not been rewarded. He was disgusted with himself.

He had lied to her tonight. When he said he did not need her power. He did. Perhaps he did not *need* it, but he craved it. The thought of her sourced to another—the idea of her trusting a dragon that was not him with her power, giving it freely—was what had set him, as Nhemith so irritatingly identified, brooding.

Nhemith's hand was in his hair, her nails scraping over his scalp. It sent an alarming tingle along his neck.

"What are you doing?" he growled.

"Distracting you." She shrugged against his back, "unless you would rather be alone with your dark thoughts?"

It was...effective. He raised no protest.

"I thought not. Now, shall I tell you what I heard today?"

He made a noncommittal noise.

"You were more fun before you left," she sulked.

"I was just the same."

"My memory of you is certainly fonder."

"Very well, what did you hear?" He sighed, wondering if he was going to regret engaging with her. He usually did. *I am a fool to continue to do so.*

"I heard you roar clear across the hill. Do not try to deny it, I know your voice."

"I do not deny it," he said, shoulders stiffening.

"There is no need for that," she snapped, her nails painful on his skin. She softened, trailed her hand to his shoulder, along the side of his arm. He relaxed slowly. "Better. The other thing I heard..." She paused, raked her nails down his side causing him to tense back up at the crawling sensation under his skin. "...is that your girl was so distraught she made herself sick."

"Where did you hear that?" Stekin demanded, eyes flashing.

"Calm yourself," Nhemith said, her nails digging into the soft space below his ribs. "I have not yet told you the last thing I heard. Speculation about what you are doing to that girl."

Stekin snarled. A mistake. Nhemith growled back, her teeth scraped his ear. He froze. Something skittered down his spine, twisted and tightened a deep part of him. He remembered to breathe. Then recognized the sensation. Something he had never felt in this form, an aspect of this biology that had never functioned. Not just for him, but for any of his kind who took human form.

What is happening to me? The demon-metal is gone, why are my senses still confused?

"Nhemith, please leave," he said, his voice quiet and hoarse. "Now." The heat of her at his back, her hand on his side, were too distracting.

She huffed a sigh and pulled away. He heard her stand, her terse words, the door open and shut. Heard her across the hall, settling into his sandpit, back in her true form. But it was long after her breathing settled into sleep that his skin forgot her touch. Longer still before he would forget her words and their distressing implication.

THE MORNING CAME TOO EARLY, in a riot of pre-dawn bird-song that set Stekin's jaw clenching. He gave up trying to sleep, went out onto his broad balcony, and transformed. He stretched—revelling in the *rightness* of his shape, the weight of his wings, and the perfect balance of his tail. He watched the depths of the valley slowly brighten, the sun finally gilding the tips of the opposite mountains as it rose behind him.

Last night, while he had fought for sleep, first against his borrowed biology, then against his jealousy over Arten sourcing to another, he had decided to spend more time in his natural form. Usually, staying in the human form kept him more rational, though that was not why he wore it. *But,* he reasoned, *clearly I am emotional, among other things, in that form. I have been wearing it almost ceaselessly for thirteen years —perhaps there are side effects that have not yet been discovered from such constant exposure to foreign biology.*

Whatever the cause, keeping to his true form would

eliminate whatever malfunction his borrowed form was experiencing.

Though when Nhemith commented on his form, he responded, "It is time to be kaz, and so I must be." She swelled at that, happy he was taking her advice. He hoped she believed it was only that.

Good to her word, she healed him before they left, easing an ache in his chest he had already grown accustomed to. He tried his wings—they stretched at the healing skin under his scales, but Nhemith addressed the places he was concerned about, places he had re-injured flying to his compound the night before. And then there was no avoiding it.

With a resigned sigh, he thrust himself into the air. He was still recovering, and his muscles had deteriorated, especially his flight muscles, which he had barely kept functional during his long exodus. The flight to the amphitheater was humbling and, frankly, embarrassing. He landed heavily, for once grateful of Nhemith's insistence on pageantry. The dragons were not due to assemble for another quarter-hour, so there were no spectators to witness his botched landing nor how winded he was.

"You will never keep up with me like that," Nhemith frowned, shuffling her wings in agitation. "I hope you have not lost your grace permanently."

I should never have encouraged her, he thought as he watched from under heavy lids. She righted the stone cairns that had fallen over, dusted the stage with great backdrafts of her wings, and removed bits of twig and debris that had blown in. *Kylik has told me enough that I know she has not been at a loss for partners.*

If he is to be believed, she nearly took a consort. So what is she really after? It is certainly not the fight and the flight—there is nothing new there between us.

New or not, he was not so deep in denial as to think he was not anticipating flying with her again. It had been quite a long time—they had not flown since their daughter was born.

"I hear the first arriving." Nhemith's voice cut through his thoughts. "Stand up."

"I will stand when they are assembled," he said through a yawn. "I have slept on much worse than this clean stone in the last thirteen years. No one will care if my scales are a little dirty when my all my ribs show through."

Nhemith made a frustrated noise, but then took up a statuesque pose at the center of the amphitheater. She was beautiful, there was no denying that. Her scales were glossy and smooth, her long body softened with fat, her legs still as fine in her age as they had been her youth, her wings unmarred and supple. He knew he looked scruffy in comparison. Most of that would fade as he recovered. His ribs would fill out; his scales would shine up. But the jagged edge of his left wing, the twisting scar down that same leg, the slight crook in his tail where it had not healed quite right, the barely noticeable scars checkering his belly where scales now grew misaligned—those would remain with him. Reminders of his past and who he sometimes had to be to protect his people. Reminders that could be hidden when he donned a human body.

A sizable group had assembled by now. Most of them were staring at Nhemith, who was scanning the crowd, demanding their attention with every line of her body.

It is a shame she is unsuited to be kaz. She plays the role so well. But perhaps that has always been her problem—that it is an act, not a conviction.

The first bell of morning pealed. He listened as she reminded them, needlessly, that he had been gone, had returned, and of some of the *great deeds* he had done in the past. The ones no one but the two of them had been alive for. The thought dragged at him. He stood.

"Enough," he said, "I will speak."

Nhemith glared at him, her eyes burning with white light. He stared her down, despising the contest, despising that it was necessary. Always necessary with her. Nhemith acquiesced, bowed, and gave way. And in it, Stekin saw what she tried to hide—the hesitation, the moment when she wondered if she should stand and challenge him. He tucked the observation away and took her place in the center of the stage.

"It is good to see so many of you." His voice carried up into the cliffs where dragons perched in the nooks and ledges carved out for them. At first, they seemed to be too few in number. But then he noticed the human faces dotted amongst the dragons. A few score of his people had donned their human forms for this. He thought it odd, felt his mind puzzling at it, his brow drawing down as he scrutinized them.

Nhemith's huff reminded him as to why he was here.

"I have a few things I wish to say, so thank you for coming to hear them." He curled his tail, an automatic habit to hide the kink, and swept his wings back and down to cover the scar on his leg that would be visible from even the highest perches. He imagined Nhemith's approval in the intent stare she had fixed on him.

"First, I want to apologize." A rustle of wings and scales met this announcement. He suppressed his irritation and reminded himself, *If a kaz is infallible, then I cannot be one.* "When I left, thirteen years ago, some of you felt I had abandoned you. Some of you are surprised I am alive and that I have returned. No doubt, some of you no longer consider me kaz. I am not here to convince you of anything but to give you facts I believe to be relevant.

"In the point of my leaving, the facts I wish you to know are three. First, that at the time of my departure, I had no reason to anticipate it to be a lengthy trip. Second, that I weighed heavily the cost of leaving and determined, for reasons I shall not disclose, it was in the best interest of our community for me to do so. Third, that when I left we were peaceful and prosperous and I had not been relied upon for several years. I was confident New Respite would continue to thrive without me, and I was ignorant of the true scope of my search.

"You may be wondering if I found what I sought. Yes, I did." And here, the lie. The twisting of the truth that they must believe. "I found a powerful artefact in the south. Tomb divers uncovered it and were trying to operate it. I discovered them at long last and destroyed the artefact."

The story was true, but the artefact was not the thing he had sought.

"While I was searching the continent, I took the opportunity to check in on various network nodes. I uncovered a disturbing pattern. The number of travellers flowing through the southern nodes did not match with those reaching the northern nodes and did not match with those reaching our city.

"On my return journey, I encountered a source fleeing through the network. I travelled with her, using her, with her consent, as bait to draw out any nefarious elements. We uncovered several nodes that intended her harm. Without my intervention, she would have never made it here whole or alive.

"I tell you this to explain why I plan to clean out the network. Our sources are precious enough without losing them on their journey here. We must keep them safe in New Respite; we must keep them safe in the network. However, the network is vast; it will take considerable time to thread protected sources through it all. So I request of each of you: speak to your sources, ask them to come forward, to report to me any difficulties or concerns they had on their way here. If we know which nodes are dangerous, we can excise them before more damage is done.

"The numbers we are losing inside the network do not, however, fully explain the decrease in our source intake in the past years. Arten, the source with whom I have just returned, discovered the cause of that, as well.

"About twenty-five years ago, you may recall, our sources here in New Respite experienced a series of attacks. A source named Ergin was the perpetrator of those attacks. He underwent voluntary erasure, and we released him. Ergin, in short, has been capturing and murdering our sources with increasing frequency ever since. Arten found his lair, and I killed him. This act alone should double our source intake to the levels to which we are accustomed.

"Which brings me to my final point. Arten, though I travelled with her and now instruct her in taming her wild power, is not my source." And another, small deception: "While we were in the network, I offered Arten, in exchange for her continued assistance, after someone attempted to murder her, the right to choose to whom she sources. This means that any of you may contend for her, but the decision will be made by Arten, not the source council. I have no intention of taking a source at this time and will not be part of the choosing, regardless of what you may have otherwise heard.

"That is all. Thank you for coming. If you have questions, please come forward."

The questions were largely what he had expected. Was
he dying, how did he know the source problem was fixed,
what was his plan for flushing the network. A few came
through about Arten, and he deflected them, insisting any
questions should be asked directly of her. The second bell of
morning tolled before he had answered his ten questions.
Nhemith gathered the attention to herself again, told them
to drop by with any further enquiries while Stekin paced
away.

Once he was out of sight, he labored into the air, angled
back towards his house. Where Arten would be waiting for
him. He quickened his wingbeats.

ARTEN WAS WAITING FOR HIM, Claude announced upon his
return, in the library. Stekin elected to walk there instead of
fly; his back and sides were burning, the healing tissue
inside prickled sharply with every breath. He found her in
his human-sized nook, one of his journals in hand, peering
at the pages. He knew she could not read it—he had
obscured the writing in all the books of import before he
had left years ago.

"That is private," he said, coming up behind her, his
claws silent on the carpet.

She jumped, hand diving into her pocket as she spun
around. She hissed a shocked breath up at him, and her
eyes lingered on his teeth for a moment, exposed as he
grinned at her reaction, but she recovered herself with a
rapidity that pleased him.

He took the small book from her hands, slotted it back into the shelf with careful claws. "Come," he said.

He stretched out on the carpet runner in front of his windows, wings folded precisely along his sides, while she settled in the high-backed chair. He could see she was agitated from the way she fidgeted. He searched for what to say. Decided on, "It is done. I have announced that the choice of who you will source will fall to you, and that I have withdrawn myself from consideration. You may be approached by some of my people. If they are bothersome, let me know."

"Yes, Kaz," she muttered mutinously, staring at the toe of the boot she was digging into the carpet. The honorific irritated him. Especially after their talk last night. *Bringing it up will serve no good purpose,* he reminded himself and did not correct her.

Her power was bright, filling her. He felt a quiver of anticipation, his teeth itched to pull it away. If she reached for it... He stopped himself with a firm thought, *No, she is too upset to try this now. If she cannot master herself, I will send her home.* He felt a bitter swirl of righteousness and disappointment.

"You are distracted," he said.

"I'm fine." She shrugged, her voice deadened, still looking away.

"That is plainly untrue."

"Can we just get this over with?" Her hands curled into fists.

"No." He stifled a sigh. *I am too tired to coax her into talking today.* "Go home, Arten. Come back when you are calmer."

"No!" she yelped, jumping to her feet. "I can do this. I want—I need to tame my power."

Why does she sound distressed about that? He knew she would not tell him.

Instead he said, firm and wintry, "You are too emotional. You will only incite your power further. Go home." He kept the part of him that was eager for her power locked in his core.

"I can do this," she protested.

"I know. But I will not prise your thoughts out of you, nor will I permit you to endanger yourself by reaching for your power in your present frame of mind. Return when you are ready."

She snarled, turned on her heel, and stalked away. The doors shook in their brackets, shuddered as she slammed them closed.

He sighed and put his head down on the backs of his long-boned forepaws. *Nhemith would know what was bothering her,* he thought. *Perhaps she will agree to talk to Arten...*

He would seek Nhemith out for counsel on this, but first a small rest. Then Kikkyo was due to drop by and inform him of her progress on the network agent acquisition. There were few enough of the humans willing to risk venturing outside the city and none that Kikkyo had been able to find thus far willing to go as far south as was necessary. But Stekin knew that the prospect of money was sufficient to motivate most humans, it was merely a matter of finding the quantity. His fortune was made; his income was sufficient to run the network three times over. He would increase the stipend for the network council and authorize Kikkyo to use the new funds to purchase assistance. After all, what was his fortune for if not to protect his city and his people?

He only wished the problem of Arten were so easily solved.

9

TOO MANY DRAGONS
ARTEN

Arten sat at the top of the stone stairway, legs braced on the third stair down. A chill breeze flowed down from the mountains, plastering her tunic to her sweat-slick back. Her head drooped between her knees as she rested to catch her breath.

I must be getting sick, she thought, panting. *I wasn't even running this time.* She shivered as the wind gusted, reminding her that autumn was upon them. She stared down the hewn steps. *I wonder how long this training will take? If climbing up these stairs is terrifying now, how about when they're covered in ice?*

She shuddered.

I'll just have to tame the Words before then, she decided, her mouth set in a grim line. The next thought followed immediately: *How am I supposed to learn when Stekin refuses to teach me or let me practice?*

She simmered. Thought that if she had a dragon's eyes, they would be flashing right now. Defiance sparked in her, grew into a flame.

Before she knew what she was planning to do, she had

plunged her *hands* down, wrapped them around a rope of her power. The Words paused, flickered. She felt an instant of intention there, the tiniest glimmer of—what? Intelligence? *No, the Words aren't sentient*, she reminded herself.

But it was already too late. She felt her anger resonate in the strand of power, felt it ripple through her, magnified. Felt it grow and compound and feed on itself until it was an inferno of rage that screamed for release. For escape. For relief. For vengeance.

Her ethereal *hands* vaporized in a flash, something inside her seared. Something else constricted. She couldn't breathe, she was being smothered. She fought to draw breath, scrabbling at her chest and throat with ineffective urgency—but she was breathing, she could feel the motion, could feel the panting heat of her exhale on her hands. And yet she couldn't breathe, even though she was. A dark haze clouded the sky, Arten felt herself falling sideways. Her thoughts stopped as the world faded.

SHE WAS IN HER BED—NOT the pallet on the floor, but the proper bed in her suite. She opened her eyes, pushed herself upright with a groan. Her throat felt like she'd been screaming.

"Foolish!"

She recognized the disapproving hiss. But why was Nhemith here?

"You are fortunate it was I who found you, not Stekin," Nhemith snapped in response to her fumbled question.

"Why?" Arten croaked.

"You cause enough scandal for him as it is. The last thing

he needs is a report that he brought you home fainted and limp as a dead thing!"

"Why?" she repeated, confused. "What scandal?"

Arten gingerly felt her throat, fingers instinctively feeling for the lumps of gravel that must have lodged there. She winced as the probing irritated sensitive tissues.

Nhemith frowned, her beautiful features twisting with disgust. "It is not unnoticed how much time he spends in your company alone. That you travelled together is bad enough. But then the days he lived with you here, in our very midst, were shocking enough to make the former immaterial. Now he is visiting in the night, giving you secret lessons from which you leave so depleted that you are ill?"

Nhemith's expression, the *way* she said those things— shame crawled along Arten's skin, heated her face, recoiled through her thoughts. She couldn't protest, the words of denial rang small and impotent in her mind against the force of Nhemith's censure.

Arten stared down at the sheet balled and twisted between her hands. Felt Nhemith's eyes on her. Tightened her grip on the tortured cloth.

Nhemith's gaze slid away. "What happened to cause you to fall unconscious at the top of the stairs?"

"I," Arten began, remembered, stopped herself, "nothing."

"Do not lie to me, human." Nhemith's teeth snapped together. Arten risked a glance, saw her eyes blazing whitely. "Tell me what he did to you."

"Who, Stekin?"

Nhemith growled a wordless assent.

"He didn't do anything. I'm not lying!" Arten protested at Nhemith's sharply indrawn breath, "I'm not! I...he told me I couldn't practice reaching for the Words today. Said I was too emotional. But I...well, I was angry, and I just want to get this over with so people stop acting so strange around me."

"Foolish! You reached for your power while angry?" Nhemith sounded amazed—like Arten was particularly gifted with stupidity. "You will burn yourself alive."

"I didn't know that," Arten muttered mutinously.

"That will not save you," Nhemith dismissed with a snort. "Though," she added, thoughtful, "how you did not flare out...?"

Arten waited for her to continue, but she said nothing further for several minutes. Nhemith rose abruptly from the chair she had positioned beside Arten's bed, moved towards the door.

"Wait," Arten called, then quailed under the reproachful look Nhemith turned on her. She rallied. "Tell Stekin...tell him not to come."

"Why should he come here?" Nhemith's pale eyes narrowed.

"Because he always comes," she blurted, unthinking. Amended when Nhemith's eyes flashed: "When my power flares. That's what happened, right?"

"Yes, that is what happened. You may rest easy—if he did not come in the hours you lay passed out atop the cliff, he will not come now."

Arten started—*hours?*

"You are fortunate my man came across you."

Arten barely noticed Nhemith leave. Kept thinking, *Hours...I was there for hours. And he didn't come. Why didn't he come?* Stekin had always known when her power was flaring, had appeared in time to drain it from her and prevent her flare-out. So why hadn't he this time?

Maybe Nhemith was wrong. Maybe I wasn't in danger. But she knew it wasn't true. The force that had overwhelmed her had manifested differently this time. It hadn't burned her, but she recognized it. Recognized it as the same conflagration that had nearly killed her twice before, the one that had always summoned Stekin. He said he could sense when she was about to flare. *But not this time. What does that mean? That he really doesn't want me to be his source? That he doesn't care if I die? Or that it wasn't powerful enough to be a threat?*

Or maybe the little training she had done had tamed it somewhat.

Arten swung her legs over to the side of the bed, her booted feet touched the ground. She felt a weakness in her limbs, a ghost of what she normally felt after the power transfer to Stekin. It was mild enough that she ignored it, got to her feet, and went in search of a distraction.

SHE FOUND her distraction in the form of Emilette. It was *not* what she'd been hoping for.

"Arten!" Emilette cried, rushing in from the back patio.

Arten grimaced, ears ringing. "Why were you out there talking to Nhemith?" Nhemith speared her a glance through the glass doors that Emilette had just closed behind her —*She probably heard me*—then spread her wings and lifted away.

"Oh, that? That was nothing," Emilette said, rushing to Arten's side. Arten found herself propelled to the couch, pushed down into the corner Stekin had occupied the night before, her feet propped up on the cushions. Emilette was saying, "She told me to take good care of you and not to let that dragon bother you."

"What dragon?" Arten asked, overwhelmed by the buffet of solicitous attention.

"Are you hungry? You slept all the way past lunch! It's nearly two-afternoon," Emilette rambled.

"What dragon?" Arten repeated, more firmly.

"Oh, you know. *That* dragon. I'll go talk to the cook, get her to make something else for you."

"*What* dragon?" Arten ground out through her clenched teeth.

"*You* know. The *kaz,* of course. Now just you wait here, I'll be back in a flash!" Emilette darted off, her rapid steps echoing from the long hall back to Arten through the crack in the doors.

Arten was irritated. She flailed, dislodging the tightly tucked blanket Emilette had wrapped around her, scattering the small pillows that had barricaded her into the corner of the sofa. Freed, she left the comforts where they fell, not caring at all that she trod over the blanket as she left the suite.

She made it all the way to the kitchen without seeing Emilette. The scent of baking apples and sugar reached out to wrap around her, pulled her in.

The cook greeted her brightly. "Ah, I'm glad to see you're feeling better."

Arten slid onto a bench beside the long worktable, staying out of the way while the woman rolled pastry dough out flat.

"Would you like a fresh one?" she offered, nodding at a rack of cooling pies. "The ones under the cloth should be cool enough."

Arten's stomach rumbled a plea, so she indulged it. While she nibbled at the hot treat, the cook talked easily.

There was a big celebration on Saviorsday; oh, had no one told her? How thoughtless of them. The harvest came earlier, up in the mountains as they were, but it wasn't just a harvest festival. It was a thanksgiving, where sources celebrated their new lives here, the family of their compound, the community of other sources. It was the one day out of the year that sources had fully to themselves, where no dragons would descend from midnight to midnight.

Arten felt herself growing heavier, more isolated, the longer the woman spoke. Her own family wouldn't be celebrating the harvest for weeks yet. She imagined what it would be like—her mother scowling at whatever imperfections had occurred in the preparations, her brother in the perpetual soured mood he carried everywhere these days, and her father...

Will he miss me? I know Mother and Deric don't care that I'm gone, but Father...surely he does?

Again, she felt a wave of homesickness.

"What's wrong, dear?" the cook asked alarmed. "Why are you crying?"

"I'm not," Arten protested, scrubbing the betraying moisture away with her sleeve.

"Well then," she said, patting Arten's arm roughly, leaving doughy crumbs, "that's good."

Arten stood abruptly, thanked the woman for the pie as she pushed the bench back in. The kitchen had become too small, the air thick, stifling.

"If you're going out," the cook said, turning back to folding apple paste into triangles of dough, "will you take that sack of pies over to my compound? It's three down across. Be sure to hold the bottom so it doesn't split, that's a dear."

Arten picked up the sack, braced the sagging underside against her arm and, with perfunctory thanks, left. She hadn't intended to go out beforehand, but the thought of staying cooped up inside this mausoleum was oppressive.

As she made her way to the cook's compound, she wondered where Emilette had gone. She was so distracted by wondering why she cared, she didn't notice the change at first. She felt vaguely that something was different as she crossed the boulevard and approached the cook's compound. Felt unsettled. But it wasn't until the door opened in response to the rap of her elbow that she saw it.

A woman, branded like the cook, opened the door. Her eyes immediately went to Arten's unmarked brow, that small, guarded frown that Arten had grown accustomed to flickered into being.

"I was asked to bring these over," Arten said, holding out the sack. Then it registered with the woman who Arten was. A flash of shock, then disgust, passed over her features, then nothing. The woman looked past her, peering into the street as though looking for who had knocked. "Hello?" Arten said, confused. The woman shrugged and shut the door, leaving Arten on the step, sack in hand.

Arten's patience snapped. She dropped the sack, not caring that the bottom split open and pies scattered across the flagstones. She pounded on the door, shouting, "Hey, hey!" as her anger crackled. But no one responded. *I'm sick of this! I try to meet people, try to be helpful, and this is how they treat me? It's getting worse, not better.* When her hand hurt from striking the door and it was evident no one was going to open it, she kicked it, kicked the sack, and stormed off.

She didn't make it very far. Beyond the compound gate, the entire boulevard had fallen silent, staring at her. No whispers, no darting glances. Open, mute, hostile stares. Her face burned. She looked around for anywhere to escape, but a piping voice cut through that intention.

"Look, look, there she is!" the excited cry carried to her. Down to her. She looked up. Three dragons darted from the sky, landed in front of her, screening her from view of most of the street. "Arten! It's Arten, right?" the dragon in the middle said, practically vibrating with excitement, his hummingbird-green scales flashing.

"Yeah," she acknowledged, peering around him. Movement through the forest of wings and tails had caught her eye. The women in the street, almost as one, were turning their backs on her. Not to resume their conversations, but in silent purpose. All of them.

"I'm Rengath," the dragon introduced himself.

Arten felt the hostility pouring off the sources' backs. It was that hostility she'd dimly noted on the way over but this...this was so much worse. She wanted to scream at them, wanted to demand to know what she had done wrong to make them be so horrible toward her, wanted to defend herself against whatever charges had been laid against her. But if they hadn't talked to her before, it was clear they wouldn't now.

"Are you...are you unwell?" Rengath was asking anxiously.

"I'm fine," she said through gritted teeth. Forced herself to look at him. "Why are you looking for me?"

"Well, well! I heard—we all heard!—about how gallant you were in the network, and how you discovered the one who has been taking our sources," Rengath gushed, "I just had to meet you and thank you!"

"Please keep your voice down," she hissed. *Not that it matters, just more fuel for them to throw on their dislike of me. They've already decided.* "Can we go somewhere else to talk about this?" she muttered.

"Oh, of course, if that is your wish! I have a lovely garden..." he began, but a hiss from one of the other two dragons had him backpedaling, "but perhaps one of the public courtyards would be better."

"Fine," she said, fists balled at her sides. "Lead the way."

"I could fly you..." the brown dragon to her left offered smoothly, an eager glint in his blue eyes.

The thought of the dragon's claws closing around her, bringing her in range of his teeth, made her chest tighten.

"No," she said quickly. "No, that won't be necessary."

Arten followed them out, unable to avoid seeing how the backs turned to follow her, until they were a wall propelling her through the arch. The dragons flanking her were oblivious. The walk to the stairs seemed longer than this morning, and by the time they got there, Arten was tired.

She sat on the steps at eye-level with her three-dragon escort and said, "I'd appreciate it if you didn't talk about all that in front of the other sources."

"Oh, but why not?" Rengath cried.

And the brown dragon, who had introduced himself as T'nathax, offered, "Surely you wish them to know how brave and strong you are?"

"I think the female sources little value those things," the third dragon spoke finally. Arten was surprised that it had a rich, distinctly female voice. She was larger than the others, her body shape bulkier—*More like Kylik than Stekin; nothing like Nhemith*—and Arten had assumed that meant she was male. The dragon bowed her head to Arten elegantly, and finally introduced herself, "I am Kikkyo." Arten managed a polite acknowledgement, still adjusting to the idea that she was female.

"Did the kaz warn you to expect us?" Kikkyo asked.

"No," said Arten.

Kikkyo inclined her head, an apology. "Then you must be wondering why we are here."

"A bit, yeah."

"The kaz announced this morning his unusual agreement with you. These two," Kikkyo gestured with the wave of a mottled-gray hand, "are here to express their interest in being considered in your decision of whom to source."

The pebbled-brown and sleek-green heads moved, sending affirming undulations down their long necks.

Arten said, "Oh."

"Perhaps," Kikkyo offered, turning to the two dragons beside her, "you should tell her a little about yourselves."

Rengath pounced on the opportunity, told Arten of his compound, his three sources and their superior personalities. T'nathax interrupted to speak of *his* compound, and his wealth and the intelligence in his sources. Then Rengath commandeered her attention to say that it was well and good to have wealth *now,* but he had generations of good breeding and a strong family history of compound responsibility. To which T'nathax swelled, spreading his wings, and retorted that good breeding just meant inbred these days, and his mongrel ancestry made his line more viable long-term. By then, they had largely forgotten about Arten and were posturing at each other, hissing boasts and insults.

Kikkyo tried to settle them, to redirect them, but they would have none of it. And their commotion had attracted attention. Other dragon-shapes dotted the sky, descended to land. Began voicing their own boasts and qualifications for Arten to consider.

There were five, then eight, then twelve. She lost count at twenty. The swirling mass of legs and wings and tails and necks, light flashing off scales in a rainbow of colors, voices raised to deliver cutting or triumphant remarks, was dizzying.

"I do not see why," a sonorous male voice cut through the

noise, "you are all here, scrabbling like animals over the kaz's cast-offs." The sea of legs and wings parted, revealing a hulking black dragon, larger than even Nhemith, with flashing orange eyes. He stared at her, his lips pulled back, revealing his long, white teeth. The way he approached her, stalking, trying to dominate her with his predatory stare, had her rising, her hand going to the knife in her pocket.

This one is dangerous, some part of her knew. The part that had recognized the workshop men.

The black dragon's nostrils flared, his pupils dilated. His mouth parted a fraction and he drew long, gulping drafts of air. Drawing in her scent. And, by the way he looked through her, he was also assessing her power. Something none of the others had done. He let out a low hiss of approval, stepped closer. She wanted to back up, to retreat up the stairs and away from those teeth, but she held her ground as he came within striking distance.

"You're as bad as those you insult, if you're here," she said, her voice steady and steely, unlike her quivering insides.

"No," he purred, "I am much more than this rabble. The kaz may not want you," again he swept his gaze through her, "but he is a fool. I will take you."

Arten's hand spasmed around the hilt of her knife. She reminded herself that drawing it would do her no good, not against a dragon. But his words, the *arrogance* in them. As though he had the right to claim her. She felt soiled and crawling under his gaze. The other dragons, she noted peripherally, had drawn back, deferring to him.

"You won't," she heard herself say.

"Oh? Do you think so?" He grinned, wicked and amused. Something about that voice, that expression—reminded her of her brother, Deric, when he'd been in his cruel phase.

The black dragon was about to say more when another voice rang from the rear of the assembled crowd. A voice crackling with icy calm.

"Arten has spoken, Graug. You will respect her wishes."

"Kaz," he greeted lazily as he turned, his tail lashing, wings flared as though to keep Arten tucked behind him. Stekin approached through the path that had been cleared for Graug. Assembled dragons were looking anxiously between the two of them. Some took off in a flurry of wings.

"She is not yours," Stekin said, with an edge she had never heard in him before. It demanded obedience.

"Shall we settle this? Ancient ways for the ancient: will you fight me for her?" Graug laughed, a rolling, wickedly delighted sound as dark as his scales.

"No. She makes her own decision." They were circling around each other now. Stekin looked pathetically thin and battered next to Graug. The black dragon crouched low, his face calculating, his muscles quivering with restraint. Stekin didn't match his stance, but stood tall and unbowed, denying the challenge that was clearly being made.

"We shall see, kaz." Graug's words were calm, patronizing. But he took to the air, darting away with a buffet of wings that nearly sent Arten staggering.

When he was gone, Arten looked down to find all the dragons staring, their eyes flickering uncertainly between her and Stekin. Except Stekin, whose attention was locked on her; the disappointment pouring from him, palpable.

"I didn't need your help!" she shouted at him. Angry, because she had.

"I am aware," he said, rime coating the lie in his words. He looked away from her, cast his voice out over the assembled as he said, "I would like to have a private conversation with my ward."

A few voices hissed surprise at the word *ward,* but nearly as one they took off, scattered like seeds on the wind, leaving Arten shielding her eyes for all the dust their wings kicked up.

"What was that?" she demanded, stomping down the steps as she closed on Stekin.

"Hush," he snapped, watching the sky as the dragons dispersed.

"Hey—" she started, but he hissed at her to be silent and, fuming, she waited.

Not long.

"Now, no one is looking. Be silent," he warned again as he grabbed her up in rough grasp and launched himself into the sky. "Make yourself smaller," he muttered, his quiet words filtering back to her through the air currents. She flattened herself against his neck and chest, hid her face from the wind, as he drew his arms close to his body.

"What are you doing?" she demanded over her shoulder, but he only hissed back.

He took her not far. To his white-stoned mansion, glowing like Nhemith's eyes in the afternoon sun. They landed on a dragon-sized balcony. He pushed her towards a door, shielding her from view of the rest of the valley with his body.

"Go," he hissed. "In."

She was shoved through the entrance. Dragon claws pushing against her back turned into human hands with a hiss of scale and some odd popping. He followed close after. She barely had time to recognize the room as his bedroom before he had rounded on her.

"What were you thinking, leaving the compounds?" he growled, pulling a dressing robe around himself with agitated jabbing motions. He threw open a wardrobe and pulled out a pair of trousers. He stared at her pointedly until she turned her back.

Arms crossed, Arten retorted, "What do you mean what was I thinking? Am I your prisoner, now, as well as your slave?"

"You fool!" he hissed, right behind her. She spun around, startled at not having heard him approach. She expected the glowing eyes, expected the lines of agitation in his posture. Didn't expect the fear, nor the arms that snatched her and crushed her against his chest. Too tight.

She tried to push away, but it was like trying to move a stone. "What is wrong with you?" she snapped. "Let go of me!"

"Shh," he warned, "You will attract attention."

"So? Who cares?" she demanded, still struggling.

"It is improper for you to be here," he said quietly, "and if they know you are, there will be talk. There is already talk."

"If it's improper, why did you bring me here? Against my will, I might add."

"Shh," he warned again. Then his voice turned quiet but pointed, and he wielded it like an awl, pierced her with his warning. "Stay away from Graug."

"Why?"

A hiss like the dull-edge of a knife cut across her scalp. "He is dangerous."

She scowled, suppressed a shiver. "Aren't all of you?"

Stekin froze. He said, with careful neutrality, "Not anymore. Graug...is intelligent. Perhaps the most intelligent dragon alive. I have been the only one to ever check his recklessness, and since I have been gone... He is hiding something. I do not trust him, especially not with your safety."

His arms spasmed tighter, then he released her.

She ducked free of him, backed away until she was out of reach. Accused, "I thought dragons had to take care of their sources."

"Yes. For most, it is a privilege to do so, but Graug has always been inconvenienced by his sources. If he hurt you..." He forced his shoulders down, blanked his face of the violent thoughts there. "I apologize," he said stiffly, "I am not quite myself these past few days."

"What is going on?" she demanded, nonplussed. She'd never seen him quite this—erratic.

"The demon-metal," he found his way to a chair in the corner, sat heavily in it, "is somehow still fouling my senses. As well as my emotions, it seems," he added ruefully.

"I thought it was gone?"

"Yes," he said heavily. He passed a hand over his face in one of the most human gestures she'd seen from him. Gave himself a little shake and insisted, "Arten, you are not a prisoner. But you must be more cautious when you leave the compounds in the future."

"It's not like I asked them to come and talk to me," she protested.

"No, I expect not. However, in the future, I would prefer if you spoke with no other dragons outside my presence."

"Why?" She bristled. "So you can intimidate them into silence?"

His words splintered as he said, "That is absurd! I am still your guardian, and it is my duty to keep you safe. From my own people, especially."

"I can handle myself," she lied.

"No, you cannot. Your posturing may appeal to your dragon audience, but Graug would have bested me today if he had forced a challenge. Only his desire to draw out my humiliation kept him from doing just that. You must keep clear of him. And you must never approach my people in a group like that. Have you not been reading the book I gave you?"

"I have," she huffed, "but I don't see what that has to do with this. This is about you trying to scare away the people I'm supposed to choose from!"

"This," he corrected firmly, "is about me keeping you alive. Tell me, what is the most common theme in the book of our history?"

"What does that matter?" she snapped.

"Answer," he said icily.

"Battle, I guess. Or bloodlines. It's always going on about how this clan fought that clan and how many died and who was gloriously victorious and how many children they had with whomever. But you said those dragons are all dead."

"The dragons you meet nowadays are not capable of such a life, this is true, but it still runs in the core of our natures. You saw this today—the urge to fight is no longer over familial bloodline but over sources. Sources, especially you, are coveted, and given enough time together, they will fight. And the winner will make a claim on you, which cannot be honored by the laws. The claim will cause more conflict between that dragon and whichever dragon you ultimately choose."

"You say *they,* like you're not one of them," she said, suspiciously.

"I am subject to the same base desires and failings as any of my people." He sighed. "I have just had longer to live with them, understand them, and ultimately constrain them. Do you think—" he began, his voice suddenly crisp, lurching to his feet, but stopped himself. Took steadying breaths.

A seed of recklessness had her pressing, goading, "Do I think what?"

He stared at his hands, which were opening and closing reflexively in front of him, as though they were foreign. "Do you think," he forced out, "that it was easy to watch them bickering and boasting, trying to impress you? Do you think I did not want to take Graug's throat in my jaws and lay it open?" His voice had gone rough.

"Yes," she admitted.

He looked up sharply, his eyes smoldering with emerald fire.

"I thought...you don't want me as a source," she stumbled around the confused lump in her throat.

"Of course I do." His words were as raw as a wound. "But this..." He looked back down at his hands, still clenching and relaxing. "This is dangerous," he finished, as though to himself, "for both of us."

"Why?" she asked, her voice irritated.

He looked at her. She thought she saw something golden move behind his eyes, but it must have been a trick of the light that glowed there. "Did you know I fought in a clan war? When I was younger."

She shook her head.

"No, how could you... Well, I did—not that such a thing was special. There was always a clan war with one neighbor or another. But now, not even Nhemith can make that claim.

"I remember the thrill of it, the crackle in the blood, the lust in victory. I hated it. The blood, the death, the monstrous joy. I have worked...diligently..." His voice faltered for a moment. "...to keep that part of our nature contained since we arrived here. I am proud that I have been successful, that I am the only one with memories of these feelings." His hands had stopped spasming. One shook. He clenched it into a fist, held it with the other against his chest.

"You," he said, looking down at his hand, not at her,

"make those memories surface, for some reason. You remind me what it feels like to have a reason to fight. But I have no wish to fight my own people, not even Graug. It is best you source to someone else, so whatever it is that affects me around you is strangled before it matures."

"But—" she started to protest.

"I gave you this choice," he interrupted, "and I will not rescind it. But I must also serve my own people in this. I cannot allow them to fight over you. You must follow where I lead, Arten. You must be more careful."

The pit inside her yawned and closed around her, smothering her anger, leaving her cold. She took a step forward, rested her forehead against the too-prominent ridge of his sternum.

I don't want to source to someone else, she thought miserably, as his hands came down, one to her head the other across her shoulders. They stood there in silence, Stekin's chest moving a bit too rapidly, as though he struggled still to breathe.

I...I think I really mean that. Not just because the thought of another dragon pulling her power was intimidating, not just because the small herd of them today had repelled her. And not at all because he was kaz and whatever supposed social prestige that awarded her.

She thought she would tell him—tell him she wanted to source to him, that she had changed her mind—but when she opened her mouth what came out was a muffled, "I hate it here."

His fingers twitched in her hair. "Tell me."

"They all hate me. The other sources. And every time I leave the compound...it's terrible." The bitter flow of words, now released, wouldn't stop. "The only part of the day I look forward to is getting out of that *source pen*," she spat, "and now you're telling me I can't do that. I guess that means I can't come up here for our lessons. Not that you'll ever let me practice."

Not that I want to tame my power if it means I'm going to be saddled as a source to someone else. The thought stopped her.

"You can practice when your emotions are under control, otherwise it is too risky," he said firmly.

"So I learned," she said miserably.

His hand stilled.

Oops.

His palms lifted her jaw, his eyes were sharp, alert. "Did you?"

She didn't answer, but couldn't look away.

"Yes, I see you did. Tell me," he insisted.

Embarrassed, she told him of reaching for her power after she'd left this morning, of how the anger had magnified and she'd passed out. His eyes flashed.

"Nhemith took you home?" he repeated.

"Yes." She realized his anger wasn't directed at her. *Why is he mad at Nhemith?*

"You could have flared-out," he snarled and his attention was back on her. "You promised you would not reach for your power outside our sessions!"

"And *you,*" she hissed right back, "promised to train me and then sent me away."

"You were emotional," he bristled, his fingers tensing behind her ears.

"Of course I was! And you were an unfeeling b—"

"Shh!" he hissed, straightening, his eyes snapping to the door. She hadn't even noticed that he'd been leaning over her, the way he did when her power flared, until just then. While she was puzzling over not noticing, and wondering why he had been doing so when the Words were not riled, he grasped her by the arms, lifted her and placed her in the shadow of his wardrobe. He held a finger to his lips and she nodded. He stepped out into the hallway, sliding the door closed behind him.

"Claude," she heard him say.

Then, softer, Claude's voice less resonant than Stekin's, "Sorry to disturb you, my lord kaz, but two sources have arrived. They said you wish to speak with them? Shall I show them to your library?"

A pause, then Stekin: "No. Take their names and the names of their compounds. I will visit this evening. If they wish to speak privately, still take all names, but tell them to return tomorrow before noon."

"Yes, kaz," Claude said, then there was the sound of boots trotting away.

Stekin re-entered the room. He came to the corner where she stood and took her hand, pulled her back into their conversation.

"It does us no good," he said, releasing her, "to cast blame. Do you now understand the risk and why I asked you not to practice away from me?"

She nodded reluctantly.

"And so you understand why I ask you to come free of emotion or to speak to me until you can be rational-minded?"

She nodded again, staring at the floor.

"Then we will speak of it no more."

She nodded again. Wondered if it would be so easy. Felt his fingers curl through her hair, then trace a pattern on the left side of her brow. She looked up, caught the fleeting edge of a wistful expression before he could hide it.

"You must return," he said.

"I don't want to go back down there. Can't I stay with you?" she asked, seized with sudden desperation.

"No," he said, his voice a temperature that she was starting to understand meant he disliked to say it. "Please do not ask again."

"Why can't I?" she asked instead.

He stopped his fingers tracing the pattern across her temple again. She felt him pulling away, closing off, even as the pit inside her dragged her back under.

"Go," he commanded. "There is a door under the stairs that leads to the garden. Try not to be seen."

He stopped her before she made it to the door.

"Wait." He was struggling with something. Finally said, "I will meet you at the top of the stairs and walk you home. It is not safe for you to go alone right now."

STEKIN WAS BACK in his dragon form, waiting at the top of the stairs as promised. Arten noticed, for the first time, a scar twisting down his left leg. Wondered what had made such a gruesome mark. He stood guard at the top of the steps while she eased her way down them, then paced beside her down the road.

With each footfall, she felt heavier and more morose than the last. When they finally walked under the arch, Arten was braced for the worst. But she wasn't greeted with the wall of backs turned to her, which surprised her at first. Until she realized they didn't need to physically turn on her in order to ignore her. People called out brightly to Stekin, bowing to him, "my lord kaz"-ing him, expressing their delight at seeing him so well. And yet, they looked straight past Arten.

Stekin hadn't seemed to notice, but when they reached his compound and were parting at the gate, he said, "Why is no one acknowledging at you? They greet me but not you—I find this behavior rude."

"I don't know," she said, honest and bitter. "Ask them. Then tell me if you figure it out." She was tired, more tired than she thought she should be, and just wanted to take a nap. "This is how it always is."

"I will look into it," he assured her, grim. "And," he lowered his voice, brought his head down, "if you are willing, I would like to drop by tonight after I have spoken with the sources who called upon me."

"Sure," she said.

"Very well." He straightened. "Goodbye, Arten."

"Goodbye, Stekin." She imagined a susurration of censure travelling through the sources, but that was impossible because they were ignoring her. She stumbled inside. Pushed past a nearly hysterical Emilette, found her bed, and collapsed into sleep, uncomfortably warm in a shaft of afternoon light.

10

SOMETHING IS ROTTEN
STEKIN

After he left Arten, Stekin skulked back along the empty boulevard, keeping to the midnight shadows which easily swallowed his human form, his light footfalls silent. He knew this place as no other, knew how to enter and leave unseen. Felt a little guilty at using that knowledge.

I should not have to hide that I went to see her, he fumed silently, *she is my ward and my pupil. But they will see it otherwise.* And, if he was honest with himself, he wished a little that it were otherwise. Wished that her power had flared and he had drawn it from her.

But it had not and he had not. His arrival had interrupted her rest, and he had read to her of the history of his race until she had fallen back to sleep. *But if they knew, they would find scandal in it.*

That was not why he was angry, however. *This is what you wanted,* an ancient part of him murmured, a wry undercurrent to the sharper emotions at the surface of his mind, *a community that kept itself in balance with new ethics.*

At the beginning, he snapped back, strictly in the confines of his thoughts, *when we were too many and our sources cowered from us like frightened animals.*

He remembered the sight of those first sources clearly, just after he had unlocked the secret of their power, after he had shared his discovery with his people. Years of experimentation had made him familiar to the small group of sources, and he had won a wary truce with them. However, he had been so triumphant at his success, so optimistic about how siphoning the sources' power would save his people, that he had made a huge mistake: incaution.

He had gathered his people, all that remained—not even three thousand left of his entire race. He remembered the war within him between despair, at their tragically small number, and relief and pride, at his discovery.

He remembered the nauseating wave of fear that obliterated all else when the dragons responded to his news. Chaos. They had devolved to beasts in minutes. The truce and peace of this haven he had created for them forgotten. Clans had banded together. Old rivalries had found new life. The echoes of that brief war had rung through their mountains for days.

Most of all, he remembered the sources. The ones he had been too late to save, torn apart as his people fought to possess them. The others pressed into nooks of the shanty houses they had erected, consumed with terror, the stench of their bodies and bowels revealing them in their hidden places. They had screamed and run from him when he had intervened to save them, not recognizing him at all. Run away from him into the waiting, feral claws of his citizens.

Three had survived. The three that had trusted him and allowed themselves to be herded into his shelter. But even though they had survived that day, and Stekin's rage and talons had kept them safe from abduction, they had not lived out the week. Three sources for three-thousand dragons. The wellsprings of their power had broken like clay pots under the strain. And Stekin had learned just how precious and fragile these sources were.

Source-lover, the insult sneered through him in a long-dead voice. An appellation he had embraced, had turned into a point of pride. Had turned into a way of life.

This is what I wanted, he acknowledged. *My people keeping each other in check, keeping us accountable for our actions to our sources. Sources cherished and beloved.* If that balance had become more *human* than he had anticipated, more moral than reasoned, the benefit was still there for all.

He was inconvenienced by the social norms of these new sources who had never known the dark reason for them. However, that was not what scraped under his scales at the moment.

It was the behavior of the sources on the first circuit that had his anger sparking. He had queried them, after leaving Arten, but they had all smiled and been utterly polite and deferential as they denied any knowledge of seeing Arten with him. He had finally confronted the matron, landing on her patio as was only Kylik's right, causing quite a commotion.

"They are shunning her, my lord kaz," Pasha had explained patiently.

"I can see that!" he had snapped, perhaps unwisely. "Why?"

"Well, they believe she is acting like she's above the rest of us. And that she is using you ill."

"How can she *possibly* be using me ill?" he had growled.

The matron, to her credit, had not quailed but had said calmly, "She stays in your house, and you go to great expense to keep her there, and she lifts not a finger to help herself. They believe she is squandering your fortune and playing you for a fool. It has reached us that she will not be your source. Instead of doing the honorable thing and moving out now that you have announced your intention, she has made no move to do so nor expressed any remorse for her actions."

"It has not even been a day," he had snorted, "and where would she go? Why it is any concern of the rest of you what I do with my money and my compound?"

"It is not our concern, but you must understand: we have only just had you returned to us. Naturally, we feel protective of you. We want you to have only the best sources, only the most loyal and worthy. And Arten does not match that description. In their minds," she had hurriedly added at his dark look and bared teeth.

And the men had been affronted for even less reason. "She doesn't dress properly," a few had been candid enough to tell him, and, "She don't know her place." For once, Stekin was glad he was a shadow of his former self.

If I had my full power, I would have razed the whole circuit today.

He could not remember sources being this petty, this closed-minded ever before. Unified against *his* kind, yes, but not against each other. *From where has this poison sprung, and how can I cleanse it?* He took the steps three at a time, reached the top swiftly. Thought about transforming and flying the rest of the way but needed to work off his irritation.

The other thing that was itching at him was Nhemith. *She knew Arten collapsed, and she did not inform me. Why? What purpose can hiding this from me serve? Unless she seeks to spring it on me later, when she needs to have the higher altitude.*

Which led him to the next, chilling thought, *Does she suspect how important Arten is?*

He turned his wan power in tight bands around himself, soothing it, as he thought and fumed.

NHEMITH WAS WAITING for him in his bed.

"Leave," he commanded, throwing her robe at her.

Nhemith made a disgruntled noise. "I have been patient," she said, "but if you are well enough to have *her* in here, surely you will not refuse *me.*"

"You are being intentionally crass."

"Or perhaps," she murmured, standing, "I am jealous."

"You are not." Stekin snorted, turned to open the door, heard her behind him. Dodged just in time to avoid her lunge. But she twisted, grabbed his clothing on the way down. They tumbled out into the open hall. Nhemith, for all her intuitiveness in her human form had never taught this body to fight, had never depended upon it for survival. Stekin easily subdued her, pinned her to the floor, his arm across her throat.

"You forget," he grinned down at her, "I am stronger in this body."

Her eyes flashed, she grinned back. "Are you?" she gasped around the pressure of his arm. She released her grip on his forearm with one of her hands, reached down between them. He twisted to avoid her, wrapped his hand around her wrist. But she had only been distracting him. Her wrist grew thicker under his fingers, her skin paled as the color leeched from it. He jumped away.

Not far enough. Her dragon-sized hand lashed out, pinned him against the wall. "If you do not fly with me tonight, Stekin," she growled, her breath a hot gale, "I will carry you out of here, drop you in a lake, and freeze it over." She was bluffing; she did not have enough power to freeze an entire lake. But he knew she was not bluffing about the rest. He was not strong enough yet; he would be pressed to keep up with her. But he found his fingers already working to free him from the fastenings of his clothes. They dropped to the floor behind him as he ran after her, transforming, his wings cupping the night as he followed her up into the skies.

Not very much later, Nhemith bore him to the ground in a neighboring valley. He was gasping and wrecked, but she breathed over him and sent a wave of power through him like a rejuvenating mist.

"It has been too long since I have outflown you," she said, rubbing her cheek along his.

"I wish it had been more of a contest for you," he apologized.

"You are the competitive one." She raked her teeth along his neck, sending a long shudder through him. "The flying is for you, anyway."

It was true: the flying was what completed him. The memory of it, the victory of it. And tonight he had flown like the weakened, half-starved person he was, and he had been borne down. Nhemith said nothing of it and did not pressure him, as she was usually wont, for the rutting he would have refused anyway.

AN IMPATIENT NUDGE awoke him near dawn. He felt heavy dew on his scales, rocks under his belly, then remembered where he was and who was nudging him. He groaned.

"You have only yourself to blame," Nhemith said.

"I recall." He remembered the decision to sleep before heading back. It had seemed smart at the time. "I forget how old I am."

Nhemith made a noncommittal noise and rose to her feet easily, drawing her wing away from him. It was cold without her presence radiating into him. That, more than anything, got him to his feet and moving. Only the knowledge that he had to return before Arten arrived for her lesson got him in the air. Once he was aloft, his muscles slowly warmed up and relaxed and everything was a little less torturous.

Before they parted ways, Nhemith called over, "Next time I expect better."

He hissed in her direction but she had peeled away. He managed to make it home, though the landing on his balcony was jarring. He shuffled into his other bedroom—the larger one across the hall—and sank into his heated sandpit with a sigh. He basked as warmth baked deep into his stiff joints and twinging muscles.

He must have fallen asleep because the next thing he knew, Claude was announcing that Arten had arrived and had, in fact, followed him up and would she please wait outside and let the kaz enjoy a little privacy.

"She may enter, Claude," he said, wincing at the volume of his own voice. Everything hurt, even his thoughts.

"You look awful," she said, from somewhere near his head.

"How can you tell?" he growled, but was curious. It had taken him years of study to learn human body language—Arten had known him only months, only weeks in this form. What had she picked up on in that short time?

"Well, you can't open your eyes for one. For another you look like someone stepped on you."

"Ah," he said, disappointed.

"I can go," she offered. "Come back when you're feeling better?" He had no need to open his eyes to know that she was not eager to make good on her offer.

"No, stay," he said. "I will rest while you practice."

"Okay," she said. He heard her settle down on the stone beyond the pit, her boots scraping as they crossed under her legs. He laid his head down, neck outstretched, edged it closer until he felt the warmth of her against his scales.

"When you are ready," he rumbled, already drowsing. Felt a frisson of delight when she rested a hand atop the bridge of his nose. Allowed himself a small smile.

"My lord kaz?" Claude was repeating, utterly polite, interrupting Stekin's drowsing.

"Yes, Claude?" He held in his sigh as he stretched his neck and wings with a luxurious arch. He had not slept so well in years.

"There is another source to see you. Arten left about a quarter-bell ago. She did not wish me to wake you."

Stekin made a discontented noise. "Very well," he said. "Show the source to my library. I will dress and be down shortly."

"Do you require assistance in your preparations, sir?"

Stekin declined and hauled himself out of his sandy bed as Claude's pattering feet trotted down the open hallway then muffled as they reached the carpeted strip on the stairs. He shook himself, flinging away the sand from his scales, then crossed to his other bedroom to stuff himself into a human body and human clothes.

The source was fidgeting in one of Stekin's tall-backed chairs. He jumped when Stekin stepped silently into view, then cowered.

"Be easy," Stekin soothed, his brows drawing together. *Am I so intimidating?* "Thank you for waiting."

"O-of course," the man stammered, dipped his head in an awkward bow.

"There is no need for that. What is your name?"

"C-C-Carl," he wrenched out. Stekin's eyes picked out details—the too-large clothing, the prominent cheekbones and clavicle, the tremor in hands as thin as his own, the brand of Alectros on his brow.

"You are here about the network, Carl?" Stekin asked gently.

"N-no, not the net-net-net-network." Carl's eyes were wide, darting anxiously around.

"Then what brings you?"

"It's in the f-food," he moaned.

"What is in the food, Carl?" Stekin asked, concealing his growing conviction that this source might be mad.

"The p-p-p-p-poison. They're k-kill-kill-killing us!" Carl had jumped to his feet, but Stekin grabbed him before he bolted. The boy screamed and writhed in his grip, lashing out with frail fists and bony joints. Stekin loosened his grip, wondering if he was inadvertently hurting him, but Carl continued to scream.

Claude rushed in, breathless and alarmed. "My lord kaz!?"

"Fetch Kylik immediately!" Stekin called, sending him pelting away. "Calm yourself!" he shouted at the writhing Carl. But the source was beyond reason. His nails and teeth tore at Stekin's skin as he fought to escape. Stekin struggled to contain him, to restrain him without hurting him. He managed to band an arm around the boy's writhing torso, pinning Carl's arms between them. Stekin cupped his other hand over Carl's mouth, keeping his head still and his teeth at bay.

"Easy," he said, "I will not harm you, Carl, but you must calm yourself." He continued talking to him, assuring him that he was safe. The boy stopped struggling, but the madness did not leave his eyes, which Stekin held unblinkingly. When Kylik finally arrived, Carl lost the little composure he had regained. Kylik was compelled to put him to sleep.

"You must examine him thoroughly, Kylik," Stekin commanded, laying Carl's limp body out for the healer to inspect. "Check for poisons and brain diseases. And see if there is a reason he is so thin."

"I know how to do my job," Kylik snapped, already engrossed in his examination, his typical nervousness around the kaz forgotten.

Stekin went to his worktable, leaving Kylik the space he needed. He took down the last volume in the series of books Arten had picked up before—his journals—and began to record what had transpired so far in the incident, including the exact words the man had said, his presentation and behavior, notes on the examinations Kylik was performing, and the injuries Stekin had acquired. *It may turn out to be nothing*, he thought grimly, *but I doubt I will be so fortunate.*

It was done in short order—years of research had informed Stekin's record-keeping, and he was efficient. He watched Kylik, felt the tightness in his mouth and across his brows as the healer's body-language grew agitated. Kylik was rigid with something—A*nger? That is uncharacteristic of him*—when he left Carl's prone form and faced Stekin.

"I want you to look at him—look into his core," Kylik said, his voice flinty.

Stekin raised his brows. "That is unethical," he warned.

"I have already done it," he dismissed with a flick of his wings, still in that uncharacteristic, hard tone, "I want you to confirm my findings. As for ethics, this breech is minor, if you find what I think you will."

Stekin stood, a warning tingling at the nape of his neck. A ludicrous desire to transform, to cover the weakest part of his spine with his natural ruff of horns, flashed through him. He went to Carl's side, crouched. Unlike Kylik, who had honed the skill of power-perception as necessitated by his profession, Stekin required eye-contact and a physical connection to view deep enough to see the source of a person's power. Such an act often revealed intensely private facets of a person and was thus strongly discouraged for those who were not healers.

Kylik would not ask this of his kaz if it were not important, he reminded himself, his hand on the boy's skull, thumb on his eyelid. He pushed the flap of flesh up, revealing an unfocused, narrow pupil. With a steadying breath, Stekin drove a tendril of his power down like an extra appendage, twisting towards the dim source of the man's power. And it *was* dim.

Shockingly dim. *What has happened to him?* he wondered, growing uneasy. Not just his power, but Carl's very soul was darkened. *A malady?*

He edged closer, careful not to brush the foreign power that curled in weak, twisted tendrils. Thinned his exploring power to narrow ribbons, threaded closer until he could *see* what had happened.

He fell back into himself with a jolt, kept falling backwards onto his hands. Stopped himself before he scrabbled away.

"What did you find?" Kylik pressed, urgent and distressed. Stekin now knew why.

"That...what did that to him?" Stekin's biology was torn between sickness and rage. All he could do was stare at the now-closed eyes of the gaunt source.

"Later." Kylik hissed, "Tell me—what did you *see*?"

Stekin composed himself, dragged his gaze away, refocused on the healer. "His soul has been...carved? No, nothing so precise. Chipped away. The damage there is horrific."

A silence followed. Kylik broke it with a pressed, "And?"

"And I will have Alectros answer for this!" Stekin said. He rose to his feet, brushed off his trousers, felt a deep scowl on his face. Knew his eyes were glowing.

Kylik made a strangled noise. "That is all you saw? I suppose...well, it is a relief, I suppose. Perhaps I was wrong."

"About what?"

"The wellspring of his power. I must have mistaken the damage to his soul for something more serious."

"*More* serious?"

"Well, yes, of course. What you saw is unusual, I will grant, but nothing particularly alarming. I had thought— well, I suppose it does not matter. Though," he added to himself, "I should like another professional opinion. No offense to you, kaz."

"Not alarming?" Stekin repeated. "This is source-neglect, if not outright abuse!"

"No, not particularly. It *is* abnormal for it to be quite so progressed in someone his age," Kylik mused, "but he will have a good eight years left if I am not mistaken. He will not be the youngest we have lost. It takes them all differently."

Stekin's voice was rising in volume as he said, "*What* takes them differently? You are making no sense, Kylik. Explain, precisely, why you are not concerned about the state of this person's soul!"

"Kaz, why are you so distressed? You of all people should know the soul-toil our sources experience." Kylik looked genuinely confused.

"Soul-toil? *Explain*, Kylik!" He had never heard of such a thing. Never seen such a thing.

Nor have I looked for it.

"Of course, kaz," the dragon said, crouching in a submissive way. His voice was tentative, as though worried he was doing something wrong, as he explained, "You know that our sources die younger than other humans? Yes, well, that is because of the soul-toil. Their souls get whittled away, just like you saw in this one," Kylik nudged his nose in the direction of the still-sleeping Carl. "As I said, he is quite young for that amount of damage—but they all decay differently. Most of them experience the wear over about twenty-five years. He looks like he will only tolerate about ten years total before the transfer kills him." Kylik peered at Stekin nervously, shifting on his feet.

Stekin felt winter in his veins. "You mean," he said carefully, "that our sources are *all* damaged like this? And you have never thought to tell me?"

"I—we assumed you knew!" Kylik protested in surprise. "With all your research—and with all the healers before me —how did you not know? It has always been this way, my master said the soul-toil was posited very early on."

"This soul-toil," Stekin was fighting to keep the thing inside him still, "tell me what you know."

"Well, we do not *know* much, we have only supposition. We know that when the soul wears out—the breaking point is slightly different for each source, but can be roughly predicted—the body will die. We suspect that only sources have this type of damage—but we have not dealt extensively with other humans. And, we suspect that the act of power-transfer causes the damage. We thought you knew," he moaned again, a supplication for forgiveness.

Stekin paced as he wrangled his anger. *The transgression is not his. It is mine. I have been complacent and blinded; sources are living so much longer than they once were, I never thought to consider if that was a sufficient life-span for their kind. How long do other humans live? How have I never seen this?* He knew the answer to the last—he had only rarely looked into the core of his sources. Except Arten, all of them had been his primes, and all in the early days when he had been actively forging them. He had never looked later. Had never needed to, never thought to.

"Be easy, Kylik," he said, though frost still crisped his words. "Tell me: if the transfer causes this soul-toil, does it not follow that this one's damage is higher because of increased load? That is to say, that more transfers than normal have been performed on him?"

"It is possible," Kylik mused, "As I said, each source experiences the toil differently, but we cannot know for certain."

"Unless he tells us," Stekin murmured to himself, eyes narrowing. There was something else that needed to be asked. "If this is not what alarmed you, what did?"

"I thought, I still think, that the wellspring of his power has been disrupted, damaged. Though what caused it," Kylik amended quickly, "I would not guess. I think only of whether it can be healed."

Stekin thought about going back for another look to validate Kylik's concern, but just the thought left him with a crawling feeling under his skin. *The demon-metal effects are still not gone?* "Get your second opinion," Stekin said, "and return to me when you have it. Take him with you, admit no one to see him except me. Do you understand?"

"What about Alectros?" Kylik all but whimpered.

Stekin's eyes snapped to the brand on the source's face, they flashed. "Especially not Alectros. Not until we have some answers."

"Yes, my kaz." Kylik bowed his head. He scooped up the limp human in an arm, cradled him against his chest with a long-practiced expertise, and hobbled out.

Stekin paced a long time before he recorded the remainder of the encounter and his thoughts.

There was a pressure building in him, an urgency, a fear. This was to be Arten's fate. Her radiant, strong soul worn away to a dim, pocked thing like Carl's. He snarled and slammed his notebook closed. He could not let that happen to her, could not allow her to be shredded to nothing. *But what can be done?* He was pacing again. *She must source, her power must be relieved. I have squandered all these years, fumbling in blindness! And she will now pay for my failings.*

His rage echoed back at him from the stone walls.

THE AFTERNOON SUN baked warmth into Stekin's scales as he glided on a high wind current. The wind was from the south; it tasted of crisped rock with a tang of sulfur. Far below him, New Respite clung to the floor of the valley, three little birds warily sharing a nest. The curved oblong of the compounds, clustered together around the three arteries that kept them connected, cowering in the safety of the cliffs. The wild tangle of the Hill, dragons living unnaturally close, weaved together like strangling vines, each keeping the others in check and upright. The humans in their divided city, huddled to the side, carefully not touching the others, focused inwards—as divided as the dragons and sources in their own right.

I must check on my properties soon, he reminded himself, *and on the governor. He did not call upon my return. Perhaps another governs now.* The humans were so fleeting, so busy in their impermanence, and he cared little for their schemes.

His people schemed as well but on a larger scale. It made the humans seem like children by comparison.

Nhemith, for instance, is up to something. But she has concealed it well from me. I can only wait for her to make a mistake. And she would—Nhemith always did. She was ambitious and impatient and invariably overreached. It was why she had failed as kaz, why his people had turned back to him even as he was unfit to lead.

He turned his thoughts away from that time, away from Nhemith. It was not she who had driven him to mull on-the-wing. It was Carl. And Alectros. And the confirmation Kylik had brought that the wellspring of Carl's power was riddled with fine cracks in various stages of healing. Which meant one of three things: either Alectros was abusing his source, another dragon was stealing from Alectros, or a human had learned a way to siphon power. None of which were acceptable.

It is unlikely a human is responsible; Ergin was the only source I have neutralized in perhaps sixty years. What other human would have motive to drain power?

Stekin was most proficient at the erasure, but that did not mean others could not do it. He made a note to inquire with Ktet whether any crimes had warranted that punishment in his absence.

Which left him back with the likely scenario that a

dragon was interfering with Carl. *Alectros was one of the five who engaged in source-theft,* he remembered from the list Nhemith had named to him. The list that included Hirany-ath. That Nhemith had given them all sources after their crimes still angered him. Especially because sources being in such short supply was the crisis that had precipitated their deviancy in the first place. *Perhaps if it had not been her daughter, she would have acted more strongly,* he thought, but did not believe it true.

The wind shifted east, and he veered away, angling north again. North, the only safe direction to fly. North, where the snow voids and the ice mountains stretched without end, where humans dared not go. Not with the predators and natural obstacles he had cultivated for hundreds of years to deter them, at least. The brisk, dry air closed around him, caressed his scales. It reminded him of the teeming herds of shaggy arctic deer. The seasons of endless night chased by those of endless sun. The carved-ice palaces of his clan. Of hanging off a spire, barely fledged, scanning the horizon for the flap of out-clan wings. Of the bodies, still frozen there, dead these long centuries.

The north was no refuge, not anymore. His kind were as crippled there as the humans now. He was the last who had flown those skies. He dipped his wing and turned back.

I cannot confront Alectros, not without evidence, he thought, turning his mind back to a different type of danger. Carl had mentioned poison—it should be simple enough to validate that claim. He could also monitor the boy, see how often he was intersecting with Alectros or if he crossed paths with another.

I also need to check with Nhemith, or perhaps Ktet, and find out who exactly has learned to transform in my absence and what their human forms look like.

His records were out of date, and if dragons were stealing sources again, it was imperative he learn to recognize them in all their skins. He wondered how Hiranyath and her compatriots had acquired their forms. Another thing to ask Ktet.

THE SUN WAS NEARING the far rim of the valley when Stekin returned. He angled for Ktet's house, far up on the side of the hill, the new construction modeled more closely after human city dwellings. He called out a greeting as he circled overhead and landed on the roof when Ktet called out a welcome.

Ktet hopped up from a hole in the floor of the roof—he had no need for niceties like stairwells since his servants all lived off-premises.

"Kaz," he greeted, inclining his head with deep respect.

"Ktet," Stekin acknowledged. The dragon's vibrant orange scales had dulled a few shades since Stekin had left, and the black slashes on his wings, flanks, and tail had similarly deepened, making him look less eye-watering. In the sun, the change was more striking than it had been in his library.

"What can I do for you, kaz?" Ktet asked, polite but with a tone that told Stekin he was interrupting something.

Stekin was immediately on alert. Ktet had always been one of those that had looked to him with awe, the dragons, like Kylik, whose spines weakened in the presence of the kaz. The old Ktet would have flown through a lightning storm instead of walked to answer Stekin's call.

"When you are free today," Stekin said, with feigned

indifference, "please bring the census over. I wish to review it with you."

"Oh?"

Stekin heard the faint click of talons below as they inched closer to the hole in the roof.

"Might I ask why?" Ktet pressed, calling Stekin back from the few steps he had taken towards that void.

"I have been gone for many years, and much has changed. I wish to know how our people are doing," Stekin equivocated. The dragon below had gone silent, and Ktet was hovering nervously, trying to look as though he were not. "What do you do when it snows?" Stekin asked, to cover his interest, peering around Ktet with a gesture toward the roof doorway.

"I put up the awning," Ktet said, with a thread of relief in his voice. "Would you like me to demonstrate?"

"Please, yes." The contraption was rather clever and would solve the problem of moisture falling into the dwelling below, but Stekin was more interested in the silence emanating from the interior and Ktet's nervousness.

He said a farewell once the demonstration was done and rose into the sky. Surreptitious glances back showed him that Ktet watched him until he landed on a sunny ledge out of earshot. Then the orange-and-black dragon hopped back down into his home.

Stekin slid off the ledge in silence, only the faint sound of wind flowing over his wings betrayed him as he dove. He opened them gently, easing into a fast glide that took him near but not over the house.

Ktet's voice carried up to him, "...just the awning. There is no cause for concern."

Stekin banked, making a turn around the dwelling, his

breath held as he strained to hear the other occupant's reply.

"You are too confident," a familiar voice said, full of suspicion.

"Why can we not just tell him about us?" Ktet complained.

"It is not yet time."

Stekin had heard enough. He banked away, angling for his own home.

Nhemith's quiet laughter followed him. "Are you jealous?" she asked Ktet. And his muttered affirmative.

Something had gone still and utterly calm inside him. *Why is Nhemith skulking in Ktet's house? Why has she pursued me since my return if they are together?* He searched for some jealousy inside himself, some drop of envy that would once have diluted through him. There was nothing. *If she means so little to me, why am I indulging her in her attentions?*

He had no answer, not yet. He pondered the situation into the evening, staring out his library windows, unseeing. He knew that Nhemith was lying to him, lying to Ktet, or lying to both of them—that much was apparent. But why? What did she have to gain from this deception, this game?

And did he have more to gain by playing it or refusing?

HE WAS FORCED to put his musings aside when Kikkyo arrived.

"My kaz," she greeted him with her elegant bow, "you are looking well today."

Stekin acknowledged and dismissed the observation with a stiff huff of his wings. "You did not come to tell me that."

Kikkyo gave him a short look of disapproval normally reserved for errant dragonlings, then seemed to remember that he was kaz and smoothed it away. But it had the intended effect.

"My apologies, Kikkyo, for my rudeness. What brings you?"

She smiled, mollified, and said, "Good news, I trust. With the increased funds, we have found six more who have agreed to become network agents."

Stekin felt a small frown lodge on his brow. "So few? How many does that bring us to?"

"Eleven, including the ones who volunteered before." She hesitated then added, apologetic, "We did agree to pay the previous volunteers the increased wage as well, to prevent a strife that was brewing."

Stekin nodded. "I expected no less. Expect to increase the wage for the existing agents as well—we cannot afford to lose them. For those who are using the network activity to further their own businesses, like the importers, I think a small increase is sufficient—if they protest, you can tell them they will get the same wage when they devote their full time to the network but not before. And perhaps a compensation scheme should be generated to reward those who do the work we most require—bonuses for those who take territories in the south and west, for instance, and bonuses for detailed and timely reports."

Kikkyo was nodding, looking thoughtful but cautious. "Are you certain, kaz? These increases will be costly..."

Stekin huffed out his irritation through his long nose. "Then consider your operating budget doubled."

Kikkyo's eyes widened. The network was the most expensive part of their society; keeping it running was easily twice as expensive as the maintenance of all the compounds combined. Every dragon paid in if they wanted or had sources, but those contributions were whatever the person could reasonably afford and in aggregate accounted for only 23% of the operating costs. The rest was funded by Stekin. His offhanded donation was more than most dragons would earn in a lifetime.

"That is...quite generous," Kikkyo said, her voice rippled with shock.

"No. It is *necessary.*" Stekin heard the hardness in his voice and with an effort gentled it again. "I expect you to use it, Kikkyo, every scrap of it, to cleanse our network and keep it safe. You must do whatever you can."

Kikkyo nodded, a slow gentle undulation of her neck. She was not looking at Stekin, but thinking. "I have some ideas," she said, "that I will surface to the rest of the council when I tell them of the increase you have given us. They may not work...?"

She was looking for permission. He granted it. "As long as you control the damage, experiment away."

Excitement was beginning to spread through her, washing away the hesitation. "Yes, my kaz!" She rose to leave, but he raised his wings to forestall her.

"Eleven," he said, "is not enough. We need twice that number, at least."

She settled, caught his somber mood instantly. "Do you have suggestions as to where we should be looking?"

Stekin thought then said, "Ask the mercenaries and the houses of religion; they will know."

"An excellent idea, my kaz! I shall do so immediately."

"Wait." He halted her once more. "I have news for you, as well."

Stekin recalled to her the reports of the few sources who had come forward about problem nodes in the network.

Kikkyo listened, promised to notify the relevant agents and have them venture out as soon as possible. They talked logistics of training up the new agents for a few minutes, then Kikkyo left.

I like her, Stekin decided after she had gone. *I regret not getting to know her better earlier.* Why had he not? He had always thought she was empty-headed and vain. Thinking on it, now, though, her eccentricities were different from other people, but they all had them. Even Stekin, with his research and his insistence on walking in a human form more often than not.

Perhaps, he struck on it at last, *I have been simply envious that she has a wealth in her children.* Something he would never have.

HE WAS in the courtyard eating his evening meal when Ktet arrived. The space dwarfed them both. Ktet landed and joined him, though he fidgeted uncomfortably.

"It has been a long time since I have seen this place filled," Stekin said innocuously, licking a claw clean. Ktet nodded a wordless agreement around his shank of roasted meat. "Did you call the court here while I was gone? Or was it held at the amphitheater?"

Ktet waved a talon in negation. "We called no court, kaz."

"Not even for the source thefts? I find that irregular. You are not generally irregular, Ktet."

Ktet's tail jumped. He shifted and avoided Stekin's eyes. "It was...a volatile time. We were concerned that a formal court and trial would cause even more harm. We had already broken up several scuffles during the allocation process. One ended in a torn wing; we were fortunate that Kylik was able to save it."

"Who was kaz?" Stekin asked before sipping at a bowl of stewed vegetables. It had taken him many years to learn the trick of it in his natural form.

"You were," Ktet said guilelessly. "Nhemith insisted you would return. She counselled patience."

"So you looked to Nhemith for guidance?"

"Yes, I suppose," Ktet mused, his voice growing cautious.

"But she refused the honorific?"

"As I have said."

Stekin made a noise of curious dismissal which belied the importance that acknowledgement held for him. *Nhemith has always aspired to be kaz, and when it is handed to her, she refuses it. Then she clings to me upon my return. Oh, Nhemith, towards what far horizon do you fly?*

"There were five thieves, I am told?" Stekin said blandly between sips, watching Ktet from the corner of his eye. "Tell me what happened."

The story Ktet told mirrored Nhemith's. There were a few more details—the number of times each of the five youths had been denied a source, the number of days between source arrivals, the squabbles and altercations that had broken out between petitioners of the source council. One of the five had been the dragon whose wing had been torn. Her recovery had been rough, and she had not flown well after that. She had been the ringleader of the little band. And she had killed herself when she fractured another dragon's prime.

"It was horrible," Ktet remembered, his voice wavering. "She flew as high as she could on that damaged wing— higher than was safe for her, so we were, most of us, watching, wondering what she was up to. It was before we knew what had happened to the prime. Anyway, she got up there and...and she turned the last of his—the source's—power on her wings and shredded them. Just charred the membranes clean off. I can still hear that scream, sometimes. It was horrible," he said, staring into the space of memory, pupils tiny dots even in the low light. "Horrible. She fell—with that scream—and I felt the ground shake with her impact, and then it was quiet. So quiet.

"Until the sources started shouting. That's when we learned about the prime she shattered the night before. His compound-mates had just found his body." Ktet shuddered.

"Whose prime was it?" Stekin asked.

"Nhemith's," the orange dragon said, then explained that Nhemith had been outspoken against granting the dragon a source on account of her wing. If she were unable to fly well, she would be unable to produce strong offspring, and so, Nhemith had counselled, sources should first go to those best able to support the community as a whole.

That sounds like the Nhemith I know, Stekin thought.

"And yet, Nhemith counselled generosity for the transgressors?" he prompted.

"Yes," Ktet nodded, coming back to himself a little. He toyed with the femur in his hands. "She felt personally responsible for the extremes to which the perpetrators had been driven. To restore the peace, she thought the best solution would be to give them what they had been denied. What, in less lean times, they would have had."

"The best solution for the city," Stekin mused aloud, "or for her daughter?"

Ktet went still. "Both," he said with a hint of a challenge.

She definitely has him, Stekin now knew, *but why does she need him?*

He made a noncommittal noise and steered the topic,

"You mentioned Graug as one of the band of five—how can that be? I recall him being granted a source shortly before I left."

"You are correct; his source died about six years ago. He had been on the list for nearly three years and was impatient. None of the others had ever had a source, just Graug. I understand why he did it, and frankly, I was surprised to learn he was not the instigator."

"I suppose he was the first to be allocated a source?" Stekin hazarded.

"N-no. We did not want to set a precedent..." He quickly added, "Alectros was first."

"Hmm. What is his source's name?"

"I have it in the census exactly, but it was Carl or something like that, if I recall correctly."

Stekin cleaned his claws with feigned indifference. "And the others?"

Ktet named the dragons and the sources they had been granted. Natalia to Hiranyath, Raccard to Graug, Viktor to Nyyrikki. It aligned with what Nhemith had told Stekin that first day. The last source, Viktor, had only been granted last fall—nearly two years after Alectros had been given Carl.

Stekin steered the conversation to other news, kept Ktet talking of who had taken consorts, which unions had been dissolved, what children had been hatched, and how many had failed to make it out of the shell. His community was small, and Stekin asked after the news of each by name. A feat which kept Ktet at his side until the stars wheeled overhead. Only then, when his guest had been worn down by relaying the minutia of thirteen years, did Stekin ask his last question.

"I understand many of us have learned to take the

human form, while I've been away. Are you still cataloging those?"

"Oh, yes," Ktet said around a yawn, patting the census book as he had been with increasing frequency as the evening stretched on. An unsubtle hint that Stekin should educate himself instead of forcing Ktet to feed him all the information already contained in that volume.

"Very good," Stekin said. "Well, I think I have kept you from your consort long enough. If you would be so kind as to leave the census, I will return it to you in a few days."

"I—I have no consort!" Ktet sputtered, coming awake.

"Do you not? I must have been misinformed," Stekin lied. "A mate? No? Hmm, my apologies. Do leave the book. Goodnight."

Ktet's black-striped wings flashed in an ancient pattern of warning as he took himself home. Stekin allowed himself a smirk as he took the census book into his library, placed it carefully beside his chair, then flew up to his own bed. He was not surprised to find both of them were empty of Nhemith.

Tomorrow, Kylik will likely release Carl. Tomorrow night, I will tail him and see what I can discover of this poison, see if my suspicions bear out. Which meant he must convince Nhemith that tomorrow would not be the best evening for an aerial rematch. In some way that did not arouse her suspicion.

If Kylik is correct that the transfer causes this soul-toil, then it follows that more transfers equate to increased soul-toil. Graug's source died after about twelve years of use. And now Kylik thinks Alectros's source will expire similarly early. Nhemith's prime was shattered. If the other two sources have similar soul-toil, I will know what is going on. But how could he prove it? And how could he stop it?

No, it is too early to be thinking of a purge, he cautioned himself. *It could be nothing.* But there was a pattern unfolding here, one he had seen before. One that he had been forced to end. It was pointless to wish it were not so. He had to face it, he would face it. It was why he was kaz: he kept his people alive, kept their society functioning.

And now, he was also guardian to Arten. *I will not allow her to source to anyone who will treat her poorly. And I will pry into the private lives of every dragon here, if I must, to ensure that.* His vehemence unnerved him. He did not manage to sleep until after the second night bell.

When he awoke in his sandpit in the morning, it was to Nhemith curved around his back, her wing thrown over him, her foreleg and neck draped over his own.

11

A PURPOSE?

ARTEN

W hen Arten awoke in the morning, it was to Emilette panicking about something. After forcing her eyes open and prodding her thoughts into sluggish action with the help of her morning ablutions, Arten gathered that the fuss had to do with the cook.

"What about the cook?" she asked, perhaps unwisely.

"She's *gone!*" Emilette cried, hands buried in the hair at her temples. "Oh, what are we going to do? You're late, again, to see the kaz, and there's no breakfast."

"I'm not late." Arten sighed, combing her fingers through her hair. She pushed Emilette out of the room, then stuffed her legs into a clean pair of trousers and wriggled into her blue tunic. Someone had managed to get the speckle of Stekin's blood mostly out of the cloth.

"Ugh, when are you going to get some proper shoes?" Emilette lamented, not for the first time, as Arten stuffed her feet into her boots. Boots that, admittedly, were in rough shape. But they had taken her through the network; they had walked with her hundreds of miles.

become a terror. She stomps around here, a black cloud following her, shouting at the servant girl, treating her very ill indeed. I worry that she will turn her abuse on me next.

I find no fault with you, my lord kaz, for I am certain you have been misled about her character and temperament. However, I can no longer sit by and watch you be taken in by whatever ploy this girl has used to so deceive you.

Further, I feel it is my duty, as someone in your employ for a short while longer, to inform you that there is much Talk about this situation between you two. It seems odd that you would continue to house and provide for (so splendidly!) someone who you do not want as a source (which, it now occurs to me, may mean that you are not deceived in her character after all!).

People are also seeing these other dragons come up to your door, soliciting her attention, and it is, frankly, alarming. It is unnatural. Dragons do not enter compounds that are not their own!

They think you would be better to send her away, to one of the unused compounds on the third circuit, and avoid this alarm and confusion. I have heard many people wonder, in my hearing, if this signifies a broader change. You can understand, I think, why it would cause worry to think that strange dragons could enter our compounds at their will.

Thank you, again, for permitting me to serve you. When you have a proper source, I will be happy to do so again.

IT WAS SIGNED NEATLY. At a glance, it looked fine, the writing handsome and even—not like her erratic scribblings. Arten would not have thought such venom could be contained behind something so pretty-looking.

"These work just fine," she said. It wasn't true—the leather was worn at the toe on one and let the weather in, and the outer soles were thin and cracked. Puddles were misery, but fortunately it didn't seem to rain much here.

"You *must* tell the kaz today to buy you some shoes. He can't refuse you *that!* Not with winter coming..."

"He hasn't refused me anything," Arten bristled at the implication, "I haven't asked."

"Well, you must! Oh, but you're late, hurry, hurry!" Emilette ignored the fact that she was the one slowing Arten down, with her insistence on brushing Arten's hair and whisking off imaginary dirt from her clothes. But Arten was growing used to that. It was easier to submit and just leave when Emilette was ready, despite her verbal rush.

They came across Natalia at the base of the steps. More accurately, Natalia came across them. Arten was sitting on the bottom stair, taking a rest, when Natalia approached.

"Hey, Arten," she greeted, in her usual brusque way.

"'Morning," Arten said.

"You look awful."

"That is *so* rude!" Emilette snapped, aghast.

Natalia turned her pale eyes on Emilette, narrowed them, and the battle of wills began. Arten might have found it amusing if she wasn't so preoccupied with how tired and winded she was. She watched as Natalia said nothing but clearly conveyed her disdain without a sound in response to each outburst from Emilette. Emilette's face, Arten noticed for the first time, rarely changed from an expression of large-eyed shock, even as her words dribbled out in all manner of intensity and emotion.

Their one-sided argument continued when Arten was able to drag herself up the steps, throughout her rest at the top, and then along the lane until they reached Stekin's pedestrian-gate. Arten observed but didn't interrupt—mostly because she thought Natalia was winning. Natalia must have thought so, too, because she smirked when she told Arten, "Later," and shot Emilette a look of cold triumph.

"Well!" Emilette gaped, but could, for once, find no other words.

Arten relished the silence as she rang the bell and waited for someone to admit her.

The door slid open just as Emilette jumped and said, "Oh! Arten, you're so forgetful, you almost left this!" She pressed a folded sheet of paper into Arten's hand, saying, "It's from the cook. For *him,*" then scampered away.

Arten fumed, stuffed the paper deep into the pocket of her tunic and stomped along behind the boy who led her to the library. It was empty, but the boy assured her the lord kaz would be down soon. She plopped into her chair and kicked the legs of it while she waited. The large book on the table between the chairs drew her eye. She pulled it onto her lap and opened to a page in the middle.

It had lists of words that she couldn't decipher, with numbers next to each. She had to flip through a few pages to understand that the lists were of assets, and the numbers represented the value. Most of the assets seemed to be buildings, but here and there she saw "eqin & cart" or "mine - salt" and other, more arcane entries. Sometimes the lists changed to be only symbols. Others seemed to contain the names of people, some of which were crossed out. She finally realized what she was looking at when she saw a familiar symbol inked at the top of the page—the symbol branded into Matron's skin. It was an inventory, she realized, of Kylik's assets. Including—her finger stopped on Pasha's name—his sources. About half of the names of his sources were crossed out.

The list disturbed her, but she didn't quite know why. Found herself wanting to see if Stekin was in the book, what the list of his sources said. Wanted to know if her name was on it, and how many names had been crossed off.

She turned to the front, expecting to need to page through and match symbol-headers to the memory of the one on Stekin's compound gate and door, but was pleased to find an index. But it was hardly necessary—his symbol was the first entry. She turned to it—saw that a note of "Deceased?" had been struck through next to his mark on the first page—and began reading through his lists. She read for about five pages, then began turning the pages more rapidly.

Demons, I knew he was rich, but is there anything he doesn't own in this place? The lists of properties were mostly marked with street names and lot numbers that she didn't know, but the "New Respite" at the end identified them clearly enough. He also owned several mines, the paper mill, and half of the printing press, along with properties in other towns she had never heard of. She wondered if they were network houses. She skimmed over his land resources—grazing land, forest land, water rights—but stopped when the list of symbols appeared.

The heading read "Genetic Distribution" and it had three entries, two of which were crossed out. She didn't know what it meant, and the next section, "Source Assets," drew her eye away. It was completely empty. But the author of the book had left two blank pages to hold entries before the next dragon's lists started.

What did that mean? *That Rya was right, maybe, about*

what Matron said—he hasn't had sources in a while. I wonder when this book was written. And why would they leave so much blank space? It's like the author was expecting him to have a lot of us. She frowned vaguely into nothing.

Silent hands lifted the book from her lap. She jumped. Stekin closed the volume and set it back on the table.

"What did you learn?" he asked, his face and voice neutral.

"Nothing I didn't already know," she said. It was mostly true. "You look better." That was definitely true. He was dressed in his fine, if dated, clothes and boots. No robes today. He was buttoned up and alert, his cheeks looked less hollow, his eyes had more spark. It was difficult to believe that only days ago he had sat in that same chair and looked like death was upon him.

"You do not," he said bluntly. "Are you still not sleeping well?"

"No," she said. *I'm not sleeping well. Is that why I'm so fatigued?* She felt a twist of relief at the thought. That must be it.

"What do you need from me?" he asked.

I need you to make them stop ignoring me, she thought, but it was impossible and needy so she didn't voice it. "I don't think you can do anything," she said, instead. His hand reached over and long, thin fingers squeezed her wrist before drawing away. It helped, a little.

"You can talk to me," he offered, noting her agitation, "or go home." It was meant kindly, she heard no ice in the words, no ultimatum.

"Can I just stay here for a bit?" she asked unhappily.

"Of course," he said. "You may stay until Ktet arrives, then I must attend to other matters." He picked up the tome and settled it on his own lap, opened it to the index. "You must tell me what you require," he cautioned, "because otherwise I cannot know."

"I know," she said. He nodded, taking her at her word, and turned his focus wholly to the book. But she didn't know what she needed. She kicked at the chair legs a little longer, then tried pacing. Neither helped. She wondered what she could say, what might ease the conflict in her. *The faster I train up, the faster I get sourced to someone else,* she thought miserably. *But I can't tell him that.* Her face burned, embarrassed at the mere thought of saying such.

She sank to the ground at his feet, rested her head against his knee. A hard edge dug into her stomach. She fished the folded note from her pocket. The first line read, "*My lord kaz,*" but she read it anyway.

My Lord kaz,

I thank you for the opportunity you have provided. However, I will no longer be able to fill the role you have hired me to do. Not only has my prime requested that I resign, but I feel that it is my moral duty to do so as well. For as long as I am working for you in this capacity, I am showing a measure of support for the situation here. A support that I do not feel and can no longer lend.

You know, I am sure, how Arten's superior airs garner her no friendship from those of us who know our place. You may not know that she has become increasingly moody and destructive. She volunteered to take some pies over to my compound, pies that had taken me days to make in preparation for our Unity Festival, and then dropped them on the doorstep and kicked the sack over. Half of them were ruined! And behind closed doors she has become a terror. She stomps around here, a black cloud following her, shouting at the servant girl, treating her very ill indeed. I worry that she will turn her abuse on me next.

I find no fault with you, my lord kaz, for I am certain you have been misled about her character and temperament. However, I can no longer sit by and watch you be taken in by whatever ploy this girl has used to so deceive you.

Further, I feel it is my duty, as someone in your employ for a short while longer, to inform you that there is much Talk about this situation between you two. It seems odd that you would continue to house and provide for (so splendidly!) someone who you do not want as a source (which, it now occurs to me, may mean that you are not deceived in her character after all!).

People are also seeing these other dragons come up to your door, soliciting her attention, and it is, frankly, alarming. It is unnatural. Dragons do not enter compounds that are not their own!

They think you would be better to send her away, to one of the unused compounds on the third circuit, and avoid this alarm and confusion. I have heard many people wonder, in my hearing, if this signifies a broader change. You can understand, I think, why it would cause worry to think that strange dragons could enter our compounds at their will.

Thank you, again, for permitting me to serve you. When you have a proper source, I will be happy to do so again.

It was signed neatly. At a glance, it looked fine, the writing handsome and even—not like her erratic scribblings. Arten would not have thought such venom could be contained behind something so pretty-looking.

"What is that?" Stekin asked, his fingers stilling in their track through her hair.

The pit in Arten opened, she began the slide into it as she handed the paper up. *It's better to get it out of the way,* she thought miserably. *If he's going to cast me aside, I'd rather know now than later.* She heard the rustle of the paper between his fingers, felt the lightness where his hand had been resting on her head.

"Tell me what happened with the pies," he said. He read much more quickly than she did, so the question came too soon. But she stumbled through an explanation. Of how she had been pressed into the chore, how the woman who answered the door had pretended not to see her and shut the door in her face, how she'd been angry and kicked the sack.

"But only a few of them would have been ruined." She glowered at the hem of her tunic, picking at some loose thread. "Not *half.*"

"I see," he said, in a voice that sounded full of disappointment. "And the shouting at your servant?"

"Emilette," she spat, "is hysterical half the time. So, yeah, I've shouted at her, trying to talk through whatever fit she's worked herself into."

He made a noncommittal noise. "The dragons?"

"After I took the pies over, those three descended on me. You were there for that. Then yesterday a few dropped by to talk at me. I sat on the step by the door and listened."

"They were in the front garden, then?"

"Yeah."

"In view of the boulevard, at all times?"

"They were huge, so, yeah."

He made another noncommittal noise. It echoed

through her, like the clank of a demon-metal collar closing around her neck.

"Where are you sending me?" she asked, heavy and dull.

"What do you mean?"

"It's fine," she said. "She's right. I'm not your source, I shouldn't be in your compound. Just tell me where to go and I'll leave."

"This interfering woman's words are nothing to me," he snapped. She knew the anger was not directed at her. It warmed her but only a little.

"It's fine," she said, still deadened. "Maybe things will get better if I move. I'd rather be forgotten than watched every day." A small hope stirred.

"I will not acquiesce to this." She heard a snap of paper, then he made a thoughtful noise. "However..." His hand touched her head. He fell silent, his fingers moving absently.

She glanced up, saw the look of intense thought on his face.

His eyes flicked to hers. "I have been investigating a report of source-neglect." His words were cautious, but his eyes clear and arresting. "We may be able to turn this situation to the advantage for both of us. If you are willing to assist me?"

"I—"

"It might be dangerous," he cautioned.

"Will it get me away from these people?"

"A move would be necessitated, yes, though you would still be on the circuits."

She didn't have to think. Whatever it was, whatever he was so carefully weighing, that statement told her all she needed to know. She wouldn't be shut in a box, and she would have some purpose.

was boiling in the sun. They were only halfway, but Arten had to stop and rest. It was a mistake—getting started again was so difficult. Only Natalia's increasingly terse commands kept her placing one foot in front of the other. Until she fell into her bed.

Somewhere far away, Natalia was snapping at Emilette, telling her to get out and leave Arten alone. That no, she wouldn't be moving tonight, did Emilette not have eyes to see how sick she was? Arten couldn't even smile.

12

BETRAYAL & PREPARATION
STEKIN

Stekin was unhappy to find Nhemith in his bed, but unsurprised. He slid the door closed behind him, concealing his sigh. He heard the sound of sheets shifting as he draped his clothes over a chair—Claude hated when he dropped them on the floor—and left his boots by the door. Claude would take them away and shine them up again before Stekin awoke. Before he had lived amongst the humans, before he had been the only one to attend the small tasks of cleaning and mending clothing and shoes, what irritated Claude would have been nowhere in Stekin's awareness.

There was a time previously, he remembered, pulling the sheets back, *when I was conscientious of the humans around me. I wonder how long before I take them for granted again?*

He lowered his head to the pillow, stared into Nhemith's open eyes. Saw another time, another valley, another woman.

He did not share those thoughts. Instead he warned, "I am tired."

"I can see that. What has kept you so late?"

"I went to see Jackson," he said. The source council and one of the Gatekeepers had ambushed him this afternoon while he had been trying to negotiate for the property where Arten would soon be living. They had been concerned that, despite his assurances, no other sources had come since Arten. It had been more than a week, and was he certain Ergin was taken care of?

He was, but that did not mean that their concern was unfounded. He and Arten had found Ergin, and although it was unlikely there was another danger on the road between the final network house and New Respite, it was not certain. So he had flown out until it was no longer safe to fly and remain unseen, then walked the rest of the way to the last stop in the network.

Nhemith made a thoughtful noise, "Trouble?"

"No." Jackson had been happy to see him, thinking Stekin was bringing news of his replacement. He was less happy when Stekin brought no news on that front and asked after sources. He had gotten defensive and indignant and ranted about how he had 'been doing this for decades' and 'never lost a source' and how one cannot rush the boiling of water. In short, no other sources after Arten had come through, but he was expecting one. It had taken a good hour to calm the man down and assure him that no one was dissatisfied with his performance.

At least I was able to fly directly home. Tomorrow I will need to finalize the arrangements for Arten. He had spent all morning after Arten left and a large part of the afternoon property scouting. Ktet had given him the names of the owners of various properties on the third circuit, properties that had belonged to dragons who had inherited, and subsequently moved into, more prestigious locations when other genetic lines ended.

"What troubles you?" Nhemith asked. Her hand came up, fingers touched his face.

"I was thinking of how many empty compounds there are now. I am wondering if we have enough species diversity left to survive. Especially since Kikkyo is responsible for such a large percentage of our hatchlings."

"Kikkyo spawns like a fish," Nhemith said with haughty disdain. Stekin smiled a little in the dark. "It *will* be tough in a generation or two to keep her offspring away from each other. But," she continued in a different tone, full of smoke and teeth, "if you are concerned, why not contribute some eggs of your own?"

He snapped, "We have been through this."

Her eyes flashed dimly. "Foolish! You pride yourself on your logic and your research, but in this you are more superstitious than a human."

"My *research*," he scowled, "clearly shows that my offspring are inferior."

"Three is not statistically significant," she countered, angry. He felt his heart beat a little faster, felt his teeth bare at her.

"Stop," he asked. "I do not wish to argue about this again."

She moved against him and he felt the heat of her, pulled her closer until her skin warmed his. "I know," she said finally, "that you do not want more eggs. But I do."

"We are not bound," he said and, distracted by the scent of her, almost said too much. "You may have eggs with," he caught himself, "whomever you wish."

"I do not want whomever's eggs." She snorted. "I want yours. We are the last, Stekin. Our line would be strongest."

It was something he had often thought himself, as those who survived the Sundering had dwindled in number. It was what had convinced him thirty years ago to give Nhemith an egg that had hatched into Hiranyath. Hiranyath, who had become a source-thief, one of the most heinous crimes a dragon could commit. More proof that he was not meant to reproduce.

And there are four, not three, he thought. Though he would never tell Nhemith of his first, his tragic daughter. Even as he curled himself around her warmth, he thought of Ktet, wondered what she was planning. Wondered if she meant what she had said, or if she had said it for his benefit.

Will she ask Ktet to sire her offspring when this game of hers is done?

He wondered if it would bother him if her children with another dragon turned out better than theirs had.

"What are you doing?" he asked, jolted out of his thoughts. Her hand was moving along his back, down and behind his thigh.

"Is it unpleasant?" she asked, not stopping but reversing direction.

"It is...the demon-metal is still affecting me," he managed, his skin crawling in a distinctly *not* unpleasant way. Her hand continued its movement. He felt a response in this foreign biology, one which he recognized earlier, and pushed Nhemith away, rolled onto his other side.

Nhemith moved faster than he thought she could, had him on his back as she sat across his legs, her fingers digging into his shoulders. "Why do you continue to insult me," she hissed, "with that lie?"

"What lie?" He bristled, his hands gripped her forearms, ready to heave her away.

"Demon-metal!" He started to protest, but she interrupted him, "The demon-metal has not been in or near you for the better part of a week. Yet you keep insisting that this

—" She moved, his breath caught. "—is some sort of afflic-
tion. What prevents you from just admitting you are
attracted to me in this form? Or—" Her eyes flashed. "—is it
too old for you?"

"What?" He struggled to wrest her away, more against
the primitive instincts of this biology than her. "This is not
attraction, it is a malfunction," he snapped, even as his
nerves clawed at him to be closer to her.

She snarled and struck, he felt the skin along the ridge
of his cheek tear, smelled the tang of his own blood. Her
teeth were around his throat, her incisors digging towards
the arteries, not sharp enough to do damage. But he hardly
felt it, barely noticed the heat of her breath and flick of her
tongue, because she had aligned herself with him. He was
paralyzed, could not move, half of him recoiling in fear, the
other half now subsumed by the mindless need of his
borrowed form.

He reached deep, called a desperate plea to the beast
inside. Nothing answered. Only perfect, diamond stillness.
In that moment which stretched longer than the moment of
Sundering, he froze. Hesitated. Said, "Wait. Nhemith, stop."

But his hands, clawed into her thighs, now, did not push
her away. They could have, had he been resolved. He could
have easily extracted himself from her teeth, but he did not.
There were so many things he did not do. Perhaps because
failed to believe she would continue. Perhaps because he
was shocked that she wanted this—and again at the way this
body was responding when it had never done so before the
demon-metal entered his lungs. Perhaps because of the
deep abhorrence that was pulsing through him, knotting his
power. Certainly out of gut-twisting terror at the consequences of such an act.

The moment slid past. Slid away from him like a wriggling eel. And the next came. Came with the sensation of Nhemith's voice vibrating through his throat. With a cracking inside him, like a rusty door being pushed open. He knew, with that first shuddering jolt, it was a door that should never have been opened. He smelled fear, human and stinking. An eternity of flashing thoughts later, the crack gaping wider, he knew it to be his own. No, it was not a door—it was his skin being peeled back, laying his nerves bare to the world. As though his scales were being cut away, leaving only human skin underneath. Human skin that was so much more delicate and sensitive than it had ever been. He could feel the racing of his heart, heard it pulsing in his ears, felt like both would rupture under the strain.

Raw, overwhelmed, confused, he was beyond action now. As vulnerable and frozen as when he had been Sundered. But instead of Lien goading him into action, there was Nhemith, eyes flashing, teeth bared in victory as she pinned him down.

Faster than thought, a wave of fury consumed him. Icy, implacable, and stronger than stone. The diamond beast was awake. Was under his skin. Was gripping Nhemith with strength that crushed. Was throwing her away, across the room.

Nhemith hit the door hard enough something cracked. Before she could pick herself up, he was standing over her. She looked up at him, eyes blazing with fury. Something she saw made her go pale, her rage dried up in an instant. She gulped and ducked her head down and away—an involuntary motion of subservience—then fled the room.

THE SUN ROSE the next day. Stekin heard the birdsong that heralded it. He had not slept since the beast had retreated. But dawn meant Claude would be by soon to retrieve his laundry and boots, to lay out his clothes for the day, to do all those small things that now seemed so meaningless.

The idea of being found marinating in the result of his fear got Stekin out of bed. He stripped the bed—the room—of anything that held a hint of that distinct malodor and tossed the mess into the corridor. Nhemith's fine silk robe he dropped into a trash bin. Then the only reeking thing left was himself. His skin was slick and grimy with the biological residue of fear. He'd seen it in those early sources enough to recognize it. Enough to despise it.

He fled the room, letting his natural form emerge as he ran. He flew west, high up amongst the clouds, letting the early rays fall on his face. Usually the sun on his scales was the reassuring touch of an old friend. Today it was not. He banked, followed the erratic line of a ridge until it joined others around a narrow twist of a valley that was home to a few intrepid rock goats and a glacial lake. He dove into the lake, crashed against the rocks at the bottom, clung there until his breath gave out, then pushed for the surface.

He washed, several times in each form, abrading skin and scale with fistfuls of gravelly sand, then let the sun bake him dry. It helped, but the grime still clung to him, as though the memory refused to be forgotten. What drew him home was not a feeling of absolution or relief but a remembrance of duty.

He needed to sign a lease for Arten's new residence. He needed to check on Carl's progress with Kylik—he had been unable to do so yesterday with the requisite visit to Jackson. Which only reminded him that he needed to talk to the network council about Jackson's replacement. The world had not stopped, even if he was cracking. He pushed past his dread and winged back to New Respite. Left only the lake and the valley behind him.

A PACK of dragons was mobbed in his courtyard, circled around what was certainly a human. He bristled as he recognized Claude at their center. He spotted Ktet's distinctive markings near the middle, Kylik's bulk hesitating on the outer ring.

"What is the meaning of this?" he roared as he dove down, swiping at heads and limbs to clear a place for him to land behind Claude. He mantled over the poor man, who was now crouched down, protecting himself from the backdraft of Stekin's wings. Claude was smart, though, and stayed small and still as Stekin turned in circles, swiping with claw and tail until all the dragons had backed away. Some took to the wing, but most stayed, warily out of range, eying him with a guarded expression.

"Explain yourselves!" he roared again. Claws clattered, wings rustled, tails hissed over the stone tiles, but no one spoke. *There is one who will answer me,* he thought, eyes flashing. "Kylik!" The large, green dragon shuffled forwards, crouched under Stekin's glare.

"Yes, kaz?"

"Tell me why you are part of this rabble who are harassing my staff." He wished he had the power to spare to actually frost the air with his words, but in the long centuries he had learned to modulate his tone in the absence of power. Kylik flinched.

"You were gone," Kylik offered.

"And that gives you warrant to behave in this appalling way?"

"No, kaz, I spoke poorly," he agreed quickly, "You were gone, and we—well, some of us—thought that you might be *gone.*"

"And?" Stekin demanded.

"And—we were worried? We thought this servant might know if you were *gone* or just gone."

"You are speaking nonsense, Kylik," Stekin hissed.

Ktet stepped forwards a pace, made a noise of polite interruption, "If I may, kaz?" he said, inclining his head. Stekin made a gesture of impatient acquiescence. "What Kylik is attempting to say is that we did not know for how long you would be gone this time." There was a slightest emphasis, just the right insidious drop, on *this* in his words.

Stekin's anger cooled and a flood of shame took its place. *They thought I had abandoned them again,* he realized, looking into the faces that surrounded him. That strange look now made sense—it was disbelief and relief mixed together. *They are afraid. They do not trust me to remain.* His power twisted into pained knots. He quickly memorized the people that had come. *I must find a way to mend this.*

He did not let his discomfort through as he said stiffly, "I understand you. However, as you can see, I was only gone on temporary business," he lied. "I have no intentions of leaving again for any lengthy duration, and if I do so, I will be certain to inform at least two people of the circumstances that draw me away. Now," he continued brusquely before sentiment could take hold of any of them, "since you are all arranged, and since you owe me reparation for harassing my staff..."

He named four of the crowd, sent them to fetch the members of the network council. Then he named three others to send word to each of the three compound-owners who he needed to conclude his business with today—one of whom would walk away with a lease.

"Kylik, wait for me in my study. Ktet, a word if you please. The rest of you—I am busy for the rest of today, but if you wish to stop by tomorrow, I will be happy to discuss any business with you then. Good day." They were reluctant, but once the first dragon was in the sky, the rest cleared out readily. Ktet remained.

Stekin turned his eye-flashing glare on the black-striped dragon. "I expect better from you," he said witheringly.

"Yes, kaz," Ktet demurred, making a low gesture of apology.

"You help make and keep the law here," Stekin continued with icy contempt, "and if you do not act to actively keep peace, you are useless in your position." Ktet bristled, strained to keep his wings down but his tail lashed. "I have no cause at the present to call for your removal," Stekin warned, "but if you fail to act again, I will leverage any and all of my influence to see you replaced."

"Yes, kaz," Ktet said, his voice perfectly neutral though Stekin saw the flash of mutinous anger pass over his face.

"That is not a threat, Ktet," Stekin said, drawing himself to his full height, "it is a fact. Our race may have fallen, we may be shades of our former selves, but that does not give us license to revert to mindless beasts. Panic, fear, greed—left unchecked, they bring us death. Your position in this community, your whole purpose, is to combat those enemies with law and justice.

"Today, you stood with the crowd. You gave their fear gravitas it would not have otherwise had. You should have been at the head of it, dispersing them. Next time, you will do the right thing."

"Yes, kaz," Ktet said, a hint of chagrin about his mouth and in the cringe of his bow.

"Good," Stekin said, inclining his head in farewell. After Ktet left, Stekin settled his wings and reached back to touch Claude's still-huddled form. "Claude?" he prompted.

The man made a strangled sound but did not move. Trauma, Stekin guessed. It was not unexpected, given the circumstances. *Thirty dragons converging on one is enough to frighten even some of my own people.* He picked the man up, tucked the tightly curled ball of him against his chest, and went into his library.

Kylik was pacing, his wings fluttering nervously. He stopped when Stekin entered, started to speak, but Stekin interrupted.

"What can you do for him?" he asked.

The healer examined the man, sang a brief song that sent him into a deep, restful sleep.

"That should calm him and help him sleep for now. After that, it is up to him," Kylik said with a regretful dip of his head.

"Very well," Stekin acknowledged. He flew Claude to the servant quarters, in the main building. He waited as one of the kitchen staff fetched two young men to carry Claude back to his room. Then he returned to Kylik in the library.

"Kaz, I—" Kylik started as soon as the door rumbled open.

"No," Stekin stopped him. "I have something I need to say."

The green dragon's voice quavered as he said, "Yes, kaz." He crouched in that annoying, nervous way of his.

Stekin had used the healer's awe of him to his advantage in the past, he had traded on it, encouraged it. Because it was useful to him to have Kylik both in his service and within his control. He had never seen the harm in exploiting that awe to ensure the betterment of their race. Until today. When he had seen Kylik's miserable cowering in amongst all those other faces full of fear.

Kylik is not mine to manipulate; none of them are. Perhaps if I had realized that thirteen years ago, if I had been less arrogant, the source-panic would not have happened. They are so different, so young—I always think of them as children. Ignorant and grasping. But they are not children, nor do they need to be controlled and sheltered. Those days are past.

He had long known that in some ways, these new generations of dragons were more advanced than he was. He was a relic of a time that would never be again. *Even if I am successful with reunification....* His eyes flicked to the bookshelf filled with centuries of his research and notes. *It will not be as it was.*

These new dragons had known peace, had lived in harmony with each other and humans, had a purpose beyond battles and eggs. Even if that purpose was things the clans would have considered silly, like art or music or cataloging insects.

"Kylik," Stekin said gravely, approaching the healer. He sat in front of him, took his jaw in his palms. The embrace unnerved Kylik, his eyes went wide but he did not pull away. "I have failed you." And then Stekin apologized.

He told Kylik how much he valued his ability and dedication. Told him how often he had thought of him while out in the world—and he had, even before meeting Arten had made those thoughts turn more practical. Every time he had come across an interesting food or medicine that the humans subjected themselves to, he had wanted to bring a sample back for Kylik to study. Every time he had spoken with a human doctor or medic or shaman, he had tried to learn something Kylik might be interested to know. Stekin did not go into all the details, there would be time for that later.

Instead, he said, "I think of you as a friend, Kylik," though he had not realized it was so until a few moments earlier. "And as a friend, I should have informed you when I left to find Arten and that I suspected it might take some time to locate her. I regret my thoughtlessness has caused you such distress. Then, and again today. You have my word I will not choose to leave in the future without first informing you."

Kylik made a small noise of surprise and awe. He was clearly uncomfortable with the intensity of Stekin's regard. Stekin pulled Kylik's head down, pressed his forehead to the larger dragon's, then released him.

"I also wished to inquire about Carl," Stekin said then, in his normal tones, stepping out of Kylik's personal space casually. "Have you released him yet?"

"I have," Kylik said, the edge of nervousness in his voice cut through Stekin. "Last night. I had no cause to keep him longer."

"I understand," Stekin said, then mused, "Is there cause to check up on him later?"

"I would very much like to," Kylik agreed. "Why?"

"When you do, if you find reason to examine the sources that share his compound, I am interested in your findings."

"You suspect something?"

Stekin made a noncommittal noise. "It would be best if you kept any thoughts on suspicions I may have to yourself for the moment."

"Ah, very good, kaz," he agreed.

"One more thing before you go," Stekin said. "I spoke with your prime—it was a breech, and I will make reparations to you both for it, but it was necessary. She was helpful in illuminating the behavior of other sources towards Arten. Ah, she has told you of the shunning, then? She also informed me there is a perception that it is indecent of Arten to live in my compound when she is not to be my source.

"I would like you to inform Pasha that I have taken her words under advisement and I will be moving Arten into a different premises. As Arten's guardian, I am still responsible to her for the next three years. No, I did not expect you to know that; I was not in a state to widely broadcast it upon my return. Would you like to see the document?" Stekin fetched it from the bookshelf, extracted it from the tiny tube with careful claws and pinned it to the table for Kylik to read.

"She is indentured to you *and* you are her guardian? It is a good thing she is not also your source," Kylik said, "or your relationship would be quite tangled."

"Hmm," Stekin said, pushing the paper back in the tube, "I fear it is tangled sufficiently as it is. Now you understand, I hope, why I must ensure she is housed and cared for. In bowing to the wishes of the other sources and removing her from my compound, I expect they will cease this shunning. Will you relay this to your prime?"

"I will, kaz," Kylik assured as they walked to the library doors together, "and I will speak with Alectros about checking on his source's health in four days. Is that agreeable to you?"

"Yes, thank you."

Stekin waited in the courtyard, watched the squarish form of Kylik vanish over the high, tiled roof of the walkway that bounded the space. He wanted to check on Claude, wanted to see Arten. His thoughtless escape this morning meant he had missed her visit. He wondered how angry she would be. He automatically cast out for her, searching.

He could sense the burning of her power from here. It was the beacon that would always guide him to her. Now it was a tempest, surging and pushing, trying to be free. She was fighting it, somehow. Fighting more effectively than she had ever done before. He didn't understand how it was possible. She should be flaring under the strain, but she only clamped down tighter. But if it meant she was controlling it, that was all to the good. She would be sourced sooner.

Once she is sourced, he reminded himself, turning his power calmingly, *I need not worry about her falling prey to the schemes of people like Nhemith and, perhaps, Ktet. How many others are there? How many resent my return, want to punish me for leaving, or simply preferred having no kaz to scrutinize their actions?* Only patience and time would reveal them. Both of which he felt were in increasingly short supply.

It had only been two weeks since their arrival here, but already the three years that remained to him as Arten's guardian and indenturer felt too short. *I must convince her to assist me with reunification. I must determine why her power calls to me as it does—me and no other. I must make this a place she can live happily. If I fail...what is the cost?* He did not know except, with diamond certainty, that it was too high.

The noise of wings interrupted the frustrated pressure that was building in his mind. He looked up. The network council was arriving, Kikkyo already circling to land. He switched his thoughts to those of Jackson's replacement and the training of new network agents.

STEKIN GOT nothing accomplished that day. The network council had been riled to alarm by those who had gone to retrieve them; he and Kikkyo had spent the greater part of the rest of the day soothing the others and listening to them repeat their concerns over all number of previously visited issues. He knew it was a reaction to their deeper fear of his desertion, a fear that none had been willing to broach, and that he had spoken to only perfunctorily. But it had wasted his time.

Consequently, he had been forced to move the premises negotiations to tomorrow morning. The inheritors were not pleased at the delay, and he sensed tomorrow would bring a repeat of the sidelong glances and trembling of wingtips. But he would deal with that, then.

After everyone left, Stekin ascended to his rooms, shifted into his human body, and penned a note to Arten, keeping his back to the newly covered bed. He wrote that she should not come by tomorrow morning because he would be otherwise engaged, and, with a word and a thought and a small thread of his power, transported it to the floor in front of her bedroom door. He would have put it at her bedside, but she kept the book and the candle there and he did not want to accidentally complect the paper with either of them. He should have had a servant take it to her, but at this distance it was a trivial usage of power.

He wrote a few more notes, equally brief and equally guilty, to Kylik and the dragons he hoped to sign that contract with in the morning, informing them that he would be in his library by second-morning bell.

He pulled on his tattered travel-robe, tied it closed, then left the room. He would not be sleeping here tonight, but he had one more thing to do before he left. He descended the staircase, his bare feet muffled by the narrow band of carpet along the outer edge. He followed the pathway Claude traversed several times a day, taking in the silence all around. Even the night creatures had not yet begun their songs. As though the world held its breath.

He never entered the servant quarters without invitation on principle, and he did not do so now. A child disappeared within and a woman was summoned out. She led Stekin back to a smallish room, which he knew to be generous in size and appointment, though it was too confined for his own liking. Claude was sitting in a chair. He looked a little unfocused, but when Stekin stood in front of him and asked how he was doing, the man blinked a few times. He looked from Stekin's feet up to his collar, frowned vaguely.

Then said, "My lord kaz, your nice robe is in the wardrobe. Shall I fetch it for you?"

"No, Claude," Stekin said, placing a hand on his shoulder to stop him from rising, "this is sufficient. I have come to tell you that you are not to work tomorrow." He gave a few more commands—the usual enjoinder to rest and recover. In the coming days, they would have to see if Claude would be able to stand the presence of a dragon. Until he could, or until Stekin could find him other employment, Stekin would have to remain in his human form.

Something that normally would have given him no concern.

Now, the thought of it made his skin crawl.

He left as quickly as was polite. The woman escorted him out in silence.

Claude's wife? he wondered. He realized he did not know if Claude was married. *Too much has changed; it is difficult to keep track.*

He thought of the census book in his library, of all the changes within. Consorts taken and refused, businesses started and closed, eggs laid though not necessarily hatched.

His steps took him to the courtyard. He transformed, tucked his travel robe amongst the branches of an urn-dwelling bush, and pushed up into the sky. The world dropped away, and he angled for a high peak. It was a good stretch away, but not so far he could not be back by morning. There was a little cave, a tight squeeze for a dragon of average size, but he would have a little wing room and the space would warm up quickly. He wanted to be away from here, far from Nhemith and his human form and his bedroom with the new sheets. Away from the consequence of his panic.

He forced himself to think about other things. About the number of eggs that had hatched while he was gone (three), the dragons who had died (five). About the lists of sources acquired, sources lost. About the decreasing life expectancy of sources. And the dragons who had acquired human forms in his absence. Which made him wonder why they needed them, what had caused the sudden interest. Which led him to Hiranyath and Alectros and their compatriots, and the reason *they* had acquired human form.

It cannot be a coincidence, he frowned, scanning for the dark notch of the cave opening, *that there are more dragons learning to take human form and that the source-thefts happened. But is there causation or merely correlation?* Were there source-thefts because a higher percentage of dragons taking human form led to more opportunities for deviance, some of which had been acted upon, or were there more human forms taken because the deviance had gone unpunished? *And is there anything I can do, at this point, to correct the situation?*

He sighted the cave, landed, squeezed in. He settled

himself in its dark interior, pushing at the floor to roll an offending rock to one side. *I must investigate Carl's misman-agement, that is certain.* He sighed to himself, once settled. *Further than that, do I want to press?*

No, he did not want to. But he needed to.

If he is being overtaxed, I must know. I must stop it. Alectros must answer for the deplorable state of his source. If Alectros is not responsible, I must find and stop the one who is.

If Alectros was not responsible, it meant someone else was stealing from his source. That would not surprise Stekin, especially not if the culprit was whomever Alectros had stolen from in the first place. But such retaliation only compounded over the years, and Stekin must end it. If Alec-tros *was* responsible, that was a trickier situation.

No, it is not tricky at all. The thought snaked through him, leaving him heavy and cold. He knew what would have to be done.

I had hoped to never face this again.

A foolish hope, perhaps. But one that had allowed him to banish the specter of guilt and shame.

It is just Alectros, he told himself. But the words mocked him as false.

STEKIN DID NOT SEE Arten the next day. He checked on her frequently, monitoring the restrained inferno within her, alarmed at how violent it was becoming. It should have flared before now, and he kept his senses extended, alert for the possibility that it should do so at any moment. He did stop by his compound after the noon bell, but the maid servant had informed him Arten was unwell and sleeping.

Which did nothing to lessen the itchy concern under his scales.

He had signed the lease, finally, and employed a few sources to clean and prepare the place. It was small, but the roofs were intact and aside from a copious amount of dust and a lack of niceties, it was serviceable. The compound would only hold four and had no prime quarters to speak of.

With just Arten, it will be enough.

The rest of the day had been spent in conference with the neighboring dragons as he bartered with them for various aspects of her upkeep. None of them were well off, their compounds not yet self-sufficient, and their personal wealth in early stages. One agreed to bring her chopped wood and other necessities, in exchange for which Stekin agreed to assist him in turning his investments around so they provided enough income to cover his compound expenses. Another agreed to lend their sources to perform the various structural and sanitary maintenance chores necessary in exchange for a discounted publishing rate on his next book of poetry. Another would be by once a week to clean the place, in return for which Stekin promised to outfit the dragon's three sources in warm winter clothing.

The last, Hiranyath, agreed to help with laundry if Arten would help in the kitchens. Although a minor agreement, it was the one Stekin most carefully arranged—because it was necessary to get Arten inside that compound. Hiranyath and Alectros's compound. Inside, Arten would be able to observe Carl firsthand, observe the comings and goings in the household. Then she would report her observations back to Stekin at night.

The real reason he had selected Arten's new residence in

particular was that it had one feature none of the others did. It was not adjacent to the property Alectros and Hiranyath shared, it was not the best kept, nor the most desirable save for that one feature. At the rear of the property, the brick wall and the cliff joined. Over a century ago, the compound had been inhabited by particularly troublesome young men who had sought to dally in the town against all warnings and rules. They had knocked loose a stone at the join and replaced it with a hollow fake, then transplanted a broad screen of bushes on either side to allow them to enter and exit unnoticed.

They had had their fun, but one of them went too far and flared out, taking his lover and half a building with him before the flames were subdued. One of the burned companions had confessed to only the kaz of their secret exit. Stekin had placed a trap around the fake stone, told the men of it, and they had not ventured out that way again. He allowed them to think it was a magical trap, but in actuality it was simply a vicious, noxious mixture he had concocted with some plant oils that would cause human skin to break out in a stinging, purple rash. If any of them had moved the stone again, the evidence would have been plain.

A few generations afterward, the compound's owner had inherited and moved his sources to the second circuit. Since then, the place had lain empty. Stekin continued checked the stone every few years, but it had not yet been moved.

And so, once the sun went down, Stekin went out to do more work under the cover of darkness and protective gauntlets. The soft rumblings of the stone he was working free went unnoticed, but he remained cautious. The nearby compounds, those that were occupied at least, seemed to be celebrating. *No, preparing to celebrate.* He overheard their chatter, carried through the cracks at the join on the wind, eventually pieced together enough to realize that tomorrow was the Unity Festival. He frowned and worked a little faster. Annoyed that he had forgotten.

I will not be able to see her tomorrow, he scowled at the half-freed stone under his palms. *Then I must see her tonight.* He looked for her automatically. She was there, in the same place—had she moved at all today?—blazing silently.

Something pulsed through him strongly enough to make his knees give way, and he caught himself on the wall. He looked at the pale, shaking hands that supported him, disgusted. A violent shudder followed as he remembered Nhemith's teeth around his throat, the vibration of her sounds traveling through his neck, the shuddering wrenching as his protections had been ripped away. *Protections from what? What is happening to me?*

He sank to the ground, rested his back against the sturdy stone of the wall, which was still a little warm from the afternoon sun. He felt like claws were gripped around his chest, squeezing too tightly. He was panting through his nose, his heartbeat was palpable under his bones. *What is this?* He stared up through the screen of the bushes, unseeing, focused inwards. *It is strangling. An emotion can do this?* The thought was horrifying.

I must be ill, he decided. Nhemith was right: the demon-metal was long out of his system, and its effects would have subsided instantly upon the last shard's removal. *Perhaps Kylik missed some.* But that did not seem correct—his power was flowing normally; it was no longer chaotic as it had been when the demon-metal was in his body. Everything felt fine. Except—

Except that I can feel that an insect has climbed onto this foot, I can feel the breeze on my scalp and in this hair. I can feel this...fear?

No, not fear, but close. He had been thinking of seeing

Arten tonight since it would not be allowed tomorrow. Thinking of how it had been two days since he had seen her —of how long that now felt. He had never noticed these things with his sources in the past. *I was wondering what was different this time, why I am so invested in one who will not source to me.* He had instinctively looked for her. Noted she was in the same place she had been all day...

Worry, he realized with a start. *This? Surely not.*

But the claws around his chest tightened further, and he found the thread of thought deep in him that drove it.

Is this how humans experience emotion? he wondered, awed and appalled. It would explain much about them. His thoughts jumped to Claude. It was no wonder he was still dazed; if a simple worry could have this impact, what would terror do to one? Stekin frowned, the dragon in him already intrigued by a new line of inquiry to answer these questions.

He remembered Arten. *She was frightened to enter those last few nodes in the network.* He had seen the trembling in her, smelled the chemical residue of her battle.

He had always thought it was a mental deficiency that all humans were born with. *But I was afraid with Nhemith. And my body betrayed me, it could not act.*

Were emotions a structural weakness, then? Were these unarmored forms too fragile to contain them? *Does my natural biology protect me from this internal wound?*

The thought was discordant in him.

It was not as though he did not feel emotion, nor even strong emotion. After the Sundering, he had felt so strongly the diamond beast inside him had been created, forged from that pain and loss and anger. He had needed its detachment to survive. So many had died from their grief.

No, he decided, *we feel the same things, there has never been confusion about emotion expressed by humans.*

This force which gripped him, he decided, was rude. Perhaps because humans were shorter-lived, they needed their bodies to be hijacked in order to pay attention to their situation. Whatever the cause, he would master this as he had mastered all other things.

He turned his power in broad bands, set his jaw, and pushed himself back to his feet. He would finish his work, then he would see Arten and prove that this concern was foolish. Whatever was happening to him, he would not let it rule him.

He had survived the Sundering; this was nothing.

By the time he finished, it was quite late. Arten was asleep. Her forehead was hot under his hand, but that was not unusual for her. Her power churned in her chest, awake and agitated, but was also somehow stable. The fourth bell chimed and he left.

M*IDNIGHT TO MIDNIGHT,* he reminded himself, sliding the false stone back in place. He scrubbed his gloved hands with fistfuls of dirt to remove the chalk from them—chalk to soften the sound of his entry and egress. He hurried away, moving around the base of the cliff until he was hidden from the compounds and the intermittent houses that dotted the lower part of the valley. Only a few cattle saw him transform and glide silently back to his house.

He devoured the food waiting him on the balcony. Someone had remembered his duty today, even if he had not, and thought to lay out his meal in the middle of the night. He made a note to discover whom and thank them. He dropped off his robe and gave himself a quick scrub over his scales with his sand, then was away again.

Back to the compounds. But this time, to the archway over the entry to the first circuit. He circled above, waiting for the midnight bell to sound. Below him a few sources—a very few, he noted, and all old—had gathered just inside, forming a sparse line across the road.

Once, they formed a wall here, he thought unhappily. *What has changed? Why have so few come? Who has been maintaining the vigil in my absence?*

That question did not take long to answer. For as soon as the bell chimed, four of the sources went out to the great gate that was always open, its iron bars hugging the stone on either side. They looped ropes around the bars with familiarity and began leaning into them, heaving on one side of the heavy gate, straining to break rust free of its hinges. They had budged it about a handbreadth—a human handbreadth—when he landed and approached.

"May I enter?" Stekin voiced the ritual greeting, keeping the anger from his voice. The four sources outside the archway jumped, dropping their ropes, and looked at each other nervously, uncertain how to refuse him. *They have never had to make the refusal,* he saw. Even as he prepared to explain his role in this, one of their few rituals, to them, someone stepped forwards from the line.

Matron Pasha bowed to him. "My lord kaz," she said with a strong, unwavering voice, "you may not."

"I demand to enter," he said, with the haughtiness and entitlement of his race.

"O revered dragon, I say you may not," Pasha refused him again. A few heads nodded, expecting this, but most looked to her in shock. Some backed away.

"I *will* enter, and none will stop me," he threatened. The reaction of the sources in front of him—the disbelief and alarm on their faces—caused his words to come out with more of an edge than intended.

"Lord dragon, you are mighty, and if you so choose, we cannot stop you," Pasha acknowledged with another bow. "However, this is our day of rest and rejoicing. We ask to celebrate in peace, and we will stand firm against you if we must."

"Your words are brave, cherished source," he intoned, "and I see your resolve and the resolve of your fellow sources. Go back to your celebrations; you need not stand against me. I will hold fast this gate until midnight next."

He advanced, grasped one of the gates in his hands and jerked it free from the rust. It took a great wrenching to unstick it, and he wondered how four humans could manage such a feat. Metal screeched as he dragged the gate closed. Then the other side, which was much easier. The sources had moved back by then, abandoning the ropes and retreating to hover around Pasha.

"Go now," Stekin ended, "I will stand for you." He turned his back to the gates, heard Pasha marshalling her confused helpers to slat the wooden beam across the inside of the gates barricade all from entering, which finalized their part of the ritual.

As they did so, she gave a short statement of gratitude and warning. He made no response—none was expected—merely sat back and flared his wings across the width of the gate. She then turned and made another short speech to her assembled, declaring the purpose of their holiday, declaring that none shall enter or exit for the whole day.

Then, with three claps of her hand, echoed by a drum, the ritual was ended. Stekin heard some feet shuffle away, but most stayed. He heard their whispered demands of Pasha, wanting to know what the kaz was doing here, why had he interrupted their ritual. She told them he had not interrupted anything, that this was an older, more complete form of the ritual, and then sent them away. But she remained behind, he could smell her near the gate.

When all the other sources had gone, Stekin spoke softly over his shoulder, not looking at her, "I know we cannot interact, Matron, and I am not allowed to make any demands of you today. However, perhaps you will hear what I have to say and decide if it aligns with your own goals."

There was only silence, so he continued. She would not have remained if she did not wish to communicate something to him.

"It seems that my arrival was unexpected tonight," he mused, looking up at the stars.

"It is good," he heard her say in the same thoughtful way, "that the lord kaz has returned. We have not had the Refusal and Resistance since he left, and I am one of the few who remember that a dragon once played the role of Gatekeeper."

"I am saddened at the number of things that have been neglected in my absence. I hope my role as Gatekeeper is the beginning of restoring some of the order that has been lost. I wonder if anyone will remember that the Gatekeeper does not only watch the gate, but also the skies. I hope our sources will call upon the Gatekeeper to enforce their privacy on all fronts."

"It is a relief to have a dragon Gatekeeper again," she said, the breeze carrying her words back to him. "Most respect the sanctity of our day, but some have forgotten." They both knew it was not forgetfulness. "I do wonder if it would be wise to call upon the Gatekeeper to protect the skies. No dragon likes to be told they cannot do as they please, and it might be more harmful in the long run to those who source to turn the one they turn away."

Stekin made a thoughtful noise and said, "I trust our sources to do what they think is best." Matron made a noise of agreement. He heard the soft sounds of her slippered feet over the smooth boulevard as she left. With no one now observing, he lowered himself to the ground, pulled his wings in, and tucked his chin to sleep.

His role was mostly ornamental. When the Unity Festival had first been established, he had been necessary to repel those few people from the city during the day, and the occasional dragon who tried to sneak in at night, seeking to make their displeasure with the new law known. Back then, the sources had been willing to put up a cry to summon him if they saw a dragon near the compound. But they had also kept the boulevards lined with torches and had come *en masse* to the Refusal and Resistance ceremony.

It will take time, he reminded himself, *to repair the trust broken by Hiranyath and her ilk.*

Tomorrow night, I must be alert.

He expected no trouble tonight—if any of his people had wanted to draw from their sources, it was trivial to do so before the midnight bell. The second night was when they tried to slip in. It was ritual now but was rooted in that old necessity. Even after those making political statements had challenged the law less often with faded conviction, youngsters had taken up the role of law-breaker for a night, the allure of the forbidden enticing them. He had never punished anyone who broke this law on this one night, as long as they allowed themselves to be turned away. He wondered how many would permit themselves to be turned this year, and if he would need to revisit his policy of leniency.

Especially since it seemed that Matron would not encourage her people to send up a cry if one of his slipped in. He would need to be especially alert. His role may seem ornamental to the others, but to him...

Rosa.

Which meant he needed to sleep and quickly.

13

THE UNITY FESTIVAL
ARTEN

I t was not Emilette's usual hysterics that awoke Arten but a sonorous, incessant pounding on the front door. She dragged herself out of bed, noticed she was in the tunic and trousers she had worn yesterday. It saved her the effort of getting dressed, but even so, she was already dragging by the time she reached the door. Everything had become much more difficult over the past few days.

I hope I get over this soon, she thought, *whatever it is.*

She opened the door. Was greeted by a group of hostile faces and one reluctant Rya.

"Sorry, Arten," Rya said, flushing, not looking at her.

"What's this about?" Arten asked carefully, her hand still on the door.

"Err, the lord kaz is at the gate," Rya mumbled, "and they —" Someone jostled her with an elbow. "—we want you to ask him to go away?"

She glared at the group gathered, both men and women, all branded. They all looked away to avoid her eyes. She'd spread the news she was moving, and Stekin had made it known where she was going. And yet they still treated her like she was doing something wrong.

"Tell him yourself," she said, sliding the door closed.

"Wait!" Rya cried, thrusting her hand out to stop the door, "Please? We've already tried, but he won't acknowledge us. But he'll listen to you."

"Fine," she said, intrigued despite herself. Why would Stekin be ignoring them?

She followed them to the archway over the exit. Was surprised to see it barred by a gate. On the other side, sitting on the section where the boulevard narrowed into the lane, was Stekin, his wings thrown wide. Her wakeners lagged behind, leaving her to approach the gate alone.

She thought to open it, to go outside, but the wooden beam was too heavy for her to move. When she tried, Stekin's head swung around. It jerked back, just a fraction. *Why is he alarmed to see me?*

"What's going on?" she demanded of anyone, leaning against the gate. Demons it was already hot, and barely morning. She felt sweat sliding down her back, wiped the back of a hand across her brow. No one answered. Stekin was looking at her with a calculating expression.

"Fine," she groused, "then I'm going back to bed." The thought of even the short walk back to her compound left her feeling queasy, but she didn't want to be in the middle of whatever this was.

Let Stekin ignore them for all I care.

"Wait," Stekin said, his voice reminded her of how cool his hands felt on her face. "Tell them to fetch the matron here."

"Why don't you tell them yourself?" she demanded.

"I cannot interact with any source today," he said.

Arten felt the invisible wedge between her and the

others grow wider. Her fingers touched her temple, found the unmarred skin there. She felt the pit closing around her. The damage was done. She may as well wait and see what this was all about.

"Go get Matron," she said to Rya. The girl ran off.

Arten lowered herself against the gate, felt the cool iron press against her back. Refreshing but not enough. "Stekin," she started, but he made a noise of dissent so she closed her eyes and waited.

Matron's brusque tones startled her out of the doze she'd dropped into.

"What is the meaning of this assembly?" Matron demanded. Unlike Arten, she got an answer.

"We wanted to know why the gate is barred, and why the lord kaz is outside it preventing us from leaving!" one of the sources spoke up.

"Today is the Unity Festival," Matron snapped, like that explained everything, then pushed through them. She approached the gate, spoke loudly as she asked, "Gate-keeper, how many have passed the gate?"

"None have entered, none have left. None shall pass through the gate on my watch," Stekin replied in a formal way.

"I thank you for your service, Gatekeeper," the matron said with a bow, then turned back to the group of sources knotted a few paces away. "The lord kaz has taken up his traditional post as Gatekeeper today. As he has done for many long years before any of you ever came to this place." Her words were whip-sharp. "Now, go back to your compounds and trouble him no further."

"We've never needed a dragon before," one of the men jeered.

"Yeah, and why are we locked in?" a woman demanded.

Matron snapped, "We have *always* needed a dragon on this day, and we are fortunate that the lord kaz has taken up this role again! The gate does not lock us in; it is symbolic of us locking our dragon lords out. Which all of you would know if you actually listened to the primes who tried to teach you our ways. What need have you to go out today?" Matron addressed the woman who had objected. She admitted that she had none. "Then cease this interference and return to your compounds. Do not bother our Gatekeeper again."

The matron sounded angry, so Arten was surprised when Rya spoke up in her small voice. "Matron?" She hesitated. "Dragons can fly."

"The Gatekeeper will protect us on all fronts," Matron said, but there was a hardness to her tone that made Arten doubt she meant those words. "Go, now, all of you." The group began to move away, muttering to one another, then slowly dispersing. "You, too, Arten."

"Why?" Arten asked, tired.

"What do you mean?" The matron bristled. "It is the Unity Festival," she said, like that meant something.

"I have no compound, so it's not like anyone's missing me," Arten argued.

"Then spend the day with your friends."

"What friends?" Arten barked a bitter laugh. "The people who only stopped shunning me to have me come demand Stekin leave the gate?"

"Then spend it alone," Matron snapped, "but leave this gate."

"Why?" Arten demanded, angry at her suddenly. Matron had done nothing to intervene, had done nothing to make her feel like she was a part of the community here, had only ever criticized and chastised her. Like she was some errant child. But Arten had done nothing wrong, and she was tired of being punished. Tired of being spoken to like she was contemptible.

Matron snapped, "Sources and dragons do not interact during the Unity Festival. You must go away from here and not tempt our lord kaz into breaking his vow."

Arten felt that bitter laugh bark free again. "Good thing I'm not a source, then." She heard the low rumble behind her, and said, "Do you hear that? I think right now the one who is tempting the kaz to break his vow is you. You'd better hurry away, Matron."

"You are setting a bad example," the matron warned darkly.

"Great," Arten said carelessly, "at least this time when people complain about me it will be for something I actually did."

Matron stared at her, face red, jaw working as she stopped herself from saying what she wished. The growl was still building in Stekin's chest. Matron spun on her heel and stalked away.

Arten sagged back against the gate.

"You should not have antagonized her," Stekin warned once the matron was out of earshot.

"You were the one growling," Arten shot back over her shoulder.

"I did not like the tone in which she addressed you," he said, the edge of a growl still in his words. She heard the clatter of his claws on stone, knew he was pacing.

"It's fine," Arten said half-heartedly. "I've gotten used to it. At least she still looks at me, unlike most people here."

"They know that you are moving!" he hissed, "Why has this treatment continued?"

She had no answers, so she offered none. Instead she said, "This Unity Festival is strange, isn't it?"

"In what way?" His pacing stopped.

"Well, how do you have unity when you're closing the gate and trying to keep the world out?"

"Do you know the history of the festival?" His voice was quiet, closer. She looked over her shoulder. Saw him settled in the shade of the arch, his scaled shoulder near her own.

"How could I?" she asked, the words caustic.

He made a noise of agreement and began to tell her. His voice was quiet and low and sounded like snowmelt. She felt the radiating cold of him, moved until his bulk was behind her, his scales barely brushing her back through the bars, let the chill of him seep into her.

He told her of an uprising of the sources. When she asked why they had risen up, he did not answer. Instead he spoke of the peace that was eventually brokered and how this festival marked that peace. He was talking of the history of it, the rituals and meaning and how they had changed over time. She was having trouble paying attention. Found herself drooping, her eyes closing.

SHE AWOKE hot and sticky with sweat. Stekin had moved away, was sitting quietly in that odd wings-wide pose. The sun had moved, eating away the shade so that she now baked in it. She was too hot. She pushed herself upright from where she had slumped with a groan. Immediately regretted it as her body flashed with heat and sickness.

She tried to calm herself, tried to drag her weak, flushed body into the shade. She made it, but only after emptying the contents of her stomach onto the dingy white stone. She felt the bulk of a cool body behind her, heard a frantic voice.

"It's okay, Stekin. I'm fine," she heard herself say. It sounded like someone else talking. "I'm fine. I'm just hot. It's too hot outside," she rambled.

He was shouting something. She kept repeating that she was fine, even as darkness was pulling her down. There was a commotion, hands were touching her. Not Stekin's—they weren't cold enough to be his.

There was a hiss. "She's burning up!" a voice cried.

Matron's voice, tinged with something unfamiliar and wobbly, "Grab her, take her to my rooms. Fetch an ice bath." Arten was being borne away. Behind her, she heard Matron talking to someone, a gatekeeper. Heard the gatekeeper's response. But it was wrong, somehow, and worried her.

"Be still," a voice above her hissed. "If you don't quit thrashing, we're going to drop you. There, that's better."

There were more voices, then a dark place. She sighed, relieved to be away from the sun. Then something wonderful—a cocoon of cold wrapped around her, hugged her tightly. She revived a little, felt a cold hand on her forehead.

"Stekin?" she asked, trying to focus on the owner of the hand. It was an unfamiliar woman with a scowl she didn't have to have seen before to understand. It reminded her of her mother, even though they looked nothing alike. The hand moved across her head, slick and small. Not a hand, a shard of ice. There were shards of ice all around her, floating in the water.

She finally felt cool again. Sighed with relief and fell away.

14

TAXED

STEKIN

S tekin forced himself to stay at the gate. To let them bear Arten away and not fly after. To respect the boundaries he had set so long ago. To be a symbol of respect and gratitude. To play the role that was expected of him. Even if he were the only one who expected it any longer.

He had felt this before. Not the sun on his back, the ache of holding his wings spread for so long, but the sense of helplessness. Not often—only three times. First when his daughter, his first daughter, was taken from him. Then again with his wife. But it was the third time that he now remembered.

Rosa.

His prime. His last prime. He had not thought of her in too many years. But she came back to him, now. The iron in her, the purpose. She was exceptional, had possessed a gift for managing his sources. She knew how much each could give, never let them overextend, kept a strict rotation and schedule. He needed only to give her two days' notice and she could ensure he had any amount of power he required.

I was blind. He could still see the roundness of disbelief in her face when she had shattered, before she sank, limp, to the floor. *When I murdered her.*

He remembered everything. The days of his demands for more power than he had ever asked for. The way she had reassured him each time, the way he had avoiding asking how she would manage it. *It was enough for me that she made the power available. I did not think I would need so much. I did not think I could do without. I did not care for her the way she cared for the others.*

Rosa had refused to draw more from his sources than they could bear, he learned afterwards. And she had refused to deny him when he asked for too much.

She was as prideful as I, in that way, he thought with a wan smile. That was what had drawn him to her, when she first arrived, what had convinced him to forge her into his prime. She never accepted the impossible.

But regardless of what her mind and spirit believed, her body had the final say. *I should have realized it, I should have been more observant. It never occurred to me she was expending herself to keep the others hale. And I did not stop and ask.*

He hissed quietly, shamed at the memory of his pride in her ability to keep so much power flowing to him without losing any of his sources. Pride that he had allowed to blind him to the truth—the only way for her to perform the continued miracle she was, was for her to endanger herself.

A prime was like a focusing lens. Carefully trained, taught to take in power from other sources, focus and hone it, then release it again in a purified, condensed form. If Arten's power was a hammer-swing that obliterated, a prime's was the delicate shaving that brought life to an ice carving. It was smooth and beautiful and satisfying. And Rosa had been a master at her craft.

But when he had demanded too much, she had spent

her power recklessly, making up for what his other sources lacked in volume with her skill as a prime.

I accepted her gift. Deceived myself as to the cost of it. Until even her skill could not keep up with his demands. Until she had tried to create too much from too little once too often. And her control had wavered. And the power she was focusing had flared. And she had not had enough of her own left to counter it.

It was so fast, he remembered, *there was nothing I could have done, even if I had seen her falter.* The borrowed power, so tightly focused, had started to ricochet, building until it shattered the carefully wrought prism inside her and speared free. *She was more surprised than I was. I think she had not believed that she could fail right up until she did.*

Had he been paying attention to Rosa, had he been thinking about how much power he was drawing and cared to ask how she was managing it, he would have stopped her long before. But he had been selfish, and she had died for it.

Arten is not dying, he reminded himself, his arms remembering the slightness of Rosa as he had carried her to her rooms. She had been so thin; if he had only looked that should have been enough to warn him. *This is entirely different.*

But the feeling he had now, sitting outside this gate, unable to cross to Arten, unable to prove to himself that it *was* entirely different... It was the same one he had experienced sitting at Rosa's bedside, watching her die. Unable to change her fate. Unable to change his part in it.

This is not the same! a part of him roared silently. *I can fly over, I can break down this gate, I can drag Kylik down here and heal her.* The part of him that had watched Rosa die, that had heard her tearful apologies at failing him—the part that had never allowed him to forge a prime again—wanted to do all of those things. But another part was stronger. The part that had made such unreasonable demands of his sources in the first place. The part that knew the price of each decision made, each action taken. The part that knew that this festival was Rosa's legacy.

The Gatekeeper.

The Gatekeeper, who was wise enough to allow himself to be repelled.

Who protected that which was most precious to his people from themselves.

Who stood as a warning to all, and especially to himself.

The Gatekeeper, who had not kept the gate in thirteen years, and in whose absence another prime had shattered and a dragon had taken her own life.

No, he would hold. Arten was not Rosa, she was not in danger. Her power was bright, with that muted roil it had had for so many days. Not flaring.

The apex bell struck, signaling noon. Sounds of celebration drifted through the iron bars to him. But he listened for another sound—that of wings. And he watched the beacon that was Arten, alert for the flickering that would signal her danger.

He had only half his vigil remaining. He would hold.

THE SOUND of wings arrived only after the second evening bell. The sun was hidden behind the high valley walls, a gloomy dusk settling in. High above there was a languid beat of leathery wings. And another. Stekin scanned the sky, saw the dragon wavering above the compounds. The dragon's head was turned, scanning the shadows of the gate, searching for him. Obligingly, Stekin leapt into the air with a roar and arrowed towards her.

She fled higher into the sky then veered back, racing away from him. Stekin was not yet at his full strength, he could not catch her. So he chased her with his voice then glided back down to his post. Below him, glints of white eyes from upturned faces followed him. The boulevard had fallen silent.

Gradually, the laughter and chatter returned, the younger sources could be heard playing games. Scents of roasted meats and confections wafted through to him, reminding him how long it had been since midnight last, and how long it might still be before he would eat again. He looked for Arten's power reflexively.

She was back in his compound, unmoving. Pasha had come by, after her fever had been lowered, and explained the current situation to a source she had brought with her. Within contrived hearing range of Stekin. That the matron was having her checked on and had issued orders to be alerted immediately if Arten's situation changed was a relief to him. It freed his attention to listen for wings, though he still was counting down the hours until he could assure himself of her condition.

Another dragon tried to sneak in at the fourth bell, gliding in. Stekin heard the soft whistle of air over scales, was grateful that there was no wind to cover the minute sound, and leapt towards it. His roar split the night, interrupting the revels—louder, and a little inebriated—below again. He clawed through the air towards the shape of the dragon he could not identify in the darkness. He saw a flash of wings as it turned away as silently as it had come.

As the clock neared midnight, he tensed and coiled, waiting. They would come early. Someone would test him tonight, the truth of it resonated inside him. And, with ten minutes left until the single strike that would end the evening and start the night, he heard three approach. He met them in the sky, his challenge warned them away. But the one in the lead position of their little formation ignored him. Dove down towards the third circuit.

Stekin followed, bellowing to those below to clear the boulevard. Humans froze then scattered as he closed on the dragon. Only when he was close enough to reach out and snag a wing in his claws did he recognize her.

Hiranyath roared when his claws pierced the membrane of her left wing. She faltered. Tried to slow, to recover, but he crashed into her and bore her to the ground, his teeth tearing at the small horned ruff that protected the fragile joint of her neck. Not to kill, but to frighten.

His daughter lumbered to her feet, crying out in confusion and pain. He allowed her to shake him off then chased her back into the sky, snapping at her tail and the ends of her wings. When he was certain she was not going to double back, he relented and let her escape. One of her comrades called for her, descending from the clouds to fly at her wing, voicing concern.

Which meant the other had taken advantage of his distraction and slipped past him. Angry, his power and blood churning at the aborted fight, he sped back to the compounds. Passed over the gate, followed the cliffs, eyes scanning the brightly lit gardens and patios. Looking for the glint of scale, the flutter of a wing or tail, a dark bulk in a shadow. He barely noted the absence of sound, the wide eyes staring up at him, so focused was he on his hunt.

He reached the wall behind the third circuit, climbed for altitude and came back for another pass down the middle of the circuits. There was nothing, no sign of the third dragon.

Stekin reached the gate, climbed and rounded for the next pass, over the wall-side. But he reached the end wall again, without seeing anything as large as even a horse. He snarled, tail lashing, as he readied for one more pass.

It was nearly midnight now. He heard the sound of wings circling above, waiting for the intoning of the bell. None descended. He was just passing from the third to the second circuit when a sharp whistle reached him. His head snapped to the sound.

A source was waving her arms, drawing his attention. His eyes flared as they caught hers. The source made a jabbing motion to her temple, which was bared as her other hand pushed golden hair away. She pointed again to the dark word on her skin, then thrust her arm out pointing towards the bottom of the third circuit. His eyes followed the line rapidly. Picked out what she had been indicating: the face with no brand. With an infuriated roar he swept down.

The face that belonged to no source twisted into a hate-filled expression, then the body turned and sprinted away, casting sources to the ground where they impeded him. But his human form was no match for Stekin on wing. Stekin swooped down, snatched him up in his claws, angled his wings and shot back into the sky.

"Who are you?" Stekin growled, holding the man at arm's length, his hands tight around the frail torso but not crushing. After all, he could be a bystander.

Before the words were gone from the air, a bolt of power lashed at Stekin's face, dazzling him. Stekin snarled and flung the human body away from him. *Definitely one of my people.* Moments later, the roar of a dragon split the air from below. Stekin pivoted and dove towards the sound, relieved in a small way that his opponent had transformed success-fully and not fallen to his death.

"Kaz!" the dragon bellowed, his eyes blazed orange, illuminating the black scales of his face ominously.

"Graug," Stekin growled, recognizing the twisted expression on that face. A wisp of memory sent a pleased jolt through him: Arten, hand in her pocket, clutching the hilt of Ergin's knife, bristling with her rejection of this same dragon. Terrified, yet brave. "I had not thought you a coward!" Stekin taunted, his blood singing for a fight.

It had the desired effect—Graug roared and lunged for him. Stekin twisted away, striking out with claws and teeth, which were met in kind. It was brief and fierce. Graug scored on Stekin's flank. Stekin got lucky and hooked his claw under a plate scale across Graug's chest and pierced the flesh there, then when the black dragon back-winged to pull away, his teeth cut a line through the soft scales under Graug's eye. There was a tangle of sound as Graug readied his power to lash out. Stekin disengaged quickly, folding his wings to drop—he had nowhere enough power to counter or absorb whatever his opponent had planned.

He fell a wing-length away; the bolt of power crackled through where he had been, caught the edge of his back, singed his scales. The midnight bell tolled. Stekin's role as Gatekeeper ended, and he had no further reason or jurisdiction to continue this conflict.

Graug acknowledged this truth by stopping his attack mid-swing. They both drew away, still circling each other warily.

"You should not oppose me again, kaz," the black dragon warned, "The next time you do, I will not be so lenient."

Stekin said nothing. His opponent sneered and dove for the ground, landing dramatically on the third-circuit boulevard—now cleared of pedestrians where Stekin had forced his daughter to ground. Stekin banked, leaving the odious dragon behind. He returned to the gate.

Matron was speaking the closing words of the ritual. Stekin landed quietly, stood facing the gate. He played his role, speaking the required words automatically, though most of his attention was on turning his power and calming himself. When the wooden beam was lifted, Stekin pulled the gates open, pushed them back to their wide-flung positions, and exchanged some more expected words with Matron, hiding his impatience.

Because now it was after midnight, and he could enter the compounds once more. His tail tip leapt, betraying his agitation. The taste of Graug's blood was on his claws, the sense of Arten's power filled his awareness, he could almost smell her. The few minutes it took for Pasha to conclude her statements were endless. Until they were done and he was free. With only a brief word of thanks for her prior assistance, he shot into the sky.

SECONDS LATER STEKIN was on Arten's patio. He burst in through the patio door without even the pretense of politeness. She was in her bedroom. He snatched a throw blanket from the couch and tied it around his waist—humans were strange about bodies—as he strode to her bedroom door. His fingers trembled and he chided himself for being so emotional. He shoved the door open and stepped through in one, urgent movement. Two bounds later and he was at her side.

He touched her arm. It was hot. Her face was scalding under his hand. He pushed at the corner her eyelid, revealing a sliver of pupil, and peered deep into her. Her power was bucking and surging, more violent and wild than it appeared from a distance.

She is unconscious—the power within her should have been freed. Why has it not? He looked for answers in the flow of her power, his chest constricted by that invisible grip. He spread his hands above her, felt her power crackle just beyond his fingertips. Something held it back, but what? Muscles jumped in his jaw as he attuned every sense to her, turned his considerable will to a single purpose: discovering what ailed this precious human.

At last he found it. He opened his eyes. The room was fully dark, sweat prickled all over him. He did not need light, she shone too brightly to him. And there, winding around her power, trapping it in a fragile net, was something else. Something foreign. He reached out a tendril of power and touched it lightly, testing.

It sent him reeling back in horror.

The net was alert, a foreign power lodged in her, strangling her own. And that power was his own.

He had emptied himself to prevent her from flaring out. A kindness, he had thought. A kindness that was now killing her.

He knew he did not have the strength to remove the binding and transmute her power. There was too much. He would be too weak after breaking the net to handle the backlash of wild power that would surge free from her. *It would consume us both. But I must do something. I refuse to lose her!* But what else could be done?

Whatever it was, he must do it soon. She was burning up —more slowly than a flare-out, but he had no doubts that the condition his power had put her in was any less fatal.

He leapt to his feet, paced, hands entangled in his hair, pulling it unknowingly. He could not remove the net, he could not leave the net. His thoughts ticked rapidly past, creating and discarding options, until he began to despair. Even Kylik would be no help to him; only Stekin would be able to dismantle the net without harming Arten. It was his power that bound her; if he could reconnect with it—if such a thing could be even done—he might be able to draw it away. Anyone else, even someone as skilled as Kylik, would have no option but to try and obliterate the obstruction and hope Arten did not sustain lasting damage in the process.

Such a blow could shatter her, he knew. *I cannot risk that.*

Then something struck him. What if—what if he left his power in place and siphoned off some of her power. If he could do that, he would be able to transmute a little at a time until he had enough of his own power back to remove the net.

And if my power does not respond to me? the thought rose unbidden. He snuffed it out.

It must, he told himself, baring his teeth.

He bent his focus to her once more, fell deep into her until he hovered just beyond the knotted wisps of his power that contained the riotous miasma of her own. He prodded the net, letting it recognize him. When at last it did, he let out a long breath he had not realized he was holding. He urged it gently, one strand at a time, to loosen, working it into a new shape, something he could use. His power did not like being knotted; it wanted to return to the stretchy bands it had once known. With a patience outside of time, he shaped it to his will.

Then—there was a gap. The storm in her surged against the breech, desperate for freedom. Her eyes flew open, and she screamed silently, unseeing, her back arched off the bed. He stooped over her, jaws wide, drew her power in. It seared past his teeth, licked flames at the places inside him that had been soft and cool for too long. When he could hold no more and still maintain his connection to his own power in her, he closed the net.

She groaned; the inferno inside her flared but the net stretched and tightened and subdued it. It subsided into the seething, endless maelstrom. He closed his jaws, rubbed the pained joints under his cheeks as he sat heavily beside the bed. His limbs were heavy and feverish as his body fought to transmute her power. The cool stone was, for once, refreshing against his legs. He rested an elbow on her bed and propped his head against that arm. He found the strength to lift the other arm to the bed, curling it around her shoulder. His fingers found her hair.

"I will fix this, Arten," he croaked. "I will fix this." The battle inside him hurt. His throat and mouth were scorched. His insides burned. He struggled silently, wondering if he had gone too far, taken too much, if her power would overcome him. But slowly, painfully, he won. It had cost him every step of the way, but at last he was himself again.

He opened his eyes—it was dawn—saw her face. A little less rigid with pain. He caressed her head and slept at last.

THE SOUND OF BOUNDING FOOTSTEPS. A voice: "Arten! Are you *still* in bed?" A door sliding open, "You—" A soft sound of startlement.

Stekin opened his eyes, turned his attention to the young woman in the half-open doorway. The maid. He spared her only a glance.

He unfolded himself from the ground, touching Arten's forehead before he stretched, straightening his back. She was still fevered but cool enough to touch, at least.

"Tell me," Stekin said calmly, turning his attention back to the servant, "why should I continue to employ you?"

"I—I don't understand, Kaz Stekin," she stammered, shifting her weight to bolt.

"Arten has been like this for...?" he prompted.

"A few days? She hasn't been like *this* before!" the girl protested. "She's just been, you know, tired."

"And you did not think to inform me?"

"Well, no! I mean—you already knew. But I guess you didn't know? I thought you did," she rambled, her eyes flicking between Stekin and Arten. "She was always worse after she saw you." There was a hint of something sly in her words.

Stekin's eyes flashed, he turned his full attention on her.

"What are you implying?" he asked, icy daggers in his voice.

"N-nothing. Just that.... Well, just that I thought you would *know* so I didn't have to *tell* you." The woman recovered quickly, he would grant her that. She was not unafraid of him, he could hear her rapid heartbeat, but she was putting up a good front of bravery. He had admired those same qualities in Arten—but there was something about this one that made him leery instead.

He put the thought aside. Arten was not out of danger yet, and he had much work ahead of him drawing off her power to safe levels.

"Bring me water," he said, "and something to eat." He waited until she had scampered away to examine Arten more closely.

She was still unconscious, but her heartbeat was stronger, though her breath was still coming in small pants. Her skin and hair were gritty with the residue of sweat. He found a basin, filled it from the small water jug next to it. Sat on the edge of her bed and began wiping away the salty crust with his moistened fingers. He washed her face and neck, marvelled again at the fragility of human bodies. Her pulse threaded under his fingers; he could stop it with one blow, and she would never wake, never have the opportunity to defend herself.

Not that he ever would. But someone else could. Another dragon. A servant. Anyone. The invisible bands tightened around his chest, he felt his throat work as he swallowed. He laid his hand along her jaw, brought his forehead to hers. *Arten...* her name echoed through him.

The door slid open. Stekin straightened, stood. Faced the woman bearing a filled tray. Her eyes were full of hard suspicion, raking down his body. She covered it quickly, the vapid expression snapping back into place. She rambled some polite nonsense, placed the tray on the table at the other side of Arten's bed.

Stekin came up behind her as she fussed over the tray, clearly stalling. He placed a hand on her shoulder. She jumped, squeaked. "Leave," he said. She scampered out the door, avoided his gaze but speared a glance at Arten's prone form before she left.

Stekin latched the door behind her. Returned to Arten's side.

He sat cross-legged on the bed beside Arten, then leaned over her, his fingers scenting for the net. He caught it, opened it, and pulled away more of her wild power. He was stronger this time and could hold more. He closed the net when he felt his arms trembling as they supported him over her body. He dropped back, drowned the ash in his mouth with desperate gulps of water, forced some food down, then fell over slowly. His leaden fingers found Arten's wrist behind him and he clasped it. Her pulse was still too fast.

He gave himself over to the struggle inside.

He slept, woke, and carefully freed her power twice more. He was weary, some part of him drained away, but her transmuted power sizzled under his skin, denying him real rest until his task was complete. How long had it been—two days, three? He couldn't recall. Sometimes it had been night, sometimes not. Now it was day.

He stirred to wakefulness, slowly. Somehow he had ended up here, curled around her each time he awoke, as though she were freshly hatched and his arms sheltered her like wings. He had thought at first his instinct was a natural response to her warmth. But this time, his skin barely missed her—with her power, he had drawn some of her heat into himself, and their internal temperatures were nearly aligned. He withdrew the arm that encircled her abdomen.

She was almost lucid, a frown crossed her features and she stirred as he moved away. The chaos still roared in her but like an animal, caged, pacing its confinement ceaselessly.

He got to his feet, did not replace the blanket that had fallen from his waist—it was just Arten here, and she was in no state to perceive its absence, and it only tangled around his legs. He paced the room, fighting the desire to transform and fly away. The half-wild energies in him eddied at cross-purposes with his own, agitating him. He had not had time to tame them fully. He was bloated with her power. Needed it to submit to him, needed the sky and the wind rushing under his wings to remind him of who he was.

Her power corded and knotted with his, wanted to move

to her rhythm not his own. He worked at it some more, forcing it to disperse one rope at a time, forcing it to respond to his will. Until the knots were loose, confused snarls, until the cords were torn into smaller threads. They would rebind soon enough. And he would obliterate them again, and again, until the power forgot her and knew only him.

He was not certain how much more he could take from her. She needed it to be done, but even in the short amount of time he had just rested, her power had forgotten him. At some point, his power would not be enough to subdue hers, and he would be overwhelmed. Diamond scales scraped at his core, alert, waiting for him to falter. He would not die—the beast inside him had protected him from that in the past and would do so again—but Arten?

Her power is what threatens me. If it takes over, the beast might view her as an enemy, might lash out at her.

He could not let that happen. Neither could he leave her in this volatile state.

Weary, he leaned over her once more, arms supporting him heavily, and pushed aside the net. *Once more*, he thought, *should be enough. Let it be enough.*

He coaxed the power out, did not care when it scorched him. He channeled it into himself, until he could hold no more. His arms shook. He couldn't stop, not yet. The wild power still oscillated out of control inside her. If he stopped, it would continue to build, continue to consume her. He found more reserves.

Then—he was not pulling at the power. It was being pushed to him. His eyes snapped open. *A gift?* She lay still, but he saw the stirrings of wakefulness on her face. Somehow, at last, she'd found the way. He accepted the offering gratefully and the tamed power flowed into him. It mingled with its wild brethren and spread calm where it went. The flow stopped; she was finished. He pushed the strands of the net back into place and collapsed heavily beside her.

The powers swirled in him as he stared towards the ceiling; coiling, intwining, then merging. He felt the alchemy throughout his entire body, in his toes and eyelids and deep in his core. It was—glorious. *How could I have forgotten this?* He no longer felt overfilled; the power roared through him, twisting and spiraling in ways he knew so well, filling him more fully since—perhaps since the Sundering. *As long as that?* He needed to fly, to remember what it was like to be a dragon in his prime. Not so old at all.

A fierce joy bubbled up in him, and he laughed, the sound strange in his ears. But there was time enough, now—he allowed the ecstasy and fatigue to bear him away. He saw a face at the window, its wide-eyed expression. But then it was gone. And he forgot it in the sensual curl of his power.

15

CHOICES
ARTEN

S he awoke, weak as a kitten. There was something heavy
pinning her down. She struggled against it, but she was
disoriented and dizzy and couldn't free herself. It took her a
moment to realize what it was and longer to believe it.

"Stek...?" she ventured, her voice a croak. No more sylla-
bles would come out.

He lay, half beside her, half draped over her. The arm
and leg that pinned her in place were relaxed into sinuous
curves. His head lolled back and away, exposing the long
curve of his throat. A pulse thrummed there. He looked
wild, primal, and she was reminded that he was not, in fact,
a man.

"Stekin?" she said again.

An answering rumble filled his chest and from a great
depth he roused himself. His head shifted her way, his eyes
opened to mere glimmering slits, but all else was still in
him. "I am here."

"What happened?" she asked. The change in him bewil-
dered her. "Why are you," she paused, realized the implica-

tion of the skin she was seeing, gulped and finished, "on my bed?" The last words quavered.

"Your power was bound, and it built." His voice was melted wax, alarming her further. "I had to pull it away." He groaned as he congealed himself back into muscle and bone. "Too long..." he murmured to himself as he flexed his fingers slowly, marvelling at them.

"Stekin?"

He looked at her through heavy, narrow eyes.

"Are you all right?"

He smiled. A wide, beatific expanse that erased the sharp edges in his face, making the precise lines of his teeth all the more ominous by comparison. "I am so much more than that." He sighed, the rasp of silk in his words. "You..." He dragged his arm up until his palm rested, hot, on her forehead, his fingers swimming through her hair. "You did well. You did very well." His eyes burned through their lids, then dimmed.

She felt a squirming in her stomach that had nothing to do with her power. What had happened to him? His hand on her head was not the hand she knew. She pushed it away, confused and alarmed. She didn't know what was wrong with him but she did know she wanted him to go. He had probably saved her from herself again. And she wanted him gone. Guilt added to the rest of the discomfort in her stomach.

He rolled away from her and rose to his feet, his limbs rippling like water. "Rest," he said, then, over his shoulder as he flowed through the threshold, "I will be gone...for a few days." Her door slid quietly closed behind him, she heard click of the patio door. Then the sound of air caught in taut wings.

She was sitting there, still dazed, when Emilette burst in.

"What has he done?" Emilette cried.

"I don't know. Left."

"And before then?" Emilette demanded, her face shrewd.

Arten flushed, wondering what Emilette had seen and what she suspected had happened between them. *What did happen between us?* she wondered, a little panicked. *Surely I would...know, if anything inappropriate had... But he wouldn't. Why would he? He wouldn't. But then...why was he sleeping all over me like that? And what was that smile?* She drew her knees up, wrapped her arms around them.

She couldn't remember what had happened after she went to see Stekin at the gate. She'd been feeling so terrible. But she didn't anymore. *He said he had to draw my power away. But I don't remember it flaring?*

Emilette was still staring at her, fists on her hips, demanding an explanation. Arten had none to give. Nothing made sense. She curled up and went back to sleep.

ARTEN SLEPT POORLY, in intermittent dozes until Emilette burst in with a proclaimed, "I'm back! Oh, were you sleeping?"

"Not well." Arten sighed, giving up. She pushed herself upright, swung her legs over the side of the bed. She was still dizzy, her limbs felt oddly blank, like they were half-asleep. Her clothes were creased and rumpled and a little damp, but she didn't want to waste energy changing them.

"Oh, good." Emilette sighed her relief. "Let's have some lunch, then. Can you make it to the dining room or will I have to bring it in here?"

"I'll make it." Arten set her teeth and levered herself to standing. Once the room stopped spinning, she was able to move slowly towards the dining room. Emilette chattered the whole time, and Arten ignored her. She sank gratefully into the dining chair at long last, and tried not to focus on the weak trembling in her limbs.

Emilette disappeared into the kitchen and returned with a generous sandwich, which she cut in two and divided between them. Arten didn't think she was hungry until the she was licking the crumbs from the plate. Then she realized she was ravenous.

"Is there more?" she asked.

"I suppose," Emilette said with an unhappy sniff.

"Why am I so hungry?" she groaned, wrapping her arms around her angry stomach.

"You haven't eaten in three days, and who knows what *that dragon* has been doing to you in there!"

"What?" Arten's head snapped up. "What do you mean?"

"Oh, never-mind-that," Emilette said airily, breezing back into the kitchen. When she returned with another sandwich and some a plate of pastries and cookies, she plopped down into the chair beside Arten with a heaving sigh. "I *shouldn't* tell you this," she cautioned in a conspiratorial way. Arten's mouth was too full to demand she do so, but Emilette obliged her anyway. "I *shouldn't,"* she repeated, "but you are my dearest friend and so I feel I *must."*

Dearest friend? Demonsfire, Arten thought, alarmed. She made a gesture for Emilette to continue.

"The blonde one stopped by—Natalia?—anyway, she stopped by while you were shut up in your room with that dragon. And she said...oh! I don't want to repeat it! But for you, dear Arten, I will!" Emilette visibly calmed herself and pressed on. "She wanted to know how you were doing, and I told her that the kaz was looking after you and she said—

can you *imagine?*—she said, 'Well, I hear that dragon has been doing some weird things to Arten.'"

"What is that supposed to mean!?" Arten shouted, her face flushed with outrage and no little shame. She pushed the food away from her.

Emilette protested from around a fruit tart, "I don't know, that's all she said, and of course I tried to get her to say more, but you know Natalia. So terse."

There was a long silence, then Emilette said, "I know that's upset you, and I'm sorry, but you really have the right to know, I think. Especially if your friends are spreading vicious rumors like that. It is..." She grasped Arten's hand. "It *is* just a rumor, right? He hasn't...*done* anything to you, has he?"

"Don't be absurd." Arten snatched her hand away. She didn't think so, but she didn't remember and he had been so *strange.*

"Not that you would tell me, I know. But if you *did* tell me, I would never breathe a word. Only then you wouldn't be alone."

"There's nothing to tell," she snapped.

"Of course not. No! The kaz is a very important dragon, he would never risk his reputation, his standing, on people like us. But if something *were* to happen, I just want you to know how much I care about you."

Arten made a noncommittal noise and quickly changed the topic. "What else has happened?"

Emilette spoke around a bite of honeyed pastry, "Well, nothing really. Nothing *ever* happens down here. Sources are so dull, you know? Although...I suppose you're the exception. You're lucky that I keep an ear out for you or you'd never know all the scandal you cause. But it's much better to be the *cause* of scandal than the brunt of it."

"What scandal?" Arten asked reluctantly.

"That dragon locking himself in your room, of course!"

Arten's face burned, she stared down at the table as Emilette prattled on.

"It has *quite* overshadowed the resentment that you're *still* living here, even after that dragon got your new place to live all ready. I mean, the *first* day, after that silly celebration where I got locked out, everyone was cross that you hadn't moved yet. But then the *second* day it got around somehow —I didn't tell them, you *know* I didn't!—but someone started saying that the kaz had been here for two nights already and was still here. And then *this morning* he was *still here!* And I didn't know what to do, but I thought I might break down the door and tell him he had better leave you alone! But then I saw him coming out of your room and I was so startled—you know he was *stark naked?*—I just didn't know what to even think."

Emilette had paused, was leaning towards Arten expectantly. But even if she'd known what had happened, why she'd awoken with Stekin puddled over her like that, why he was so transformed, she wouldn't have told Emilette.

When enough silence had stretched for Emilette to clue in on Arten's unwillingness to confide in her, she breezed on, "Oh, I've forgotten to tell you—some of the girls up in the town are putting on a little pageant tonight, and they've asked me to help out. Just making sure no one tramples on each other behind stage, that sort of thing. I was going to surprise you with it, but then you were ill and it flew out of my head. I would stay with you, but they're so depending on me and you're just going to be sleeping, really. You don't mind, do you? I can go and get one of your little friends to come by and keep you company tonight."

"Sure," Arten said, uncaring.

Emilette smiled and chattered some more over goodbye and then dashed out the door.

Arten pillowed her head on her arms, pushing the dishes aside and napped right there, her heart heavy. It was so peaceful without Emilette that she drowsed there into the evening, the sun warm on her back as it streamed in from the windows. She awoke to a gentle shake.

It was Rya. Bearing a covered basket, the smell of hot food wafting from it.

"Emilette asked me to come by," Rya explained, her face worried and nervous.

"Oh," Arten said, sitting up. "You didn't have to," she said, knuckling sleep from her eyes.

"Are you...are you feeling better?" Rya asked, like the question was a snake.

"I suppose I must be. Tell me," Arten said, irritated, "what you've heard about me in the last few days."

"Oh!" Rya blushed, looked away, "Oh, nothing I believed."

Arten ground her teeth and reined in her anger. Rya wasn't the problem, and she shouldn't take her ire out on her. *She's so meek, even the thought of creating or spreading rumors would be too much for her.* Arten thought of Maruko— her neighbor and best friend before she'd fled into the network to escape the temple and the dedicates. *Maruko would know how to fix this situation. She'd do...something! Something bold and brilliant and have them all eating out of her hand afterward. I wish...*

She stopped herself before the wish emerged.

Wishes could come true, and no part of her would ever wish for Maruko to be here. Because for Maruko to be here, it would mean she was cursed with the Taint, that she would go through the network and face workshop men and all of that alone, and then she would become a slave to a dragon just as Arten was going to be.

She would, at least, have only one master.

"I'm not surprised," Rya said, breaking across the dark trail Arten's thoughts were headed down, "that you're still here."

"What do you mean?" Arten stood belatedly, helped Rya clear away the dishes from lunch and place new ones down.

"I mean it doesn't surprise me that the lord kaz has not moved you into the last circuit yet. He clearly cares for you very much." The words were simple and frank and, for some reason, sent an alarm racing along Arten's spine. Rya continued, unaware, "It's more curious to me why he would announce that he has no intention to take you as a source."

"Why?" Arten managed through her frozen jaw.

"I haven't been here that long," Rya demurred, "but from what I've seen so far there's a blind possessiveness our lord dragons have for their sources. It can take a bit to kick in." She hid behind the fall of her hair as she removed dishes from the basket and added more timidly, "It was a whole season for my lord Kylik to...to care that much about me." She continued hurriedly, "But it seems obvious that the lord kaz is...well, that he feels that way about you. To me, anyway," she amended.

"Is it?" *It's not to me,* Arten thought.

"Well, yes. Why else would he nurse you through your illness and entrust your care to no one else?" Rya blushed again and looked down and away. "Especially with all the... talk it caused. Matron said it was foolish of him to shut himself up with you, that he knew better and knew what would come of his actions. And he does seem to be wise from what I've heard of him, and thoughtful. So why else would he do it, but that he was inattentive to the consequences? Which leads me to believe he was responding the way any dragon would if their source were threatened." Her voice got quiet and wistful. "It's flattering, really."

"I'm not his source," Arten protested, "I'm just his slave. He paid a lot of money for me. If anything he was protecting his investment."

Rya's words were tempting, but Arten couldn't allow herself to be deceived by them.

Rya dropped the matter quietly.

They ate in silence at the long table. Arten couldn't help but notice the difference from the warm, family atmosphere at Kylik's compound. It was hard to imagine these stone walls ringing with laughter, humming with contented conversation. It was a place as cold and unnerving as its master. Had sources past lined the sides, identical plates in front of them, eating in silence, the clinking of utensils the only conversation? Or maybe they were all like Natalia, barbed and aloof, cutting comments behind each other's backs. Or maybe, her thoughts moved away from the sting of that image, there had never been anyone at all. Maybe she was the first slave to be penned here.

Rya stayed only a little after supper. She returned a book, borrowed a new one. They talked a little of nothing important, then Rya packed her basket of empty dishes and went home. To her family, to her dragon, to the people who would miss her if she was gone too long.

Arten trudged down the hall to her room, the silence and the wan light of her candle her companions. Slid the door to her bedroom open, and stopped. She saw the ghost of a languid body draped over the empty sheets of her bed, felt a strange hand on her head. She pushed away the memory. Found enough energy to bundle her few things into her travel pack, and tuck *A History*, which was too large for the pack to hold, under her arm.

I hear that dragon has been doing some weird things to her.

She put the room to her back and trudged out through the echoing corridor, past the empty rooms, across the still common area. She pushed the great door open, heard its rattle and groan for the last time as it closed behind her, and went out into the night.

SHE WAS SO focused on staying upright and continuing to put one foot in front of the other that she made it all the way to the start of the third circuit before she realized she had no idea where she was going. A part of her had assumed the compound would be marked with Stekin's symbol, that she would know it from a distance. But that didn't make sense, since she was not Stekin's source. *Marking the compound would put me in the same situation that I'm in now, just with less snobby neighbors.*

She thought about going to Natalia's, begging a room for the night but she remembered what Natalia had said to Emilette: *I hear that dragon has been doing some weird things to Arten.* Arten flushed and resolved to go back to Stekin's compound before she relied on Natalia's hospitality. She found a rock, artfully placed under a tree, and sat, shrugging out of her pack, to think. She had just decided to do a single loop around the circuit to see if any of the compounds jumped out at her as being particularly newly maintained, and if not to return to the first circuit, when she heard foot-steps on the stone of the boulevard.

A man ambled up. Old—or as old as people seemed to get around here—and alone. He greeted her neutrally, his eyes roving over her face, taking in her short hair and unbranded temple, then he noted her pack and a spark of recognition lit his features.

"Ah, you must be the kaz's ward," he said, with warmth. A smile creased his face. "What brings you out this late?"

She debated what to say. But he had recognized her and smiled—no one had done that before. "I'm moving."

"Ah, I see," he said, nodding. "You mean to say that is not my business, but are too polite. No, no, you are right. It takes more than that to offend me. But here, let me carry something for you. You are clearly exhausted. I insist—of the two of us, I think I am in better shape at the moment. Good girl." She handed him her pack, which he slung across his shoulders easily. "Now, where to?"

"I...I don't actually know," she admitted, unable to meet his eyes as her face burned.

"Ah, our dragons can be forgetful of these little details, can they not?" His smile didn't falter. "Fortunately, I can show you the way. Your arrival is much anticipated on this circuit."

She followed as he led her around the curve of the boulevard, her steps lighter than before. "Is it?"

"Oh, very much so. I am glad you will be joining us. It is such a blessing that I came upon you tonight!" He pointed with his chin, a gesture that was somehow familiar to Arten, and said, "Look, there. The one where the cliffs turn away."

Arten looked upon the building. It seemed small in her eyes so recently adjusted to the grandeur of Stekin's compound, but she knew that even half a year ago she would have been dazzled by it. *It's a good thing I'm getting away from Stekin's wealth before I become more used to it.*

The man walked her up to the splintery wooden gate. It had probably once been metal, like the rusted fence that stretched away to either side, but it had clearly been wooden for some time. The boards were ribbed from exposure but freshly painted. She could see the ghost of a symbol under the paint—a dragon's mark that was not Stekin's.

"Here you are," the man said, opening the gate for her. "Can I help you get settled in?"

"Thank you, but no," Arten said quickly. He seemed like a nice enough fellow, but she wasn't feeling sociable and didn't want to drive him away before he had a chance to know her.

He handed her pack over with a bow. "I hope you will not be too cross with an old man if I come by and check on you now and again?"

"Not at all, but wait," Arten halted his turn. "Who—who are you?"

"Oh dear, how silly of me. Forgive me, my dear. Micah," he bowed again, "at your service."

"It was nice to meet you, Micah. I'm Arten."

"I know." He smiled broadly, his eyes crinkling almost entirely closed.

"Um, well, thanks again." She returned his smile nervously. They spoke a few words of farewell, then he ambled off. She turned to the compound, closing the gate behind her with an organic thump. It was a large house, really. Made of stone throughout, she was certain, but this stone was coarse and local—it matched the color of the cliffs—and the joins weren't seamless and tight the same way the compounds on the first circuit were. The door was made of freshly painted wood and rattled open on squeaky wheels; it didn't have a spring-closure so she had to haul it back shut on the other side.

The air inside was still, the place dark. Even with the few

windows at the front of the house, little light filtered in. She dropped her pack, rummaged through it briefly to find the candle and striker she'd stuffed in the top. Made herself a light.

It's not so bad, she told herself. It really wasn't. The room was small, but everything was going to be small compared to Stekin's place.

It's better to compare it to my parents' home, she reminded herself. Their rooms above their shop had been spacious, compared to the living quarters of other children in her village. Except for their neighbors, Maruko and Juro—but they were wealthy. As she went through the compound, she decided this place was somewhere in between her parents' and their neighbor's.

There was a proper kitchen, not just a stove in the center of the room, and a fireplace in the common room. Downstairs there was a small sanitary room and a room with a desk and a keyed lock on the door. Upstairs were five doors and four bedrooms, three of which were as narrow as her own had been growing up, but each with external access to the hallway. The last, at the end of the hall, was larger—it ran the full width of the house, though was just as narrow. A bed lay opposite the door, a stool crouched in one corner, a two-drawer chest in the other. The biggest luxury was the windows on either end, already propped open and coaxing a breeze into the room.

She closed the door behind her and dropped her pack against the wall. The book she placed down on the dresser top, shoving a wash basin into the corner to make space.

In the candlelight, she almost missed the door in the wall panel. It didn't slide, but pushed inwards under her hands, startling her for a moment. She swept the candle around, revealing another room. Two chairs, another window—smaller. A low case for books. A door to the hallway that was just as stuck from this side as it had been from the other.

A whole room just for reading? It didn't matter that it was narrow and awkward, she was pleased. It was a little sanctuary. The bolt on the swinging door meant she could keep out anyone she wanted.

A yawn cracked her jaw and set the candlelight wavering. She could explore tomorrow, she decided, and left the little room, closing the door after her.

She sat on the bed, was pleased to find it as plush as the one in her room at Stekin's, more pleased to find the pillows were also the same. She tucked the sheets around her. They were crisp and smelled fresh and clean, were cool against her skin.

Fatigue pulled at her. She blew out the candle, expected to fall asleep immediately. But couldn't. The night sounds were wrong. There was the scrape of twigs against the tiles of the roof. As the moon rose, the soft dapple of light moving across the floor had the wrong shapes in it. The roof was too low, the stone walls too close.

SHE AWOKE, panting from a dream that she was back in the network, with the workshop man pulling up the wooden ladder, leaving her huddled in the bottom of that cell with no way to get out. Laughing as he sealed her in.

"All is well," a voice said, waking her promptly.

She yelled and backed away, pressing herself against the wall, reflexively throwing the only thing at hand towards the sound. Her candle hit a dark form, then the metal base clanged heavily against the stone tiles of the floor, the hollow tinkle of the candle following.

"Was that necessary?" The shape bent, picked up the candle and its base. There was a muttered word and light flared at the tip. Stekin stooped, frowning at her through the doorway of her reading room, his fingers and the edge of his body visible around the door.

His voice was still too soft, too warm, but his face at least looked more normal.

"Come," he said and turned, closing the door behind him, taking her light with him.

Arten snatched her blankets around her and stomped after him.

"I thought you were going to be gone for a few days," she snapped, unreasonably angry at his presence, her heart still racing from the dream.

"I was. But I did not need as much time as I thought and was already on my way back when I saw you leave the compound. Why did you not wait until morning?" he asked, looking down at her.

She didn't know how to answer that, didn't know how to describe the emotion that had rolled over her remembering the feeling of his limp limbs, the vulnerable sight of his throat pulsing with life.

"Why were you on my bed this morning?" she countered, instead.

"I needed rest after drawing away your power," he replied, emotionless, his eyes hooded.

"And you needed to be naked for that?" she demanded, dropping into one of the chairs and drawing her knees to her chest. She cocooned herself up to her ears in her blanket.

"What are you asking, Arten?" He sat in the chair next to

hers, clinking the candle down on the little table between them. A part of her felt an echo of the familiar and realized this was a re-creation of his library.

"I'm asking," she said, more boldly than she felt, "*what* you did. I don't...I don't remember."

His teeth bared, caught the candlelight. "Nothing," he said with a rime that was, finally, Stekin, "that I have not done before when you have asked me to. I drew your power away, that is all."

"I've never asked you to..."

"To what?" His teeth bit the words from the air. Something—*What is this, relief?*—rolled through her.

"To—" she started, faltered. To sleep beside her? That wasn't true—they had huddled together at night for warmth in the mountains, and during the deluge when she'd been half-frozen he'd tucked her against his side. And it's not like she was particularly squeamish about his nakedness—dragging him back from Ergin's cave covered only in ribbons of blood had put an end to that. It was just a body, as he always said.

So what had disturbed her so much? She saw again the limp limbs draped over her, felt the weight of his body pressing against her. Shuddered, and knew.

"I thought you were dead," she said to her knees. *And then when I knew you weren't, you were like someone I didn't know.*

"I regret that I have distressed you," he said. Out of the corner of her eye she saw his fingers twitch once and then still. "I will leave if you wish."

"No," she said, hugging her knees tighter. "Not...not yet?"

"Very well." He settled back into his chair, folded his hands into his lap. His shoulders seemed more relaxed than usual, his spine more curved. "What is the last you remember before this morning?" he asked, his face turned to the window, away from her.

"Talking to you at the gate."

"How long have you been ill?" he asked. She saw the muted flash of green on the arch of his cheek.

"I don't know. A few days?"

"You did not tell me."

Why does that bother him? "It was just a cold." She shrugged.

"Was it? When did you first feel unwell?"

She frowned. "It's been getting worse gradually. I don't know." But she was thinking back. "I was sick in the lane," she remembered. "Natalia helped me home. I'd been running, we were arguing about something, I remember you roaring. But I was just scared and overheated, that was different. The weakness and fatigue didn't start until a few days later."

"You vomited at the Unity Festival. Were you overheated then as well?"

"Yes. But it was a hot day and I fell asleep in the sun— that doesn't have anything to do with it."

"It was not a hot day, Arten," he said gently. "Did you not notice? The other humans are wearing long sleeves and light coats at night. I should have seen that you were different; I should have known it was important."

"What are you talking about?" she snapped. "It was just a cold," she insisted.

"No. They bathed you in ice three times to get your temperature down. Some of the people who tended you have frost burns, but you were unscathed. I am told that even fevered patients do not transfer their heat into the bath enough to warm the water as you did.

"What afflicts you is not a cold. It is more serious than

that. And," he added, ice cracking through his words, "it is my fault."

"I don't—?" She didn't know what to say. Heard the fear in her voice.

"I was worried," he admitted, "when you collapsed at the gate. I wanted to go to you right then, but I could not. As soon as midnight passed and the ceremony ended, I came to you. What I discovered..."

He told her about how her power was trying to flare out but was being prevented by something. A net of his power. About how he had manipulated the net somehow and pulled her power away over three days.

"This net—it came from when you gave me your power that one time?" She remembered it with a shivery thrill.

"Yes. It was...a gamble. Whether it saved your life at the time, we will never know. But clearly the longer-term consequences are dire. I have failed you, Arten. I sought to protect you, but the risk I took has only endangered you."

She had never heard him despair before. He was so somber, so distraught...

"Am I going to die?" she asked quietly.

"This transfer, from dragon to source, has never been done before. The outcome cannot be known. What I do know is that your power continues to grow. The net contains it. When the amount of power within you exceeds the capacity of your body to hold it, under normal circumstances, you would flare out. This net prevents your power from releasing externally and turns it back on yourself."

"Oh..."

"There are two options that I see, though I would like Kylik to examine you in case I have missed something. The first option is to keep the net in place. Since the net is made of my power and it is proven that it still responds to me, I could periodically open it and draw away your power. However, there is no guarantee that the net will continue to respond to me, and, as your power grows, so will your dependence on me. I think you will not enjoy that.

"The second option is to dismantle the net. The earlier we do this, the better. But it may not be possible. Even if it is, we have no guarantee of success. My interference could disrupt your power. It could kill you. Or it could restore you. I have only speculation.

"Both options are equally dangerous. Leaving the net is risky longer term. Destroying it risky now." He turned back to look at her; her breath caught at the anguish in his eyes. "Arten, you must know by now, but let me state it plainly for you: if this can fixed, I will see it done no matter the cost. If it cannot, I will make your life as long as comfortable as possible. You have only but to ask and I will grant you anything in my power."

"What if I just want to go home?" said the knot of pain and fear inside her that wanted nothing to do with her Words or dragons or anything more complicated than her father's hand on her head and his nod of approval as she ran his shop. That longed for her friends and their acceptance.

Stekin stiffened. She expected him to say something caustic or simply, 'No.' She could not have anticipated the tears that started tracking down his face.

"I apologize," he said, struggling to keep his voice even. "This body is malfunctioning lately."

She touched his cheek, felt the moisture there and a crackling spark that made her jerk back, before she even realized she was even reaching out. His jaw tightened, a brief twitch spasmed across his features.

He brought his hand up, covered his face, turned away from her.

"Do you know what you are asking?" he said, wintry and remote.

She hadn't, but his reaction...she now realized the magnitude of what she had asked. If he let her go home, he was risking the safety of his entire people. She stammered, "I—I'm sorry. I didn't mean it."

"If it is what you want, when your power is safe, I will take you home," he said. Sounded like he was being torn apart. He stood abruptly. "You must make your choice of how to proceed with the net. I expect your answer in the morning in my library." He was crossing to the hallway door, "Thinking on it any longer will not make the decision easier."

"Wait, Stekin," she said, but he did not pause as he slid the previously stuck door open and stepped through.

"Goodnight, Arten," he said, closed the door behind him. She didn't even hear his steps in the hall, just the skittering of her thoughts, like fallen leaves in a gust of wind.

ARTEN TRUDGED to Stekin's house, heavy and uneasy. Physically, she felt better than she had in weeks; even though the walk was longer from the third circuit, she had no trouble with it. It was appalling to think how difficult the simple act of getting around had become, and how she hadn't noticed. Even the gauntlet of judgmental sources—longer today than ever before—was not what weighed her down. She barely noted the cold reception, tuned out the gasps and fierce whispers. She had bigger things to worry about.

Like what she had asked of Stekin, what he had promised. She'd always thought him impervious to small things like emotions. He grew irritated, could be angered, and clearly cared about his people. But he'd always seemed driven by duty and expediency and his need to keep his people safe.

So why did he say I could go? After he paid so much and risked so much to bring me here? He needs me for something, so he keeps saying. How is it in his best interest, or that of this city, if I leave?

It wasn't. Any way she looked at it, it wasn't. So why had he not told her no?

And the tears—she shied away from thinking about that. About thinking of Stekin as a feeling person. *If me leaving causes...that reaction in him, why would he allow it? Unless...*

Unless he knew she could not endanger them.

He means to place me under a compulsion. She felt like she'd been kicked in the gut.

Of course. It made sense. Why wouldn't he compel her to not reveal this place? He would, to protect his people, to protect the secret of their existence.

So the tears...? 'When my power is safe,' he said. Did he mean that he would make it safe, the way he did with Ergin? By ripping it out completely. But she'd asked him to do that before and he'd denied her. Because Ergin's soul had broken in the process and he'd slaughtered hundreds of sources in his impossible need to get the power back.

I know he felt responsible for Ergin's madness. It makes sense that he wouldn't want to have to do that to me. But then why hadn't he adamantly denied her, as he had when she'd made the request to have her power taken away the first time. What had changed? She didn't know, couldn't guess. Tried to think about something else.

Her thoughts did not drift far, though. They turned to the decision she had made last night, after he left. A decision that would impact the rest of her life. *I can still change my mind*, she thought, going over her reasoning again. Every time she did, she came to the same conclusion. *I guess that means it's the right choice.*

She sighed, letting herself through the gate and into his yard. The sky was full of clouds, casting his gardens in a rich light. It had rained last night; the plants looked refreshed even as some of them were transitioning into their winter slumber. The grass under her feet was springy, the flowering bushes potent with honeyed fragrance as she passed.

The knocker was cold and rough in her hand. The sound of it striking was too loud.

A young boy answered the door, trotted with her to Stekin's library. Where he was waiting, sitting in the chair, only his long fingers tapping at the armrest were visible as she approached.

"You have come to a decision?" he asked.

She stopped in front of him. "Yes," she said. But there was something she needed to ask first. "If I keep it, how does that impact this choice I'm supposed to make?"

Stekin thought on that, his brows coming together. "It delays it. Makes it more difficult for you and the one you would source. We would need to find someone who could draw your power once I opened the net." Something unpleasant twisted on his face then passed.

Even if I'm dependent upon him, he has no intention of taking me as a source. That made her decision easier.

"I want you to break it."

He didn't ask her if she was certain, didn't ask for her reasoning, didn't remind her of the dangers. Simply said, "Very well," and stood. He placed a hand on her shoulder and shepherded her outside. She glanced up at him, not certain what response she was looking for.

A challenge? An admonition about how important this decision is? What was it he said to me?

After the workshop man, he'd said, *'I expect you to, now and always, know your own mind.' But people say things all the time, it doesn't mean they act on them.* And yet, here they were... A decision that impacted her life in a monumental way—and he wasn't challenging it. Doubting her.

"Kylik will be here shortly. I have asked for his opinion on how best to proceed."

The question escaped before she could stop it. "Will you really let me go home?"

He flinched, cut three words from the air: "If I must." His eyes caught her and held her as he said, "Please, do not mention that to anyone just yet. I must remain kaz a little longer. There are still evils I must right."

"Why would that—" she started, but a squeeze of the fingers on her shoulder silenced her. There was the sound of wings; Kylik had arrived.

ARTEN SUBMITTED TO THE EXAM, which was simple on her part. Kylik had her raise this arm then that on command as he paced around her and peered through her from all sides. When he was finished, he and Stekin fell into intense discussion that Arten only superficially followed. Stekin wanted to break the net, Kylik was concerned about the backlash from it. Kylik argued the risk was too great to both of them. Stekin argued it could be mitigated.

"There is a reason we do not force adolescence!" Kylik hissed, his tail jumping. "The complications are universally fatal. In one year or ten, the damage will assert itself."

"This is nothing alike," Stekin dismissed the concern with a gesture.

"It *is*," Kylik insisted, looming over the human-sized kaz, his teeth too large and close for Arten's comfort, though Stekin appeared unfazed. "Save that the power is yours and not her own."

"What do you mean?" Stekin asked, intrigue taking the place of impatience.

"This is the same seal juveniles have to prevent their power from manifesting when they cannot control it."

"Is it?" Stekin looked at her sharply, looked through her. She was already getting tired of that look.

Kylik huffed and said, "Yes. But because it is your power, she cannot assert control over it and absorb it back into herself."

"Yes," Stekin mused, "I see. But if she could?"

"She cannot, so it is immaterial," Kylik said.

"Humor me."

"She would, theoretically, be able to winnow it away until it dissolved, as happens naturally in our kind." Kylik paused and lowered his head to peer down at Stekin before asking unhappily, "What are you thinking?"

Stekin stalked to her side, wrapped his fingers around her upper arm and lifted her arm up. He extended his own alongside it. "This," he said, bringing his arm closer. Until a tingling crackle moved under her skin where it almost touched his.

"What—?" she started.

Kylik interrupted, "It might work. But you must do it now before you transmute any more."

Kylik peered through Stekin, then pulled his head back sharply, his pupils lost in the field of his amber eyes.

"How much did you draw?" he gasped. "How did you surv—?"

"That," Stekin cut across him, "is sufficient, Kylik, thank you." He let go of Arten's arm. "I will proceed now. Will you monitor?"

Kylik ducked his head shyly, "Of course, kaz. I am honored."

Stekin made an irritated noise, but turned back to Arten. "Do you understand?"

"As much as I need to. How confident are you that whatever this is will work?" she asked, hope and uncertainty hopping in her stomach.

"Moderately," he said. Which told her absolutely nothing. He touched her cheek, traced a crackling line down it. "Are you ready?"

Her mouth was dry, so she nodded.

WITHIN MOMENTS ARTEN was sitting in her chair in his library while he knelt in front of her.

"This is delicate work," he said. Was that an apology? "I need to be able to see."

She realized what he was asking. "Okay," she agreed, surprising herself. Let the jade pools of his eyes overpower her, consume her.

She felt him searching the depths of her. Before, she would have torn her gaze away, hidden from him, afraid of what he would churn up. Afraid he would learn about Tizzy and despise her. Before, his presence had been a violation. But now she felt unexpectedly...reassured. She sensed the tension in him, though, and in their silent onlooker. She would have been embarrassed to have Kylik observe this—

whatever this was—between her and Stekin, if she were not so frightened.

"This will be unpleasant," Stekin said without preamble, and his eyes began to burn.

She felt his hand press against her sternum—too warm, still—his fingers splayed wide and curled sharply into her chest, as though trying to grip something inside her. His breath came shorter, his hand trembled once against her, she smelled the tang of sweat. His or hers, she didn't know.

Then, with a startled cry, he threw himself away from her. He panted, looking at her queerly, something glinted behind his eyes, shifting. He mopped his brow, drawing his arm across it, then, tearing away from, her strode to the workbench. In all their travel during the summer, had she ever seen him sweat?

"Kaz, what is it?" Kylik asked anxiously, crouching nearby, his wings pulled tight to his body.

"A complication," Stekin said darkly, throwing various ingredients into a small heap on the table, from the jars and boxes strewn there.

"Kaz," Kylik hissed, then with a glance at her, lowered his voice.

They had a low, frenzied exchange which ended when an unfamiliar bell pealed across the valley. On the first note, both of their heads snapped up, fixed on an invisible point in the south. Not the clock chimes; a deeper, three-toned sound which repeated twice more. Stekin dropped his head back to his task, leaving Kylik scenting the air.

"Go, Kylik," Stekin commanded. "Tell them I refuse. Whatever you do, keep them away from here. I cannot be disturbed."

"No, I will stay," the healer said, wrenching his head back down. "Allow me to assist you."

"You serve me better by preventing the disruption that is about to descend upon me."

"Arten is my patient," Kylik protested.

"Arten," countered Stekin, his hand snapping out to grab the dragon's nose and pull it down until their eyes were level, "does not need a healer right now. But *I* need a friend."

Something tense passed between them, but ultimately Kylik dropped his gaze.

Head drooping, he acquiesced. "Write it and make your mark. They will not believe me otherwise."

"Done," Stekin agreed, grabbing up a pen and a square of paper from a stack. Papers flew off the table, some items clattered to the floor in his haste, but Stekin didn't seem to notice. He dashed his pen against the paper, rolled it rapidly, and thrust it into the dragon's waiting palm. The scaled hand closed and the paper disappeared entirely. "Hurry."

"Yes," agreed Kylik with a worried glance at Arten, then he scurried away.

Stekin had turned back to his mishmash of ingredients before the healer had taken his first step towards the door. The only evidence he was aware Kylik had gone came when he flung out his hand and growled some rough words. Arten heard the groan and thunk of huge locking pins falling into place.

She stared at him, wide-eyed. He had healed her before, done small things with his power like the lighting of the candle the previous night, and even big things—like running faster than a horse carrying her on his back. But this, for some reason, struck her in a way those things had not. *This power inside of me...is magic.* She looked down, as though she would be able to suddenly see the power flowing inside her as he could. There was nothing. But she could feel it. The Words, the Taint—her power. Churning and coiling inside her. Leashed and molten.

Magic shouldn't be this...angry, she thought.

Stekin made a satisfied noise, drawing her attention. The small mound on the table looked like something swept from under a bed but with a few flashes where flecks of a shiny substance reflected the light. He brushed this into his hand, crunched it into a fist, and chanted in that rough growling tone. The Words within her boiled suddenly in excitement. She felt something inside her constrict, restraining them. For the first time she knew what that was.

His fist was opening, pushed apart from within, until his fingers curled around a transparent sphere, coated in an oily sheen. He placed it in the crease of an open book, balancing it carefully, then he dashed back to her, pulled her up from the chair by her arm.

"I apologize, Arten," he rasped, voice rough from the low chanting. His free hand moved through her hair, absently. "This is going to hurt."

His hand tightened in a vise around her head, tilting it back. His other arm moved, wrapped around her, his fingers digging into her ribs as he crushed her against him. She couldn't move as he looked down, through her.

She felt a tugging that spasmed around her chest and abdomen. Another tugging. It felt like the entirety of her insides were about to be pulled out from above. Then there was something, a force, pressing the mass inside her back down, while pulling, tearing at something else. She felt it being ripped away, like the skin of a peach sloughing off. She heard herself scream as it was yanked free, ripping away chunks of her core where the force pushing down on her was not strong enough to restrain it. She felt like she was bleeding inside as the skin jerked free at last. Her legs had given way, her arms and wrists hurt—she'd been hitting Stekin, trying to break free. But the bands around her head and chest held firm. She felt the sharp exhales of his breath past her ear as a he panted heavily through his nose.

The slack mass was being pulled up through her throat. She felt it as a great knot, forcing its way up. She wanted to vomit, to help it along, but was unable to. She heard his mouth open, jaws cracking wide. She couldn't see past the dimness in her eyes. She felt his teeth graze her lip, the edges too honed to be human. She wanted to recoil but couldn't. Then it was through, in the back of her mouth, being drawn forward over her tongue. It tasted like blood and honey. It passed her lips, passed between his teeth.

With an audible snap, he clamped his jaws around it and dropped her. She fell to the floor, her legs unable to react in time. A new pain in her ankle cleared the fog from her vision. She saw him lunge for the nascent sphere. It disappeared into his mouth. She squinted, saw a shimmering wall in his throat, pushing back on something darker and smokier. The shimmer faded, and he spat the sphere out.

The last thing she remembered was seeing him stare down at it, disheveled and sweaty. His pupils flashing from small to large, again and again, his mouth twisted open in horror.

16

TRUTHS SPOKEN
STEKIN

W hen Arten collapsed, Stekin shoved the orb into his pocket and leapt to her side. Her power, freed at last, swelled and flared out of her, leaving her body lurching in pain on the ground. Stekin lunged, caught it, his jaws cracking with the effort. It tried to coil around him as he drew it in, singeing his robe, searing his skin. He fought it for long minutes, drawing it more and more into himself, out of Arten, protecting her from its destruction.

Finally, his teeth closed around the last of it. He pulled it deep inside, plunged it into the rivers of half-transmuted power inside himself. He slumped onto the bench, rested his head on his arms as he turned his focus inward, fell into the battle raging there. He frayed the ropes of her power, ripped apart the knots, forced the broken remains to join his own, to respond as his own. Again and again and again. Until everything else was forgotten, and his whole existence was defined by the destruction and transmutation of her power.

Then there was someone talking. He could not listen, was too deep in his power to have room for things like words. The talking continued, then stopped. Time stopped again in his interminable battle.

There were more words. An acrid scent shot up his nostrils, sending him reeling up out of himself. His hands were already pushing away the larger, scaled one. He coughed, eyes stinging.

"What?" he managed, a rasp, before coughing some more.

"You went too far," Kylik apologized, stoppering the small pot in his hand and packing it back into a chest full of other pots and boxes and packets.

Memory bubbled up through the sludge that his thoughts had become. "Arten!" he cried, jumping to his feet. Immediately sat back down when the world canted and swam.

"She is sleeping."

"You...?"

"Yes, I examined her. She is doing as well as can be hoped, given the circumstances. It is too early to tell for certain if there will be lasting damage, but I have healed what I can. You, however, are going to heal yourself. You are bursting with power, so you will not even need skill, just do as I say."

Stekin, still half-dazed, followed Kylik's direction, sending his power wherever Kylik's power tapped, setting up small healings to repair the more extensive injuries. Four days of battling Arten's power had been more damaging than he thought.

"That is enough for now," Kylik announced. "Come, you need rest more than anything else right now." The weakness in Stekin's knees when he stood was enough to convince him not to argue. He did not even protest when Kylik insisted on picking him up and flying him to his room.

"I trust," Kylik said, pulling the door open with his claws, "that you will force yourself to sleep. I will be right here until I have deemed you both well enough to be removed from my care."

He pushed Stekin through, closed the door behind him.

Stekin's bleary confusion lasted only until he saw another form lying in a tight curl on his mattress. He eased himself down on the far side of the bed, careful not to disturb her. He lay on his side, watching her, his hands tucked under his arms. Until his eyelids drooped and closed. Then he watched her with his other sense. She was dimmed, her power depleted, but he felt scorched just being near her.

Despite his fatigue, despite the slow drain of his power into his healings, despite the ardor of the continuing transmutation battle, he could not sleep. He felt the weight and smoothness of the orb where it rested against his thigh. It was dark to him, did not shine with her power despite being made of it. As though it were dead.

I can only hope it is, he thought with a shudder, wrapping his power tightly around himself. *Let it be dead. Let me have extracted it early enough.*

He opened his eyes to look upon the human sleeping across from him. Again, he saw another human, in another valley, in another time. *I will not make those mistakes again. I will tear apart the world to stop it...* He wanted to take out the orb and assure himself that it was inert. He wanted to hurl it away from him, smash it open and destroy it. It stayed in his pocket, silent and still. *Dead, or waiting?*

His insides clenched painfully. *Curse these human emotions! What has happened to me?* He was relieved that it was Arten, not Nhemith, across from him. His skin crawled at Nhemith's remembered touch, he found himself bearing his teeth. They had not spoken, he had not even seen her, since that night. Had not wanted to see her.

Her game with me must be finished. Or perhaps entering the next stage? Why else would she end not only her pursuit of me, but her close counsel to me. She has barely respected my privacy since I have returned—until now. Nhemith was not the sort to be put off by his rejection. Their long history was filled with him turning her away, by force usually, when her demands were more than he wanted to give. That night when he had thrown her away was mild in comparison.

She tells me she wants our line to be strong and pesters me daily to that end. She positions herself as a key counselor upon my return, and her presence drives others who would fill that role away. Meanwhile, she keeps a relationship with Ktet hidden from me—a relationship in which he feels jealousy, though that could be professional jealousy. She also feigns or experiences jealousy over my connection with Arten.

It made no sense. This was too shallow, too false for Nhemith. Even if she was, for some deranged reason, jealous of Arten and wanted to keep both himself and Ktet vying for her attentions, she would not approach it in this way. *She would pit us against each other subtly, undermine my confidence in him, undermine his confidence in the kaz.*

Has she done that? he wondered, remembering the lecture he had given Ktet, remembering how he felt the need to conceal his investigation into the source-thefts from him. *No, her claws may be in Ktet but they are not in me. She is one of those I am purposely keeping this investigation from; she cannot have influenced me there. No, this is something different.*

Why get close to him if she had no intention of destabilizing him as kaz? She had every opportunity to become kaz while he was gone—why had she not? Was it that she no longer desired to lead? *Perhaps she learned patience while I was away and was merely waiting for me to cease communication for a sufficient period of time, to ensure I was not coming back, before accepting the title.* That would set her up as a savior, not an usurper, as one who stepped in to lead them at a critical moment—a moment that she would no doubt engineer.

So what does *she want? What does she gain from*—his chest constricted, his gut clenched—*what she did?* He could not see it, did not yet have enough information. His thoughts travelled the same track a few times before the orb dragged his attention away once more.

A shiver prickled along his spine, swept down his arms tightening his skin into tiny lumps. He rubbed a hand over his forearm, angrily.

The anger galvanized him to stand. He slid his door open. A mass of moss-green scales walled him in. He thumped his fist against what turned out to be Kylik's side, until the healer shifted and allowed Stekin egress.

"Why are you not resting?" the healer demanded, his voice pitched not to carry.

Stekin slid the door closed; relief pooled through him. *Just being in the room is intolerable,* he growled silently to himself. To Kylik, he said, "This body is malfunctioning."

Kylik asked, as he leaned in to peer through Stekin, "In what way?"

"In this way," Stekin snapped, and out of Kylik's view reached into his pocket and grasped the sphere in his hand. As his fingers closed around the orb, those tingly bumps stood out from his arms again, his legs trembled. He held his forearm up to Kylik. "What is causing this?" he demanded, releasing the sphere back into the depths of his pocket.

Kylik sat back, looked at Stekin from the corner of his eyes. "What were you just thinking of?" he asked carefully.

He would not tell Kylik of the sphere, of the terror it summoned in him. Instead, he said, "The Sundering."

Kylik grimaced involuntarily. "What other symptoms are you experiencing?" he asked.

Stekin told him of the band around his chest, of the various pains and wobbling that wracked inside him, of the weakness in his limbs, the spells of dizziness, the extrusions of sweat and tears, the rapidity that seized his heart.

"You are not malfunctioning, those are simply human emotional experiences."

Stekin snapped, "I know that it is an effect of emotion! But I have been taking human form since before the Sundering and never experienced this before. I originally thought it was due to the demon-metal shards in my lungs —but those have long been gone. I need you to find the source of this and correct it."

Kylik's eyes flicked away and he rustled his wings nervously. "I cannot correct it," he muttered. "You will grow accustomed to it. It may become less potent in a few years."

"You know it then?" Stekin advanced a step, his eyes flashing.

Kylik leaned back, "Yes. Most of us have been affected."

"Stop being coy," Stekin growled, "and tell me you know. Is it a disease? What is its source?"

"It is not a disease," Kylik said, glaring at the floor. "It is more accurate to say that your human form is functioning more correctly than it ever has before. Your biologies are fully aligned for the first time."

"You are not making sense," Stekin said, even as a chill raced down his spine.

Kylik huffed a note of bitter amusement. "I am making perfect sense, as you well know. Ask anyone who can take human form—and they will tell you the same. There are only a few I know of who are unaffected—and they may be concealing the truth from me. Because it is not an illness, there is no way to diagnose who has been fully aligned and who has not."

"How does this...this alignment happen? Why is it only occurring now?"

Kylik nodded heavily, like he had been dreading the question. "It is not natural, as you have already suspected, nor is it caused by demon-metal. The alignment—it is something done to you. Usually with consent..." He avoiding finishing the statement. Stekin knew where it was headed—clearly his consent had not been granted else they would not be having this conversation.

"By whom? To what purpose?" But a memory was strong upon him: the feeling of teeth around his throat, the vibration of sound into his neck, a body holding him down, the wrenching of a door being forced open inside him.

Nhemith, he knew. *And before that time, when I first returned—I awoke to her song, to her hands on my chest. It was never the demon-metal. How many times did she try before she succeeded?* Was that why she had come to his room so many nights? Was that why she had not been back?

She succeeded. But why?

"I do not know," Kylik admitted, cutting across his thoughts. "At first, it was a novelty. But when we realized it was permanent, it began to feel more like a plague. I have transformed only a few times since your daughter inflicted it upon me years ago. The edge of it has dulled in those years, but I still cannot stand the intensity of feeling in that form."

It took Stekin a few moments to realize he meant

Hiranyath. *Nhemith and Hiranyath...* "How did this start? Why has it not been stopped?"

Kylik shrugged his wings, shuffling away a bit more at the glow in Stekin's eyes. "No one knows where it started. No one will admit to being the first. It is...shameful."

"Someone knows," Stekin growled, but did not press the healer.

Later, laying back on his bed, staring through the dark to the small human across from him, he reflected on Kylik's word.

Shameful.

Yes, it did feel shameful, these visceral emotions. To be unable to control himself was embarrassing. The way his body had betrayed him, what he had almost done with Nhemith, was so close to deviant as to be indistinguishable to him. This body was his refuge and penance; he wore it to enhance his analytical mind, to keep his strong instincts at bay, and to remind himself of the cost of failure.

Nhemith knows that—at least in part—*and she has taken it from me.* To make her bid for kaz at last? Betrayal and anger roared through him.

He saw Arten's peaceful face reflect the green light of his eyes. *If this girl can master herself, so can I. Kylik says it can fade —I will discover how to make that happen, I will conquer this.*

A part of him felt doubt. He was already overextended on his investigations. *Between convincing sources to come and speak to me about the network, investigating the neglect of the source Carl, determining a link between soul-toil and power-theft or mismanagement, training Arten in control of her power, keeping Arten safe from those who would use her against me, and trying to remove the animosity against her amongst the sources, how much more can I realistically take on?* He was already neglecting his estate, had not made the time to go around and speak to his people since his return, had not met the new governor, was not building his strength up the way he ought to be. He had not picked up his research since he returned, *and this sphere is going to demand my time as well.*

Arten has complicated my life, he realized with a frown. *If her power had never called to me, if I had not gone to find her, my time would be much better managed.* And, he knew, she would be dead. *And I would still be adrift.*

The thought arrested him, his hand stopped inches from her jaw. *I was adrift,* he knew. *Chasing the summer wind.* What had changed?

Why is she so important to you? His knuckles brushed along her jaw; her power under his skin tingled. The question was in Nhemith's voice. He ignored it.

A crease formed between her brows. "Juro?" she whispered.

A bottomless ache, a searing lance of pain. Stekin withdrew his hand. "No," he said.

Her eyes flew open. "Stekin?"

"Yes."

Her eyes flicked over his face like she could see it. He pulled his power and turned it in tight bands, dimming the glow of his eyes to nothing.

"Is it gone?" she asked, her eyes moving down to stare into the dark.

"It is," he said neutrally, trying to wrangle the wild emotions that were responding to her voice and tamp them down. He wanted to tuck her against him, mantle over her, hide her away. Something inside him was shouting, *Protect!* "How do you feel?"

"Like there are rivers of fire and pain inside me," she muttered, rubbing her chest and ribs.

"Kylik is outside. Shall I summon him?"

"No," she said with a shiver.

He drew the covers up around her from where they had slipped down.

"Your hands are warm," she said quietly.

"Yes. I have transmuted a significant amount of power from you in the past few days."

She said nothing to that, just stared into the dark between them.

He needed something from her, did not know what it was, so he pressed, "Juro—that was your neighbor."

"Yes. He was my friend."

He hated the loss and pain in her voice.

"What else can I do, Arten," he pleaded, "to make you happy here?"

She did not answer for a time. Eventually said, "How will it work?"

"Hmm?"

"When I become source to someone else. How will that work, being a slave with two owners?"

"Sources are not our slaves," he corrected. "We provide and care for them in exchange for the transfer of a power they have no use for, which is also harmful to them."

"But we can't leave, we can't change our minds if our dragon or their sources turn out to be horrible."

"No," he agreed, frowning. "But both our people need order and society. Without the compounds, there is chaos and death." He remembered the way it had been before, knew they must never go back.

"So I just have to live with it," she spat through a clenched jaw. "And what happens when this dragon that I'm not-slaved-to-but-can't-refuse demands I serve only them? What happens when your demands of me upset my not-master? People hate me enough as it is..."

There was something else there, in her tone, in the lines of her face. Something Stekin could not place. "Arten, what are you trying to say?"

She was silent, a struggle played out in her features.

"You do not wish me to impose upon you once you are sourced," he guessed.

She turned her face into the pillow, muttered a muffled, "That's not it."

"Then what is it?" he heard the snap of irritation his words.

"Why did you cry," she demanded, her fists balling in the downy softness of the pillow, "when I said I wanted to go home?"

A test. "Because I want you to stay here. With me. It was painful to hear you wish for something different."

"So why won't you take me as a source?" She was tensed, straining to hear his answer. As though she were holding tight to herself, the same way he banded his power around himself.

"We have been over this." He scowled. "If I contend for you, you will not have a choice—others will stay away."

"I don't care about the stupid choice!" she cried, the sound muffled by the pillow.

"You said—"

"I *know* what I said," she snapped.

He smelled a salty tang.

"I was mad at you for bringing me here. I was lonely, I wanted what everyone else here seems to have: a family, people who care about them." Her back shuddered under the hand he had placed upon it as her breath guttered.

"I am trying to get that for you," he murmured, his failure heavy around him.

"You can't," she muttered. "The sources don't like me, no

matter what you've done. Whatever compound I join, they're going to treat me just the same. And that will be my life. Trying to prove to everyone that I'm not as horrible as they think. I don't...I just...I'd rather be with you."

He stopped, his power, his heart, his breath all paused. With a lurch they started again. He could not stop himself as his arms reached out, closed around her, pulled her close. She stiffened as the power under his skin reacted to that under hers, but relaxed when the sizzle faded. Her hair was soft against his face.

"Arten," he breathed into it, "I do not want you to source to another."

"But?" she prompted, her forehead against his chest, speaking to the arms she still had wrapped around herself.

"But it is too dangerous for you to source to me."

"I don't care," she muttered.

"I do." He told her, then, a little of his fear. Of his contentious history with Nhemith, and that she had already moved against him—though he did not specify how. "If she knew of how important you are to me, if you were my source, she would not hesitate to entangle you in her schemes. And there are others, ones I do not know about. Ones that hold a grudge against me for decisions and judgements made long ago.

"But more than that, Arten," he admitted finally, "I do not trust myself. Your power is so strong. I do not trust that I would not become accustomed to it and ultimately demand too much of you, that I would not use you ill. Even now," he admitted reluctantly, moving his hand across her back, feeling the charged prickle under his fingers, feeling her skin twitch beneath her tunic in response, "there is a part of me that would draw more, even knowing how damaging it would be to both of us. Fortunately, I can overrule that baser part of myself most of the time. But it would take only one lapse...and I cannot do that to you."

"Is there someone you would trust me with?" she asked, bravely he thought, considering what he had just said, how tightly he was holding her, how his teeth had bared and the flat of them pressed against her scalp.

"Absolutely not," he hissed.

"Then isn't it better for me to source to you?"

"No," he said.

But she had given him an idea.

An ambitious, yet dangerous plan.

He voiced it to her.

"Do you think that will really work?" she asked, her tone caught between hope and distrust.

"I am certain of it."

"And you...would do that? For me?" Again, the hesitance.

"Yes," he said simply. Was rewarded with a fierce hug. "Now," he cautioned, extracting himself from the embrace before the possessiveness that was stirring in his blood grew any stronger, "you must rest."

He caressed her head once, drew the covers close around her, then left her to sleep. Humans were less tactile with their offspring and close relations than his own kind, and for the first time, Stekin was understanding that. With this new...biology alignment, with his instincts so strong and skin so sensitive, he could now understand how touch might be uncomfortable.

He found his way downstairs, into the servant hall, to the kitchens. There he found Claude, as he had expected. They played cards in silence until dawn. The orb lay heavy and wrong against Stekin's leg, but his thoughts were only of Arten.

17

THE FUNNY CAKE
ARTEN

Arten healed slowly. She couldn't stop remembering the slick knot moving up her throat and out her mouth. Her gorge rose every time she thought of it: the barest edge of sharp teeth, the wall of Stekin's power... The oily sphere. The cocoon of glacial cold.

She ached inside where his power had taken hunks of...*something* when it had been stripped away. But she was no longer sweltering all the time, no longer had constant fatigue dragging at her. Kylik came to visit her daily for a while, then every few days, until he declared her healthy and stopped coming altogether.

She slipped into a routine without becoming aware of it. Life was...easier. People mostly left her alone now. Partly because she was out of the way and so out of their minds, partly because there were fewer people down here on the third circuit, and partly because she didn't venture outside her small sphere of comfort. She saw Natalia daily and found a wary peace, if not a friendship, there—though Arten had never admitted to the older girl what Emilette had revealed to her. Micah, her moving-day rescuer, continued to drop by at unexpected intervals, but Arten was either on her way out the door or on her way to bed, so they didn't end up talking much. Just the fact that he dropped by to say hello was enough to lift her spirits.

Then there was Stekin. Whom she now saw twice a day.

Once in the early afternoon, after her morning chores in Natalia's compound were done and before the evening chores began. Arten had started helping prepare the meals at Natalia's in the mornings and evenings in return for assistance with her laundry. She and Emilette generated a considerable amount of laundry for two people, which Arten blamed on Stekin—if he would come around less often or were not so infuriatingly sensitive to smell, she would have a quarter of the work. Natalia seemed to have the same amount for a compound of four to Arten's two.

When Stekin came during her midday break, they would sit together on her back patio, the sun baking heat into his scales even as the wind stole it from her, filling the air with the scent of dragon and dying leaves. As the weather had gotten colder, even though she'd been strong enough to make the journey up to the Hill once he'd removed the net, he'd insisted on meeting her down here. She would practice touching her power—which was so much easier now than it had been—and he would snap criticisms at her. But then he'd angle a wing to shield her from the wind or rumble an approval, and she'd know he was more pleased with her progress than he wanted to admit.

He'd fly away, she'd go back to Natalia's compound and finish out her chores, eat with them, then back to her own rented compound. To while away the hours until Stekin came again. Under the cover of night, silently stealing in through the false stone in the back wall he'd shown her. How he managed to cross the yard without her ever seeing him, or to enter the house and her reading room with barely a sound, was always a source of wonder to her. There was a hidden latch in the hallway door that only he could open, and he always entered that way and never crossed the threshold into her room.

He was always careful—waiting until Emilette had gone to bed or gone out for the evening. Sometimes he waited so long that Arten had fallen asleep in her chair, locked into the little room, safe from the world. Since Arten had moved into the new, third-circuit compound, Emilette had found more and more reasons to stay out late, sometimes staying away all night. Stekin had been unhappy about this behavior but permitted it since it meant he had more opportunities to visit Arten unobserved.

It was imperative no one discover these late-night meetings. Stekin had told her what people would think was happening between them if they found out, and it had been mortifying enough just having that conversation with Stekin that she was determined no one else would ever know. After that distinctly uncomfortable talk, Arten often blushed to remember the days he'd spent in her rooms after the Unity festival and what people probably still thought.

All of the things he'd mentioned, the *deviancy* as he called it, were far from the truth. Both then and now. But the truth was something she couldn't tell.

Because what really happened in those nightly meetings was a detailed accounting of her day in Natalia's compound.

Arten was a spy. She was spying on the closest thing she had to a friend. It felt horrible, sometimes, and if Natalia ever found out... But she reminded herself, when guilt seized her, that it was for the best. Stekin had refused to tell her what he suspected or what exactly he was looking for, only that he was trying to protect the four sources living in the compound. He wanted to know the times that each of the sources left and returned; where they went, if she could find out; how tired or energized they were upon their return; and what and how much they ate. He was especially interested in any time they went up the Hill, and she had learned to pay special attention to their state upon return in order to satisfy his interrogations.

She was also to report to him anything suspicious or strange, no matter how innocuous it seemed.

Her observational skills improved drastically, and she began to see patterns in the movements of the household. She began to be able to predict when Stekin's brows would pull down, when suspicion would tighten his mouth at her report. Not that he ever said anything, told her anything except, "Every observation is helpful."

It was frustrating, not knowing what was going on. But the way he looked at her after her report, sometimes—like she was *important*. How he would sometimes say, "This helps more than you know." Made her feel needed, useful. Made her feel less alone.

But nothing suspicious had happened in her month here. And they were both getting frustrated with the waiting.

WINTER CAME ABRUPTLY, screaming down from the mountains, coating the valley in ice and snow overnight. Emilette had not banked the fire the night before, when she'd slunk in after midnight bell, so the compound was frigid this morning.

Emilette, predictably, was sleeping in, leaving the morning to Arten. With the snow outside, the world seemed hushed, waiting. She didn't bother with the fire—Emilette could fix it when she got up—but bundled up in the winter gear and new boots Stekin had bought for her and traipsed out into the untouched world.

Three compounds down on the wall-side, she shoved open a familiar gate, breaking apart the snowbank around it, and blazed a path around the side of the house to the back door. An unsmiling blond face opened the door to her knock.

"Good morning, Viktor," Arten said.

He hated door duty; Arten was beginning to suspect that's why he'd been given the task by his other compound-mates. He said nothing. Arten expecting nothing else.

Viktor left Arten in the hall and retreated upstairs. Arten sighed and unwrapped herself, hung her long coat on the stand behind the door. Wondered if today was going to be a good day.

Some days Natalia was fine, seemed to enjoy Arten's company. Other days, she was as frigid as the blizzard last night and treated Arten like a burden. To Arten's eyes, there was no discernible reason for these shifts, but she kept them open and reported all to Stekin.

Arten stamped her boots free of snow then made her way down the tight hall to the kitchen. It was warm, the fire hot, griddle cakes sizzling on the inset stove. Natalia had her back to Arten, chopping something into furious bits.

"You're late," Natalia said, her voice as hard as her chopping. That didn't bode well.

Arten knew what was expected. She pulled up the short stool to the fireside to turn the flatcakes.

Considering how skinny Carl and Viktor are, I can't believe how much food they eat, she thought, carefully turning the densely packed cakes one by one. Carl was still emaciated, no matter how much food she and Natalia tried to force down him. Even Natalia was thin, and she ate as much as the rest of them. Only Raccard seemed to be healthy. She brushed the outline of Ergin's knife under her clothes, reassured by its presence and weight.

Raccard hasn't tried anything, he barely even looks at me—so why am I still nervous around him?

She was thinking of how he had cornered her in the back yard, how small and alone she had felt, and not about the fragile cakes. One on the end split, half of it sliding into the fire. She scowled and marshalled her thoughts back to her job. By the time she had finished flipping them, the first ones were nearly ready to come off. She got a plate, stacked the crisp cakes on it, balancing them in a precarious tower. She left the broken one to last, nibbled on it as she took the plate to the sturdy table and plunked it down in the center. She was licking her fingers of the grease and to cool them when Natalia shouted:

"What do you think you're doing? Those aren't for you!"

Arten jerked, startled by the anger on the girl's face. "Sorry? It was a little mangled piece. I didn't think you'd mind. I'm hungry."

Arten's breakfast was always ready when she arrived but she hadn't had time to eat it today because she'd been late.

"These," Natalia speared her knife at the platter of hot cakes, "aren't for you. Those," she jabbed it to the far end of the table where Arten's two individual cakes were waiting on a plate, "are for you. Look," she snarled, "if you're not going to help just take them and get out of here."

"I'll help!" Arten snapped, jumping to her feet, "What's the big deal? I'm sorry I ate your precious flatcake, but it's not like you said anything to me! How was I supposed to know?"

"Yeah, you are sorry," Natalia sneered. Arten's face burned. "Just get out," Natalia shouted, "I don't need you making a muck of things today."

"Fine!" Arten shouted right back. "I don't need you talking down to me, either."

She stormed out of the room, barreled past Viktor in the hall, sending him crashing into the wall. She heard his confused question, ignored it, throwing her coat and hat on. Heard him demanding an answer from Natalia. Natalia was just laying into him when Arten threw the door closed behind her and stomped back the way she'd come.

But she couldn't stay mad. Walking through the snow, the burning in her legs and lungs, reminded her of Maruko and Juro and their winter excursions. She missed them fiercely.

Just when I thought I was finally finding a friend here, she lamented, *Natalia turns into a total jerk. What does she mean, screaming at me like that for eating a stupid flatcake?* It was as abrupt and heart-wrenching as when Juro had declared he was too old to play with 'little girls' anymore and cut her out of his life.

But he apologized for that, eventually. Natalia is much prouder than Juro, though; I doubt she'll *apologize.*

But it wasn't about the apology, not really. Juro had explained why he'd pushed Arten away—his family's expectations of his marriage and how he was coming to regard Arten as more than a friend had made him think it was best to distance herself before either of them got hurt. Never mind that she was years from being marriageable at the time.

Well, I know Natalia doesn't want to marry me. If for no other reason than because sources weren't allowed to marry. *I've never gotten the feeling that she was interested; it's more like she can barely stand me some days. On the good days, I think she just likes having someone to talk to. But it's not like she's happy that it's me, just someone.*

Arten kicked a snowdrift. *So why'd she act like that?*

She reached her temporary compound, considered going back in. Knew Emilette would still be asleep and Stekin wouldn't be arriving for another two hours for her lessons in taming her power. She imagined his disappointed scowl as she told him she'd stormed out, imagined the lecture he'd give her tonight about how every observation was vital.

She had no desire to sit in a cold house and dwell on Stekin's censure, and the air and snow were invigorating, so she crouched down in the yard and drew him a quick message in the snow.

"Went to city."

She used his symbol, or as close as she could approximate it from memory and with only her mitten for drawing. *He'll find it and wait, or come after me. Either way, I'm not sticking around here.*

THE CITY WAS FARTHER AWAY than she expected. Whether because the snow slowed her down or because it obscured landmarks, once she passed the icy cliff-stairs, it seemed to take forever before the first wooden buildings peeked around the edge of the cliffs. She walked a little faster, following the curve of the road until the whole cluttered city was before her.

It seems so small, she thought, disappointed. After being around the compounds and up the Hill where everything was built to accommodate dragon-access, the buildings seemed tiny and too-close together. The road narrowed as it entered the town, buildings pushed in on each other on all sides. It was still wide enough for a dragon Kylik's size to walk down, she noted as she walked along it, but he would have to keep his wings tight. Nhemith wouldn't fit.

And it's so fragile, she thought, imagining Kylik's wings tearing the wooden shingles off storefronts as he shifted them, his tail pulverizing glass windows as he twitched it thoughtlessly. How long since she'd seen dwellings made of anything but stone? *The last house in the network.* It made her realize that it had been half a year since she'd left her home. It seemed so much longer than that.

She stared around her, drinking in the sight of the human town. The streets were clogged with snow, but it was clear people had stamped down trails as they moved about. Smoke curled out of surprisingly few chimneys, but as her eyes moved up, she saw that atop the cliff rested another half of the town. More smoke was apparent there, and the buildings seemed a bit broader and sturdier.

She'd started to feel strange when she passed beyond the first rundown buildings but dismissed it as nerves—it had been a year and a half since she'd gone with her father to Laird, the nearest town with a respectable merchant faire. And the buildings in Laird had not been so tall, nor so pressed-together, as these. It was noisy in the streets, the sounds of industry and people mixed together, spilling out of doorways and windows, even if most people she passed were rushing to keep out of the snow today. But by the time she reached a grand stone staircase that marched back through the side of the cliff, she knew her feeling wasn't nerves but something physical.

She stumbled, then sank on the bottom-most stair, leaned her back against the artificially smoothed cliff-wall, and wondered how she was going to get to the top. She wasn't going to let a bit of a weird feeling stop her. The stairs were snow-crusted, and based on the evidence under her, had a film of ice below. Unlike the steps to the dragon's Hill, these were wide and generous, and there was a groove cut into the cliff-stones that traced the slope at hand-height. The problem was more that the world was spinning a little and she felt like it might fall away.

It slipped, but the snow caught her. *Thoughtful.* She smiled.

"Hey, kid." A face interrupted her musings on an icicle-crusted roofline. "You okay?"

"I feel funny," she admitted.

"Yeah, you're acting funny. Why don't you come inside and warm up a bit?"

"You have a nice voice. You're a nice person. I like you," she said. The man belonging to the face had pulled her to her feet, had one of her arms over his shoulder and was walking her across the street to a little shop.

"Sure, kid," he muttered. He pushed open a door and got her inside. She ended up on a stool, leaning against a wooden counter that was more a table than anything else.

"Do you live here?" she asked.

"No. It's my shop," he said, from behind the counter. She heard sounds of him rummaging through something.

"Oh," she said. "You know it's all wrong."

"What do you mean?" He tucked something around her —a blanket. She snugged it close with a noise of appreciation.

"Why are you frowning?" she asked. "Did you know your eyes are the color of that bird I met?"

"How could I know that?" He sighed, a hand passed over his face, then rubbed his temples.

"It screams like a lady."

"That's interesting," he said, not sounding interested at all. "Hey, what's your name, kid?"

"Arten."

"Arten, great. I'd like to get you home, Arten. Does that sound good?"

"I want to go home," she agreed, "but I can't."

"Sure you can," he urged, "you can always go home. It can't be that bad."

She frowned and drew herself up. "What's *your* name?"

"Tam."

"Well, Tam. You're very nice. And I like you a lot. You can't help it if your eyes look like that bird that almost got me murdered. And you seem like a good person, even if your shop is all wrong. But I can never go home, and you saying I can is just going to be upsetting to me. So I wish you wouldn't."

"Sure, kid," he said hastily, nonplussed. "You just, uh, stay here as long as you need."

"You're a nice person, Tam. Thank you. Have I said that?"

"Yeah, kid."

She rambled on for a while, unable to collect her thoughts, unable to stop talking. Tam's face grew more and more alarmed the longer she stayed.

"Kid, you sure no one's looking for you?" he asked, dodging her question about why he had so few customers coming in.

"Oh. You're right, he's probably looking for me! I should go," she said, sliding off the stool. She fumbled out of the blanket, got it draped over his shoulder after two tries.

"Hey, I can't let you go out like this!" His hand closed around her arm. "If you go to sleep in a snowbank again, you'll freeze to death."

"Then I won't sleep in a snowbank. I'm not stupid. I'm just...I'm just....I don't know what I am. But he's going to be worried if I don't get back." She pulled towards the door, but Tam held her back.

"You're in no shape—" he started. Was interrupted by the door slamming open, wintry wind rushing in.

"Unhand her," a voice growled.

"Excuse me, sir." Tam bristled, but Arten interrupted him this time.

"Oh, you're here! Good, I don't have to look for you."

"You know him?" Tam asked.

Arten felt a wave of spontaneous gratitude towards the shopkeeper and gave him a hug. Tam was startled enough to release her. "Thank you!" she said, then tripped over to Stekin. "Why are you frowning like that? It's not his fault his shop is so bad. Well...I guess it *is* his fault, but it's just because he doesn't know better."

"Arten, you are unwell," Stekin said, his frown deepening.

"I know," she lamented, "I feel squishy inside. And I really want to hug you, but I know you wouldn't like that, so I'm not. And I can't stop talking. But this man has been really nice, even if his eyes look like that bird."

"Come," he said, shooting a dark look over Arten's head at Tam.

Arten followed the look in time to see the man raise his hands as he said, "I didn't see anything, you were never here."

Stekin made a low noise—a threat?—then pushed Arten outside, his fingers strong on her shoulder, propelling her ahead of him. Not into the street, but to the stairs. He switched his grip to her arm as he walked her up the stairs.

"Where are we going?" she asked, trying not to slip. Stekin seemed to have no problem with traction.

He didn't answer, instead said, "Tell me what happened this morning."

She told him about Emilette forgetting the fire, about Natalia shouting at her, about feeling strange once she got to town.

"You ate something?"

"That's why Natalia yelled at me," she complained. "But I *always* eat those cakes for breakfast. How was I supposed to know *their* cakes are *special* cakes and I'm not allowed to eat them? They're the same thing! So what, does she think the cakes'll get dirty or something if I touch them? It's stupid!"

"I see," he said. His fingers tightened on her arm as her foot slipped to the side. "These special cakes—there were enough for everyone?"

"Yes!"

"So it is safe to assume that all four members of the household ate them today."

"Yeah. It's the same number I always make. Well, except for the one that half-fell in the fire and I, burn me on a pyre, ate."

He made a hard noise. They were at the top of the stairs. "Climb on my back. We have little time." He knelt and she hooked her legs through the crook of his waiting elbows, clasped her arms about his neck. Then he was up and jogging away, his long legs clearing the snow more easily than hers had.

"Where are we going?" she asked, making herself small against his back. Her stomach churned unhappily.

"To Kylik."

"Oh," she said, but before she could ask more she

became distracted. "Your hair is softer than it used to be. How did that happen?"

"Is it?"

"Mmm. And you smell nice."

"Please stop sniffing me," he said, jerking his head away.

"I can't," she said. "It makes me feel fuzzy. Like a hug for my nose." She pressed her nose against his neck. How had she never noticed he was cuddly, not prickly, before?

"Enough," he snapped. "If you cannot control yourself, I will put you to sleep."

"Fine." She huffed a sigh, resting her chin on her shoulder, looking away from him. She managed to make it to Kylik's without giving in to the desire to smell him or touch his hair or, once, bite him. She didn't know where the strange impulses were coming from, but Kylik gave her something which tasted terrible and made her vomit. And after that she fell asleep.

THE RUMBLE of too-large voices awakened her. She cracked an eye open, saw unfamiliar stone walls. Their distance and the makeshift pallet under her indicated she was in a dragon's home. The walls were reddish-green, the floor a burgundy marble so polished, she thought she would be able to see herself in it. She started to lift herself to an elbow but quickly sunk back down into the nest of tough leather pillows. Everything ached. She closed her eyes again, resigned to wait for another try.

The voices rolled over her. That was Kylik's voice, and it was raised in agitation.

"—right away. There is not a moment to lose!" he was saying.

"Even if it is as you say," an unfamiliar voice said, full of haughtiness and disdain, "I cannot bring charges on so little, tangential evidence."

"Are you not listening?" Kylik snapped, "They are in danger *right now*. You must do something!"

"What would you have me do?" the other huffed.

"Fetch them out! Allow me to examine and treat them!"

"That is dangerously close to interference with another's source..."

Kylik snarled. "Are you being intentionally obtuse?"

"Are you?" the voice drawled back, then sharpened. "By your own admission, you suspect this is not the first time these measures have been employed. Clearly, the sources involved survived then, and they will do so again. If I accost them now, on the scant evidence of your testimony and the kaz's, any charges will be overturned during the trial. It is better to wait and observe, gather more concrete evidence."

"I care nothing of your trial and charges," Kylik yelled, "but of those lives that are even now in jeopardy! Kaz, you must stop this at once."

"Do not council the kaz to folly," the other voice snapped. "His concerns are much greater than the lives of a few sources."

"Enough," Stekin's voice rang out, an icy dagger.

Arten felt a loosening in her back, as tension she hadn't noticed seeped away. She felt a little silly at thinking Kylik, no matter how angry, would let harm come to her. And embarrassed that Stekin's mere voice had reassured her so easily. *He's a dragon,* she reminded herself. But the caution rang hollow.

Stekin's words were hard and clipped as he said, "Ktet, this is happening. I want you there in your official capacity, to bear impartial witness to what we find, but I do not need you. Your objections have been noted," he silenced the beginnings of protests. "Kylik, prepare your treatments for travel. As for you, Ktet, I expect your support or your silence."

Arten heard the faint clicking of Kylik's dulled claws as he trotted away. Then the light scratching of longer, sharper claws. The movement of scales over stone. The soft noises of wings shifting.

Ktet's voice was strained with bitter politeness as he said, "I will join you. If this is to be official, I must retrieve my medallion. I would not want my *official* presence to be mistaken for *personal interest*."

There was a small growl of warning from Stekin, then wings bearing someone away.

Someone approached with a two-beat gait. Arten's eyes darted to the high, arched doorway. Stekin seemed so tiny as he passed between the shiny marble pillars. She pushed herself upright, stifling the groan as the muscles in her chest and back protested loudly.

"What's wrong?" she asked when Stekin's glossy black boots paused just beyond the spill of rough leather. They were almost as reflective as the floor. He crouched, his hands reached out, found their place along her either side of her jaw. They were warm.

"Do not concern yourself," he said, but there was no bite in his words. "You are safe here until I return. No dragon would risk Kylik's wrath by intruding into his infirmary."

Somehow that didn't reassure her. She rubbed her aching ribs. "What happened? I remember...Natalia. I was angry at Natalia. We shouted at each other...and I left? But I don't... Why am I here?"

"You found it," Stekin said quietly, his thumb tracing over her cheek in small, anxious strokes. "Carl's poison."

"I did?" She didn't remember that. "Is he...are they...?"

"I am going to retrieve them as soon as Kylik returns." He brought his forehead down to rest against hers, the field of his eyes filled her vision. She saw a shimmer of golden light moving behind his irises, and the black curve of his pupils. Couldn't look away. Didn't want to.

Her hand reached out, cupped around the sharp, impossibly smooth angle of his jaw. His pupils flared wide, an eager maw that pushed the emerald bands into thin rims. Once, it would have terrified her.

The stiff line of his nose was pressed against her cheek, his breath was a hot stream down her face falling over the cliff of her jaw. *What is this?* she thought, even as she remembered: Nhemith in a shaft of sunlight atop the hill, Stekin reaching up for her, pulling her face to his, their brows pressed close. How she had looked away, embarrassed at the intimacy.

The Words inside her churned, fraying free of the ropes she'd been carefully training them into under Stekin's guidance. They dissolved to chaos. Something dark in her shifted, separated. Pressed upwards, driving the Words before it.

Stekin's eyes went wide, alarmed. He wrenched himself away—she hadn't realized she was the one pulling them closer until that moment. The shadow in her stilled, drifted back down. She felt it settle, mold back into a place at her core that was carved just for it. Then disappear, so that if she hadn't just felt it, she would never have known it was there. She saw her shock mirrored on Stekin's face where he sprawled on the floor.

He had one arm was thrown up between them, as if to ward her away, the other he leaned on, recoiling. His cheeks were flushed, his teeth bared as his breath heaved. She could see the rapid throb of his pulse in his neck. Was he frightened? They just stared at each other, wide-eyed, confused. Then all at once he went rigid, jumped to his feet.

"Wait," she whispered. He didn't pause in his turn from her. Then she heard it: the sound of Kylik's claws. Stekin was stalking away. "Let me come with you?"

He said nothing, and she may have imagined the falter in his step. He was through the archway, disappearing down the hallway beyond. The soft sound of his boots met those of Kylik's claws. Some low words were exchanged, then the heavier sound of wings and human feet running.

18

THE KAZ RESTORED
STEKIN

S tekin ran. Not towards Carl and his compound-mates. Away. Away from Arten. Away from the cold tingling that was raking daggers along his spine. He clenched his hands into fists, nails digging into his palms. But it didn't erase the memory of his fingers curved behind her ear, pulling her closer to him. Of that moment, just a fraction of a second, where he had seen not Arten but Lien.

Stop it! he snarled at himself. He was bounding down the icy steps, Kylik winging overhead. The wind tore at him, stealing away his heat. *This is not the time. You need to focus on what is waiting for you in that compound. Not Lien. Not Arten.* But he could feel her, behind him. Could sense her power moving, coming after them. He was half-tempted to turn back and stop her. His foot slipped on the ice, he came down heavily on his other leg, sending pain shooting through his ankle.

Focus! he snapped at himself.

He thought about shifting into his natural form, but it would take more time to sort out the limbs and clothes during the process than it would to sprint, and the power loss to fuel his sprint over this distance was negligible. He managed to scrape together enough presence of mind to arrive outside Alectros's third circuit compound without further injuring himself.

Kylik was circling to land. Ktet was dropping from the clouds high overhead. How had Ktet arrived before them? *His mother was descended from the desert clans,* Stekin remembered belatedly. He had forgotten that, with Ktet's jungle clan coloring. She had been a terrifically fast flier, with as much grace as a duck. She had been strangely suited to the lumbering oaf that became her consort and Ktet's father, though Stekin had wondered when they first mated how they would manage the flights. He had never been crass enough to learn, and Ktet had been born, so clearly they managed.

Stekin shook himself mentally. Ktet and Kylik were both on the ground, the former bundling a fur-lined robe about himself, positioning his medallion of office over his shoulders. It was made for his dragon form, so the heavy bronze plaque drooped down below his hips, but it clearly declared his legal capacity here. Which was all Stekin needed. A witness who could not be denied.

"I will intercept any who leave," Kylik offered. Stekin understood his unwillingness to shift forms and simply nodded. He gestured to Ktet to proceed.

Ktet's control over his human expressions was unpracticed, and the curl of his lip and fingers told Stekin all he needed to know about the dragon's willingness to be here. But his voice was strong and loud, and he stated formally:

"There has been an accusation that the sources at this compound are being neglected. The complaint comes from Kaz Stekin, backed by findings of Kylik the healer, and is levelled in specific, to Alectros who claims Carl as a source,

and in general, against all dragons who claim sources herein
—Hiranyath, who claims Natalia; Graug, who claims
Raccard; and Nyyrikki, who claims Viktor. We will be
lawfully entering the premises in one minute with the intent
of removing all sources for a health examination and to
verify the living conditions of all inhabitants."

The seconds ticked by with agonizing slowness. Stekin
expected the dragons to come boiling out, protesting. He
expected sources to emerge, pleading for refuge. Neither
happened. At twenty-three seconds, there was a small cry
from inside. Only one, and very faint. At forty seconds, footsteps approached the door. At forty-four seconds, it opened,
and a dragon emerged.

"It was an accident," Alectros pleaded, his eyes too-wide,
staring at Stekin. His human face was ashen, his hand trembled at his side.

"What have you done?" Stekin roared, his voice too weak
in this puny form to convey his anger properly.

"It was an accident," Alectros repeated, his eyes unfocused as he retreated into himself.

Stekin lunged for him, but a noise of protest from Ktet
stopped his assault. If Stekin attacked Alectros now, he
would prove bias against the dragon he was investigating,
and all his efforts to this point would be undone. Everything
they found inside that compound—whatever had shocked
Alectros to insensibility—would be for naught.

Stekin constrained himself to restless pacing. Counted
down the seconds.

At the minute mark, he sprang forwards, threw Alectros
aside, and darted into the compound. At a minute three, he
found Carl.

Stekin dropped to his knees, took the dead body in his
arms.

Carl was still warm, his face twisted in alarm and pain, no indication there of how Alectros had killed him. Poison? Then how could it have been an accident? More likely, Alectros had drawn too much and broken the delicate wellspring of power.

Stekin closed Carl's eyes, smoothed the lines from his face. It was a useless gesture. He rose, Carl's limp form lolling in his arms.

"This is your fault," a female voice croaked.

Stekin looked about for the first time. Noted the pallet and its rumpled occupant, blankets drawn tightly around her, pieced it together with the scents in the air and Alectros's shock.

"Yes," he agreed. "I should have moved sooner."

"No, you shouldn't have given him a minute. He panicked. And Carl's the one who's dead," she shot back. A knife of guilt wrenched in Stekin's gut.

He noted her brand, would have recognized her without it from Arten's investigations. "You are Hiranyath's," he said. Natalia just glared her hatred out at him. "Will you testify? You witnessed what Alectros did to his source. Help me end this. Tell us what happened."

"No. You sentenced me into *her* servitude. Figure it out yourself. Fix it or don't. Just leave me alone."

A weak part of himself wanted to protest, *Not me, I was not part of this.* But his absence had caused this. He was kaz. His people had strayed. She was right—it was his place to fix it, not hers. His place to find the truth of what had happened in this room, of the poison, of the source thefts. Of what these dragons were hiding. What Natalia had been through he could only guess, but he would not be the one to put her through more.

He turned to leave the room, Carl heavy and still against

him. "Dress yourself," he said over his shoulder, "your health must be examined."

"Burn on a pyre," she snarled.

"THIS IS FOOLISH," Ktet hissed, hours later.

Carl's body had been examined by Kylik, then taken away for burial. The healer had confirmed Carl's power had been ripped from him and the shock of it had killed him. Which made sense, given the state of the body and the timing of the death, but left Stekin consternated because it didn't explain the poison or why Natalia had been in the room.

Kylik had been so incised by the evidence of Alectros's neglect that Stekin had only just managed to calm him. Fortunately, Ktet had performed his duties as expected without the kaz's supervision.

Causing the death of a source was the most heinous crime in their law. As such, Alectros was confined within an abandoned house on the Hill; a much more comfortable cell than most were afforded. He was under oath and guard to prevent his leaving. In accordance with their law, Alectros was now in a state of *finding* where his interactions would be limited. Although he had guards around the premises, they were forbidden to interact with him as he was with them. His consort and mate, if he had one, the kaz, and his accuser, were it not the kaz, would be able to meet with him, but all meetings would be supervised by the judicial council. He would remain in *finding* until the judicial council had gathered enough reports and evidence to form a judgement.

Normally, the *finding* dredged up the details of a person's private life and character. It illuminated the dark corners the person sought to keep hidden as well as the brighter ones that defined them publicly. The judicial council would weigh the whole person, determine whether the accusations were valid, and agree on the reparations. In situations where the crimes put the community at risk of exposure to the outside world or jeopardized the health of its members, the individual at fault could not be allowed to continue the behavior. They would be executed.

Alectros's crimes, the murder of his source and endangerment of Natalia—not to mention the previously dismissed source-theft—were of this latter nature. He would be executed. But not without the investigation that was his right, not without uncovering the extent of his deviancy.

Deviancy, in this combined culture of dragons and sources and unpowered humans, could mean many things, from the relatively innocuous thoughts, like coveting of objects or persons outside one's race, to more severe actions, like murder or allowing a source to copulate. Stekin understood deviancy and the treacherous path from thought to action as no one but Nhemith, who had witnessed the terrible consequences of it alongside him, might. At the core of it, all deviancy came down to a betrayal of the safety and sanctity of the sources. It was a rot that took hold in the mind and slowly corrupted one, making unthinkable transgressions possible.

In a community as small as Stekin's, once revealed, there would be no hope of hiding the truth of Alectros's deeds—it would spread through their number as though borne on the wind; it would be as pervasive as the alignment that now cursed nearly all of them.

The things revealed would be shocking, horrifying— and they would open his people's minds to possibilities. Possibilities Stekin had sacrificed so much to expunge. Even the most honest and law-abiding of people could be tempted once their minds were open, once they had been shown how easy deviance could be...and how difficult to detect.

Stekin could not risk his people being exposed to the knowledge of Alectros's deeds. He had spent too much blood in cleansing the rot from his community in the Great Purge, washing it from their minds and souls, to let them be corrupted once more. He needed a third option.

He needed Alectros to agree to a trial by combat.

Ancient ways for the ancient—Graug will be pleased. Stekin's lip curled at the thought.

Ktet, still awaiting Stekin's response, bared his teeth; his wings went loose as he misinterpreted Stekin's reaction. "It is my right and responsibility to investigate this fully. We deserve the truth! Alectros must not be allowed to escape this crime."

"With respect, Ktet, you fail to understand what is at stake," Stekin countered. "If he is allowed to testify, I may not be able to contain the damage. I must speak with him and convince him to forgo the investigation."

Ktet huffed back, "With respect, *kaz*, I know my duties and station. Our people deserve the truth of this matter."

Stekin snarled and wished he were in his true form so he could lash Ktet with his teeth and release the anger that boiled inside him. "Your pride blinds you! This is not about you and the glory of your investigation. This is about the continued existence of our race. If the details of Alectros's deeds become known, the rot will spread. It is bad enough that people will know how he murdered his source. Do you wish them to know *why* that happened? To know of the poison? To know he was complicit in, if not present for, his source copulating with another source? We do not yet know what motivated Alectros, but there are no valid reasons for any of his crimes. A *finding* would force us to make the answers public. Do you wish to be responsible for necessitating the next Purge?"

Ktet reacted with a moment of genuine fear at the word 'purge'. "Surely not! He is just one...a purge? No...you are overwrought, kaz, and not thinking clearly."

"*You* are the one not thinking!" Stekin growled. "You have never flown these skies, and I refuse to allow you to jeopardize my people with your willful ignorance. Step aside, or I will remove you."

Stekin did not have to specify from *what* he would remove Ktet, but he put enough weight into the word that Ktet gulped, and the contraction of the younger dragon's pupils and wavering of his wingtips showed he understood Stekin's meaning.

But Ktet did not step aside. "I do not contest that you would have been a match for him once," Ktet offered, conciliatory, "but now? Kaz...you will throw away your life, and he will go free. Whatever atrocities he has committed, he will be pardoned to continue. You cannot dispute that such an outcome would be worse than the risk that his deeds become known."

Stekin felt his eyes burn, felt himself straighten. In this form, Ktet dwarfed him, yet still he managed to stare Ktet down, teeth exposed. "You forget yourself, Ktet. You forget who I am, the lengths to which I will go to protect my people and this city. You know nothing of the Great Purge, you know nothing of *me*. But you will." His tone darkened, and he saw the swallow travel down Ktet's throat. "I will make an example of Alectros, and I will not allow his deviancy to spread. And you will call to your ancestors and, if you are intelligent, listen when they tell you not to get in my way."

Ktet's wing-tips trembled. "Yes, kaz," he whispered.

"Now," Stekin snarled, "take me to him."

"Yes, kaz," Ktet agreed, relieved, and miserable.

KTET TROTTED to keep apace of Stekin as he stalked up to the house that was Alectros's jail. Stekin's feet were silent over the broken, dirty flagstones, despite the sweeping pace he set.

Alectros was at the center of the house, in the open courtyard. He stared not up into the sky or at the near mountains but at the ground, as though the murky, weed-speckled mosaic with its shattered tiles held answers for him. His eyes rose from the floor with a slowness that seemed almost reluctant, and eventually met Stekin's. By the time Alectros had roused himself from his stupor, Stekin was standing in front of him.

"Kaz," Alectros acknowledged.

Stekin knew his eyes were burning, and he glared his anger and disappointment at Alectros. Was rewarded with a shudder that ran the length of Alectros's neck and sides. He was afraid. *As is ought,* Stekin thought grimly.

"Carl is dead," Stekin said, harsh and unfeeling. Wanted to add, but could not yet legally, *You killed him.*

Alectros sounded empty as he said, "I know," but he flinched as though struck, and there was a brief spear of pain across his features before it was wiped away with the blankness.

It was enough to convince Stekin that Carl's death had indeed been accidental.

"Regardless of intent, your actions caused Carl's death. Then there is the matter of the poison. And there is no possible justification for what Hiranyath's source was doing with yours. You will be investigated, your full deviance will be discovered, and your name will be a blight in the minds of all who have loved you," the kaz threatened.

Alectros blinked slowly, then acknowledged, "This I know."

"You will be found guilty and deviant, and I will execute you. Everyone will know the extent of your weakness; everyone will know your shame. You will submit to me, for all to see, and bear your throat like the coward you are. When I rip it open, our people will be *relieved* that someone as unworthy and base as you no longer taints our species. No one will mourn you, even those who found redeeming qualities in you before. Your bones will be discarded."

Again, the impassive, "This I know."

Stekin paused, scowling, letting the silence press down on the captive. Letting him turn that last phrase over and over in his mind.

Your bones will be discarded.

Since the Sundering, his people may have stopped consulting their ancestors out of shame, but they all hoped to join them on the wind at the end of their days. A new faith had begun to spread in the past two generations—a belief that once freed of their Sundered bodies, they would become whole and unified, and all else would be wiped away. Stekin could not know if it were true; he was the first and last of the Sundered from his own line, so there were none to answer any call he might make.

Regardless of whether the spirit reunified in death or remained Sundered for eternity, Stekin had promised that Alectros would know neither: *your bones will be discarded.* He would not receive the death rituals, his bones would not be carried to their rest, his spirit would not be freed from them. His flesh would rot, his bones turn to powder, and he would never join his ancestors.

Stekin saw the heaviness of this truth settle over the captive. Saw the tightening in his chest and throat as he held back emotion.

Then Stekin said, "However," his voice and face twisted with unfeigned disgust, "while you deserve no kindness, I will grant you a boon."

Alectros blinked slowly.

"If you choose to forfeit your *finding,* I will permit you a trial by combat. An opportunity to prove yourself a dragon, not a snake. To die with a dignity you do not deserve."

While his bones would still lay where they fell, it gave Alectros a chance at redemption.

It was common legend that death in combat would purify and free the spirit, even without the death rituals. Stekin had seen it happen once. He could still feel the scrape of foreign scales against his own as the dragon's body had fallen from the sky, crashing towards the icy plain below them. He could feel the shivery trails of something else as it whispered around him, rising. It had coalesced at his wing, nothing but a shimmer in the air, had paused there for a moment, as if assessing him, then had blown apart on the wind.

For all the dragons he had witnessed die in combat, Stekin had witnessed an ascension only that once, and that before the Sundering. He had no doubt Alectros's spirit would not ascend, though he would not tell him so.

Alectros blinked. Then again, faster. "And if I should win?"

Stekin grinned, mirthless and fierce. "You accept my offer, then?"

MORNING DAWNED late and cold and clear. False-winter was upon them; the slice of daylight was dwindling, the north winds were biting. Stekin crouched upon his balcony, watching the valley lighten below him. The wind wrapped fingers around him, drawing away his warmth, drawing hints of scent across his snout. Small promises of stunted pines, un-melting ice, and vast darkness. His power, his blood, stirred, remembering a time long forgotten.

It had been summer last time. And as much as the winter wind rejuvenated him, it would do as much for Alectros. Alectros was one of the last from the alpine lines. They were each of the last.

And this morning, we will be one fewer. A waste.

And the first of many. He knew. He had been here before. Exactly here, standing on his balcony, waiting for the sun to rise and the gong to ring and his role as executioner to begin. He knew exactly how many mornings he had been here, with these thoughts and doubts and anger. He remembered the names, the faces, the taste of each he had killed. He remembered the sounds of their bodies breaking against the ground.

He hated Alectros for the abuse of his source, for the deviancy that led them here. He hated Nhemith for pardoning the source-thieves and giving them sources of their own. He hated himself for the person he was about to become, for the devastation he was going to bring. Why had they not learned? Why were they forcing him into this position again?

What will happen to my people once I am dead? he lamented. *I leave for thirteen years and rot takes hold. What of the eternity after my death?* But he knew the answer. They would die. Slowly at first, then rapidly once the sources were scarce and the fighting began. He had averted just such disasters many times before. *And Nhemith, it seems, will not step in.*

He had never before felt so isolated. It had been about a century since the last of the Sundering survivors had gone, leaving just himself and Nhemith. The last time he stood here, a summer wind under his wings, execution before him, there had been hundreds who had lived through the Sundering.

Now, they were two.

I failed them all, he knew. His efforts may have kept them clinging to life, but he had not achieved reunification. He had not come close. Even with Arten, even if he could determine why she was so different, even if that got him closer to reunification, he doubted he would achieve it. He was old. The average lifespan for his people these days was a little over a century, growing shorter with each new generation.

Perhaps I have sheltered them too much from the world. We are stagnating here, seeped in our fear and complacency. The network is established, our wealth is established, our trade and resource lines are established. What do we have to strive for?

But the sun had risen, and wings of all shades and hues were stirring, moving towards the amphitheater—they were few enough to fit there, now. He raised his own—as blue as the sky and heavy as his guilt—and flew towards his duty.

KTET AND HIS charge were already there, waiting. Alectros's eyes never left Stekin. Behind Ktet stood Nhemith. Regal as always. She did not meet his eyes, looked pointedly away. It only increased the weight that threatened to drag his head down. He could not let it—he could not afford for Alectros to know how much he dreaded this.

The dragons assembled, reluctant whispers hissing through the crowd, tails and wings scraping at the rocks. Ktet would wait until more arrived, Nhemith would have advised that. Stekin scanned the crowd, meeting the eyes of any who sought him. There were a few, a precious few, who remembered the last time. Those were full of respect and apology. Others were curious, some even hostile. There were two pairs that did not belong, peering out from the shadow of a boulder. Arten and the girl who had been with Carl —*Hiranyath's Natalia,* he reminded himself.

Arten looked confused and afraid. He wanted to send her away but did not want to draw attention to her. He forced himself to move past her. Natalia had eyes only for Alectros, and they were full of hatred.

Hiranyath, he noticed, was not in attendance. Graug was there, and his orange eyes raked over Stekin like he was a fat goat in midwinter.

Nhemith made a small noise; Ktet took the cue.

"We are assembled today," he said smoothly in a clear, ringing voice—a voice Stekin could never replicate. A voice of calm and reason and persuasion. *Is this butchery the only reason I am kaz?* "We are assembled today to hear the charges against Alectros, as brought by Kaz Stekin and witnessed by Kylik and myself. Alectros has refuted the following charges: source-theft; neglect of his source, Carl; endangerment of a source that is not his own, Natalia; interference with a source that is not his own, Natalia; and murder of his source, Carl."

A susurration of shock and anger swept through the assembled. Stekin paid particular attention to those whom it did not touch. He noted them, committed their expressions to memory.

I will find your secrets, he thought viciously.

"Any one of these crimes warrants execution," Ktet was saying, "if the *finding* reveals them to be true."

He sounded sincere and regretful—*Nhemith's coaching at work,* Stekin knew, sparing her a glance. She was carefully impassive.

"Alectros," Ktet said, turning to him, "you have waived your right to a *finding* and have requested a trial by combat, is this correct?"

"Yes," Alectros hissed, tail lashing. Eager or frightened, Stekin could not tell. The air was filled with the sound of shifting scales and rustling wings, a formless whisper of confusion from the onlookers.

"Kaz Stekin will carry out your trial. If he fails, you are considered acquitted of all charges. If you fail to acquit yourself, your name will be recorded with these crimes forever in our record, all other reparations you owe will be invalidated, and your bones will rest where they fall. Do you understand and agree to the terms of this trial?"

"Yes," Alectros hissed again, his eyes flashing as he studied Stekin.

Eager, Stekin decided.

"Kaz, do you accept this duty with full understanding that if you fail, Alectros will be pardoned of all crimes stated today, all reparations you owe will be invalidated, and your bones may be removed by your loved ones to a place of rest?"

"Yes," Stekin agreed.

"All assembled today: have you witnessed the contract that has been made here?"

"Yes," rumbled a hundred throats. Some more enthusiastic than others.

"You may not interfere with either party at any time, even after the execution has concluded. Any interference will allow the wronged parties or their survivors to demand reparations of any severity. Is this understood?"

The assembled rumbled agreement again, unhappily.

"The execution will begin at the strike of the gong," Ktet said, backing gracefully away, leaving only Stekin and Alectros on the platform and Nhemith crouched in the rear by the great gong.

Alectros's eyes were blazing. He was so suffused with Carl's drained power that Stekin could see the faint shimmer of it under his scales. They squared off.

They were roughly the same size and build. Alectros was also alpine, though a descendant of clans in a different part of the world. Their powers were of the glaciers and frost and would be weak against one another. Alectros was younger than Stekin; his physical energy was naturally higher. And Stekin was still not the strongest on wing—he was still building his flight muscles from the long years of atrophy. But he had been frugal with Arten's power, and though he had less to work with than Alectros, and less than even a month ago, he had survived without a source's power for a very long time.

Despite his weaknesses, Stekin had one thing that put him ahead of Alectros. One thing that Alectros would spend all his physical power, all his magical power, combating. Stekin knew how to kill. Not just fragile humans, but dragons. Dragons of all types, all sizes, all powers. He knew how to kill Alectros a hundred times over. He only needed an opening, and it would be done. As he had done so many times before.

The wind pulled at him, his power roiled with the scent of home, the scent of death. His world narrowed to the alpine dragon mantling at him.

Then Nhemith's tail struck the gong, and they took to the air.

ALECTROS CLOSED ALMOST IMMEDIATELY. He knew, as well as Stekin, that this would be a physical contest more than anything else. Stekin fought to keep tooth and claw away, using his weight to throw his opponent off balance, forcing him to withdraw.

They closed, withdrew, closed again. Only minutes had passed, but they dragged on Stekin's wings like hours. The next time they closed, Alectros's rear claws hooked into a loosened scale on Stekin's barrel and ripped it away, gouging into his flesh.

He roared with pain.

Teeth darted for his throat, but Stekin writhed out of reach. He climbed for altitude, the younger dragon snapping at his tail, the scent of his blood heavy in the air.

Alectros was guarding his spine well, and his horned ruff was keeping Stekin's teeth at bay. And he had not yet touched that reserve of power. Stekin needed to get Alectros to use it so that when he made his move—whatever it would be—Alectros would have nothing to counter with.

Stekin folded his wings and dropped from the sky, darting past open jaws that raked along his flank. Alectros did not follow, not wishing to sacrifice the higher altitude

Stekin had given him. Stekin rolled in the air, released his power in a burst of tiny lances, then snapped his wings open and swooped up even as Alectros shoved his attack back at him.

The ice needles passed harmlessly beneath him. But Alectros was now circling above, wary, his tail thrashing.

He is wise not to attack with his power, Stekin thought with grudging respect. *So I must make him defend with it.*

He kept to the lower position, created wide openings along his sides and back to taunt Alectros into attacking, even as he fired off small, sporadic attacks of his own. Tiny lances of ice that he threw at Alectros's eyes and nose, small sharp hail that he released into the wind to pepper at his wings, all the while increasing that wind, drawing the frigid northern air to him, drawing it over both of them.

Alectros turned the first volleys back on Stekin with great shoves of power, but soon realized he could not keep that pace up. Stekin's attacks were small, targeted, and Alectros was countering them with wild flailing.

He went for small shields instead, and Stekin nibbled away at the edges, forcing him to expand them. Then Alectros shifted to dropping the shield between attacks to conserve his power. So Stekin made his needles smaller, sharper, sent them zipping towards him at terrific speed, forcing Alectros into spending the power anyway in throwing the shields up and tearing them down.

The dragon was getting irritated, his wings were pricked in myriad places, hot drops of blood flung out from them when they beat. Below, they pattered against Stekin's scales, misting him on all sides as he spun and twisted in the air. His own wound was sluggishly closing, he felt the sticky tightness of clotting blood when he stretched that side and rolled to feint another attack. His wings were strained, he did not know how much longer he could tax them. He sent a small band of his power through each, healing strained muscles. He needed just a little longer for Alectros to lose patience.

It took three more circuits, seven more stinging attacks, two of which landed. Stekin exposed his wound as he turned, seemingly careless, and Alectros snarled and fell from the sky darting for the weakness. But Stekin did not flee from the attack. He twisted and caught Alectros, binding with him, claws scraping for purchase against scales.

Alectros struggled, tried to break free. But his movements were sluggish, his wings and limbs stiff with cold. The north wind howled around them, biting at them.

Then, too late, Stekin saw Alectros understand. While Alectros had been circling, using up his power on protections, Stekin had been keeping warm below with his antics. The drain of Alectros's power had lowered his core temperature, removed his protection from the cold. And the wind had stolen his heat away, had chilled his blood in his wings and claws. And now he was outmatched by Stekin, whose body was still warm and loose.

Alectros struggled to free himself, struggled to stop their plummet to the ground, but Stekin was dead weight, pulling him down. Stekin could almost hear the strain on Alectros's wings but did not relent. There was one avenue left to him. Only one way to free himself from Stekin's entanglement before they both were shattered against the mountain.

He opened his jaws. Stekin waited. Waited until he felt the crackle of power under his claws, the sudden shock of frost just before the attack. Waited until Alectros was fully committed, until his jaw was loosened to expel the power.

And in that moment, Stekin reached out, grabbed Alectros's muzzle and lower jaw in an iron grip. Wrenched them apart.

The joints dislocated, then ripped in an instant—in *the* instant when Alectros was directing his power out. His power leapt free but was no longer directed. The bolt of power meant to stab Stekin through the chest turned into a formless cloud of frost and hail. Stekin released Alectros, kicked free, took the brunt of the attack on his shoulder as his cupped wings caught the air and arrested his free-fall. Ice coated his shoulder and the leading edge of one wing, shot cold pain through him, faltered his flight.

Through the cloud of his power, Stekin saw the confusion and rage in Alectros's eyes. Then the ice pouring from him closed fully over his face. Whether he was wondering how Stekin had gotten the better of him or why he was pulling away, no one would ever know.

There was the sound of shattering and a heavy impact, and Alectros was no more.

Stekin landed heavily beside him, unable to fully stop his own fall, jarring his legs and spine, cracking the ice on his wing free. He looked down at the already-glassy eyes of his almost-kin. Blood pooled under his former-opponent's rimed blue scales, turning the shattered remnants of his icy tomb into rubies.

Stekin climbed out of the snow crater, leaving Alectros to the wind and the sun. He left Alectros's bones to rot, left his name to be lost to time, left his spirit in the confines of his flesh, never to fly free with his ancestors. As he had done so wrenchingly many times before.

As someone would one day do to him.

Especially if they ever learned of the thing they could never be allowed to know. Of the guilt that drove him. That shaped his every action. That kept him alive when everyone else had let their soul fly free. That had crushed him until it turned his will to diamond. His choice that had doomed them all.

The kaz pushed through the loose snow as he made his limping way home.

19

THE CHOOSING
ARTEN

A rten bundled herself up. Winter was well upon them now, and it had snowed again last night. She would need to clear the path to the second circuit. She pulled her mittens on, glancing over at Natalia as she did so. Her blonde hair was streaked with orange from the fire on one side,and white from the snow-crusted window on the other.

"I'm headed out," Arten said cautiously. Natalia was hard and blank, said nothing.

"I'll just stay in today," Emilette chirped back. That had become her refrain since the snows had started falling. Since Natalia had moved in with them. She pushed a piece across the strategy board. Natalia's eyes flicked down to it, the line of her mouth hardened further. She moved her own piece with slow deliberation in a counter. Emilette made a noise like an angry cat. Natalia went back to staring at the opaque window, ignored the maid's sputtered protests.

Arten sighed, pulled her hat down around her ears, and left them to their game. Somehow Emilette managed to get Natalia to do things. Perhaps it was sheer irritation, but Arten suspected that wasn't it. Emilette was a little different with Natalia—not as loud, not as flighty. She could coax Natalia to eat, to dress more warmly, to play that infuriating game. Arten didn't understand how someone as quiet and private as Natalia could stand Emilette's incessant chatter.

But just last week, Natalia had started speaking again. Just a little. Only to Emilette. It was a start. Kylik had examined her multiple times before she'd refused to see him again. She was in good health, by all accounts, except that she'd gone inside herself to a place where no one could reach her.

Except, it seemed, Emilette.

Arten took up the snow pusher, cleared the path to the gate. The previous night's snow was sticky and heavy and would crust over tonight. At least she wouldn't need to clear the back garden today. Before she left, she slogged through the unbroken yard to the kitchen window and ran the flat plank of her snow pusher against the pane, knocking down the brittle crust that clung there. When she waved through the pane, Natalia didn't wave back.

Arten pushed her way to the cleared path, then out through the squeaky gate. She leaned into the handle as she walked, the angled plank shifting the wet muck to the edge of the path. She'd cut it two tracks wide this time, but it had been a while since the last stretch of warmer days, and the path had narrowed to only a little wider than a single pass could handle. She wondered if it would be worthwhile to cut it three-wide next time.

She seemed to be the first one out today, and she ended up clearing all the way to the join with the second circuit. She leaned her pusher against the big tree there after shaking down some of the snow from its drooping lower branches. The second circuit was cleared by its own denizens, much more thoroughly than the third circuit, and on the first you wouldn't know that it had snowed at all.

The road was plowed by a nice man from the town and his team of cart horses, and he was quite an early riser, so she rarely saw him but always thanked him when she did. The stone steps were the trickiest part, but the new boots of her winter outerwear had grooves in the soles to grip on ice. She went up and down on all fours though, just in case.

Her boots slushed through the heavy top layers, crunched on the harder-packed snow beneath. Her breath clouded the air and echoed in her ears, strained. By the time she arrived at Stekin's door, her legs burned, and a stiff line of pain shot through her side.

A familiar face greeted her.

"Good morning, Claude." She smiled.

He smiled back, though there was a tension around his eyes. He led her back to the library, paused at the door. "When you've finished, drop by the kitchens for a moment."

"I will, thank you." Since Natalia had moved in, Arten had largely taken over meal preparation for the both of them—Emilette rarely ate with them. Clearly, she had some other source of food that was less burnt and adequately spiced. Arten didn't blame her; she took advantage of every scrap Stekin's cook offered with desperate gratitude.

Claude's face softened briefly, then tensed again as he opened the doors and gestured her through. She noticed the quick, worried glance inside, the working of his throat. Stekin was standing at the windows, as tall and thin and stiff as if he were an extension of the architecture. Claude loosed a shaky breath.

Arten padded down the thick carpet which had been changed from the usual blue to a deep red in the same swirling patterns. The soft weight of the doors rumbled shut behind her, the room felt a little warmer. As she slipped into her chair, she caught the edge of Stekin's profile, stark from the glare of the snow, his mouth a grimace, his eyes fixed the hands before him, clawed against the stone window sill.

I wish I knew why he's so unhappy, she thought as she plunged down into the ropes of her power. Since Stekin had removed the block, it had become almost trivially easy to manage. What had once felt like an exercise in plunging herself into a furnace to try and grow accustomed to catching on fire was now like wrapping her hands around a candle flame. Warm, comfortable, friendly. Alarming feelings to have about what she had always considered to be a force intent on killing her.

She spun the ropes thicker, twisted them around one another into weighty cords. Thinned them out again into mere strings. Collected the strings in her fingers into yarn and looped it around under her skin like Maruko had always done to measure a foot—three times around each finger drawn snug.

"You are smiling." Stekin's voice interrupted her warm memories. It was tepid, like a stagnant pool. *Today is a bad day.*

"Am I?" she said, reaching up with her real hand to feel her mouth. It didn't feel like she was.

He tilted his head to the side the slightest amount, the jade storm of eyes the only life in his features. He turned back stare out the window, said nothing more.

He'd always been remote and strange, but since he'd killed that dragon—the one that had looked so much like him she'd not known whose body had rocked the ground until Natalia had said her last word, "Finally"—since Alectros had died, Stekin had been different. Some days he didn't talk to her at all. Some days he would pace the windows in long bounds, stopping only to race to his work-bench and make notes in impatient, jerky motions, only to finish and stalk the windows again. Some days he sat in his chair and watched her, his face full of things she had last seen on her father's the night he'd learned she was Tainted.

Those were the hardest days. The ones where she wanted to be sitting on the tall stool, smelling the oil as she rubbed it into the counter until it gleamed, her father greeting red-cheeked customers brought in on a gust of wind scented with cedar. Instead she was here, in this room that sucked away any warmth and cheer, or in another, smaller one that did the same back at the compound. Surrounded by people as fragile as last year's pine wreaths.

Fragile.

The thought stopped her. Her power paused in her ethe-real fingers, then stuttered to a start again. *They are. Stekin, Natalia, Claude. I feel like I'm balancing eggs when I'm around them.* The wrong word, the wrong tone of voice, would send them smashing down. And she didn't know how to prevent it. *Balancing eggs in the back of a wagon, and I don't know when the next hole in the road is coming.*

She missed Maruko, Juro, even Deric. She missed the customers coming into the shop, missed the rivalry with the MikNeilsons, even missed the unappeasable countenance of her mother.

I miss people. Normal people. Not sources and dragons and all this... She wanted to talk to people who didn't treat her like she was diseased, didn't look down on her, didn't need anything from her.

She was building and shredding the ropes inside her reflexively. Knew she was scowling, now. Felt Stekin watching her but ignored him. She could tell he was about to say something. The silence was gathering around him expectantly. Before he could, a bell chimed out of time—the source bell. The built pressure around Stekin broke, drained away.

"Come," he said. "That is enough for today anyway."

His hand was icy on her shoulder, gripped too tightly for comfort. She felt the bones of his fingers even through her coat as he walked beside her, propelling her up the hill to the amphitheater. Dragon wings snapped and caught, the sound carrying in the frigid air. Below them, the compounds would be boiling with people all busy preparing for the new arrival. One dragon flew overhead, going down to the compounds—Kylik, she knew, going to fetch the matron.

This was the fourth source that had arrived since her own arrival. This would be her third time attending the ritual. Stekin insisted she go, wanted her to see how the choosing normally went. Fortunately, he didn't insist that she stand near him on the stage. He tucked her away in a gap under a ledge, the tightening of his fingers on her shoulder his only farewell. While he descended to the flat depression at the base of the curved cliffs, dragons dropped from the sky to settle on surfaces, both natural and carved, or to crowd near Stekin without crossing the circle of rocks that surrounded the amplified space. Snow splatted down from the ledge above her just in front of someone's swiped tail. It heaped in a slushy pile before her gap, hiding her even more from casual view.

She wrapped her arms around her knees and waited. It could take a while for the source to cross the valley, even if Matron had been able to arrange the wagon in this snow. They always arrived at the compounds first. Stekin had told her it was to reassure them that people were happy and healthy here, that they were safe. Then, the matron would escort the new arrival to the amphitheater, explaining enough so that the sight of more than a hundred dragons didn't come as a complete shock.

From what Arten had seen, that talk was largely ineffective to its purpose.

The drone of large voices buzzed through her rocky niche, carrying snippets of conversation to her. Dragons gossiping and speculating as much as her own people did at Decaday gatherings. She heard a voice nearby trying to set a wager on whether Stekin would accept this one or not.

"No, I would be foolish to take that bet," a second, deeper voice responded with a huff from massive lungs. "Kaz Stekin is caught up in his new source. He has proven he has no interest in others."

"Listen to you! Talking like you know him. He has spoken to you all of, what, twice?"

"Three times, actually. Four if you count the time he spoke to me in my shell."

"I do not," the first dragon snorted. "You have no proof that even happened."

There was a low, disgruntled noise. The laughing apologies of his friend.

"Here, is he looking this way?" the first dragon said, encouragingly.

"Do not tease me," the second mourned. There was a hiss of indrawn breath, then his voice was alert as he said, "You know, I think he is!"

Arten knew Stekin couldn't see her, that the snow in front and the shadows around her kept her hidden here. But his eyes still found her, then skimmed away. A message —the new source was arriving. Arten tucked her hands under her arms, hugging herself against the cold. She reached for her power, turned it carefully, was rewarded with a current of warmth inside her. Stekin's eyes flicked back, flashed a warning as they bored into her for a heartbeat.

You would do the same thing if you were stuck under a rock shivering, she thought angrily, glaring at him. Until she passed his tests to prove her control over her power, he had insisted she not touch it outside their sessions. *And if anything happens, you're right here.*

He was already looking away, monitoring the crowd, answering questions from nearby dragons with as few words as possible.

Above her, the dragons had gone quiet. "Did—did you see that?" the deep-voiced dragon asked, breathless.

"Yes," the other said cautiously, "but Thok—"

"He looked right at me!"

"Yes, but—"

"Twice! And did you see that? His eyes—did he...?"

"They probably just caught the light."

"But he—why are you looking at me like that?"

"Thok," the first said, and Arten recognized the thick unhappiness in her voice, "do you regret mating me?"

"What? No, of course not. Why do you ask that?"

"This infatuation with Kaz Stekin... You want to fly with him, you talk of him constantly...it was all I could do to keep you here, safe, these last few years. I kept thinking I would wake up one day and you would be gone, chasing after him. Now that he is back...maybe you are wishing you were free to pursue him?"

"I am not same-bent, Cylia. This infatuation, as you call it...do you not know it? Look at him! The last *real* dragon." His voice was full of longing and awe.

Arten felt the Words in her stir, rising in response to his plaint.

"We are all *tame,* Cylia! Echoes of stories trimmed down

in the telling, similar only in shape. To what we should be. To *him*. Tell me you do not feel it—the thrum in your blood when he is nearby, the call to something greater."

The one called Cylia did not answer, said instead, her voice stiff, "He is not the last."

"Nhemith? She is no dragon."

"Do not speak so!" Cylia hissed, the words quiet and anxious.

His next words were quieter, and Arten strained to catch them, "My grandfather told me she was just a child during the Sundering, so she has no real memory of life before it happened. His father, who lived through it, told him the Sundering broke everyone in different ways. And that Nhemith, being broken so young, learned how to hide it, but she's a reptile among us."

"Hush!" Cylia hissed again. But then added, reluctantly, "And Kaz Stekin? How is he broken?"

"Grandfather would not say. He told me I should ask him myself."

Cylia snorted. There was the sound of claws on stone, bulk moving.

"If he offered you an egg, would you no longer take it?" Thok asked.

"That is different. Now hush, they are coming."

Thok rumbled a wordless complaint but didn't press the matter. Other conversations died just as abruptly, scaled noses pointed to the footpath that wound down through the amphitheater, waiting for the two humans they could scent coming, to appear. There was an expectant energy drawn in the muscles of limbs and wings, the craning of necks, as though battling against a pull in their noses. Even in Stekin's limbs, as he leaned slightly towards the path as though drawn.

"Are you going to try for him?" Thok whispered.

"You are hopeless," Cylia hissed back, "that is a female."

"No, no, two leg tubes means male, one leg tube means female. Clearly this one is male."

"You cannot sex them based on their clothing." Cylia sighed, then hushed him again.

Matron and the new source were visible to Arten now. The new source was clearly female, somewhere in her late teens, though she had cut off her hair and wore scrubby men's clothing to try and disguise it.

Is that what I looked like when Stekin brought me in? Her hand itched to reach for her own hair, still not as long as her fingers. She wondered if the new source would have as much trouble as she had, *but Matron isn't glowering at her like she always did with me.*

In fact, Pasha was patting the girl's arm encouragingly, and the new source seemed to take strength from it. She raised her chin, straightened her back and squared her shoulders. She looked at Stekin, not any of the dragons around her, and walked towards him. He stared back, his eyes dark and unblinking, his face blank. Arten felt something clawing inside her, dark and raw and angry. She shoved it down, wrapped her power around it, binding her core in molten ropes. Stekin saw nothing but the new source.

She was nearing him, only a few strides away. Stekin extended his hand to her. Matron pushed her gently forward. With only a brief glance back, the source closed the distance. His fingers closed around her hand. Arten cinched her power tight, where the wave of jealousy had knocked it loose. Because even from here, she had seen the sharp smile, the line of teeth—a ghost of the hunger she had seen on him only when her power was flaring.

Stekin was leading the source to the center of the stage. She recoiled a little as Kylik looked through her, but he kept his distance, and Stekin kept hold of her hand so she didn't flee. Kylik announced to the assembled dragons the compatibility of her power, but Arten didn't hear past "alpine." There was a roaring in her ears, drowning out sound, and all she could see was Stekin's gaze fixed on the new source, the cage of his fingers around hers.

The source council separated from the wall, replaced Kylik on the floor.

"Kaz Stekin," the leader said, as he had all the times a new source had been announced compatible with Stekin's power, "the source council grants you right of first refusal."

Stekin looked down at the new source. A brief horror, betrayal, flashed over the girl's face, she jerked her hand back at the same time Stekin released it.

"I have no intention of taking a source at this time," he said, as he always did. He drew a little away from her but stayed nearby, turned his attention away. Once again, his eyes found Arten, flashed a warning. Then moved on to scan the assembled, roving over them alertly.

Above her, Thok had gasped. Cylia was telling him that the kaz had not signaled his benediction. Thok was asking if she was *sure* the source was female.

"Yes, stop asking me," Cylia snapped.

"You are right, of course. Of course you are. Why would Kaz Stekin encourage me if it was a boy?"

"He was not—" Cylia started but Thok babbled on.

"He would not. No, I know that. He would not want them to combust."

"What nonsense are you saying?"

"Combust, combust! You cannot combine the female and male sources or they combust."

"That is absurd. Where did you hear that?"

"I read it," Thok said haughtily, "in a healer's book."

"I do not believe you. Everyone knows you do not combine them to prevent the fighting."

"Well, everyone is wrong. Oh!" The call had gone out for all other eligible dragons to make their interest known. On the far wall, Arten saw a pair of wings spread wide, below her two more. Above her, claws on stone, the leathery unfurling of wings indicated Thok's interest.

The leader of the source council named them, and the five dragons who had self-selected settled back down while the council knotted into a small group and deliberated.

Arten barely noticed. Her focus was turned in, her ethereal hands plunged deep into her power, spinning it smooth, unfurling the knots, setting it to curl around her core tightly. The Words inside her were agitated, sparking. She threw herself into the work that soothed them gladly. Because she didn't want to think about that pause. The pause before Stekin had released the new source. If she hadn't recoiled, would he have taken her?

No, she wasn't going to think about that. She had to focus on the Words.

"Do you smell that?" Cylia murmured distantly. "A southern breeze?"

"There is no wind," Thok replied, distracted.

"I smell warmth," Cylia protested.

"Shh, they are decided!"

But Arten was deep in herself, lost to the gentle resistance of the currents inside her as she frayed them, split them, spun them back together. She lost herself to the motion, to the unexpected joy. The Words drew her in, recognized her, protected her.

A voice snapped her back into the world. Arten raised

her head from her knees. Saw a single pair of legs standing on the rock in front of her, cut off at the waist by the over-hanging ledge.

"Congratulations," Stekin said neutrally, though Arten could hear that he was making an effort to be pleasant.

"Thank you, my kaz," Thok's voice rumbled above her, unexpectedly deep and liquid. Cylia said something polite and perfunctory, then Arten heard the sound of her wings bearing her away. "I will treasure her, as you have taught us."

"See that you do," Stekin said. She knew he was distracted. Clearly Thok didn't.

"Might I ask," Thok nearly purred, "what brings my kaz to see me?"

Is he flirting? Arten closed her mouth which had fallen open. *I didn't know dragons flirted.*

An absurd image of Stekin trying to flirt back went through her mind, and she shook her head at it. No, he was too serious, too rigid for something like that.

His next words confirmed it: "You were Alectros's hatch-mate, I believe?" Serious. Voice packed with ice and a fur thrown on top.

"I was." Thok was moving, his claws scraping above her, then beside her. Slate-gray legs climbed down into view. Two, then four, wing tips, a tail. His scales gleamed in a way she'd never seen Stekin's do. He paced in a half-curl around Stekin, glossy and shining, black nails claws scraping over red-brown stone.

"You were still in the egg when he hatched."

"I was," Thok agreed, with a hint of triumph, his voice as smooth and rich as his scales, pacing a little closer. "I am honored you remember me."

Stekin pivoted, keeping himself squared with Thok's

head as the slate dragon circled him. "Bartolok," he remembered.

"I prefer Thok."

"Very well, Thok." Thok made a pleased noise that set the hair on Arten's neck on end. "I regret that I had to take your hatch-mate from you."

Thok stilled; his voice was normal as he said, "How did his source die?"

"I did not witness it directly."

"But you witnessed something?"

"I heard a noise, as we waited to enter the compound. Seconds later, Alectros emerged and surrendered himself. When I entered, I found his source, Carl, dead. A second source, who wishes to remain anonymous, testified to me that Alectros had panicked at our arrival and pulled too much, killing Carl moments before."

Thok growled. Arten's hair stood on end, again. "Then I am glad," he said, his voice as hard as Stekin's, though many degrees hotter, "that you stopped him."

"Hmm."

"Kaz?"

Stekin's voice was stony. "There are too few of us, far too few, to rejoice in this slaughter."

"One deviant cut down is hardly a slaughter, my kaz." Thok was making an offering, but Stekin refused it with a hard noise.

"Thank you," Thok continued, the richness layering back into his tone, "for thinking of me. This has been an unhappy business."

"If you do not mind, I would like to be alone, and you have a source to greet."

"Yes, of course. But should you ever want company, perhaps to stretch your wings...?"

"I do not play games with children, Thok." Stekin released the winter and it snapped icy daggers though his words.

Thok stopped his fluid circling. "As you say," he said formally, stiffening, then launched himself into the air.

Wind buffeted around Stekin, the clap of wings receded.

Arten was frozen, her body still locked remembering Thok's too-close growl. A long arm reached in, grabbed her, hauled her out. She yelped involuntarily. Stekin's hand closed over her mouth. His eyes were flashing emerald fires, boring into her angrily.

"You are *not,*" he growled, and though his voice was merely human, it cut into her as deeply as Thok's had, "to touch your power outside our lessons." His fingers were hard in her shoulder, digging into the bone. "You gave me your word."

"How did you—?"

"I can *see* you," he snapped, "I can always see you, Arten. I can certainly see when you are meddling with your power. Especially when you are close to flaring—which you nearly did. Foolish!"

"Ow, let go!" She pushed away from him, pressing back into the ledge when his fingers loosened. "I didn't flare, did I? I had everything under control."

"Oh, did you?" he mocked. Gestured around them.

She didn't see what he was upset about, just the rocks and the snow and—and the spreading swath of bare, dry rock in front of the ledge, where there had been snow before. She looked up behind her to the surface above, from which Thok or Cylia had swept down piles of wet snow earlier; it was now dry and clear.

"What...?" she started, faltered. Felt suddenly dizzy and warm. Hadn't she just been freezing?

"This is what you call control?" Stekin said, the condemnation bitter and frozen.

"Would you rather I have flared out?" she shot back hotly.

"I would *rather* you have kept your word and not brutishly handled your power unsupervised."

"I didn't brutishly handle anything!" she yelled. "And for your information, oh great kaz, if I *hadn't* reached into my power, I would probably be *dead* right now. Not that you would care."

"Dramatics do not suit you, Arten." He bristled. His head snapped to a distant sound, beyond her hearing. "We will continue this at home," he growled, reaching for her arm.

"Get off me," she snapped, wrenching herself away. He looked startled as she slipped out of his grip. "This isn't my home, and you don't tell me what to do."

"Arten, you are not a child. Do not behave as one," he said, his eyes narrowed, mouth a hard line.

Her hands fisted at her sides. "If I'm not a child, don't try to parent me when it suits you." She was flushed, her winter clothes stifling and humid. Her careful ropes of power were a disordered knot in her gut, churning with Words and heat. They surged up, scraping along her throat to freedom. Her knees went weak. *No no no no no! Not now, not here. Don't prove him right.*

He reached down, grabbed her arms in that too-tight grip. His eyes were bright with triumph and greed, his teeth bared in a smile.

He wanted this! she thought, rage sweeping through her. *He wanted me to flare out because I haven't given him any power since he removed the block.* She wanted to slam her fist into his face, wipe that ravenous look off it.

And she knew. She would not give him the satisfaction.

She would not flare out, would not let her power escape. *It flares because it's wild, because I can't control it,* she reminded herself. *But I can control it—didn't I just do that earlier?* She set her jaw, planted her feet on the ground and her hands on Stekin's chest, and shoved.

He staggered back, gaped at her, his hand coming up to touch his chest where her palms had connected. Then she ignored him. Plunged other hands deep into her power, scalding them as she grasped it, forced it back down. She hadn't brutishly handled it before, but she did so now, strangling and pummeling it back, shoving it into motion away from where it wanted to go. She was sweltering, couldn't breathe. She shed her outerwear; the cold air cut through her tunic found its way down her collar, wicked away the sweat from her skin.

She dove back into her power, gritting her teeth as blistering heat met raw hands. The power, the Words, formed a snarl, searching for the route to freedom with starts and jumps in random directions, confused. She picked it apart, tamed it to her will, sent the threads twisting away into ropes. Too slowly. But a refreshing breeze touched her skin so far away, gave her some strength.

Her phantom fingers were blistered, beyond pain, but she kept going. Then she was halfway through the snarl. Three-quarters. It unravelled faster, now, almost like it didn't want to be separated from the rest of her power. Then she was done, climbing back out of her core, leaving the crisped, raw husk of her inner-self, moving back into her skin and bones. Looking out of her own eyes. Into Stekin's wide ones.

His face was open, a book she could read for the first time. There was loss, and pride, and a question pleading there. She pulled his hands away from her face—they had been the breeze that revitalized her. He remained where she left him, like a pose-able doll, his hands still partly raised, like he'd forgotten how to move, how to speak. Only his eyes followed her as she gathered her coat and climbed out of the amphitheater. She felt them on her spine until the rock rose between them.

SHE TRUDGED BACK through the wide streets on the hill, deep in thought. No longer angry—that had been burned away. When she thought about it, she felt a little foolish for thinking Stekin would intentionally provoke her into losing control when his entire concern had been that she *would* lose control. The drawing off of her power had always been a private thing between them. Was private between all dragons and sources, if Matron were to be believed. He wouldn't have wanted a public display any more than she did.

But I stopped it, she thought, drawing her coat back on. The heat was fading rapidly as her power calmed back into dormancy. *I controlled it. I didn't need Stekin.*

The thought thrilled through her, she found herself grinning but somehow colder. There was a sense that something was shifting under her feet, something she didn't understand. She pulled on her hat and mittens.

She should have been at the stairs by now, but when she looked around, she didn't recognize the lane or the dragon-houses set back from it. She frowned. *I must have missed the turn,* she thought, her triumph deflating. *Maybe I should turn around?* But it wasn't even midday, and the lane was well-travelled by human feet. *I'll just see where it goes,* she thought, and felt a thrill at the freedom in it.

Stekin would have wanted her to go straight home. Matron would have told her she was being intrusive. Emilette would have had paroxysms of distress at her being out alone, in the cold, on an unfamiliar path. She mentally gave them all a rude gesture she'd learned from Juro and walked on.

As she wound down the hill, admiring the dragon estates crusted with snow, dangling long icicles from the corners of the roofs, she wondered who lived in them, what they did. There was a whole realm of people up here that she didn't know at all. Just Stekin, with his library and his mysterious research and his councils. They couldn't all be like him. Surely some of them laughed? Kylik, she remembered, had been full of sighs and softness in the privacy of his compound. Was he the same here, on the Hill?

Her boots were no longer crunching on snow; the trek of many feet had cleared it from the path except a few patches of dense ice. The dragon homes had gone from palatial to nice to careworn to ramshackle. She passed one that was barely more than walls with a partial roof closing off some rooms. Then, just a few short turns later, flanked on either side by gardens that had overgrown to the point where she could no longer even see the houses through them, the walls and gardens stopped and the lane opened to rocky plains on either side, giving Arten a view all the way to the town.

She broke into a jog, following the lane as it wound down into the upper town. People—normal people!—lived there, and she couldn't close the distance fast enough. She was tired of dragons and sources and magic and intrigue. She didn't slow until the tall, fine houses rose up around her. Far too grand to be anything she'd grown up with. And yet, compared to the compounds and the disproportioned splendor of the houses on the Hill, it was like coming home in a way.

She grinned to see people moving about in the street in their fine, impractical clothing. She didn't even care that they were gaping at her and hurrying past. She pressed on, seeking the center of town.

Maybe they'll have a merchant market, like Laird! But no, that didn't make sense—there was no one to trade with, no one who knew this place existed outside this valley. The thought dampened her enthusiasm only a little. Because there were shops now, windows presenting wares that glinted in the sun. Restaurants and bakeries that wafted warm, tantalizing smells throughout the street, sending her stomach growling, reminding her that she hadn't stopped by Stekin's kitchens to see Claude. But the sights, the people, the goods distracted her from that small guilt.

The locals ignored her and avoided her, but it was different from down in the compounds. There was no malice, no intent behind their actions, just the casual indifference of strangers. She immersed herself amongst them, wandered the streets aimlessly, ranging towards whatever caught her eye. Found public gardens, crossed a massive stone bridge that arced over the river, paused at its middle to watch the waterfalls flow, half-frozen, over the cliffs upriver. She was turned back at the far side of the bridge by a burly man with a long, temple-like belt and a disc sewn onto his coat.

But her excursion wasn't as satisfying as she'd expected. No one had talked to her, called out to her. She had no money, and the few shops she'd tried to enter had shooed her out in short order, so she'd been relegated to looking through the panes at their goods. Even in the parks, there had been knots of people—friends, neighbors, families—

talking, laughing, playing. She felt displaced, disconnected, and the sun was beating down now, making her feel hot and a little sick. She pulled off her coat and draped it over her arm.

The clock at the center of the upper town chimed three-afternoon. *I should head back.*

She sighed, stopped at a street vendor to ask for the fastest way back to the compounds, and set out following his directions. As she made her way south, the buildings became less grand. Still what she considered prosperous, but they looked a little harried compared to those deeper in the upper town. Right about the time they were becoming cramped and a little less well-cared-for, the street stopped and the ground dropped away. Below her spread more buildings, the lower town, and a wide stone stairway dropped away, cutting through the cliff face in a long diagonal.

As she descended the stairs, she had a strange sense of familiarity. The stairs were broad enough that she didn't get vertigo as she descended, though she clung to the rail carved into the stone wall the whole way down. She stopped at the bottom to catch her breath, which she'd been holding. Was about to press on when a voice called out.

"Hey, kid!"

She looked around when the call came a second time, realized there were no children in the streets. Saw a man standing in the open doorway of a shop, his shoulders hunched against the cold, huffing hot breath onto his bare hands. He gestured her over urgently.

She frowned, pointed at herself.

"Yeah, you! Come here."

Again, she got that sense of familiarity. She crossed the street.

"Come inside, kid. It's wicked out here. How are you not freezing?" He huffed on his hands again, rubbed them together, then went in, not waiting for her.

She hesitated only for a heartbeat, then followed him.

He was leaning against a doorframe at the back of the narrow shop, behind a sad excuse for a counter, his hands shoved deep into pockets of his canvas apron. She glanced around, took in the shelves of paper and pens, ink and wax, stacks of what looked like ledger books and other bits of odds and ends that were unfamiliar to her.

"What's wrong with my shop?" he demanded, crossing his arms over his chest.

"What?" she asked, confused.

"You've got that look again. Last time you kept talking about how this place was all wrong. Well, I've moved things about, but you have that same snooty look. So tell me, kid—what's wrong with my shop?"

"Last time?"

He bristled, pushing away from the door frame. "You kidding me?"

"No. Who are you? Why do you think you know me?" She edged back.

"Name's Tam," he grunted. "Guess you don't remember, huh. I looked for you, you know, after. Tried to make sure you were okay. I pulled you outta a snowbank 'bout a month ago. You were a little off your head. Makes sense you don't recall, I suppose. Tall fellow came and took you home."

Arten was looking around. It did feel like she'd been here before. She moved to the counter, touched her shoulder which felt suddenly cold.

"You gave me a blanket," she remembered, frowning, shaking her head slowly as though it would clear the fuzziness.

"Yep."

She stared at the little pots of ink on the shelf beside her. "These weren't here last time. They were over there."

"Yep," Tam said again, watching her closely.

Her hands reached out for them without thinking.

"Hey, what are you doing?" He pushed away abruptly, jumped over the counter, and grabbed for her. She stared at his hand clamped around her wrist, then at his face. His eyes had been kinder last time, she remembered, his face softer.

"They're mixed up," she said coolly, hearing a bit of Stekin in her voice. It irritated her. She snatched her hand away and deliberately went back to what she had been doing. Tam loomed at her shoulder, stiff and tense, until she stepped back.

"Why'd you do that?" he demanded; she could see him counting the pots.

He thinks I'm trying to steal from him? She drew herself up, scowled at him. "I wouldn't have to if you kept this place better."

"I keep it just fine," he protested, looking down at her with a frown, his eyes calculating.

"Sure, Tam, was it?"

"Yeah."

"Well, thank you for helping me out last time, Tam. Good luck."

Her hand was on the door when he called, "Wait! You haven't told me what's wrong with my shop."

She turned back and crossed her arms, mimicking his pose. "Why should I?" she demanded. "I had to work hard to learn how to run a shop. So should you."

"I'll pay you."

"What?"

"I'll pay you right now to tell me what's wrong with this place."

She stared at him. *He's serious!* She looked around more closely, saw a dozen things she would do differently. Even if she pointed it all out, she doubted he'd be capable of getting the place into shape. He didn't even have the discipline to stack his product consistently. But she could. It would take her...a week? It was a small shop, but she wasn't overly familiar with the writing and stationary business, so she'd have to learn it. Give herself room to experiment and check out the competition. Two weeks.

Maybe it was her anger at Stekin, maybe it was the motion of the power inside her bound and tamed into ropes she'd made, maybe it was that in these few minutes in this tiny shop she'd felt less alone than she had since she'd upended her life and thrown it into Stekin's hands. She looked at Tam, at his face that bore no symbol of slavery, his eyes which had once looked on her with concern.

"I want a job," she said.

"I'm not hiring," he said immediately, but his face was thoughtful, his hand came up and he ran his nails through the scruffy beginnings of a beard.

"Two weeks," she pressed, "and I'll teach you how to fix this place up."

"Two weeks?" He was skeptical.

She started wavering inside, considered going down to one week. But her father had always said: go into a deal with a strong will and people will bend for you; if your will is the weaker, you will bend to them.

Today her will was iron, bound by ropes of fire. "Two weeks." She stood firm, raised her chin. "And three coppers a day."

It was one more than her family had paid the interim

shop boys who helped out, but she was going to be providing a service in addition to her labor.

Tam's eyes went wide.

"No less," she demanded.

"Demons, kid, that's robbery," he swore.

Her heart raced, but she hoped she wasn't letting it show.

"Three coppers a day," she repeated, waiting for his counter.

He dragged his fingers through his scruff a few more times, the sound organic and strangely soothing. "Can't afford you full time. Half-days for a month, Firstday off."

She did some quick calculation. "Okay. Twelve coppers a week, then." His face took that alarmed look again. "You're the one who called me in off the street. You need me."

"That's not—" He rubbed his hand over his face and shook himself. "I can't possibly pay you that and live with myself." She started to protest, but he continued, "It'll be five copper a day if you get here by noon bell. Four if you're late. Late three times and we're done. You don't show, we're done. Four weeks. Get me?"

She repeated it back to him, a little dazed. *Five copper for half a day's work!*

"Agreed?" he said, holding his hand out, looking just for a moment like a competent merchant.

"Agreed," she said, slapped and clasped his hand. He clasped back and shook. And it was done.

"You start tomorrow?" he said, a grin spreading over his face. She found herself grinning back.

"Yes, sir!" she said, shaking his hand again.

He grimaced. "None of that. Tam's fine. Here," he fished into his apron pocket, took out two copper coins and pressed them into her palm. "Two now, three tomorrow.

Now get out of here, I've got work to do." But there were no teeth in his words.

Her hand closed over the coins. "Tomorrow, then."

He shooed her out the door. In the afternoon light, the coppers in her hand glinted. She stared down at them, so small in her palm and yet heavy. Her very own money. She'd had money before, a copper here or there gifted to her, but she'd never been *paid*. All this summer when she'd worked in her father's shop, she'd not been paid. It didn't seem like an important thing at the time. She'd felt like her work was a repayment on a debt to her parents.

But Deric is paid to work in the shop, she realized for the first time. *Why wasn't I?*

She closed her hand around the coins, deciding it didn't matter, and stowed them deep in her pocket. Looked up to see Tam lounging in his shop door, grinning at her between huffs on his hands. She called a farewell and trotted towards home, the coppers jangling faintly in her pocket all the way.

She felt strangely grounded, even jogging through the unfamiliar lower town which grew progressively more ramshackle. The people here were shabbier, skinnier, all a little harried, all a little haunted. These were people she recognized. That lady dragging her child through the street by the arm, scowling, could have been her mother. That man dickering with a street vendor over something nonnegotiable could be her brother. Then the lower town ended in a shamble, and she was alone on the road.

Alone, but for the first time, that didn't bother her. It wasn't the vast, aching isolation she'd grown accustomed to since she arrived. Even as she reached the compounds and the first circuit presented their wall of exclusion to her, it didn't hurt like it used to. Because tomorrow she would go back into the town, she would get out of this stagnant place, she would see real people who had bigger lives and bigger dreams than the sources here.

They are prisoners who rejoice in their chains, she thought, disgusted. *Nor will I be like them. I will not become a complacent power source, doting on some dragon, moving to his whim.*

BACK HOME, she burnt their dinner worse than usual, distracted as she was by thoughts of tomorrow and of confronting Stekin. *He owns me for the next three years. He can forbid me from working.* It was true, *but*, another voice whispered, *you can do it anyway. Would he really stop you?*

The thought of defying him left her a little shaky, but the anger burning in the core of her, the two coppers in her pocket, bolstered her courage.

"This is awful," Emilette moaned, prodding at the congealed charred lumps in her stew.

"Then you make it," Arten snapped. She was so sick of Emilette's complaints and snide comments. "What exactly does Stekin pay you for, anyway?"

Emilette drew herself up affronted. "I'm your companion!"

"I don't need a companion. I need help around here. So help out or get out. You can start with the dishes." Arten plunked her bowl down in front of Emilette, then stalked out of the room.

Emilette's sputtering protests fed the budding feeling inside her. Power and strength and defiance. Maruko would know a word for it. Maruko had probably felt it all her life.

That night Arten couldn't sleep. She felt excited by tomorrow, nervous about proving herself to Tam, exhilarated with the knowledge that she had an escape from this place. Then she'd start thinking about Stekin and be torn between hoping he would come by tonight, so she could go down into the garden and yell at him, and wanting him to stay away and give her space.

Now that she wasn't working in Natalia's compound, there was no reason for him to visit her in the evenings—she had no report to make. But he'd taken to appearing some nights and stationing himself around the house, where he waited all night, alert—for what he'd never said. She padded to the window and scanned for him but somehow knew he wasn't there. Part of her was relieved that she didn't have to face him. The new, fiery part was disappointed.

She heard Emilette and Natalia climb the stairs just after the midnight bell rang. Heard them settle in to sleep. Envied their rest. She gave up and lit a candle, pulled *A History* onto her lap and read. All the way to the end. She closed it, placed it back on the bedside table, blew out her candle. Checked the window one more time. Saw no evidence of Stekin outside.

She could tell Emilette hadn't banked the fire again by how cold her room was growing. She curled back up in bed, the sheets chilly on her feet. Remembered Stekin's angry gesturing to the cleared rock around him. *It worked before,* she thought with a grim smile. It was only a bonus that it would make him angry if he noticed what she was doing.

She sank into herself, touched her power. It scalded her raw hands, but she braced herself against the pain and set her power spinning through her. It took a few minutes, but her feet and hands thawed, the sheets warmed around her. She withdrew, sliding back into her skin.

Her last thought before she fell asleep was remembering

Thok's statement earlier: *He is the last real dragon. We are all tame.*

The last line of *A History* had been: *We have no accurate records after this point through the Founding of New Respite due to the catastrophic losses of life and history caused by the Sundering.*

An abrupt end to a tale of violence and mayhem. Stekin was nothing like the dragons in the book, even for all his frostiness and bouts of anger. Why did Thok think Stekin was a real dragon, *has he never heard the history of his people? Why wouldn't he have? And why did Stekin want me to read it?*

20

ARTEN'S CHOICE
STEKIN

He was not angry with Arten, despite how he had acted. He rubbed absently at the bruises on his ribs, the size of two small hands, as he stared unseeing into the reflecting panes of his library windows. The bruises smarted with the tenderness of a burn, and given the force she had turned on him, he was fortunate nothing was broken.

She does not even know what she did. Never mind that *he* did not know exactly what she had done. Each breath stretched his ribs, the ache a nagging reminder that he had underestimated her. He had grown to care for her, to see her as a child. Had forgotten she was something the world had not seen before. And that, more than the angry words between them, had kept him up all night.

I have been careless, but no more. She is ready. She had mastered her power, more rapidly than he had thought possible. It had been his own weakness that held her back all this time. And as frightening as it had been to watch her directing her power in the crowd of his people, knowing that if she faltered there was no way to contain the damage she would wreak, seeing her power flare and seeing her master it had left him no other option. She was ready, but he was not.

Yes, he had been afraid for his people. She was an unknown, and her power had only intensified since he had freed it from the net of his inadvertent making. Its destructive power, if it escaped her control... He shivered at the thought. Perhaps her power was no longer wild, but she would still need extensive training to control it. Training that had never before been given to a source.

But she is not just a source, he knew. And he knew two more things. That the training she was about to undergo must be kept secret from everyone. And that he would not tell her what he suspected she might be capable of. His hand rubbed his ribs, prodding the ache.

He could sense her, still in her bed. Her power moving in slow undulations around her, like a strange snake. It was well-formed and slow. Near dormant, but guided just a touch by her hand. It was already becoming instinct for her if she could turn it in her dreams. He had seen it stir to wakefulness a few hours ago, seen her curl it around herself —for comfort?

He had been afraid for his people, seeing her power flare yesterday, seeing the slow sublimation of snow around where she crouched in concealment. But that was not why he had shouted, that was not what had fueled his anger. That was the hard gem of guilt at his core, because he knew what had caused the flare, even if Arten did not. The girl, the new source—he had been tempted. If she had not rejected him, he might have taken her on. And that moment of hesitation, of temptation, was when Arten's power had surged.

It was nearly morning. There was nothing to do now but wait and regret.

When the first bell of morning rang, he went to his balcony and transformed. There were dull marks on the scales of his ribs, the pattern of palms and fingers distorted by the shifting. He hoped no one would notice.

Nhemith will.

He knew people wondered why he spent so much time in his human form. There were many answers to that question, most of them many-layered, but today it was simpler: clothes could conceal weakness.

There were five Gatekeepers in rotation, most of them new during his absence. He flew to the residence of the one on duty this week. She found his request odd, but he was the kaz, so she inclined her head in agreement. Then he flew down the Hill, to the compounds. Not his compound on the first circuit, which always drew his eye and beckoned him, but the little cramped place at the join of the cliff and the wall. Shamefully small, *but Arten has been happier there than in mine.*

He circled down, landed quietly on the boulevard. Folded his wings to wait. A good portion of the snow had melted in yesterday's sun, and the rest had refrozen last night. The icy crust on the road crumbled under his claws.

Inside, he felt Arten awaken, come downstairs. The scent of woodsmoke and later cooking grains reached him. Few people passed in the streets, sparing him nervous glances. He supposed he looked too alike to Alectros for comfort. His eyes snapped to the compound where he had been too lenient to save Carl. Hiranyath's source might be safe, for now, but the other two... He needed Natalia to speak to him of the true events of that day in order to bring charges against them. Until she or they spoke out, there was little he could do.

This whole system was designed around a community of

sources watching out for one another. Sources that could band together if their dragon was abusive or cruel. But there was no community here on the third-circuit. Only mostly empty compounds with sources that felt too isolated to have a voice. Perhaps on the higher circuits the system still worked, but down here, there was a general malaise of despair. He needed to fix it, set it right. Starting with Natalia. But not today.

Arten was in the hall, he heard her through the door giving directions to the others. He pulled his eyes away from the place he had waited, counting the seconds while Alectros murdered Carl, and dragged them back to Arten's door. Which she was emerging from. She stopped just over the threshold, seeing him, then remembered to push the door closed.

"What're you doing here?" she demanded. *Still angry. Perhaps I deserve it.*

"I am escorting you to a choosing."

"There was no bell," she retorted, crossing her arms.

"Not yet," he agreed. "Will you permit me to fly you there?"

She looked at the street then vaguely in the direction of the Hill. He knew she was thinking of the icy steps and long trek.

"All right," she agreed. He reached for her, gathered her to his chest. She was still so small, so fragile in his claws. And if he held her a little closer than usual, a little tighter, she said nothing.

He landed in the amphitheater, just beyond the ring of stones that bounded the amplified stage. Set her down gently.

"What's this?" she asked, looking around nervously.

"Yesterday you proved that you have tamed your power,"

he said. "You must still come to your lessons until I am satisfied you are in full control, but it is time for your choosing."

She was shifting from one leg to the other, her hands twisting around themselves. "Stekin," she said in a rush, "I have a job."

He jerked his head back, stared down at her.

"I see," he said carefully. "Am I not ensuring your needs are met?"

"No, it's not that. I mean, maybe it is... I need to be around *people,*" she beseeched him, "not sources, not dragons."

"I see," he said again, trying to fit this into his plans and the order of his world. She misunderstood his stillness for displeasure.

"I know you own me for the next three years," she said bitterly, "but I'm not afraid of you," she lied. "I will fight you on this. You can't stop me," she lied again. The paleness of her face, the hammering of her heart under her ribs told him the truth. Though that she would fight him, he had no doubt.

"I will not stop you," he promised. "Will this make you happy?"

Very, very cautiously she said, "Yes."

"Good. You must still come to lessons—before or after work, but you must come. Aside from that, your time is your own to do with as you please. I am glad you have found a way to fill it."

She looked skeptical, uncertain how to react to his acquiescence. He sighed.

She has persisted in this nonsense belief. I cannot let it continue.

"Arten," he snapped, causing her to stiffen. "This is important, are you listening? I do not own you."

"But—"

"Listen," he hissed, lowering his head to her level, letting his eyes flash. She stilled. "That document your father signed gave me guardianship of you. Nothing more. You have no responsibility to me, only I to you."

"But I—"

He cut her off. "It was necessary to allow me to bring you here. Without it, your father could have sent the temple after me and taken you back. I could not risk that."

"But you bought me!"

"No," he corrected more gently, "I indentured you. I paid your family for the loss of your presence in the household. And the terms of your debt to me are as I have stated before: learn what I set about to teach you, and when you are sixteen and your indenture is over, decide if you want to stay and help me."

"But the gold..."

"Is mine to spend. You owe me nothing for it." She was looking at him like she'd never seen him before. He drew back, met her stare.

"You're nothing like them," she said to herself.

"Like whom?"

She started, perhaps not realizing she had spoken aloud. "The dragons in the book," she said.

The innocent words hit him like a wall of ice. *No, I am not.*

"Did you ever breathe fire? Did you war and slaughter like...them?"

"I never tried to learn a breath power," he admitted. "My roar was enough. It could splinter the ice when I focused it correctly. And yes, when I was very young and foolish, I followed my clan to war."

His eyes unfocused, seeing once again that ancient

stretch of mountains gleaming in ice, snow swept deep into crevices. The ice palace, nowhere as grand as their own, fresh-hewn from a glacier still rough and murky. Smudges of deeper blue and purple and charcoal asleep within. His brother and his uncle had glided in on his wing, the rest of the clan were alighting on the far side of the ridges that lined the glacier. It was his moment to prove himself, to earn his name. And he did. He roared and threw all his power into it. He brought the glacier crashing down around the sleeping dragons, entombing them. The screams had haunted him for centuries, and worse, the silence that cut them off one by one.

"Once," he said, pulling himself back to the present, "I went with them once and led them in a glorious victory. It sickened me, and I left that night. My brother caught me, tried to stop me, then tried to kill me when I would not be persuaded." The twisting scar on his left leg ached with the memory. "I escaped. Learned to take human form, lived among your kind for many years. Hiding from the wrath of my clan. Until the Sundering killed them all."

"I'm sorry," she said.

He shrugged his wing. "It was a lifetime ago."

"The Sundering," she asked, tentatively, "I've heard...that it broke people. How—how did it break you?"

He looked at her sharply. That phrase—it had been said to him long ago. By whom? How had Arten heard it? He said the same to her that he had said before, but when?

"It broke my heart." He did not add, *and made me into someone my clan would have respected.*

There were more questions on her tongue, but the second morning bell rang, and in its wake, the three distinct tones that heralded a source.

"You remember what you must say?" he asked.

She nodded, tension tight across her shoulders.

"Stand in the middle, stand firm, do not let them see you flinch."

She nodded again. The heart he claimed not to have constricted. After this, there was no going back. He would never again draw her power, she would never be his source.

He wanted to snatch her in his claws and fly her away.

He wanted to transform and embrace her.

But he merely breathed over her, the touch of family, and spread his wings. She backed away, giving him space to fly, moving to the center of the stage. He jumped into the air, rose to a prominent ridge at the top of the amphitheater. A place far enough away to indicate Arten's decisions were her own but visible enough that everyone would see and hear his response.

The theater filled up, more quickly for the strange hour of the summoning. A mist-gray dragon settled beside him, though not as close as she normally would have dared.

"What is this, Stekin?" Nhemith demanded.

"It is what it appears to be," he said.

She made a disgruntled noise but did not leave. The bowl below them filled up with wings and tails and curious eyes, all looking around, not quite certain what to think about the lone human on the stage. The source council arrived, landed at the edge just inside the ring. Stekin nodded once to Arten.

She stood tall, her voice was clear and steady even in the amplification, as she said, "I am Arten. Thank you for attending my choosing."

Stekin dug his claws into the rock, forcing down a wave of possessiveness and pride. He knew Nhemith had seen the reaction. Arten was speaking again.

"Since this is an unusual occurrence, I ask the source

council to recite the law which has been entered for this occasion."

Nicely done. Just as we discussed.

The leader of the source council displaced Arten at the center, cleared his throat and began reciting, "By promise of Stekin, generally accepted as kaz at the time of this law, and with the full support of the source council..." He named all the members and their relevant dates of establishment. "...it is declared that the source Arten will, at her discretion, choose the person to whom she will source once she is capable of fulfilling her duties without danger." The elderly dragon peered at Arten. "And are you so capable?"

"I am," she said without hesitation.

"Is there any who will attest to that?" he asked.

Stekin flared his wings wide, said in a resonant voice that carried to the stage, "As the one who has been instructing Arten in taming her wild power, I so attest."

"Very well, kaz." The dragon inclined his head deferentially to Stekin and then Arten. "Proceed."

Stekin leaned forward, his gaze locked with Arten's. This was where she would choose him. And he would repeat the sentiment he had been expressing since her arrival, *I have no intention of taking a source at this time.* She would argue that her choice had been made. He would make a case that this was unprecedented and a second choice could not be forced, that the language of the law did not allow for it, nor did it specify that the dragon must acquiesce to her decision. The precedent would then be set that although she had chosen Stekin and could not be found at fault, neither could Stekin for not accepting her. Stekin would pull the source council members aside individually and, over the course of a few days, it would become generally accepted that Arten was a free agent.

It was the course they had agreed upon, to prevent her from having to source another, and to keep her distant enough from him to not be a target. It was the plan they had discussed. She opened her mouth, he tensed. But she did not say, *I choose Stekin*.

Instead, she said, "A point of clarification, honored elder."

What is she doing? Beside him, Nhemith made a smug noise.

"Not going according to plan?" she taunted quietly.

Stekin snapped at her, moving his head but keeping his eyes riveted on the stage.

"Would you repeat the part starting with 'the source Arten', please?" Arten asked, bowing her head to the source council leader in imitation of his own bow to her.

"'The source Arten will, at her discretion, choose the person to whom she will source, once—"

"Thank you," she interrupted with another bow.

The elder bowed back.

Her eyes went up to hold Stekin's again. They were bright and fierce. "The person—" She feathered the slightest emphasis on the word. "—I choose—" Did her eyes flash, there? No, that was impossible. "Is myself."

Stekin's jaw slackened, but his expression quickly shifted into one of fierce delight. He grinned down at her, the breeze rushing over his bared teeth. It had a hint of sun and remembered warmth in it.

Everyone was staring. At him, at Arten, at the source council. But the world was just the two of them. Himself and the brave girl that had just declared her independence from him, from all of them. He could almost see the shackles she had been wearing falling free of her as she stood a little taller, as her presence expanded, as she dug deep and found something he had known was there all along.

Yes, the council would argue over this. But nowhere was it written a source must be distinct from the one to whom they sourced. Nowhere did it specify only dragons could take sources. Yes, they would argue the intent behind the law had been that Arten must choose a dragon. But he would point out that the source council had written the law and could have specified dragon but left the language vague. They would argue whether humans could be construed as people for legal terms, but that debate had been won long ago, whether the current council was aware or not.

They would challenge this. But Arten would win.

He roared his approval, the sound bolstered by a touch of his power and the full depth of his pride, and at its core: the thinnest note of a keen.

AUTHOR'S NOTE

Thank you for reading *Dragon Bound*. If you enjoyed it, please consider leaving a review at your favorite online retailer. Reviews help other readers find books they like and let them know that, yes, this book has dragons. Reviews help new authors, like me, immensely.

Arten and Stekin's adventure will continue soon!

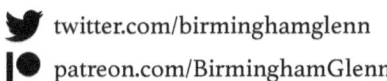 twitter.com/birminghamglenn
patreon.com/BirminghamGlenn